VAMPIRES

OF

LONDON

BOOKS 1-3

LORELEI MOONE

eXplicitTales

Copyright © 2017 Lorelei Moone,
Cover art by WriteHit.com
Published by eXplicitTales
All rights reserved.
ISBN-13: 9781913930318

CONTENTS

———◆———

Alexander's Blood Bride   1

Michael's Soul Mate   147

Lucille's Valentine   291

About the Author   435

Alexander's

BLOOD BRIDE

CHAPTER ONE

"I have amazing news!"

Cat looked up to find an excited looking Shelly standing in the doorway to their shared apartment.

"So do I," Cat responded with a wide grin on her face. The letter that had sparked her excitement lay in the center of the coffee table, just waiting to be shared with her best friend and roommate.

"Here," Shelly said, handing Cat yet another envelope. This one was different, heavy, made out of expensive looking paper.

"I've scored us an invite to the event of the year!" Shelly squealed and clapped her hands as Cat carefully opened the envelope to reveal a matching card with ornamental writing on it.

"What is it?" Cat held up the invitation to the light, noticing how the gold text shimmered luxuriously as she tilted it. The card stock itself seemed to have some texture and inherent glow as well. It was mesmerizing to look at, and almost made Cat forget about her own good news.

"This girl at work had a spare invite. Apparently this is an annual affair, been going for years now. But it's quite exclusive, not too many people know about it." Shelly's voice became more hushed as she continued to speak, like she was sharing a well-kept secret.

If there were so many printed invitations for it that Shelly got one off some random person who also worked at Superdrug, it couldn't be all that exclusive, surely!

Cat scrutinized her friend. Shelly was always the life of the party, wherever she went. Cat, on the other hand, was much more of a homebody. She didn't enjoy the club scene as much, no matter how hard Shelly had tried to convert her ever since they moved in together years ago.

It wasn't that she didn't like music, or cocktails, or even dancing. What she didn't enjoy was attracting attention to herself. Cat wasn't as popular or pretty as Shelly and for the most part, she was fine with that. She just didn't appreciate having her nose rubbed in it whenever they went out together.

"And it's fancy dress..." Cat noted.

"Yeah, obviously! What else is a Halloween party supposed to be?"

Urgh. Fancy dress was just an excuse for most people to dress up in as little as possible. None of what she'd heard so far had made Cat want to go to this thing.

And yet, the slight shimmer of the heavy card stock and the seductive curls of the golden writing continued to catch her eye. The invitation even *smelled* tempting; sweet, with a hint of pumpkin spice.

"Look, the best dressed guest will even win a prize!" Shelly leaned over and pointed at the relevant line. £1000 wasn't a small amount; no doubt Shelly would pull out all the stops in an attempt to win.

"Let me guess, you already have a costume picked out?" Cat said.

Shelly responded with a wide grin. Of course she did.

If not this party, she would have gone somewhere else on Halloween. She'd probably started thinking about her outfit months in advance. Shelly wasn't one to half-ass a costume party; she thrived on them.

"Anyway, so this seems right up your alley. What do you need me for?"

"Oh, come on! It's not every day you get a chance like this! And it'll be a hell of a lot more fun than sitting at home watching old movies all night!"

Cat made a face. "Wanna bet?"

"The card says *plus one*. Be a shame to waste it. Plus, after all the job applications you've sent out lately, you deserve to have a little fun." Shelly looked at Cat with big, pleading eyes. She could be so pushy at times.

Cat looked at the card again; every time she did, that little voice in her head screamed louder. *Stop being such a spoilsport and just agree already!* And indeed, ever since completing her degree in Art History just before the summer, Cat had been trying her best to get a job that would allow her to put her education to use. She'd been on the verge of giving up, because none of her applications had led anywhere…. Until today.

Perhaps it was a sign. After she finally received good news today, what if this party was meant to be her chance to celebrate starting a new chapter in her life?

In any case, Shelly didn't seem in the mood to drop the topic. Cat could always tell when her roommate and best friend was going to dig her heels in.

She took a deep breath. *Just this once.* "Fine. Fine! Happy now?"

"You've made the right choice. You'll see."

Cat shrugged. *Bah. Fancy dress.* "I guess now I'll need an outfit too."

"Shopping spree!" Shelly clapped her hands in excitement. "On the way out, you can tell me all about your news too, okay?"

Cat leaned forward to grab her envelope off the table and handed it to Shelly. "Read it."

Shelly did as asked. "Oh my God! You've got a job?"

Cat nodded, her chest almost bursting with excitement. "Well, an internship, but it is paid, so that's basically like a job, isn't it?"

"I told you it would work out eventually. Come here, you! I'm so happy for you!"

Cat got up from the sofa and was immediately pounced on by Shelly, who gave her a big hug.

"Here's what we'll do. First we go sort out your outfit, and then I'm taking you out for a few drinks to celebrate. What do you say?" Shelly didn't wait for Cat's agreement, instead taking her hand and leading her out of the apartment so quickly, she barely managed to pick up her coat and handbag on the way.

Alexander's Blood Bride

Cat smoothed the velvety fabric down herself as she checked out her reflection.

Not half bad.

Granted, the medieval style deep burgundy gown had been one of the very few choices in her size, and expensive to boot. But it fit Cat like a glove and accentuated her best features: her curves.

"I'm telling you, you look amazing," Shelly insisted, and rested her hand on top of Cat's shoulder.

Cat turned to face her friend and smiled. "I'll just pretend I'm meant to be an extra from Game of Thrones. That's still popular, right?"

Shelly grinned and nodded. "That's the spirit. Just give me a moment to fix my hair and we can go."

Cat watched Shelly as she fluffed up her blond curls, making sure not a single one was out of place, before pushing a flower wreath down on top of them.

Her costume was a sort of cross between stripper and fairy, with the most elaborately decorated net wings Cat had ever seen. The overall effect was impressive, if a little revealing. Of course, that was exactly how Shelly liked to dress when she went out. There was no way she'd end the night alone.

"You look great too," Cat said, as she ran her fingertips over the edge of the sparkly wings.

"They won't know what hit them when the two of us

arrive." Shelly giggled.

The doorbell rang, signaling the arrival of the cab they'd booked. You didn't turn up at a fancy party disheveled and windblown after braving the public transport and autumn rains, Shelly had insisted.

Cat took one final look in the mirror and off they went. She had no idea what to expect. The card, combined with the address at the bottom, had seemed quite fancy indeed. But if it was so special to be invited, how come the two of them had snagged a card? They weren't exactly part of London's high society.

Even the cabbie seemed surprised when Shelly told him the address. Cat imagined that it wasn't every day that two working class girls asked to be picked up from their tiny shared apartment in Shepherd's Bush and driven all the way to Kensington Palace Gardens, London's most expensive street. Luckily, the man didn't make a fuss about it.

As they pulled into the road, Cat finally did understand his reaction though. Just the size and scale of the first houses she saw were enough to take her breath away. Ever since moving to London a couple of years ago, she'd never visited this part of the city—why would she? Ordinarily she would have had no reason to.

"There it is." The cabbie pointed ahead at a beautiful Georgian villa.

As he pulled into the driveway, the ornately decorated iron gate opened by itself to let them in. The cab crawled up the immaculately kept gravel driveway and came to a halt in front of the house itself.

"Wow," Shelly said.

Cat just stared up at the impressive façade and blinked a couple of times, lost for words.

Was this really the place? She didn't belong here. They ought to turn back and forget about this whole party business.

"Come on!" Shelly urged and prodded Cat with her elbow. "Let's go!"

Cat took a deep breath and paid the driver before getting out of the car. She smoothed down her dress and did her best to stay balanced as she walked up the half dozen steps to the large double front door.

As soon as Shelly joined Cat in front of the entrance, the two doors swung open as if by magic, giving them the first glimpse of the party that was well underway inside. At least it was the right place.

Cat turned back one last time and caught a glimpse of their cab leaving. There was nowhere else to run.

Shelly took her by the arm and almost dragged her inside.

They were both speechless. They both stood there, looking up at the most beautiful carved wooden staircase Cat had ever seen. In the center of the ceiling up above was a giant crystal chandelier, its light refracting and dancing around on the walls and parquet floor below.

A waiter arrived seconds later, offering them a glass of

champagne.

Shelly emptied her glass immediately, but Cat wasn't much of a drinker. She sipped it slowly, and tried to take in as much as she could of the lush interior. This mansion didn't belong to some footballer, or other nouveau-riche celebrity. The place screamed old money.

As luxurious as it looked, it was tasteful.

Within minutes of their arrival, Shelly couldn't resist the pull of the festivities, and Cat found herself alone. She didn't mind. The champagne was lovely, refreshing with just a hint of citrus, and if Cat was left completely to her own devices, the decor alone would keep her entertained all evening.

Cat gazed at the staircase again. What wonders awaited up there? If she wasn't polite to a fault, she would have been tempted to check it out. She wouldn't, though. Not unless she was invited to.

Her eyes settled on a painting of a man on horseback that hung on the left hand wall closer to ground level. She squinted to get a better look; it seemed old, probably expensive just like everything else in here. But that wasn't what had attracted her gaze. The hunting scene looked just like the standard fare you found in country houses and palaces around the country, except the man was dressed completely in black.

She felt a chill pass down her spine as she focused on his face. His dark eyes gave the impression of being alive as he seemed to stare down at her. How handsome he was.

He would have had a striking presence back in the day with his sharp jawline, impossibly flawless skin, and dark medium length hair.

If she found nothing else of interest here—which was unlikely—this one painting could captivate her for hours. That was how lifelike it looked.

Cat had to admit Shelly had been right: she'd never been to a place or a party quite like this one before.

CHAPTER TWO

Alexander Broderick stood at the top of the curving stairwell in the center of his Kensington residence, surveying his domain. The party had started at eight sharp, with more guests arriving every few minutes.

His Halloween parties were an age old tradition, even if their grandeur and scale had evolved significantly since the early days. A hundred years ago, he'd been content inviting a few friends and acquaintances, all of them vampire like he was. Now, every year, the event had grown bigger and better, featuring new faces from all walks of life.

Eternity was a very long time to spend in isolation. He craved the change in routine, no matter how hard his maker had tried to discourage him from going overboard in the past. Of course, ever since Julius had taken over the Council leadership, he had other things on his mind than to monitor Alexander's social life.

Alexander thrived on the attention these parties afforded him. On a night such as tonight, he could step out of the shadows and into normality. Even if some guests noticed strange things around the house, they'd accept it as part of the magic of Halloween. It also helped that he kept the alcohol flowing generously throughout the night.

Tonight was the one night per year that the weird and

wonderful became acceptable.

He took a deep breath and closed his eyes. So many people. So many aromas.

His parties weren't an excuse to feed as such; no, he could do that any time. But the sheer variety of humankind at his feet was difficult to ignore.

Every vampire in attendance tonight would feel the same way. Alexander smiled as he imagined the depravity that would occur within these walls.

Sex, blood, and rock 'n' roll. Alexander couldn't suppress a chuckle.

They'd keep things clean enough, of course. Everyone here was keen to stretch the rules but not break them. They wouldn't take things so far as to attract suspicion.

They wouldn't kill.

Alexander himself would join in the festivities as well. But first and foremost, he enjoyed playing host. He was especially fond of striking up conversations with first-time guests. First he'd figure out how they'd come by an invitation, then he'd guide the conversation toward other topics that interested him.

He was a connoisseur of sorts; like some immersed themselves in fine wines, politics, or even sports, Alexander collected knowledge on the human psyche. *Zeitgeist,* as some people called it; he loved to learn about that special set of thoughts and ideas that made society tick. In gathering information about how people lived their fleeting lives, he sought to find meaning for his own.

As he slowly started to walk down the stairs, he focused on acting *normal*; that meant being a lot more clunky and obvious in his movements than his instincts dictated.

He was socializing, not stalking prey!

That was one of the first lessons he'd learned once he started inviting humans to his get-togethers. If you approached them in too stealthy a fashion, they easily got spooked.

Halfway down, his friend Michael nodded a greeting as he passed him by. The much younger vampire wasn't one to waste time; he'd already found himself two willing females to spend what he liked to call 'quality time.' Everyone had certain talents; seduction was his.

Alexander was about to continue down the steps when a presence caught him off guard. He wasn't sure what it was exactly. A quick scan around the room revealed that all the guests were quite busy entertaining themselves; nobody was looking in his direction.

He sprinted back up the stairs, faster than a human eye could see, and gazed back down to figure out what had affected him so.

The front door swung open and two women entered. One was quite ordinary, and he could hardly tell her apart from the two Michael had just led upstairs. The other, though...

A radiant sight of womanhood.

Her floor length gown was very different from the

skimpy outfits everyone else had chosen to wear. Blood red—which in itself would have been enough to entice even the most reclusive vampire among his company.

Raven hair halfway down her shoulder, which swayed with every step she took.

A face flawless, like that of a porcelain doll.

And curves. Her body exuded a richness that made every fiber in his body ache for her.

As different as they were, the two new guests couldn't have been a day older than 25, much younger than his usual choice of conversation partner.

He held on to the banister with both hands, then had to force himself to let go when the wood groaned under his tight grip. A lot could be forgiven on All Hallows' Eve, but destroying the furnishing with his super-human strength would raise a few eyebrows.

Alexander focused his hearing on the two women who still stood indecisively in the hall. One of his staff immediately approached them with a welcome drink.

"Thank you," the dark haired beauty said. *The voice of an angel.*

The blond didn't speak; instead, she just chugged the champagne and placed her empty glass back onto the waiter's tray. Alexander recognized her type. She gave the impression of a hunter among humans; she knew what she was after, and was scouting the place for the right mark.

Alexander stood frozen in place, waiting for the woman in the red gown to make a move.

The blonde had taken a few steps forward and spotted the dance floor in the reception room. She waved at her companion to join her, who refused.

"You go ahead. I'll hang back and get a feel for the place first," the medieval angel said, then took a small sip of champagne to make her point.

Alexander smiled and closed his eyes. Perhaps his senses were deceiving him tonight, but he could swear that he could catch her scent all the way up here.

A hungry vampire could smell his prey from nearly a mile away. But Alexander wasn't hungry.

At least not for nourishment.

From the moment she'd entered, the quality of the air seemed to have changed.

He knew he had to have her before anyone else. He would get to know this young woman, learn all he could about her. Take her to his chambers and bed her. He would taste her very essence. He had to. His instincts gave him no choice.

Before he opened his eyes, he knew she still stood in the same place; he could sense it. When he looked down at her, he noticed that it wasn't just him who had noticed her.

A half dozen sets of eyes had shifted in her direction.

Could they smell her too?

Alexander rushed down the stairs again, almost forgetting to follow the usual tricks to appear more human. So far so good: the other vampires had spotted her, but stayed back for now. He would reach her first. If her arrival had made this much of an impact, he would have to take it upon himself to ensure her safety here.

This was his house after all. His party.

He'd never been one to lose his tongue in company, but the closer he got to the woman, the more uncertain he grew. She wasn't just any other human to him; she was a whole lot more special than that.

"I hope you're enjoying yourself?" he said as he reached her side.

She looked up at him, her eyebrows pulled together in surprise. "Who, me?"

"Yes, Miss..."

"Uh... my name's Cat."

"Short for Catherine?" Alexander asked, mesmerized by her pale green eyes as she continued to look up at him.

She looked so vulnerable. He could hear her heartbeat, and the rush of her blood as it was pumped through her body. Being so near to her tested his patience like nothing ever had. If he'd been starving and faced with a first meal in weeks, he would have found it easier to walk away than he did now. There was something very different about this woman, though he had no idea what it was.

"I suppose, yes. Short for Catherine," she stammered.

He wasn't trying to hypnotize her, at least not on purpose. Was she under his control already?

How was that even possible?

"I said I hope you're enjoying yourself," he said, repeating his first question.

"Oh, yes." Catherine raised her glass and smiled briefly. "And what a beautiful house this is. I've never seen anything like it."

That gave Alexander his opening, a chance to get her away from all the hungry stares from every vampire in the room.

"Perhaps you'd like to see more of it?" he asked, smiling subtly to avoid exposing his sharp canines.

Catherine didn't answer straight away, instead continuing to stare at him. Hopefully, she wasn't actually hypnotized. Alexander was looking forward to having a natural conversation with this woman. Not a forced interrogation while she was under his influence.

"Don't tell me this is your place?" she asked at last.

Was she just nervous? Could that be?

Alexander winked at her in an attempt to break the tension and gain her trust. "Okay, I won't tell you that it is."

"Holy shit." Catherine immediately covered her mouth with her hand as she looked around the entrance hall again. "I'm sorry."

"You have nothing to be sorry about. My offer still stands by the way. If you want a tour..." Alexander said.

She looked into his eyes and there it was again, that strange feeling that had overcome him from the moment she'd entered his home. He had to have her, discover all there was to learn about her. Intellectually, physically, even spiritually, if that even made sense.

"I'm sorry, I just didn't expect to end up here chatting with the host of the party straightaway. Yes. I'd love a tour," Cat said while straightening her shoulders.

So she had just been nervous.

He wasn't sure why, but that pleased him. Probably because he'd been a little nervous at first too.

It was silly. He'd walked this earth for centuries and seduced plenty of beautiful ladies in his day. As delicious as this woman smelled, what did he have to be nervous about? He offered her his arm, which she reluctantly accepted. Her touch seemed to burn through his tuxedo right into his skin, almost painfully.

"We'll start with the downstairs," he said.

As Alexander led her past some of his immortal guests into the reception room, he felt their eyes on the two of them. There was no emotion as powerful to the senses as jealousy. Perhaps his nerves had been trying to tell him something. This party wasn't like every previous one. This time, he was playing with fire.

CHAPTER THREE

I'm such an idiot.

Cat straightened herself in an attempt to seem confident, even if she felt anything but. This handsome man—the actual host of the party and owner of this amazing house—had approached her and offered her a tour. And what had she done? Fumbled over her words and acted like a complete moron. Could it get any worse?

"I'd love a tour," Cat said and glanced at his face again.

Although he was wearing a mask covering the better part of his face, it was obvious that he was gorgeous. Those brooding, dark eyes... They alone spoke a million words.

And he was built too. Taller than her, with broad shoulders and a toned, athletic body which his three-piece suit could scarcely disguise.

He made Cat nervous, which was unusual. Cat wasn't the sort to get nervous around members of the opposite sex. Of course, she wasn't as outgoing as Shelly, but for most of her life, Cat had gotten on better with men than with women, platonically. Possibly that was a side effect of growing up with two older brothers...

Somehow though, this man was different. He intimidated her and made her feel out of her depth.

Was it because he was so handsome? Or so wealthy?

How shallow.

No, Cat couldn't accept that. There was something else about him which she couldn't quite put her finger on.

He guided her around the downstairs of the house. Through the reception and the dining room, as well as the very spacious kitchen. Cat couldn't be sure how the house normally looked; it had obviously been cleared out to accommodate tonight's party guests. She would have loved to see the normal layout and furnishing instead of this bare bones version.

"Would you like to see the upper floor now?" the man asked. There was a strange glint in his eye.

Cat glanced away shyly. Was that what had thrown her off? The way he looked at her? Nobody had ever looked at her like this.

"Sure, that would be great," she said.

He gestured at the stairs. "After you."

As she climbed up, she couldn't help but take another good look at that painting that had caught her eye earlier. It was even more stunning up close. Even though she could see the brush strokes in the landscape, the figure on horseback was still so lifelike. Like it was a photograph and not a painting at all. The only thing that gave it away were the fine cracks in the varnish, a clear sign that it was much older than anyone in attendance here today.

"Beautiful artwork," Cat whispered, barely loud enough to hear over the music coming from the reception room.

"Oh. Yes, this piece has been in the family a very long

time." The man smiled at her again. "If it's art you're interested in, I have some more items you might want to see."

Although she'd wanted to stop and admire that painting some more, her feet seemed to want nothing more than to carry her up the stairs. It was effortless, like she was floating.

"So this house has been in your family for a while then?" Cat asked, as she paused and held the banister with both hands at the top of the stairs. The view of the ongoing party down below, lit up by that magnificent chandelier, was something special. It made her feel powerful to be up here.

That was when she noticed a pair of red eyes burning into her from the foot of the stairs. The man, who looked to be in his mid-thirties, stood completely still as he stared at her. He didn't even blink once, which seemed unusual for someone who was obviously wearing contact lenses. An uneasy tension grew inside Cat's chest, forcing her to look away from the strange man to regain her composure.

Only then did she realize her host hadn't answered her question. And in fact, she didn't even know his name yet.

"You never introduced yourself," Cat remarked as she faced him.

He took his position next to her at the banister and looked down like she had only moments earlier. Would he notice the weirdo downstairs?

"Alexander Broderick the Third," he said. His voice

was low, like he was preoccupied with something else. So he *had* noticed.

That name, though. It was as grand as the house itself and she might have been way more skeptical of him had she not run into him here.

"Nice to meet you," she said and followed his line of sight down.

The strange man was no longer in view. What a relief.

When she turned to face Alexander again, she found that he was already looking at her with the subtlest of smiles on his lips. She couldn't help but reciprocate.

"How about I show you the master suite?" he suggested.

His proposal was forward, crossing the limits of propriety.

Cat frowned. She ought to change her mind about this whole house tour business and get back downstairs and try to enjoy the party. She really ought to... And yet, her feet refused to move.

"It's not what you think, I promise," Alexander added, raising both his hands in a defensive gesture. "There's this beautiful painting I'm sure you would appreciate."

Cat cocked her head. Nothing in his eyes suggested that he had any ill will toward her. And even if this beautiful man was indeed trying to seduce her, was she seriously about to reject him? Would it be so bad to just take a chance for once? To jump in the deep end and see where tonight would take her?

Cat took a deep breath and smiled through a fresh surge of nerves. "Okay, sure."

Alexander offered her his arm again, which she took as he led her away from the staircase and into an elegantly decorated hallway. A similar, though smaller crystal chandelier adorned its ceiling, and paintings lined the walls. There were more hunting scenes, some still lifes and portraits, though none captured Cat's imagination as much as that first painting along the staircase.

The further they went, the fainter the music became from the party below. Until one of the doors lining the hallway opened seemingly by itself, revealing not just a breathtaking array of period furniture, but also the painting Alexander must have referred to.

Cat let go of Alexander's arm and approached it. Expert brush strokes had created a completely realistic likeness of the house they found themselves in. It must have been painted in midsummer; the front drive and lawns were lined by a dazzling array of flowers which Cat didn't know the names of. She just knew they were beautiful.

"I love the light in this one," Alexander spoke behind her, his voice dreamy; he was obviously as enthralled by the painting as she was. "So realistic. A beautiful summer's day the likes of which I haven't seen in a very long time."

"You're right, the summers have been atrocious these past few years," Cat agreed. Still, she couldn't tear herself away from the image of the house.

It was perfect; blue skies reflected in the windows, just like a photograph. She leaned forward to get a better look and noticed the front doors were ajar and a figure waited just inside with its back turned. It made no sense of course, but as soon as she'd spotted it, she felt herself drawn to the house and wanted nothing more than to step inside.

Ridiculous. It's just a painting after all.

Cat turned and found that Alexander was already looking at her. He held two elegant long stemmed glasses in his hand.

"Champagne?"

Cat took a step back and scanned the room. Where had he got those from all of a sudden? Had this room already been prepped, just waiting for whoever he chose to bring up here?

She was about to protest when music started to play in the background. Something classical, she wasn't sure what it was.

Now where was the music coming from? She hadn't seen a stereo or even speakers anywhere. They'd look so out of place with all of this regency furniture that she was certain she would have noticed them on her way in.

Before she knew it, she'd accepted the champagne flute.

"To great art and great beauty," Alexander said and raised his glass for a toast.

She followed his example, even though her heart was

hammering in her throat now.

"To art," she mumbled.

What's going on here? None of this makes any sense. Was that first drink spiked?

Against better judgment, she took her first sip and felt her worries dissipate. So what if he was plying her with drinks. So what if she was alone with a stranger in this luxurious bedroom. She glanced at the painting again.

It was all worth it, wasn't it?

She took another sip and felt her confidence grow. *Who cares if he brought me up here to seduce me? This is the sort of thing that happens to Shelly, not me. If this is what it feels like to be coveted, I'll take it.*

He took the glass from her and placed it on the lacquered wooden cabinet facing the bed. Then he held out his hand.

"Would you honor me with this dance?" he all but whispered.

Cat bit her lip. This entire scenario was absurd: being in here, with this man, in this room... And now, he wanted to dance with her.

And yet...

She placed her hand in his, and he started to lead immediately.

Cat wasn't much of a dancer, and she certainly wasn't familiar with ballroom steps. Still, she found herself moving effortlessly. Her feet seemed to know what to do as the two of them started to circle around the room.

She wrapped her arm around his neck, just as his hand rested in the small of her back. They started off touching only lightly, but after a few steps, she found herself firmly in his grasp.

It didn't occur to her anymore to question what was going on.

This was amazing. She felt like Cinderella dancing through her very own fairy tale. Did that mean that Alexander was her Prince Charming? *No, that would be ridiculous.* This was just a fling at a Halloween party. Nothing less, and nothing more.

She gazed up at him, at those deep black eyes, which somehow managed to convey more emotion than any other guy she'd ever been with. How she wished she could see the rest of his face. She let her gaze travel downward to the part of his face that wasn't obscured.

Full lips, slightly parted to reveal perfectly white teeth.

His pale skin was smooth, flawless, without the slightest hint of stubble, or even a razor burn. Did rich people have ways and means to skip the inconveniences normal guys often had to deal with? Perhaps he was wearing some kind of make-up.

He asked her questions, about her family, where she was from. She did her best to answer, as she observed his every move.

Even his scent was unique: sweeter, cleaner than other guys. Not that Cat thought regular guys were dirty; Alexander was just different somehow, in a way that she couldn't make sense of.

She wasn't sure how long they'd been dancing for when the music stopped, as did the two of them. But they didn't let go. If anything, Cat thought she could feel his arm tighten around her. Similarly, she clung on to his neck and stared into his eyes.

This was the moment of truth. Now, she would find out what else tonight would bring.

CHAPTER FOUR

When the music stopped, Alexander was painfully aware that the longer they stood there, holding each other, the more awkward things might get. And yet, he couldn't bring himself to let Catherine go.

Neither did she seem in any hurry to get out of his embrace. Instead, she looked up at him with those mesmerizing green eyes as though she was trying to tell him something.

In the centuries that he had been walking this earth, he had never really focused on human attraction as a subject of study. He'd preferred more philosophical topics.

Right now, he could have really used some extra knowledge to interpret Catherine's demeanor.

Of course, it wasn't difficult for a vampire to seduce a woman simply by keeping her under his spell. But something about her demanded for him to treat her honorably.

He wanted for this amazing woman to want him back.

So far, so good it seemed.

"The music has stopped," she remarked at last.

Alexander smiled subtly. "I can remedy that."

"No, I think that's enough dancing for one night," she responded.

And yet, she didn't make a move.

He allowed his gaze to rest on her curvaceous lips. She didn't wear much makeup, just a bit of lipstick and perhaps eyeshadow. Either way, she had a natural beauty to her that was more impressive than anything man-made could ever be.

As was her scent, actually.

Her hair was fragrant; it reminded him of that display of summer flowers in the painting they'd admired together only moments earlier. In her eyes he recognized the color of morning dew on a lawn in bright sunlight, something he hadn't seen for a very long time indeed.

At first it had been easy for him to be nocturnal, but as the centuries passed, he had come to miss little things like that. In Catherine, he saw all that and more. He saw life. He saw hope.

She tiptoed slightly, perhaps without even realizing that she had, bringing her face closer to his. Her eyelids fluttered and then shut.

This was his chance.

Alexander stopped thinking about what was happening and proceeded on instinct alone. He kissed her sweet lips, which parted almost instantly, allowing him a taste of her tongue.

Intoxicating.

Excitement overwhelmed him, or was it hunger? He wanted her so badly, it became hard to focus on anything else. His senses worked at a feverish pitch; the floral scent of her skin and hair continued to egg him on. The softness of her skin under his touch invited him in for more tactile explorations. But above all, the sound of her heartbeat as it sped up, the rush of blood running through her veins—it drove him to the edge of insanity.

How could he resist her?

He pulled back and looked down at the elegant curve of her neck. That was where her jugular was, throbbing as her body pumped around what promised to be the best meal of his life.

She opened her eyes, diverting his attention back to her face.

"I'm sorry, I didn't mean to," she stammered.

Alexander smiled. "Yes, you did. As did I."

She pressed her lips together but didn't avert her gaze.

He would resist the draw of her blood a little while longer. Something told him that once he started, he wouldn't be able to control himself, and the last thing he wanted was to harm her.

"Tell me more about yourself," he whispered, as he led her by the hand to the bed and gestured that she sit with him.

Catherine paused for a moment, then looked down at his hand, which still enclosed hers.

"Not much to tell..."

"What do you do?" Alexander suggested. That was all small talk, though. What he really wanted to know went much deeper than that. Her hopes and dreams, her outlook on the world. Those were the questions playing on his mind whenever he met someone new. Most of the time his talks with humans were research to him. This was something deeper.

"Well, you know where I'm from already. I just came up here to study. Now that that's over, I've been looking for work." She looked up at him, those pale green eyes practically begging for further affections.

Alexander reached out and ran his fingertip across her cheek. Such soft, perfect skin. Was she this pleasing to the touch all over?

"Let me guess, something to do with art?" Alexander said.

Catherine's gaze darted across the room at the painting. "Yes, that's right. I like to be around beautiful things. Art History was an obvious—"

Alexander couldn't resist any longer. He let go of her hand and cupped her face, pressing his lips against hers in an attempt to still his intense desire for her. It was no use, though. All their kisses did was fan the fire within him.

Apparently, she felt the same. Though she started off a bit shy and taken aback, soon her kisses competed with his in intensity and passion. They wrapped their arms around each other and fell back onto the bed to take things to the next level.

Cat still couldn't believe where she was, and who she was with. This simply wasn't the sort of thing that happened to girls like her.

Shelly, sure. She could imagine Shelly in a room like this. With a guy like Alexander.

His hands were all over her now. And it felt so good.

While she'd started off nervous, the passion he showed had quickly encouraged her to let go too. It was all so unlike her, so deliciously naughty. She needed a night like this, perhaps more than she'd ever allow herself to admit.

It had been a while since she'd been on a date. Alexander reminded her how nice it was to feel wanted.

He caressed her curves, while she explored his toned, muscular body through his clothes. Everything felt like it had fallen into place. There was just one catch: she wasn't quite certain what her mysterious lover looked like.

And she couldn't contain her curiosity any longer.

Cat reached out for his mask and carefully lifted it off. For a moment, she was mesmerized by his symmetrical features, his high cheek bones and almost ivory skin. He was beautiful. Just like...

Oh my God.

Cat pulled back in a panic. He looked identical to the man in the painting she'd found herself staring at earlier. The hunting scene hanging by the staircase.

The work of art that was so eerily realistic, she'd found it impossible to ignore.

And as she'd passed it by on the way up here, she'd seen it up close. From the patina and subtle cracks in the paint to the style of frame, she'd been certain it had to be hundreds of years old.

How could a painting that old depict a man who was right here and now? It was impossible.

She forgot to breathe and tried to scramble away from him.

He was trouble.

He was dangerous.

She could feel it so keenly now. The nerves she'd felt before were trying to tell her that something was wrong. And she'd brushed those feelings away because she loved the attention.

All of this, it *had* been too good to be true. This man wasn't of this world. This wasn't possible.

Cat's heart raced now. Her chest felt tight, like she was about to asphyxiate.

All the while, Alexander seemed oblivious to the change in her. While she tried to get away from him, he followed and tried to kiss her again.

She pressed her lips together tightly and evaded his grasp, stumbling off the bed, landing right in between her shoes. Her bag was waiting on the dresser. She grabbed all her things and didn't look back once as she fled the room.

"What happened?" she heard Alexander's voice behind her. "Catherine?"

She didn't owe him an explanation. Her heart beat so fast she could feel it in her throat and temple. All she needed to do right now was get away.

And so she sprinted down the stairs, her shoes still in

her hand. A few heads turned in her direction as she made it back to the entrance hall, but she didn't care. Where was Shelly?

Cat scanned her surroundings and spied her talking to some guy in a pirate costume just inside the reception room. *Thank God.*

"Shelly," Cat said. "Shelly!"

Shelly frowned as she turned to face her and noticed the state she was in: messed up hair, bare feet. "What's going on?"

"We've got to go," Cat said.

Shelly glanced at the man she had been in conversation with before, then back at Cat. "Why? What happened?"

"I don't have time to explain right now. Please. Just trust me. Let's go."

Shelly turned to her companion. "Excuse us for a moment, all right?" Then she took Cat's arm and led her into a slightly quieter corner of the room.

"Did some guy attack you? Where is he? I'll sort him out!" Shelly demanded.

Cat just shook her head. "No, I agreed to go up there. That's not... Look, it's a long story. Can we please just go now?"

"So you weren't attacked?"

"No." *Not yet, anyway.*

"You're not hurt, are you? Are you okay?" Shelly asked.

Cat took a deep breath and looked down at her bare feet. *This must look pretty weird.*

In fact, people were already starting to stare at her. And now that she wasn't with Alexander anymore, the big realization she had about him seemed ludicrous. A man who was several hundred years old. That was stupid. Nobody would believe her, not even Shelly.

"I'm fine. I just want to go," Cat mumbled.

"I don't get you. You're fine—everything's fine, but you want to leave. The costume competition hasn't even started yet and I think I have a decent chance here." Shelly squinted and cocked her head to the side. "You never really wanted to come to this party anyway. Is that it?"

Meanwhile, the man she'd been talking to earlier approached them and rested his hand on Shelly's shoulder. "I'm going to get something to drink. Can I get you ladies anything?" he asked.

Cat stared at him blankly. What was he thinking, interrupting them like that?

From Shelly's expression it was obvious that she didn't share Cat's outrage. Instead, she smiled and nodded. "Champagne would be lovely. Anything for you?" Shelly asked.

Cat shook her head. Whatever.

She had nothing. No explanation. No way to convince Shelly to go. If that was how it was going to go, fine!

"I'm going home. I'll see you whenever," Cat grumbled.

"Oh come on, don't be like that! Stay a little longer! It's only just getting started in here." Shelly pouted. "And the competition starts in a few minutes..."

"Whatever. I'm out." Cat put on her shoes and adjusted her hair before marching out of the room, as well as the house. Although she'd tried to make herself somewhat presentable, she could feel the stares of the other guests burning into her back.

If there ever was a walk of shame, this must have been what it felt like.

As the doors opened, a gust of cold air stung her skin, giving her goosebumps all over. Luckily, on the drive outside, several cabs waited. She got into the first one and breathed a sigh of relief as she shut the double door behind her.

"Shepherd's Bush, please."

CHAPTER FIVE

Why had she left like that? What had he done to spook her?

Alexander paced around the room, back and forth, for at least twenty minutes, as if somehow that would help provide an answer. Of course it didn't. It just made him more agitated.

Everything had gone so well. Until all of a sudden she turned completely pale, her eyes went wide with fear, and she'd fled. Had he accidentally shown his fangs?

He wasn't a regular womanizer like Michael was, but he wasn't that stupid either. No, it had to be something else...

Out in the hallway the large grandfather clock struck midnight, and Alexander couldn't contain his frustration any longer. This was his party and if the fun was over for him, it could bloody well be over for everyone. He burst through the door and down the stairs, when the first painting they'd discussed caught his eye.

Bloody hell!

Alexander stopped in his tracks halfway down and stared darkly at the portrait. He couldn't believe he hadn't put things together sooner. She'd left the moment she'd seen him without his mask on. She had *recognized* him. From this innocuous little hunting scene he'd kept around as a reminder of another life.

In all his years living here, he'd had plenty of humans over, mostly during events much like this one. Not one of them had ever put it together like she had.

Most humans were easy to fool and not all that perceptive. But Catherine wasn't like most humans.

"Okay, party's over!" Alexander raised his voice.

Some people at the bottom of the stairs turned to give him a disapproving look, then turned to each other again and continued their respective conversations.

"I mean it! Everybody out, now!" Alexander roared so loudly the chandelier above his head trembled, as did the windows beside the front door.

The music in the reception room stopped, as did all the chatter among the guests.

Within a split second, a disheveled looking Michael appeared at the top of the stairs. His hair was in a mess and he was shirtless; clearly Alexander's outburst had interrupted him with his two lady friends. If he was annoyed about the disturbance, he didn't show it.

"Go on, gather your belongings and make your way to the exit!" Michael shouted. Whatever his vices, the young vampire was loyal to a fault.

Alexander nodded his approval and turned to face the crowd again. The first people were on their way out, while whispering to one another.

This abrupt end to this year's famed Halloween event was going to be the fodder to many a gossip, no doubt. Alexander didn't care, though. He didn't care about any of these people who just came to drink the free champagne and eat the finger food.

The one person he cared about had already left, and he wasn't even sure why he cared. What was so special about Catherine?

As the humans left, all the vampires attending the party grouped around the bottom of the stairs waiting for some kind of explanation of what had happened. As they stared up at him, Alexander was reminded of their strange behavior when Catherine had just arrived. They'd all been able to smell her. Why?

What was it about this woman?

He ought to ask them, if only he thought he'd get an honest answer. Not from any of them, except perhaps Michael. But he had already found himself some company and retreated upstairs by the time Catherine had even arrived, so he probably hadn't noticed her presence at all.

The reception room and entrance hall quickly emptied out, leaving just the staff, who were frantically clearing up, and the vampires. Still, Alexander felt more agitated, not less.

"What are you all looking at? I asked everyone to leave. That includes you too!" he snapped.

Gillian, one of the more senior vampires in attendance, glared at him.

"Your behavior is completely unacceptable," she spat.

"This is my house and I get to behave how I like in it," he said.

They stared each other down, until Michael joined Alexander's side on the landing, causing Gillian to back off.

They couldn't afford a physical altercation, not with all the human staff still around. Tonight's events would make waves as it was. The last thing they needed was to be called in by the Council for outing themselves.

Gillian knew that better than anyone.

And so, even the immortals started to leave until only Michael remained.

"I might need a moment, if you know what I mean," he said, while looking in the general direction of the bedrooms upstairs.

Alexander nodded. That was the least he could do.

"Are you going to tell me what happened tonight?" Michael asked.

Alexander folded his arms. He wanted to. He ought to.

"All right. Join me in the library when you're ready."

Within the blink of an eye, Michael was gone, leaving Alexander alone with his thoughts again. He left behind the catering staff to do their jobs and retreated, a bottle of his finest aged brandy in hand. The library was always off limits to guests during events such as this one, allowing him one true refuge from all the activity that was still going on.

Alexander sat down in one of the leather arm chairs and poured himself a drink.

Of course, his metabolism didn't allow him to feel the

effects of alcohol, but he still enjoyed the ritual of it all. This was one of those little things that allowed him to feel at home, no matter how much the world around him had changed.

So he stayed in that chair, sipping the amber liquid from an antique crystal snifter he'd had in his possession for the better part of the century, until Michael turned up.

"Sorry about that. That took longer than I expected it to," Michael said as he took a seat in the arm chair next to Alexander.

"A drink?" Alexander asked.

Michael accepted his offer and took a sip.

"So what happened tonight?" he asked, after setting down his glass on the table between the two chairs.

"It's rather difficult to explain." Alexander folded his hands and stared straight ahead. He wasn't quite sure what had happened himself.

"This woman arrived; she was unlike any I've encountered before. Her presence seemed to affect every vampire in the room," Alexander started, and closed his eyes to relive the moments leading up to Catherine's sudden change of heart. "I approached her, made a little conversation, you know how it goes."

"Right."

"Then I took her upstairs, where we danced. Things were going so well. She'd made me feel things I haven't felt in a long time."

"And this was a human woman, who had affected you

so?" Michael's voice was laden with disbelief. Sure, he enjoyed the female form more than most, but he never got too involved with any of his marks.

Alexander sighed and opened his eyes again. It was all a game to Michael. He wouldn't understand.

"She wasn't vampire if that's what you're asking," Alexander said.

"Still, it all sounds bizarre."

"It was."

"And the others noticed her too? I'm almost sad I wasn't there to see her. Almost!" Michael winked at Alexander, who just shook his head.

They sat quietly for a while, giving Alexander more of a chance to relive his last moments with Catherine.

A loud bang on the door interrupted the silence. "Open up. Council business!" a firm female voice called out.

"Come in, Lucille!" Alexander sighed again. His outburst at the party had been unorthodox, but surely not serious enough to warrant an instant visit from the Council's enforcer?

The door swung open, revealing a petite, slender vampire, who marched in with her hand on her hip.

"What can I do for you, sister?" Alexander asked, while emptying his glass with one last sip.

"Alexander. Good to see you," Lucille said, then acknowledged Michael only with a curt nod.

"Well, unless you need me, I'll be upstairs," Michael said as he got up from his chair. The much younger vampire had never been comfortable in Lucille's presence. His quick escape would have been comical, had Alexander not had other things on his mind.

"Julius sends me," Lucille said as she took the seat Michael had just vacated.

Alexander poured himself another drink, then held up the bottle at Lucille, who shook her head. "I'll never know why you like this stuff."

Alexander shrugged and set the bottle down again.

"What does our dear maker want?" he asked.

"Word has spread fast about what happened at your little soirée this evening," Lucille started.

Alexander frowned. He had Gillian to thank for that, no doubt. The old hag loved to gossip, especially when she felt wronged somehow.

"What about it? I invited people over, and then I asked them to leave when the party was over."

Lucille shook her head and smiled subtly. "Brother, why so defensive? That's not what I'm here to discuss."

"Oh?" Alexander put his glass down and turned to face Lucille properly to observe her every move. They were brother and sister, in vampire terms. After Julius had made both of them, they had even spent their first century together.

But loyalties changed over the centuries. Who knew what Julius was up to nowadays? You couldn't fully trust another vampire, only yourself; time had taught Alexander as much.

Lucille smiled again. "We hear that one of your guests was very special indeed."

Catherine. They knew about Catherine.

Alexander tried his best to feign surprise. "Is that so? Special how?"

"Don't tell me you didn't notice. We hear you were the only one to interact with her!" Lucille argued.

Alexander remained quiet. So Gillian *had* told them everything. This was the last time she'd be invited to one of his parties.

"No matter. What we really want to know is: where is she now?" Lucille asked.

"How would I know? She left."

"Right. Well she came by an invitation somehow. Where does she live?" Lucille pressed him again.

"I never saw her before tonight. Someone must have passed their invitation on to her," Alexander said, while looking Lucille straight in the eye. One of the reasons Julius had appointed her as enforcer was that she had an uncanny talent for uncovering the truth. She could always tell when someone was lying. Luckily for Alexander, he truly had no idea where Catherine might have gone.

"Well, I'm sorry I couldn't be of more help to you or Julius... But are you going to tell me what it is that makes her so special?" Alexander asked.

Lucille pursed her lips like she usually did when she was mulling something over.

"Well, I suppose there's no harm in telling you, brother.

You have been trying to cooperate after all."

Alexander leaned forward in anticipation. Any information that allowed him to understand Catherine better might help him track her down. If Julius and the Council were after her, that was bad news. She needed to be warned.

"Every so often a human female is born with blood so potent it has a profound effect on all vampires. It might be a mutation of some sort; we're not sure without further study. These women are called Blood Brides. So as you might imagine, having her walk around the city is bad news. Any vampire who tries to feed on her will not be able to control themselves. We could be outed, or worse."

Alexander's jaw tensed up. Lucille's explanation made sense. That was why Catherine had attracted everyone's attention the moment she walked in.

"So what do you plan to do once you find her?" Alexander asked, though he wasn't sure he wanted to know the answer.

"That's not for me to say. Julius ordered me to find her, so that's what I'm doing. Vampire lore has it that Vlad the Impaler was seduced by a Blood Bride sent in by his enemies. That's what led to his ultimate defeat. Hence reports of a real life Blood Bride have got everyone in the Council very worried indeed. If she fell into the wrong hands..." As Lucille spoke, Alexander couldn't detect any sign that she was lying or holding anything back.

"Fair enough. Thank you for sharing this with me. I'll

keep my eyes open for her. And if you need anything, don't hesitate to ask," Alexander said.

Lucille smiled and got up. "Thank you, brother." She nodded at him, then made a quick exit, leaving Alexander alone with his thoughts again.

If the Council considered Catherine a threat, Alexander had to make sure he found her first.

CHAPTER SIX

Cat hadn't waited up for Shelly after reaching home, not on purpose anyway. Instead, she'd gone straight to bed and tried to get some rest. But sleep didn't find her; she kept tossing and turning until she ended up on her back, staring at the ceiling.

How dare Shelly ignore her concerns and stay behind? If she was going to act like that, she could have gone on her own in the first place. But no, Cat had to come along, and she'd wasted a handsome amount on a stupid costume too.

Cat closed her eyes and there he was. Alexander.

She'd wanted to forget all about him, but for some reason her mind hadn't finished processing what had happened. She couldn't understand it at all.

Everything had been fine at first, even if completely bizarre. And then his mask came off.

In her memories, Cat thought she could see a scary red glow in his eyes. That was just fantasy, surely? Her brain had just embellished things to make him seem scarier, when actually he probably only shared a passing resemblance to the man in the painting, and his eyes had been the same damn color throughout.

She had completely overreacted and made a fool of herself.

No wonder Shelly hadn't entertained her craziness.

Cat wasn't sure how long she'd been lying in bed like this, berating herself for how she'd handled things. She could have been there still, in that luxurious bedroom, with a man who normally might not even have given her a second look. It had felt so good to feel his hands on her body, his lips on hers.

She'd panicked, plain and simple.

And now, she was almost convinced she'd made a huge mistake.

Elsewhere in their shared apartment, the click of the door lock signaled Shelly's return.

Cat took a deep breath and got out of bed. If she couldn't sleep anyway, she might as well talk things through with Shelly.

"Hey," Cat said, when she entered the living room.

Shelly blew into her hands and rubbed them together vigorously, then looked up.

"You won't believe what happened!" she blurted out.

Cat folded her arms. "Oh yeah?"

"I won!" Shelly grinned and handed over an envelope.

Cat opened it. Indeed, inside there was a check for the promised £1000.

"That's amazing, congratulations!" Cat gave Shelly a hug; the latter was so cold to the touch that it sent chills down Cat's entire body.

"You must be freezing. How about a cup of tea?" Cat suggested.

Shelly smiled and nodded. "That would be great."

Cat headed for the kitchen with Shelly hot on her heels. As the kettle boiled, she got the full rundown of how the costume competition went down, what everyone else was wearing, and who the three finalists were. The party ended right after, so Shelly had left with the man in the pirate costume.

The more Shelly talked, the easier it was for Cat to get swept up in her excitement. Why did she have to run before any of this happened? She should have been there, cheering Shelly on.

Of course, then Cat remembered what happened with Alexander and cringed. She'd handled that all wrong.

"So. Now that that's out of the way... Are you going to tell me what happened tonight?" Shelly asked, then brought her mug to her lips and took a first, tentative sip.

Cat took a deep breath and followed her example. The tea seemed to help give her the courage she needed to share her story.

"Moments after we arrived, this guy started talking to me," Cat began.

Shelly looked up, her eyes wide with curiosity. "What guy?"

"His name is Alexander. It was his party." Cat's voice tapered off into a whisper. It sounded so ludicrous out loud.

"You met the host? Holy shit, why didn't you say so earlier? You could have introduced me!" Shelly said.

Cat raised her hand in a calming gesture. "Are you going to let me tell the story or what?"

"Okay." Shelly put her index finger over her lips and nodded.

"All right then." Cat traced the rim of her mug with her finger while considering how best to continue. "Well one thing led to another..."

Shelly's eyes went even wider, but to her credit, she kept her comments to herself.

"I don't know what happened. Something felt wrong. I don't know if it was the champagne, or whatever. But for a moment, I was convinced that the guy wasn't who he said he was. I felt like I was in danger."

"Wow."

"Yeah. Well, that's when I ran downstairs and found you. And the rest you know."

"What was he like?" Shelly asked.

Cat rolled her eyes. Of course that was what Shelly had focused on.

"I dunno. Handsome, articulate, really posh. He was showing me some of the artwork around the house. And my God, he could dance. It was like we were floating."

Shelly tilted her head to one side, her eyes dreamy.

"I would have liked to meet that guy; Alexander, you say?"

Cat couldn't suppress a smile. "Alexander Broderick the Third."

Shelly let out a shrill giggle. "You're kidding me!"

Cat shook her head. "I swear, that's what he said his full name was."

"And you bailed just as you were starting to... you know?"

Cat cringed again, and stared into her tea rather than make eye contact. "Yes."

"That's... wow."

"Insane, right?" Cat whispered.

"Totally." Shelly took another sip. "I still don't get why you ran."

"Yeah. I don't quite understand it anymore either. It made sense at the time."

"Maybe the champagne didn't agree with you indeed. Or..." Shelly paused. "No, that doesn't make sense."

"What?"

"If he managed to spike your drink somehow, I doubt that's how you would have reacted. At least I've never heard of anything like it."

Cat shook her head. "He wouldn't do that."

"I thought you said he was dangerous?" Shelly asked.

Cat pressed her lips together. Yeah, she had said that. The whole situation was confusing and bizarre. Now that she was here, in the safety of their shared home, he didn't seem so dangerous anymore. The look in his eyes hadn't been threatening, it had been caring and protective.

"Well, anyway. I'm glad you're okay now," Shelly said.

Cat smiled briefly. "Yeah. I'm glad too."

Now that she'd shared her side of things, finally it

seemed that all the excitement was catching up with her. Cat couldn't suppress a yawn and put her now empty mug down on the kitchen counter. "I'm going to bed. See you tomorrow."

Shelly patted her on the shoulder. "Goodnight, sleepyhead."

Cat nodded and made her way back to her bedroom. Funny, how she'd gone from wide awake to overcome with drowsiness in seconds. Perhaps someone had put something into her drink tonight.

She didn't think about it anymore. As soon as she was safely tucked in, it was like a black cloud descended over her and knocked her out.

———•———

The crowd split and formed a circle around them. Cat looked at Alexander, whose previously black eyes had started to glow red. This time, she wasn't scared though. It just seemed... normal.

"May I have the honor of this dance?" Alexander glanced down at Cat's hand.

She placed it in his as if it was the most natural thing in the world.

The music came out of nowhere, and they started to dance. They twirled and swayed effortlessly. Although Cat was wearing heels, she felt completely steady, until gradually her legs and then her whole body started to feel weightless.

Alexander kept his gaze locked on Cat's face, drawing her closer into his arms as they floated up off the dance floor, several feet above the rest of the guests.

Cat couldn't hear anything except the seductive tones of the violins that grew ever louder.

That was when she caught a glimpse of that painting, over Alexander's shoulder, and recognized him in it.

"That's you, isn't it?" Cat asked, only this time, she didn't feel any fear.

Alexander smiled briefly. "You're very perceptive. You know your art."

Cat couldn't keep her eyes off the painting, until they twirled again and she could no longer see it. Then she looked at Alexander's face again. Handsome, flawless. His smooth skin gave the impression that he was made entirely of the finest Italian marble.

She'd never seen a man quite like him.

Was he even a man? They were floating high above the shiny parquet floor of the entrance hall now. And she was pretty sure she wasn't the reason they'd started to defy gravity.

She closed her eyes.

"You smell delicious," Alexander whispered in her ear. The tickle of his breath against the side of her neck gave her goosebumps.

She didn't respond, just held on to him tighter.

Butterflies collected in her stomach, fluttering more violently with every passing second until she could hardly contain her excitement anymore.

"You're mine," he whispered.

She smiled. She wanted to be his.

Cat opened her eyes and found that their surroundings had changed. No longer were they in the same room; instead he had somehow carried her upstairs into that same bedroom without her knowing.

She gently landed on her back on the bed with Alexander on top of her. He kissed and nibbled at the side of her neck, until suddenly a sharp pain caused her heart to skip a few beats.

He pulled back and looked down at her.

She could see the blood dribbling down from the corner of his mouth. Like red wine against white marble.

He dove down and attacked her neck again.

It hurt, but it didn't alarm her as much as it excited her further.

It was a beautiful, sweet sort of pain.

She writhed against the sheets in ecstasy, desperate for Alexander to continue whatever it was he was doing. He sucked at her skin, which satisfied her much like scratching an itch, or like a long-awaited sneeze. The comparisons that entered her mind didn't do the feeling justice.

She knew it was wrong.

She knew it was dangerous.

And yet, she didn't want it to stop.

A shrill sound filled the air. She covered her ears and shut her eyes, but the repetitive, high pitched beeping continued to increase in volume until it overwhelmed her completely.

Finally, Cat opened her eyes, only to find the familiar sights of her very own bedroom. It had all been a dream. She turned off the alarm and fell back into the pillows. Ten o'clock already. If it wasn't for the alarm, she might have slept even longer.

The side of her neck still tingled, which was odd. Cat instinctively reached for it and rubbed it a few times to make the feeling go away.

And that wasn't the only body part which still felt the after-effects of her strange dream, the details of which had already begun to fade. Her whole body seemed on edge; she was tense, aroused.

What a mess. She'd ruined the only shot she'd ever have with Alexander, and now she was obsessing about him in her sleep?

Cat took a deep breath and got up. She didn't have time for this. Tomorrow would be the first day at her new job, and she had to keep her wits about her if she wanted to make a good impression. But first, she had to head to the shops to collect a few last minute items.

This was her first real job, not counting the part time work she'd done in the past. Her wardrobe really needed the help.

CHAPTER SEVEN

Alexander hadn't gotten much rest all day. He kept thinking about what Lucille had told him.

Catherine was a Blood Bride, and now everyone was after her. And when he wasn't consciously thinking about that, he'd been replaying every moment he'd spent with Catherine in his head, as well as some scenarios that hadn't yet come to pass.

Part of him wished she'd never turned up at his party. Another, much more insistent part of him was glad that she had.

She'd made him feel alive during the short time they'd spent together.

No way was he going to let anyone, including the Council, harm the one woman who had made him feel that way, centuries after he'd been turned.

He had to intervene somehow.

He got up early—in vampire terms—just before sundown. The black-out blinds on all the windows kept him safe enough to move around freely inside the house.

So he headed straight for the library.

Somewhere in this vast collection of old books, there had to be some information, some mention of what Lucille had told him.

How would he help Catherine if he didn't know for

sure what he was dealing with?

He owned an extensive selection of historical manuscripts, dating back over half a millennium. Most of the books he'd acquired and displayed had been chosen more for their decorative value than anything else. He'd never actually read them. That was about to change.

Alexander's best bet would be texts about Vlad the Impaler. Most of the works in his collection were human accounts of history though, not vampire. No matter how many volumes he removed from their respective shelves and leafed through, Alexander couldn't find anything relevant.

It was no use.

After a couple of hours of failed research, he sat down in his leather arm chair and rested his head in his hands. This was hopeless.

"Still thinking about that woman?" a voice asked.

Alexander looked up and found Michael staring down at him.

"Have you ever heard of a Blood Bride?" Alexander asked.

Michael frowned. "No."

"Wonderful." Alexander sat back and stared at nothing in particular.

"So what's a Blood Bride, then?" Michael sat down next to Alexander as he asked the question.

"In a nutshell: a human woman with very special blood."

Alexander's Blood Bride

Michael nodded in silence and folded his hands.

"Have you googled it?" he finally asked.

Alexander gave him a skeptical look. "What do you mean *have I googled it*?"

"Well, that *is* the fastest way of looking things up nowadays." Michael gestured at the piles of old volumes stacked up everywhere. "Especially since your books clearly haven't been of much help."

Alexander still stared at the younger vampire, who finally retrieved a smartphone from his pocket and started tapping away at the screen.

"Here. Try it." Michael handed him the device.

He had already opened a search, though the results didn't look promising. It was all horror movies and cheap fiction. Alexander raised an eyebrow and held back a snide remark as he scrolled through the first page, then switched to the image view.

It would be easy to give up already, but he was determined to check out everything, if only to be able to genuinely tell Michael how stupid his suggestion had been.

Page after page of blood-splattered women in wedding dresses awaited him. He scrolled and scrolled, through what must have been thousands of images, when the very last result caught his eye: an old illustration, on what looked like parchment.

It was a woman wearing what looked to be a traditional sort of frock and apron common among the lower classes during the end of the middle ages. Surrounding her stood a few humanoid creatures with monstrous faces and fangs—not a very accurate depiction of vampires, but clear enough to be recognizable.

Underneath, in Gothic style lettering, it read: Bride of Blood.

Alexander clicked through and started to read. The entire website contained extracts from an old book the author merely referred to as the *Encyclopedia of Myth and Magick*. It wasn't complete, but the section on Blood Brides was more informative than anything else Alexander had found.

"I don't believe it," he mumbled.

"Found something?" Michael's voice was loaded with glee.

Alexander glanced up and found that Michael was grinning at him. "Fine. You were right. Listen to this—"

Alexander held the phone up and started to read aloud.

"The existence of Blood Brides was first documented by the Ancient Egyptians, who believed that they were sent down by the gods to cleanse the world of evil. The presence of one of these women would inevitably attract all creatures of the night, making them easy to control and/or capture. What is notable about these women is that they themselves are unaware of their powers and often do not understand the attention they attract, yet at the same time, they can be extremely perceptive when it comes to the world at large."

Alexander looked up. That was it. Catherine had

noticed that it was him in the hunting scene painting after all.

"In ancient Egypt, as soon as a girl was identified as a Blood Bride, she was sent off to be raised by priestesses of Isis at one of the many temples dedicated to her worship. The practice of sending Blood Brides away to become priestesses to a female deity may have extended into Roman times. Some historians believe that the Vestal Virgins of Rome in fact always had at least one Blood Bride among their ranks. There is no conclusive evidence to support this theory, though. More recently, mythical scholars have formulated a theory that the occurrences of Blood Brides in the general populace is directly linked to the amount of supernatural activity at any given time, or in any given region. It therefore follows that a Blood Bride would only be born during times of hardship or when humanity is under threat from evil forces. Therefore, it is thought that during the Great Plague, Blood Brides were a lot more common than they are today. Over the centuries, all manner of tests have been devised to identify if a woman is a Blood Bride, most notably—"

Inconveniently, that was all there was. The method for identification and specifics regarding Vampirism and Blood Brides were missing.

Alexander gave the phone back to Michael.

"So you think that's what she was?" Michael asked.

Alexander shrugged. "That's what Lucille said she was. That's why they're after her; they think she's a threat to the

Council."

"Do you think she's a threat?"

Alexander folded his hands. "I just know that the moment she walked in, every vampire in the room turned to look at her."

Michael looked down at his phone, and scrolled back and forth a few times. "None of this explains how to defeat her powers, though."

Alexander turned to give Michael a disapproving look. "I don't want to defeat her! I want to keep her safe!"

"Oh." Michael turned off the phone and put it down on the table between them. "Well then, perhaps your books will be some use after all. Isn't there some law that prevents any vampire from harming another vampire's consort?"

Alexander waved Michael's suggestion away. He'd thought of that in passing already. "That only works if the intended is willing and not under hypnosis. You forget that this woman *fled* last night."

That wasn't the only problem, though. "I don't even know her full name. How will I track her down?" Alexander mumbled to himself.

Michael knew better than to answer that last, hypothetical question, so they both sat in silence for a while with Alexander lost in thought.

His thoughts moved back to last night, and the woman Catherine had arrived with. She seemed more extroverted, more of a social butterfly. Perhaps some of his other guests knew her.

He didn't even notice Michael had left his side, until the latter came back carrying a large envelope.

"Mail for you."

Alexander was about to discard it when he noticed the logo in the corner.

Sotheby's latest auction catalog.

As cliché as it was, perhaps some high end shopping might take his mind off things.

Michael grabbed his phone off the table and started tapping away at it; his expression suggested that the time for research had passed. The only thing he would be looking for now was a companion to spend the night with.

"Well, I'm off. I'll see you later," Michael mumbled a few moments later.

Alexander waved at him absentmindedly while leafing through the catalog. Nothing inspired him until he reached the very last page of the publication.

Anyone else might not realize what they were looking at, but Alexander did. Three pieces of old parchment, torn from one side as if they had been ripped out of a book and mounted in glass frames. If it wasn't for the illustration on the first page, he might not even have given it a second look.

He did a double-take on the description, then got up and headed straight for the land-line phone to RSVP for the upcoming auction.

Then he settled back down with the catalog and studied

the image that had caught his attention in more detail using a magnifying glass to boost his already powerful vision. The illustrations bore an uncanny resemblance to the image he'd just found on Michael's phone. The lettering also followed the same style. Sadly, the image wasn't detailed enough for Alexander to decipher the writing within.

He had no choice but to attend that auction, win the bid, and study these pages in person after.

Alexander sat back and closed his eyes.

Cat smiled at him, innocently, as though she had no idea of the effect she had on him. His whole being ached for her; he wanted to hold her, love her, keep her away from all the evil in the world. She twirled a lock of her long, dark brown hair around her index finger and turned away. Alexander reached out for her arm, but she slipped away. A terrifying, guttural cry pierced the silence; it took him a moment to realize that he was the one who had screamed.

Alexander tightened his grip on the armrests of his chair, stopping only when the leather under his right thumb gave way and tore.

Great. This was the second time in 24 hours that he'd accidentally destroyed his property while under the influence of Catherine, the supposed Blood Bride.

Alexander ran his fingertip across the torn leather and got up. The longer he sat here on his own, the closer he would come to losing his mind.

All this research, all these books, and none of it would help with his main problem: he still didn't know who or where she was. He had no choice but to go out there and do the necessary footwork to track her down.

Alexander left the house in a hurry, only to wander the city aimlessly all night. He crossed Kensington, Paddington, Mayfair, and Soho, but there was no sign of her or her unique scent anywhere.

If only he got somewhere near enough, his nose would pick up on her and lead him to her exact location. He knew that.

He just didn't know exactly where to look.

Just before dawn, he had no choice but to suspend the search.

CHAPTER EIGHT

Today was the big day.

Cat had woken up a bundle of nerves, after a restless night that featured even more unwanted dreams and fantasies. The star actor in all of them: Alexander. It was as though the thought of him simply refused to leave her be. Even when she was awake, he was right there, in her mind's eye, every time she blinked.

How am I going to concentrate? Cat rubbed her eyes and got out of bed. She stumbled into the bathroom to have a shower.

When she got out, she felt slightly better, but still listless. Back in her bedroom, she put on the outfit she'd laid out the night before, and did her hair, then she made her way toward the kitchen for a much needed caffeine boost.

Shelly was still in bed, it seemed—her shift wouldn't start until ten o'clock—so their apartment was eerily quiet. Cat tiptoed around the kitchen to prepare her packed lunch, when inevitably, she spilled a big dollop of mayonnaise on the front of her blouse.

"Dammit!" Cat cursed under her breath as she tried to wipe it clean.

It was no use, the stain was still visible.

She dumped the sorry excuse of a sandwich she'd made

into a Tupperware box, and rushed back into her room to change.

A knock on her door interrupted her.

"Hey..." Shelly stuck her head inside. "Shouldn't you be on your way by now?"

Cat checked the time on her phone. Shelly was right. "Crap. I spilled something. I can hardly turn up on my first day with a mayo stain on my left boob."

"Calm down. Take a breath," Shelly said as she stepped inside. "Let's see... Wear this one."

She held up a simple white blouse.

Cat sat down on the bed. "That's all wrinkled!"

"So what?" Shelly held it up into the light. "You're wearing a jacket on top. Nobody will be able to tell."

Cat sighed and held out her hand. "Fine."

She quickly changed into the new shirt and buttoned up her blazer to hide the offending wrinkles.

"Now go. You look fine," Shelly said. "And you'll do fine too. You have nothing to worry about!"

Cat smiled bleakly. "I hope so."

"I know so. Now go before you're late on your first day!"

That was all Cat needed to hear to gather all her stuff in a hurry and head for the door.

What a start to such an important day, she thought as she rushed toward the main road. As soon as she'd run down the steps to the tube platform, she saw the tail end of the train just as it was pulling away.

Bloody great.

At least she wasn't late.

Despite everything, Cat had arrived at her new place of employment with about a minute to spare. She'd wanted to be early, of course, but you couldn't have everything in life, as her mom liked to say.

Sotheby's, one of the world's most prestigious auction houses, and *the* place to be for an art history graduate such as herself. She knew she wouldn't be in charge of anything important, but it was a privilege to be in this building, surrounded by so much wealth and beauty.

"Catherine?" A stern looking woman in her forties carrying a clipboard approached.

Cat recognized her from the first round of interviews. She took a step forward and offered her hand for a greeting. "Yes, Mrs. Pryce."

"Miss!" the woman corrected her, glancing down at Cat's hand, then turning away without shaking it. "Follow me."

Cat swallowed hard. That wasn't a great start. She held on tightly to her handbag and followed Ms. Pryce, who marched past the reception, through the corridors, and down the stairs leading into the basement at a dazzling pace, which Cat had trouble matching in her shoes.

"I assume I don't need to explain to you what it is we do here?" Ms. Pryce asked as she paused in front of a nondescript door.

"No, that won't be necessary," Cat mumbled. How was she meant to address this woman, Ma'am? No, that seemed risky, considering her earlier misstep.

"You'll be working in here, under Desmond's guidance, cataloging lots and their performance at auction."

Cat nodded. "No problem. I'm good at—"

Ms. Pryce shot her a blank look.

"Cataloging," Cat completed her sentence in a low mumble.

Of all the bosses in the world, she seemed to have hit the jackpot.

Cat glanced over at the woman, who impatiently tapped her foot and folded her arms while looking her up and down. Damn. Had she noticed her blouse was wrinkled? Or did she generally disapprove of her outfit?

Cat reached out for the knob, when the door opened on its own, revealing a frazzled looking man about Cat's age.

"Whoa, I'm sorry," he said, as he took a step back.

"Hi. I'm Cat. It's my first day." Cat stretched out her arm at him.

"Desmond." The man reluctantly shook her hand, then glanced over to Cat's left. "Good morning, Ms. Pryce."

"I'll leave you to it," Ms. Pryce said, and turned on her heel. The click-clack of her heels against the concrete floor echoed against the walls as she left, making a deafening racket.

"Well... Nice to meet you, Desmond," Cat said.

Desmond avoided eye contact and adjusted his thick-rimmed glasses. Clearly he wasn't a people person. "Uhh, yeah. Come in."

"Is she always like this?" Cat whispered, mostly to herself.

Desmond smiled bleakly. "You have no idea."

Cat reciprocated and breathed a sigh of relief. At least she wasn't all alone in this place. And with a bit of luck, they'd be working on whatever it was they were supposed to be working on without too much interference from Ms. Pryce, who probably had more important things to do.

This is only the beginning, Cat told herself. *Everyone starts at the lowest rung.*

"Let me show you what we do here," Desmond said as he waved her over.

Cat scanned the room. It was plain, like any other basement in any other building. Nothing here suggested that they were underneath one of the most prestigious auction houses in the world.

"You been here long?" It was all Cat could think of to make conversation.

"Three years," Desmond said.

His answer made her heart sank. Working your way up through the ranks clearly took a long time here. Still, this was the only job she'd been offered after applying pretty much everywhere. She was determined to make it work.

"So these racks here contain binders of old catalogs,

from before we started digitizing them. The newer ones can be seen from this computer." Desmond pointed at a workstation that looked to be at least ten years old.

"We need to prepare materials for upcoming auctions. The format is always the same: a high-res image and a detailed description. Check the previous catalogs for ideas on what to include. Once you're done with each lot, move it out of the inbox and into 'processing.'"

"Understood."

Cat took a seat in front of the desk with the computer and started poking around in the upcoming lots while Desmond explained the editing and publishing process. She was only half listening to him as pictures of exquisite artwork and antiques popped up on her screen, distracting her.

Would she get to actually see any of these items? She hoped that she would.

Within minutes, the reservations she'd had about Ms. Pryce and her prospects in this job faded, and she became absorbed in her work.

———•———

"Hey," Cat greeted Shelly as she came into the living room.

"Hey! How did it go? Did you manage to get there on time? Tell me everything!" Shelly demanded as she plopped down on the sofa without even taking her coat off.

Cat sat back and pinched the bridge of her nose. It had

been a long day. Annoyingly, as soon as she closed her eyes, random glimpses of Alexander appeared before her again. Today had gone so well! She hadn't thought of him at all until she got home.

"Yes, I was on time, but oh my God, my boss is horrible!" She turned to face Shelly, who looked concerned. "Well, one of them is. The guy I'm working with directly, Desmond, he's okay. But the woman who was there at the interview... Wow."

"Okay... Well, no one ever said it was going to be easy." Shelly rubbed the side of her neck, just underneath the collar of her coat.

"True, that."

"And what's the job all about?" Shelly asked.

Cat pulled her legs up and wrapped her arms around them. That was how she stayed as she told Shelly about her work in so much detail that her eyes glazed over.

"Well, that sounds interesting." Shelly sounded unconvinced after Cat had finished her account.

"It is, actually. Not something I want to do forever, but for now it's all right."

Again, Shelly reached for her neck, scratching at it more vigorously this time.

"Are you all right?" Cat asked.

"Huh?"

"Your neck."

Shelly stopped scratching and fidgeted with her collar. "It's nothing. Just a little itchy."

Cat leaned across and pushed Shelly's collar down to take a closer look.

Her neck was red with scratch marks, but underneath, she could just about make out two brighter dots against Shelly's otherwise fair skin.

"It's a bit late in the season for mosquito bites," Cat mumbled.

Shelly shrugged. "With global warming and all, who knows? Anyway, what are you sitting around here for? You've got a job, and survived the first day. This calls for some celebration!"

Cat blinked a few times. "What do you mean?"

"Oh come on! You didn't think I'd just let this pass, did you? Get up, we're going out!"

Cat inhaled sharply, then held her breath. It had been a tiring day. She rubbed her eyes and was instantly confronted with those same visions of Alexander she'd been battling since the party. Every time she saw him in her mind, the visions were accompanied by larger and larger doses of melancholy. She had really messed up that night.

Ugh. Perhaps the distraction would do her good. She stretched her legs, then slipped her feet into the shoes she'd discarded underneath the coffee table.

"Fine. Where are we going?" Cat got up and looked to Shelly for instructions.

The latter shrugged. "Pub on the corner? We won't make it too late. Wouldn't want you to turn up on your second day nursing a hangover."

"Fair enough." Cat put on her coat and off they went.

The walk from their apartment complex to the pub was short and through a relatively well-lit and safe part of the neighborhood. Still, Cat turned around at least three times to look behind them.

"What's up with you?" Shelly asked finally.

Cat stopped and scanned the street behind them much more carefully now. Nobody. There was absolutely nobody around.

"I thought I heard something," Cat lied. She hadn't heard a damn thing. And neither had she seen anything. Still, she couldn't fight the feeling that there was someone out there, watching her.

She must be more stressed out than she thought.

"Maybe it was a cat or something," Cat mumbled and pressed on toward their destination: the brightly lit building at the end of the road. It took hardly a minute longer for them to arrive and Shelly to push the door open.

As soon as Cat entered, she started to relax. It was warm in here, cozy. Being a weekday, and that too Monday, the pub was quiet, with just a handful of regulars playing darts in the far corner. She breathed a sigh of relief and started unbuttoning her coat to get more comfortable.

They headed straight for the bar and ordered two pints as well as some dinner to share.

"Hey, why don't you tell me more about this Desmond

guy?" Shelly suggested as she plopped down in one of the tatty looking armchairs surrounding one of the empty tables.

Cat let out a chuckle. "Really. *That's* what you want to know?"

"Look, I don't know anything about art, but I do know about men. So yeah, that's what I want to know. Cheers." Shelly grinned and raised her glass.

"Fine. Whatever makes you happy. Cheers." Cat raised her glass too, then took a sip and told Shelly everything.

No matter how hard she tried, though, Cat couldn't fully banish Alexander from her thoughts, nor the regret she felt. If only she could turn back time.

CHAPTER NINE

Alexander paced back and forth in the grand hall outside the meeting room of the Vampire Council. His footsteps echoed against the marble clad walls, which didn't help settle his concerns. What a waste of time. He didn't even know anything.

Ever since Lucille had shown up the night of the party, he knew that it was likely Julius would call him in. Alexander was the one who had interacted the most with Cat, after all. And Julius enjoyed the ritual of it all: calling in his subjects for so-called audiences, to coerce them into doing his bidding.

That was what this was, no doubt: a reminder that Alexander had no choice but to cooperate. The Council didn't tolerate insubordination.

The heavy wooden doors swung open and Lucille appeared. "You can come in now," she said.

Alexander nodded and kept his shoulders and back as straight as possible as he marched in. Lucille was a walking lie detector, sure, but convincing Julius could be even more difficult. The years had made him cynical and suspicious; unfortunately right now, he had good cause to be.

"Alexander, how lovely of you to show your face around here!" Julius called out and waved him closer from the large throne-like chair at the opposite end of the hall.

Alexander glanced around and suppressed an eye roll. The Council—especially under Julius—really did like to make a statement. Of course they'd picked an old cathedral to host their meetings and deliberations. Everything, from the tall stained glass windows and the crude forged iron chandelier, right down to the Gothic wooden throne Julius sat on, had a clear purpose: to impress and intimidate.

"Of course. I came as soon as I heard you wanted to see me," Alexander said.

Julius folded his hands in his lap and looked him up and down.

"You look well. The 21st century has been good to you."

"Thank you. You look well yourself."

Julius waved away Alexander's forced compliment.

"Enough with the niceties. You know what I want to talk about, don't you?"

"The Blood Bride," Alexander said.

Julius' eyes lit up when he heard those all-important words. If he and the Council were indeed threatened by this woman's special powers, he had a strange way of showing it.

"That's right. Of all the times and places to come across a rare and magnificent creature like her, imagine my surprise to hear one just happened to attend one of your little parties," Julius mused. He leaned forward and gestured at the two guards by the door, as well as Lucille, who stood just to the right of Alexander.

"Leave us. I wish to speak to Alexander in private."

Alexander didn't need to turn around to know everyone had instantly sprang into action. The sound of departing footsteps spoke volumes. As soon as the heavy doors creaked back into position, Julius gestured at him again.

"Come closer, my son."

Alexander walked up toward what would have been the altar of the old church, where Julius' throne now sat. He kept his head bowed slightly, following the proper etiquette when approaching the Principis, or leader, of the Council.

"No need for formalities, my son. Look at me," Julius spoke firmly.

Alexander did as asked, and made eye contact with the much older vampire. There was a change in him from the last time they'd spoken. Normally, Julius appeared calm above everything, reserved. Unless provoked, he kept his emotions to himself. Not so now. His eyes were eager and bright.

"Please tell me exactly what happened that night. When did you first realize what she was?"

Alexander took a moment to collect his thoughts. He'd rehearsed what to say in his head, but now that he was faced with his maker, he suddenly found it a little difficult to walk the line between being compelled to follow his orders, and the intense urge he felt to protect Catherine.

"I didn't know until Lucille told me. All I knew was that she was different from the others."

Julius nodded in agreement. "Ah, yes. I imagine she would have been different. Everyone could tell as much once she walked in."

Alexander nodded. "Yes. I noticed everyone looking in her direction."

"So what was she like?" Again, Julius looked more excited than threatened, rousing Alexander's suspicion even further.

"She seemed completely unaware of how special she was," Alexander said. He tried his best not to let Julius' questions take him back to that night, as he knew it would make him vulnerable, but he couldn't help it. All the images he'd tried so hard to banish from his mind were flooding back.

"I spoke to her briefly, offered to show her around the house, since she'd shown an interest in some of the artwork," Alexander continued.

Julius nodded, encouraging him to go on.

"Upstairs, I asked her to dance, which we did." Alexander blinked a few times, completely aware that he was sharing more than he had intended to, but he couldn't help himself. He couldn't get the details of his much too brief encounter with Catherine out of his head.

If only he could've convinced her she was safe with him. If only she'd stayed.

"Did you taste her?" Julius asked.

The directness of the question dragged Alexander back to reality. He made eye contact once more and saw urgency, obsession.

"No, nothing like that," Alexander said, taken aback by what he had seen in his master.

"And you know nothing of her whereabouts, or any details that might be of help for us to track her down?"

Alexander shook his head, feigning disappointment. Sure, he was disappointed that he hadn't been able to track her down, but he was glad he wasn't in a position to hand her over to Julius.

"You're certain you didn't taste her, even by accident?" Julius pressed the issue again.

"No!" Alexander protested.

"Shame. I would have loved to know what that was like. I know you still have your youth to keep you entertained, but when you get to my age... Brand new experiences are hard to come by." Julius smiled absentmindedly.

Alexander balled his fists, then immediately released them again for fear of being found out. All this talk of drinking Catherine's blood made him uncomfortable. By all accounts, a vampire would lose control once they tasted her. Why fantasize about it? Why flirt with such immense temptation? Had Julius reached such heights of megalomania that he thought to be above Catherine's powers? Or did he simply not care about what would happen?

"So you think she's a threat to our kind?" Alexander asked, hoping to steer the conversation somewhere more agreeable.

Julius licked his lips before answering. "Well, the history books tell us that women such as her have immense power. It would be irresponsible not to investigate further."

Alexander found it hard to swallow his frustration. Julius was so clearly lying. He didn't want to contain some kind of threat; his questions as well as his whole demeanor had made it obvious that Julius wanted her for himself. What Alexander had seen in him wasn't curiosity or excitement; it was blood lust.

Principis of the Council or not, that was unacceptable. Catherine was his first, and even if she wouldn't have him, he would do everything in his power to keep her away from Julius. Her safety was at stake.

"Indeed, it would be irresponsible," Alexander remarked, glancing up at his maker's face again while keeping his posture as non-threatening as possible. He had to make sure his anger didn't show.

Fortunately, Julius barely seemed to be paying attention to Alexander. Instead, his focus was elsewhere. He already seemed enthralled by the prospect of capturing his very own Blood Bride, and the inevitable blood bath that would follow.

It was no wonder Julius had wanted all the other vampires to leave for this little chat. He must have known that he would share more than he intended to. Such was the effect Catherine had on almost everyone.

Nobody, not even the most powerful vampire on earth, was able to withstand her effect, whether she was physically present or not.

Once Julius had dismissed him, Alexander didn't head home. He had already lost precious hours at the Council.

There was no time to waste; the city was vast, and finding one single human in all of that chaos was a huge task for a single vampire to take on. He didn't rest, he hadn't even fed all night, or the previous night.

The entire business with Catherine, and now the Council, was eating away at Alexander.

Where would a woman such as Catherine spend her evenings? Alexander checked out restaurants, bars, popular landmarks. It was no use. She was nowhere to be found.

Finally, when the first light of dawn threatened to cross the horizon, Alexander returned home, after another unsuccessful night.

"How did it go?" Michael looked up just as Alexander entered the library.

"No luck," Alexander said. He hated that he'd made no progress. With Julius obsessed, he wouldn't be the only one on the lookout. The Council had the manpower to cover much more ground in a much shorter time. And then there were the loyalists like Gillian. In this case, it was truly a case of one against many.

"I meant your meeting at the Council," Michael clarified.

"Oh." Alexander shook his head. "The plot thickens."

"How so?"

Alexander poured himself a drink and took a sip before answering.

"This whole Blood Bride business has everyone making fools of themselves." Alexander himself, of course, was included in this assessment. He would be the first one to go above and beyond to ensure Catherine's safety, when in fact she'd wanted nothing to do with him. It was pathetic, and completely unlike him.

He glanced over at Michael, who looked unconvinced. There was no point trying to explain any of it to him. Human women were only good for two things according to Michael: nourishment and entertainment.

Alexander looked down at the glass in his hand; its amber liquid seemed to glow in the subdued light of the library. He couldn't quite explain it to himself, either. Catherine had had a profound effect on even the most powerful vampire that currently walked this earth—and he hadn't even met her yet! How was it that while everyone seemed to just want to taste her, his own feelings were way more complicated than that?

It would have been easier had he just wanted her blood for himself, but it wasn't that. He wanted her whole being, but only if she wanted him too. But above all, he wanted her to be safe.

He took another sip and set his glass down on the table.

This urge was so alien to everything he'd known for centuries.

Was this what love was?

CHAPTER TEN

Cat had been working at Sotheby's for about a week when Desmond called in with the flu, leaving Cat to fend for herself.

For most of the day, Cat had done exactly the same as on previous days: hidden herself away down in the basement and completed some tasks Desmond had taught her.

The catalog prep was done for the week, and since they had an auction coming up, it was time to compile all upcoming lots in a spreadsheet so that after the event, they could enter how they'd performed. This data would be filed and compared to previous records of similar items.

It was all rather technical and boring on the face of it. Luckily, the lots themselves were so interesting that Cat managed to keep herself entertained.

She was almost done for the day when the door to the cramped little basement office swung open, revealing the last person she wanted to see.

"Catherine. Good, you're still here," Ms. Pryce said in a matter-of-fact tone.

"Yes, Ms. Pryce?" Cat responded almost on autopilot, as she saved her spreadsheet for the final time.

"I need you to stay behind." It wasn't a request; at least, it didn't sound like one.

Cat pressed her lips together and wondered what, if anything, she'd done wrong.

"The auction tonight. Normally Desmond would do this, but since he's not here..." Ms. Pryce clarified. "I need someone to observe the buyers, take notes on what they showed interest in, that sort of thing."

Cat's heart started to beat faster as soon as Ms. Pryce had said the word *auction*. This was her chance! And only a week into this job!

"Yes, of course I can attend tonight's auction!" Cat couldn't contain her excitement.

Ms. Pryce nodded. "I would expect no less. You might want to..." She gestured down at Cat's outfit. "Change into something more appropriate."

Cat looked down at her black trouser suit. *What's wrong with this?* It was very business-like, or so she thought.

"Yes, of course," Cat mumbled.

Ms. Pryce folded her arms and squinted at Cat. "A shift dress. Black. Heels." She nodded to make her point, then turned around and walked out again. "It begins at seven."

Cat exhaled sharply, having realized she'd been holding her breath for most of the time Ms. Pryce had been talking to her. A little black dress and heels. She could manage that. Hopefully.

A quick glance at the clock revealed she didn't have much time, certainly not enough for a round trip home. So Cat did the only thing she could think of; she called for help.

"Hey you!" Shelly answered the phone.

"You busy?" Cat asked, ignoring her greeting.

"Just tidying up and heading home, why?"

"I have a fashion emergency," Cat said. Those last two words would be irresistible to someone like Shelly, who lived to dress up.

"Tell me more!"

Cat smiled and explained the problem. She knew she could count on Shelly. The phone call was over in minutes with a promise that Shelly would be on the way as soon as possible with a suitable outfit from Cat's closet.

Cat sank back in her chair and breathed a sigh of relief. No way was she going to blow this opportunity.

In an effort to be well prepared for the auction—and to pass the time—Cat picked up a copy of tonight's catalog and started to read. She recognized the names of the lots from her earlier spreadsheet, but the images and descriptions were all new to her.

The selection of items was vast, from paintings to figurines and tea sets to large pieces of furniture. She had no way of knowing where exactly she would be during the auction itself, but Cat was determined to take a look at some of these items in person if she could manage it.

Half an hour must have passed, and Cat had read through most of the catalog, pausing on the final entry.

The picture showed some mounted pages which appeared to be from an old unnamed book as per the description. What a strange thing to be selling. Cat held up the catalog and looked at it more closely. She couldn't explain what it was, but something about this listing intrigued her more than any of the others.

For sure, this was one she would have to see up close.

Her phone rang, startling her. She put the catalog back down on the desk.

"Hey, Shelly!"

"I'm outside."

Cat hung up and made a beeline for the exit.

Cat made it into the main hall upstairs ten minutes early. Ms. Pryce was already there, coordinating with other staff Cat had not met before.

"There you are." Ms. Pryce greeted Cat by handing her a clipboard and a pen.

"Yes, Ms. Pryce."

Ms. Pryce glanced down at Cat's outfit, like she had done earlier that evening already. There was nothing in her expression that signaled whether she approved or not.

Either way, it was too late to change anything. Cat smoothed her dress down with her free hand and awkwardly waited for her instructions.

"Within minutes, buyers will start to arrive. Jeremy and his people over here will ensure they find their seat and are given a paddle to make their bids with. Phone bids will be handled from over there beside the auctioneer's podium."

Cat nodded. It was a lot of information to take in and

Ms. Pryce's tone suggested that as usual, she expected Cat to learn quickly.

"What I want you to do is to observe any active bidders and take notes. You take down the number on their paddle, the lot number they bid on, and anything else that stands out to you. And I want you to take your own initiative on this; I'm not going to spell out what to look for."

"Understood." This was a test. Cat was determined to pass it.

"And you do it from behind the curtain, so you don't attract too much attention to yourself." Ms. Pryce emphasized her instruction by pointing at the exact spot Cat should position herself at.

Cat nodded and started to walk toward the curtain.

"If anyone approaches you, you refer them to Jeremy or myself, you understand?"

"Yes, ma'am," Cat mumbled under her breath.

It wasn't a glamorous job, but at least she was here in the midst of all the action. For that, Cat was immensely grateful. She found herself a chair and placed it just so that she could look out through a gap in the curtain without being seen by the crowd which had just started to pour in. The only other people back here with her were the warehouse staff responsible for moving high value lots on and off the stage.

The auction turnout was quite diverse; most of the people entering the room had dressed up for the occasion.

Men wore suits and women wore dresses and ensembles that wouldn't look out of place on the Duchess of Cambridge. Then there were those who stood out a bit more; Cat spied ethnic clothes of all colors and descriptions, and also some people who seemingly didn't care at all what they wore. Apparently the latter seemed to think that jeans and t-shirts were an appropriate fashion choice for an event such as this.

Cat idly wondered what Ms. Pryce would have to say about those people.

Finally, as the seats in front of the podium began to fill up, someone walked in who made Cat's heart stop.

Alexander.

On his arm was a slender, elegantly dressed woman with strawberry blond hair. Her features and skin tone reminded Cat of a porcelain doll, similar to the type her grandmother used to collect when she was still alive. A pang of jealousy surged through Cat's chest. Fine, she'd left in a hurry that night, and ruined any chance she'd had with the man. But here he was with another woman by his side, and Cat could barely contain her rage.

This makes no sense!

Cat took a deep breath and tried to focus on the clipboard in her lap. With this unexpected arrival, Cat's job was going to become so much more difficult. How could she observe the entire crowd, when all her eyes seemed to want to do was stare at one particular person?

She looked up to see where he'd sat down, and found

that he was looking right in her direction. Could he see her? That was impossible, surely! She was well hidden behind this curtain.

Cat blinked and saw that he'd looked away, making small talk with his female companion.

Ugh, what a player!

Just outside of Cat's range of view, someone—presumably the auctioneer—made a knocking sound.

"Ladies and gentlemen! Welcome to Sotheby's. You are here by invitation, since you are all valued clients of ours, so I think we can forego any explanations at this point. You all know how this works. We have an amazing selection of paintings, furniture, and numerous other objets d'art for you tonight. Without further ado, let's begin!"

Cat took a deep breath. This was it. She couldn't afford to miss a moment of it.

In a rush, she scribbled down the first lot number just as the auctioneer introduced it, and started scanning the crowd, pausing every time she hit the third row from the front, fourth person from the left. Alexander. Seeing him here brought back all sorts of memories she'd been trying to block.

He had a certain aura, a presence that was impossible to ignore. All the regret she'd done her best to swallow came rushing back. If she hadn't left in such a rush, and their encounter had come to a more logical end, would he have remembered her? Did he remember her now?

Perhaps she ought to find him later and say hello.

Then again, he was here with somebody. If she approached him, that would just be sad on her part.

She rubbed the bridge of her nose with the back of her pen and did her best to focus on the crowd again. Bidders 54 and 87 seemed to have a bit of a competition going. She noted down everything she saw, including the remark "this is personal."

The next lots passed in much the same fashion. Cat did her best to control the urge to let her gaze linger on Alexander, who had stayed out of the bidding so far, even if the shock of seeing him again refused to subside. And she wrote down whatever she could about the active bidders, just like Ms. Pryce had told her to. Before she knew it, she'd filled sheet after sheet in scribbles.

Her hand started to cramp—it had been an age since she'd written this much by hand—but she didn't miss a beat. Every lot, every bidder was carefully documented.

An hour had passed, and the auction was coming to an end. From her earlier study of the catalog, she knew that there was only one lot left.

And Alexander hadn't bid on a single item yet.

"Next up, lot 66, mounted prints from an unknown book, circa 1500, let's start with the reserve—" Cat heard the auctioneer say.

In the crowd, Alexander seemed to perk up in his chair. That was when Cat noticed the chair next to him was empty.

Alexander's Blood Bride

Cat held her breath and gripped the pen so tightly her knuckles turned white. The ache in her wrist that had started to develop soon after the auction had begun had now turned to shooting pains going all the way up through her arm and shoulder. For but a moment, Alexander seemed to look in her direction again and she thought she could see it. The passion, the care with which he'd looked at her that night. It was like a stab in the heart, forcing her to avert her gaze and focus on his hands instead.

Within moments, the bidding was underway. No matter who else lifted their paddle, almost a split second later, Alexander had his in the air. He was determined.

Cat wondered what made this lot so special. Sure, she'd been fascinated by its description herself, but Alexander seemed willing to spend a fortune on it. The higher the bids went, the more intrigued she became.

At the same time, a sense of great urgency filled her; this was the last lot. Once the auction ended, he would leave. The prospect hurt more than she expected it to.

By the end, a few framed bits of old paper had gone for five times their reserve. With her heart still hammering away and a lump developing in her throat, Cat looked down to find that she had unknowingly filled an entire page with just observations about Alexander. Most had nothing to do with the auction. Damn. No way could she show all this to Ms. Pryce; she would think Cat had lost her mind.

The auctioneer ended with some sort of announcement

about payments. Cat didn't waste any more time and sprang into action. She had to see what was so special about that lot Alexander had bought. If only to feel some sort of closeness to him, to understand what made him tick.

After catching a final glimpse of him, she headed deeper backstage to intercept that final lot on its way back into storage.

CHAPTER ELEVEN

Of course Alexander had known Catherine was there in the crowd somewhere from the moment he walked in. His sense of smell had never let him down before, and he'd recognize her special scent anywhere.

Sure enough, he'd pinpointed her as soon as he sat down; she was right behind the curtain. He could even make out those pale green eyes of hers, looking back at him from the dark.

He ought to feel triumphant; he'd finally achieved his goal of tracking her down. But as much as it pained him, he couldn't act on it. He couldn't afford to tip off Lucille, who for now seemed completely unaware of how close she was to giving Julius what, or who, he wanted.

They'd ended up at the auction together not as a bonding exercise between siblings, no. This was an unfortunate coincidence. It was his first auction in months and he had a clear goal: to obtain that very special item he'd found in the catalog.

Lucille was here because—well, he wasn't quite sure why. *Just looking for a bargain*, she'd said, which was odd, since Lucille didn't normally attend these types of events. Unsurprisingly, she hadn't bid on a single lot all night. And toward the end of the auction, she looked bored.

"All this old tat, who needs it?" she grumbled.

Alexander looked up from the catalog—only one lot remained until it was time for him to get in on the action. "It's almost over. If you don't see anything you fancy, why don't you head into the other room for some refreshments? I'll be right out after this," Alexander suggested.

They shared a look. He hadn't meant the actual snacks and champagne next door, and she knew it.

"Very well. I don't know why you'd want to stay until the end anyway," Lucille said as she got up from her chair and elegantly navigated through the row of chairs toward the exit, attracting curious looks as she went.

Alexander smiled to himself. This was her hunting technique. Lucille knew exactly how to use her talents to get what she wanted.

She glanced down at a middle aged, slightly balding man at the end of the row and shot him a subtle smile. The man, confused for a second, regained his composure and got up as well, following Lucille out into the next room.

Alexander shook his head. *There goes another poor sod.* Luckily for him, vampires didn't kill anymore, not for centuries, ever since the Council became established and laid down the rules in the Treaty of London, 1789.

No, he'd be fine, eventually. At most he'd feel hungover, and wonder what might have happened in the inevitable gap Lucille would leave in his memory.

With Lucille out of the room, Alexander could relax a

little bit and focus on the task at hand. He had to get his hands on that final lot: what he presumed to be some missing pages from the *Encyclopedia of Myth and Magick*. The more he'd thought about it, the more certain he'd been. The illustrations and lettering were too similar for it to be a coincidence.

Perhaps they'd contain nothing of use, perhaps they'd change his whole understanding of the situation with Catherine. Either way, he wanted them for his library. It was a matter of pride. And knowing that Catherine was here somewhere just strengthened his resolve further. It had to be a sign.

The bidding was furious; clearly he wasn't the only one interested in some tattered pieces of paper from an old book most people would probably reject as pure fiction. But he knew better than that. And in the end, he was victorious.

Who says money can't buy happiness, he thought with a wry grin on his face.

If only everything else was equally simple.

The auction was over, and the crowd started to leave. Only those with winning bids stayed behind to complete the necessary formalities. Alexander paid by check; he'd never gotten used to electronic transactions. The feel of the booklet in his hand, the sound of the perforated paper tearing—those little things made a purchase feel real in a way that making a phone call to a banker or pushing a piece of plastic into a machine could never do.

As the young woman accepted his check and completed the necessary paperwork, Alexander grew increasingly restless. Catherine was here somewhere. As was Lucille.

He wanted nothing more than to find and speak to her. Even if Catherine wanted nothing more to do with him, he yearned to be in her presence again.

But if Lucille found out... That would be a disaster.

He couldn't risk it. So as he waited for the receipt, he impatiently tapped his foot and scanned the room for any sign of his sister. She had to be done with that man by now. Had she caught Catherine's scent as well?

While he stood here to finalize his shopping, disaster could be unfolding somewhere behind the scenes.

Just as the woman behind the counter handed him his newly printed bill, he felt a presence right behind him.

"What did you buy?" Lucille asked.

Alexander folded the paper in half, then again in half and put it into the inner pocket of his jacket.

"Just some prints," he said, smiling at Lucille to cover his nerves.

The latter squinted suspiciously. "Prints?"

It wasn't a lie, technically. The pages had been printed, and mounted as though they were in fact works of art. Alexander nodded and smiled again. "I think they'll go very nicely in the library."

"How much art does one man need?" Lucille scoffed.

At least she seemed satisfied for now; she was still

licking her lips after her earlier human snack.

"How were the refreshments?" Alexander steered the conversation away from his purchase.

Lucille sighed. "Oh, quite satisfactory. I was hungrier than I thought."

Alexander chuckled. "It was written all over your face."

Lucille placed her arm inside the crook of his as they walked toward the exit. With every passing step, he felt Catherine's presence less keenly. Alexander turned around one last time just as they passed through the set of double doors into the reception hall. He didn't know what to feel: relief or heartache.

It turned out to be a heavy dose of both.

"Anything wrong?" Lucille asked.

Alexander shook his head. "No, all fine. I think I might have overpaid for those prints."

Lucille laughed. "Swept up in auction fever. With the years of practice you've had, I thought you'd be better than that."

Alexander shrugged. "It can happen to the best of us."

As they walked through the crowds of humans on the way out, more than a few heads turned in their direction. Men, as well as women. Such was the attraction of the vampire. Some humans were drawn to them like moths who had no idea how close they came to being burned to death.

Nobody ever sensed the danger until it was too late. Except Catherine. She'd figured it out. Sadly, her keen sense of observation might have plunged her into more danger than she could imagine.

"Now what?" Alexander asked.

He hoped she would go her own way, so that he could do the same. What if she wanted to linger, though? What if Catherine walked in here to join the crowds of auction-goers, and Lucille picked up her scent? Then what?

Could Alexander choose Catherine over his sister? He'd try his best to avoid that scenario. But if it came down to it, he supposed that he could.

"Council work, you know." Lucille brushed away his question.

Alexander nodded. With a bit of luck, he wouldn't have to make that difficult choice. Not today.

"I'll walk with you," Alexander suggested.

Lucille agreed with a nod as they passed into the darkness outside.

"How goes the hunt?" he asked, once they were out of earshot of the other humans leaving the auction house.

She shrugged. "Nobody seems to know this woman."

"Yes, I noticed the same," Alexander said.

"But our dear maker isn't one to give up easy, as you well know."

"Julius is a great many things, but he's not a quitter," Alexander said bitterly. And therein lay the problem.

They walked on in silence, further and further away from Catherine's last known location. How glad he was that he'd been able to avoid any confrontation at the auction.

Alexander didn't even notice how far they'd walked when they came to a stop in front of a rundown building somewhere in the middle of Chinatown.

"Well, this is me," Lucille said.

Alexander glanced up at the unassuming façade. Humans would walk by here and ignore this place, but he knew better. It was one of the bigger lodging houses for young vampires; in the olden days, one might have called it a coven house.

"I thought you had better taste than this, sister," Alexander remarked.

Lucille let out a chuckle. "I don't live here, silly! Just doing the rounds, making inquiries... Perhaps someone in here has come across that woman. Perhaps I can convince some of them to join the search."

Alexander looked up at the boarded up windows on the upper floors. There was no way of knowing how many newly turned immortals lurked behind these walls. The Council truly had an army at their disposal.

He shrugged. "Well, best of luck in your efforts. I'll head back myself."

"I'll see you around," Lucille said.

Her tone was innocuous, but to Alexander's ears, her goodbye had sounded more like a threat.

"Yes, see you," he responded.

As he turned, he heard Lucille's footsteps climb up the front steps to enter the building. He started walking leisurely, but as soon as he turned the corner, he broke into a sprint. What were the chances of Catherine still being there, at Sotheby's?

Slim, probably. Still, he owed it to her as well as himself to try to intercept her.

CHAPTER TWELVE

Cat couldn't believe what she'd just seen.

Even after the warehouse workers had taken the final lot of tonight's auction away, Cat still stood frozen in place, right in front of the heavy duty elevator.

Although they were hard to read, some of the passages on those framed pages had been pretty damning. They mentioned the so-called undead. Vampires. There were even illustrations to go with the text that looked unlike anything she'd seen before.

She didn't believe in stuff like that, or did she?

Cat remembered the old portrait that seemed to feature Alexander. That could have been a funny coincidence, or a very clever reproduction piece that looked a lot older than it really was.

She recalled the dream she had of him later that very night; the details of what exactly happened had been fuzzy, unclear, but it all came to her as soon as she read those pages. Somehow, her subconscious had already figured out what he was. Then there were those two funny marks she'd seen on Shelly's neck. Had she just imagined all of this stuff?

Her mind tried to rationalize everything, to convince her that the supernatural didn't exist, even if all the evidence pointed toward it.

And he'd been here. He'd bought this very item without bidding on anything else, which could potentially explain everything! Was that a coincidence too?

All around, people were rushing back and forth, finishing up for the night. Cat forced herself into action to do the same.

She grabbed the clipboard with her notes, as well as her handbag, and made a beeline for the exit. At home, she'd talk to Shelly and realize that probably she was just stressed out and all of it was messing with her head. Yes, that had to be it. Better sense had to prevail.

Nobody seemed to pay much attention to her as she left. Even the streets were unusually quiet on her way.

Still, once she found herself in a near-empty tube station, waiting for the next train, she couldn't shake the feeling that she was being watched.

Again.

She'd felt the same after her first day last week, when Shelly had dragged her to the pub.

Perhaps this was what it felt like to lose your mind?

Cat wrapped her arms around her handbag tightly and scanned the platform. Of the few people around, most didn't seem to be looking at her at all. An old couple stared intently at the board announcing the next train. A man in a business suit was tapping away at his phone. Further up, there was a man in tattered jeans and an old, faded canvas jacket, who rummaged around in one of the two large plastic bags he'd been carrying earlier.

All of them were way too busy to be paying attention to Cat.

And yet...

A gust of wind blew across the platform, adding to the eerie atmosphere. *It'll be an approaching train*, Cat tried to reassure herself. Her hands went numb in the cold so she pushed them deeper into her pockets.

After an unseasonably warm October, winter had finally come.

Or perhaps it wasn't the weather that made her feel cold. A chill slowly crawled down her back, causing her to turn around and scan the other side of the platform again. *Nothing. Nobody.*

She closed her eyes and slowly counted down from ten—an old relaxation trick her mom had taught her when she was little and still afraid of the dark.

When she opened her eyes, she saw the lights of the approaching train. Finally. She'd be safe in there, and it would take her straight home.

Cat raced at the nearest door and sat down in one of the many empty seats. The train was quiet as well, but brightly lit and a lot less scary than the station had been. There was a surveillance camera on the ceiling, aimed squarely at Cat, reassuring her further. If anyone tried anything, they'd be caught on film.

She folded her arms and kept her eyes fixed on the platform. Only those few people who had been waiting earlier made it into the train. Nobody looked out of place or dangerous in any way.

The doors closed, allowing her to breathe another sigh of relief. She'd made it. The train pulled away, slowly at first, then speeding up through the dark.

Cat rested her hand on her chest and felt her heartbeat slow down back to normal again. She slumped against the back rest of her seat and closed her eyes.

Alexander smiled at her, and she smiled back.

When Cat came back to her senses, she was no longer on the train. The street she found herself on didn't look familiar.

This wasn't her neighborhood. Had she been sleepwalking? To make matters worse, it had begun to drizzle; her hair was already damp.

She had no clue where she was going, and yet her feet kept moving of their own accord.

House upon house passed her by, each one grander and more luxurious than the last.

Finally, she stood in front of a large ornamental gate and it hit her.

She was on Kensington Palace Gardens.

This was Alexander's villa!

She wanted to turn around and run, but something gave her pause. All those dreams she'd had of Alexander were hard to ignore. The closer she got to the gate, the safer she felt somehow. At the same time, the feeling of unease she'd felt at the metro station earlier was creeping up to her again. Something dangerous lurked in the darkness behind her, she was sure of it. She shivered as the damp crept through her coat.

Where her instincts had told her to run from this place on Halloween, today they were screaming the opposite. *Go in. He'll protect you.*

It made no sense. Why would he want anything to do with her, after the way she left things that night?

The gates opened of their own accord, and she stepped inside. It didn't matter that the more rational voice in her head insisted she had no business here. That he wouldn't want to see her anyway. That he was probably in there with the woman who had accompanied him to Sotheby's. Pangs of jealousy tore at her heart.

Yet her heart insisted she had to proceed.

She turned around one last time as the gates shut slowly behind her. There was something there, across the road. Two eyes, glowing red, staring right back at her. Her heart skipped a few beats and she swallowed, hard.

Cat clutched her handbag tightly with both hands and ran up the driveway toward the house. The gravel shifted and crunched under her feet, making it near impossible to maintain her balance on her heels. She stumbled and almost fell as she reached the front steps.

One of the two large wooden doors opened and a familiar silhouette appeared in front of her.

"Catherine!" Alexander called out.

Within the blink of an eye, he stood in front of her, at the bottom of the steps. How had he moved so quickly?

"Catherine. You came," he spoke again.

Cat didn't know how to respond. She blinked a few times, almost expecting him to vanish right before her eyes. Maybe she'd fallen asleep on the train, and this was all a crazy dream?

"Someone is following me," Cat mumbled, taking a shaky step forward. Her knees trembled, and almost straightaway, so did the rest of her.

"I'll protect you," he said as he reached out for her arm, steadying her.

Somehow, she believed him.

This was crazy and completely impossible. She took a step and promptly lost her balance again. He caught her. At once, she felt weightless; they didn't walk up the steps together, they floated. All she could focus on was his hand on her arm, burning through her damp clothes and setting her heart alight.

Dream or not, if she assumed that everything she'd learned was true, and he was a vampire, did it really matter? This right here, it felt right. She'd be a lot safer inside the house with him, than with whatever was out there watching her.

As soon as they crossed the threshold into his house, she froze. There it was, the painting that had started everything and almost ended it too.

She'd been captivated by it before she'd even met the

man himself.

The door shut behind them with a loud click and the outside world seemed to no longer matter.

"You'll have questions." Alexander turned to face her. His expression was soft, almost gentle, even if the flicker in his eyes suggested something more. Was it passion that she saw? Her body's reaction to him was obvious; the elevated heart rate, butterflies in her stomach, all of it hit her like a freight train, and threatened to throw her off balance again.

"I'm not sure I want to know the answers," Cat mumbled.

She glanced down at her shoes, which were scuffed and coated in streaks of mud. Her one good pair of heels.

Cat met his gaze again and his dark eyes lit up. He didn't scare her anymore. Something about him invited her to proceed. Just like on that first night, before everything had gone wrong. Her mind went blank except for one thought: how good it had felt to kiss him.

She tiptoed and let her desires take over. Before she knew it, his arms were wrapped around her, and his lips had locked with hers. It was familiar, like they'd done this so many times before; of course in a way they had, in her dreams. Soft lips, begging for affection, their tongues twirling and darting around one another in an endless game of cat and mouse.

Cat felt feverish, overcome with sensations. This one kiss seemed to unleash all the tension and yearning she'd felt for weeks.

"I'm sorry," she whispered, in between kisses.

He didn't stop or respond. How was it that he still wanted *her*, when he surrounded himself with women such as the one who had accompanied him to the auction?

The more she drank in his essence, the less important her questions seemed. The only thing that mattered was that she was here, with him. And that he wanted her back.

Cat stumbled backward, her knees buckling underneath her. Their lips disconnected, though his muscular arms still cradled her. For a moment, she had trouble identifying her surroundings, then her eyes settled on the hunting scene on the wall next to them.

"That painting." Cat nodded at the canvas.

"That's me. Yes," Alexander confirmed, like he'd read her mind.

A sense of déjà vu came over Cat. He'd had his arms around her when she asked him this in her dream. She recalled what came next: a dance and a bite to the neck. Had it really been a dream, or a bizarre vision of the future? Her heart started to race again, but she felt more excited than scared this time.

"You are a..." She paused, unable to say the word out loud. *Vampire.*

It still seemed so crazy, so impossible. Everything was going so well; despite everything, he really seemed to be into her. She wasn't ready to slip up and make a fool of herself.

Alexander smiled and brushed a wet lock of hair out of her face. "Let's get you cleaned up. You must be freezing."

He was right; in all the excitement she'd forgotten just how sorry a state she was in. Cat nodded and slipped her arm into his. Halfway up the stairs, something changed. A fresh dose of dread came over her, causing her chest to constrict and heart to pound even harder. She stopped and scanned the hall, then paused when she saw a man staring up at her. His eyes shone deep red. *Danger*.

"There's someone there," she whispered.

Alexander paused as well. "That's just Michael. He won't harm you."

Cat frowned and bit her lip. Her instincts were trying to tell her otherwise, and yet she was inclined to believe Alexander's reassurances. He would protect her, no matter what.

"You're safe, I promise," he said.

Downstairs, there was no sign of the other man anymore, and instantly, her fear subsided.

CHAPTER THIRTEEN

Alexander could hardly believe it. After he'd returned to Sotheby's and found no sign of her, he'd come home defeated. And now, it was Catherine who had come to him.

She'd kissed him with a need that seemed to match, if not surpass his own.

Only now, her eyes were wide and fearful again. He wanted so badly to reassure her, to convince her that she had nothing to fear from him.

Was that the truth, though? As he found himself so close to her, with her scent overwhelming his senses once more, could he honestly say that she wasn't in danger?

The temptation was stronger than the last time. Every fiber in his body seemed to scream at him to go for her throat, as well as her lips.

He realized it had been days since he'd last fed; all his energy these days had gone into trying to track her down.

"You're safe," he heard himself say.

It felt like a hollow promise, even if he really wanted to believe it himself. The way Michael had looked at her from the bottom of the stairs had suggested he too had fallen under the spell of the Blood Bride. Even if his loyalty to Alexander prevented him from acting on it, and Alexander somehow managed to suppress his own urges, they still had the Council to deal with. No doubt it was one of theirs who had followed Cat here in the first place.

He glanced at her as they continued up the steps and through the hallway, a journey they'd made together before. Their destination was the same too: the master suite. Once again, his eloquence was failing him; he wasn't sure how to talk to her, especially while she looked so vulnerable.

"I know this is a lot to take in," Alexander said finally.

She didn't respond, just looked up at him, and he was overcome with desire. He ached to kiss her, hold her, and comfort her.

But despite their earlier affections, it would be selfish of him to give in. This wasn't the time. Catherine was shivering visibly now. Humans were sensitive creatures, susceptible to all sorts of dangers. The last thing he wanted was for her to catch a cold on top of everything.

"The en-suite is through there." Alexander pointed at a door leading off from the other side of the bedroom. "You'll find a robe there if you want it."

He turned and walked back out of the room to give her some privacy.

"Don't go," Catherine whispered behind him. "Please."

He stopped. For her sake as well as his own, he should probably leave. But he couldn't deny her request either.

So he did as asked, closed the door behind him, and sat down on a chair in the corner with his hands folded. Within moments, he heard the sound of the shower inside the en-suite. He tried not to imagine her in there, warm water rushing down her curves, caressing her and soothing her.

There was no way of knowing how much time they had together before Lucille would inevitably interrupt. Michael would protect them, but he was their only ally against who knew how many Council loyalists? He could only hope that the safeguards this house offered would keep them out long enough.

It was obvious what they had to do. He'd seen the ritual performed once before, many years ago. Alexander rested his head in his hands.

Catherine's sense of reality was already shattered. Although his own initiation into this world had taken place several hundred years ago, he could clearly remember how frazzled he'd been. This wasn't an easy truth to be faced with.

The click of the bathroom door snapped him out of his thoughts. There she stood in the doorway, wearing his black robe. Clouds of steam billowed around her, carrying the scents of a summer meadow in full bloom into the room with it.

A radiant image of womanhood, her expression was calmer now. Perhaps she was coming to terms with where she'd ended up? He didn't know what to say, how to broach the subject.

"There is something about you," Catherine started.

Alexander's ears perked up. That meant she had felt it

too, the inexplicable connection they shared.

"I've dreamed a lot about you," she spoke, as though she could read his mind. This very image, in fact, of Catherine fresh out of the shower, had visited him in his sleep before.

"Yes." Alexander got up and approached her while maintaining eye contact. The sweet smell of her blood was even more intense now that she had warmed up. How easy it would be to hypnotize her, to make her bend to his will right now. And how hollow a victory it would be.

"And you make me feel safe," she continued.

"I want you to feel safe." He meant it, and yet it felt like a lie.

Catherine raised her hand. "I'm not done yet."

Alexander paused.

"But at the same time, there's something in this house that makes me feel otherwise. Maybe your man, Michael." Catherine shuddered as she spoke his name. "Maybe something else." She frowned, like she was surprised at her own words.

Alexander took another step in her direction. This was his opening, his chance to explain the entire wretched situation to her. If she ran again, at least it would be after she had all the facts. "There is something you need to know."

Catherine averted her gaze and wrapped her arms around herself tightly.

"You're not like other women."

Her eyes snapped back up at his again and she raised an eyebrow.

"I'm not saying this to flatter you, I'm stating a fact. Perhaps you've noticed it before." Alexander ran his hand through his hair as he tried to find the right words to continue.

"Our kind—" He paused and rested his gaze on her lips.

"Vampires," she whispered.

He nodded. It was good to hear her say it finally.

"You'll know the stories. The immortality, the drinking of blood. But we're not murderers." He started pacing around the room as he spoke.

"No?"

He shook his head. "It's against the law. We feed just enough to sustain ourselves, but we're not allowed to harm humans. Not that I personally would ever want to even if it were allowed. We're not monsters. Most of us aren't, anyway." He was rambling. This wasn't good. He paused for a moment to see how she was taking all the information so far.

"Then why do I keep feeling like I've got death hanging over my head?" Catherine said.

"Because you do. You're different, as I said."

She walked up to the bed and sat down in the center of it. Then she looked back up at him.

"Your blood is special. Any vampire who gets close to you falls under your spell. That's why you're being stalked."

He stopped and looked down at her.

"So there are vampires after me for my blood?" Her eyes widened again, and her bottom lip trembled slightly.

So fragile, so beautiful. How could she not know the power she wielded?

"Unfortunately, in your particular case, the laws mean next to nothing. They'll drink every last drop of it, no matter the consequences."

"Except you. You don't want to... kill me?" she whispered.

Alexander shook his head.

"And that's why I feel safe with you, but not any of the others?" she asked.

Alexander ran his hand over his chin. Her conclusion was logical. He started pacing back and forth again.

"It's only a matter of time before they find you here. Whoever was out there was probably tracking you on their behalf." It hurt to admit it, but it was the truth and she deserved to know. "I'll do everything I can to keep you safe. But we are outnumbered."

"I trust you." She looked up at him, and he found himself lost in the depths of her green eyes and froze.

It was bittersweet, hearing her say those three little words. He was unworthy. Throughout their interactions, he'd been teetering on the edge of control. Even as they kissed, he was only a hair's breadth away from satisfying his intense thirst. The slightest misstep, and his dark side would destroy everything they had.

"Why?" he asked finally.

She blinked a few times and frowned. "I can't explain. It's what's in my heart."

"Maybe it's a sign," Alexander mumbled.

"What?" she asked.

He shook his head. All of this was highly illogical. Their connection, as well as the fact that he could resist her—at least for now. He might as well throw all logic out the window and follow his heart too. There was only one way out; he had to take a chance. A leap of faith.

So he walked up to her until he was only a step away from the bed. Then he fell down onto one knee and reached out for her right hand. A surge of electricity seemed to pass from her hand into his, so intense was the sensation of touching her again.

"I know this makes no sense, but I must ask. Knowing everything you do now, and considering what your heart is telling you... Would you walk the earth with me, companions in life and death, now and forever?"

"Are you... Is this a proposal?" she stammered and drew her hand back a little, though not far enough to break their connection.

Of course she was taken aback. They hardly knew each other beyond what their instincts were trying to tell them. In these modern times, they didn't make commitments anymore until much later on in relationships. He had let his old fashioned ideas get out of control and jumped the gun.

Alexander averted his gaze and was about to get up again when she placed her other hand on his arm.

"Wait. I need to know your reasons."

When he raised his head and saw how she looked at him, with those expressive eyes, overflowing with emotion, he knew that perhaps, there was hope still. He just had to work for it. Alexander closed his eyes to collect his thoughts.

"Because from the moment I saw you, you shone a light into the darkest crevices of my heart. You reminded me of what it's like to be alive. You make me feel things I haven't felt in over three hundred years." He opened his eyes again as he spoke, noting the surprise on Catherine's face at his last statement.

Of course, she knew about him only in theory, but learning how long he'd lived in his current form really seemed to hit home.

"Three hundred years? That's how old you are?" Catherine whispered.

Alexander nodded. Thereabouts.

"And in all that time, you never thought to settle down?"

"Never crossed my mind." It was the truth. Even in life, he never married, which had greatly frustrated his parents when they were still alive.

"Wow."

CHAPTER FOURTEEN

Cat didn't know whether to laugh or cry. She was in so much turmoil that her brain had trouble catching up. This wasn't a casual question, or an impulsive move on his part. He had waited for centuries for the right person. The commitment he asked of her was permanent—she could feel it. They couldn't just change their minds and get a divorce like normal people did.

What made *her* so special? Just her blood? No, then he would have simply fed on her and cast her aside.

Alexander looked up at her from his kneeling position with his hand still holding on to hers. Every time she looked into his eyes, her feelings for him deepened. He expected an answer; she couldn't drag this on endlessly.

Could she live with him and love him forever? A man she barely knew? Her heart said yes. In matters of love, it was the heart you really had to listen to, not the mind, right?

"You'll have to give up a lot," Alexander spoke softly. "I won't sugarcoat it."

Cat waited for him to continue, even though she wasn't sure anything he was about to say would sway her. Her decision wasn't based on rationality after all.

"Once it's done, you'll live here," Alexander said.

She looked around the opulent room. That didn't seem

like much of a sacrifice.

"You'll never be able to tell your family or friends about the true nature of our relationship. My powers ensure that you won't age like other humans, so when the time comes that your enduring youth will raise suspicions, you'll have to cut ties with everyone you know from your previous life."

Cat swallowed hard. She'd have to say goodbye to Shelly, to her mom as well as her brothers. Then again, if she lived forever and they didn't, she'd have to say goodbye to them eventually anyway.

"And then there is the matter of the Council." Alexander's voice turned grim.

"The Council?"

"The other vampires that are after you. By law, they're not permitted to harm you if we proceed, but they'll be furious." He paused for a moment. "Of course, I'll do my best to keep you safe no matter what you decide."

"If they're not allowed to harm me, so what if they're angry." Cat shrugged.

She knew what she had to do. Despite everything he'd told her, it still felt right.

"Ask me again," she whispered.

He did. She said yes.

What happened next was a blur. Alexander, with tears of joy in his eyes, got up and swept her up into his arms. She didn't resist; there was no need to. They kissed again, and as intense as her feelings for him had been before, they were even stronger now.

Before she knew it, he had her on the bed and crawled on top of her and assaulted her whole upper body with his lips. His movements were so fast, she had a hard time focusing, and only felt the touch of his lips after he had moved on to the next spot.

The entire experience was like a dream. Like she only had to think about where she wanted him to kiss her next, and he'd already done it.

At the same time, her hands roamed his body. His beautiful, flawless body. What she felt through his crisp white shirt perfectly matched many a naughty dream. How could it be that her imagination had got everything so spot on?

She reached out for the buttons on his shirt, attempting to open them one by one. He wasn't so patient, and tore it off in one swift move. He did the same to her robe, leaving it in tatters on the floor.

He had a wild streak in him—of course he did. He had the potential of being a dangerous predator, an animal, with urges and instincts that went deeper than any human could ever feel. Catherine had put her life in his hands. Seeing just a glimpse of what he was capable of took her breath away.

"I'm sorry, I didn't mean to scare you," he said.

"You didn't," she gasped. "Don't stop!"

Before she'd even finished her demand, he'd flipped her onto her stomach and started his assault on her back.

Kisses and nibbles all the way down her spine. He ran his hands over her curves, tickling her with his fingertips, before reaching down between her legs.

"You're wet," he growled.

She could only moan in response. His fingers knew how to play her, like an expert pianist would his favorite instrument. She wasn't a virgin, though she wasn't as experienced as Shelly was. Still, Cat was certain even Shelly had never had an intimate encounter quite like this one.

"I've dreamed of this," he whispered, as he entered her with two fingers, sending her lower abdomen into a spasm of lust.

So have I, Cat thought, but she was unable to form the words.

Behind her, the sound of further tearing fabric suggested he was ready to take things to the next level. Cat tried to raise herself up onto her elbows, perhaps catch a glimpse of him behind her. He didn't wait for her to complete the maneuver, just flipped her again, spread her legs, and dove down into her sweet folds for a taste of her essence.

She squealed and bucked her hips up into his face, savoring the feeling of his tongue buried deep inside of her. He was so good at this. Those hundreds of years of experience sure as hell paid off right now.

A strange sensation came over her, a tightening of all her muscles at once, a sweet tickle that started at the point where his tongue had just been and extended all the way through her womb.

Alexander pulled back, leaving her aching for more.

"No!" she cried out, clawing at his shoulders in an attempt to push him back down.

He straightened himself and entered her in the traditional fashion instead.

Never before had missionary felt so good. She reached out for him and wrapped her arms and legs around him tightly. His solid muscle pressed into her generous curves. They fit together like a glove.

As she ran her hands over his back, she could feel his power: muscles contracting and releasing, thrusting into her with a level of control and speed she'd never encountered before.

This entire exercise seemed effortless, such was his power and strength. While she was out of breath and coated in a thin layer of sweat already, he seemed to have endless reserves of energy to draw from.

Could she ever satisfy him the way he fulfilled *her* every need? Cat looked up at him, focusing on his eyes, which told her everything she needed to know.

Her being here with him—surrendering to him—was all he needed.

She stifled a cry, which then involuntarily turned into a scream.

"Oh, God!"

Her body did the rest, releasing a flood of endorphins into her bloodstream as her lower abdomen spasmed. Out of breath, and out of words, she lay on her back, gasping for air as her orgasm continued to wash over her in waves.

Alexander gathered her up in his arms and thrust into her one final time before erupting himself and filling her with his seed. He lowered himself onto her, his face resting on her chest until her breaths started to calm.

"That was amazing," Cat whispered.

He didn't respond, just raised his head to give her a peck on the lips. Only then could she see what toll their activities had taken on him.

"You look tired. I didn't realize vampires could look tired," she said, while running her hand through his hair.

"Not tired, just hungry," he mumbled, then gave in to her embrace once more.

Hungry? She was about to say something stupid about going down to the kitchen and fixing him a snack when she realized what he meant.

"Do you want to... you know?" She straightened her neck and gestured at it.

He shook his head. "Not yet. Not until it's official."

She kept caressing his hair while they rested. The only sounds cutting through the silence were her own breaths and the soft ticking of a clock.

"How long do you think we have?" she wondered aloud. If someone had followed her here, it wouldn't be long until they called in the so-called Council and turned up with reinforcements. "Before those people who are after me turn up?"

"They'll be here before the night is over. My security measures will keep them out for a while..." Alexander stretched and leaned up on his elbow.

The short rest had made all the difference; he looked reinvigorated. Flawless, like before.

"It's important we perform the ritual before they make it inside. Are you ready?" he asked.

Cat bit her lip. The moment of truth.

"Yes," she whispered. It was crazy to think about all that had happened in such a short period of time. But this wasn't the time for reflection, it was the time to act.

Cat took a deep breath and forced a smile.

"Yes. I am ready," she repeated, with more confidence this time.

"I'll get Michael to prepare the library." Alexander's expression was solemn. No doubt this was a big step even for him.

Cat nodded and watched as Alexander got up. What a sight. She glanced down at her own naked body, then at the torn robe on the floor.

"There's a selection of things in the wardrobe," Alexander said. "Something is bound to fit."

It was like the man could read her mind.

———•———

Barely half an hour had passed before Cat found herself next to a make-shift altar in the library, with Alexander by her side.

The other vampire, Michael, had agreed to stand guard outside in case trouble arrived. They'd have no witnesses, but apparently the ritual would be valid nonetheless.

"It's not difficult, or lengthy, but it's important we follow all the steps until the end." Alexander pointed at the numbered list in the ancient text that lay on the table next to them.

Cat nodded. She wanted to do it right, and not just because their safety depended on it.

"First, we create our bond, then we ask the questions. I'll begin." Alexander picked up the small dagger that was incorporated into the spine of the book and held it up to the index finger on his right hand. He cut himself, not too deep, just enough for a single deep red drop to form. Then he handed the dagger to Cat.

"You do the left," he said.

She hesitated for a moment. *This is the right thing to do.* She took a deep breath and pressed the sharp point of the dagger into her left index finger. Her blood flowed much more willingly, as though her body was as keen to complete the ritual as her heart had been.

They stood facing one another and held up their hands, pressing them together until the blood on their index fingers mingled into one. The realization that she was one step closer to finalizing her bond with Alexander made Cat's heart surge.

As she caught her breath, he retrieved a deep red ribbon that had so far served as a bookmark in the old manuscript, and handed her one end of it.

"This symbolizes that we will forever be connected," he whispered.

Together they placed the center of the ribbon between their index and middle finger, then started to wrap it around, threading it through their fingers and around their wrists, holding them together.

He smiled at her; she thought she could detect a hint of nerves in his expression. This was possibly as big a step for him as it was for her.

Now, it was time for the next step. The questions.

Alexander glanced over at the old book, then made eye contact with her again. Images of their earlier encounter filled her mind. Would they be like this forever?

"Will you swear on everyone you hold dear, that you, Catherine Knight, pledge yourself to me, in life and in death, now and forever?"

"They're here," a voice—Michael's—called out from the other side of the door. Sure enough, Cat could hear shouting and thumping noises, as though people were trying to break in. Her fight or flight response tried to kick in, but she suppressed the urge to flee. It didn't matter, anyway. They were on the last step and the intruders would be too late.

"I will." Her voice trembled as she spoke. "Will you, Alexander Broderick the Third, pledge yourself to me, in life and in death, now and forever?"

Her heart jumped when she saw a little change in

Alexander's eyes. The passion, the fire, it was all still there. But there was something else in there as well. Was it love? He barely knew her—how could he be so sure he'd want her forever?

"I will."

Cat and Alexander didn't stir; they still stood in the center of the library, their hands with the deep red ribbon still in place and their eyes locked on. As crazy as the past few hours had been, this was the right way forward; Cat had never been so sure of anything in her entire life.

This man—vampire—who stood before her was willing to sacrifice everything for her safety.

The ritual was done; she felt the change in her. The noise outside grew, and Alexander positioned himself square to the door, partially blocking her view of it.

CHAPTER FIFTEEN

Alexander stood tall, with his eyes fixed on the door leading into the library. The ruckus outside had grown in intensity; clearly the intruders were now right outside with only this one pane of wood separating them from him and Catherine, who stood by his side.

He glanced at her. Should he feel differently about her now? Their connection had been intense even before they made it official.

The doors swung open with a loud crash, and Catherine flinched backward. He joined her and tightened his grip on her hand.

"We'll be fine," he mumbled, though he wasn't quite certain of it himself.

"Alexander!" Julius bellowed as he marched in past what was left of the door. "Hand her over, right this instant!"

Alexander took a step to his right, positioning himself in front of Catherine. His gesture was more symbolic than anything. The sheer age difference between Julius and Alexander ensured that the former was much more powerful. If it came to an actual battle, Alexander knew he didn't stand a chance.

And worse still, Julius hadn't come alone. His position in the Council meant he had support, no matter what. Just behind Julius stood Lucille, of course, and Gillian, as well as a number of other vampires Alexander didn't know. Behind them, a disheveled and bruised Michael peeked inside with a concerned frown on his face.

But Catherine was too important for Alexander to simply give up. He would fight if he had to. From the start, he'd wanted to protect her, even if that meant going against his deepest, darkest instincts, which had wanted to experience the taste of her blood, just as every other vampire did.

"I will not." Alexander stared at Julius; the resolve was written all over his face.

"Then I will have no choice but to compel you, son." Julius balled his fists and stared back.

"I thought you said we'd be safe if we completed that ritual," Catherine whispered behind Alexander.

Looking at the determined expression on Julius' face, Alexander could offer no reassurances to comfort to her. Yes, technically she should have been safe. But all the signs seemed to suggest that Julius was in no mood to follow the rules. He wasn't used to having to face opposition. Ever since he'd taken his place at the head of the council, he had become used to his will ruling supreme.

"Julius, master," Lucille said, her voice gentle and calm, very unlike her usual demeanor.

"Yes, child. What is it?" Julius spoke quickly, impatiently.

"I see the change in her," Lucille said, her voice

growing even softer.

Alexander turned his head to look at Catherine. Sure enough, he saw it too. There was a special glow about her. Humans wouldn't see it, of course, but it was clear as day to all the vampires in the room.

"Oh, what nonsense!" Gillian protested from the back. "I don't see anything!"

"How dare you!" Julius roared. "I gave you everything, and you repay me by spitting in my face?"

"She is my wife. I knew it from the moment I first saw her, and not even you, the great Principis of the Council, can undo that!" Alexander responded.

Julius charged ahead and Alexander moved back into position, blocking Catherine from the incoming assault.

He braced for impact, but Julius stopped dead with only inches between them and his hand wrapped around Alexander's throat. His eyes, once rich with experience and wisdom collected over two millennia, now only expressed one thing: blind rage. If he chose to, his fingernails would dig into Alexander's flesh and rip out his esophagus. Although not fatal, the trauma would be enough to disable Alexander long enough that Julius would win the battle immediately.

Behind them, Catherine let out a choked sob, which tore at Alexander's heart. It had just been a few hours since she'd been initiated into this parallel world Alexander and his kind inhabited. And already, she had to deal with the threat of death or worse, at the hands of the most powerful vampire in the world. It was too much. He was responsible; if he hadn't thrown that party, none of this would have happened.

"Master," Lucille spoke again. "The laws are clear."

Julius' frustration was obvious. He waved his other hand dismissively in her direction. "I know, I know. The laws forbid me from harming her."

He turned and stared into Alexander's eyes again. "But nowhere is it written I should spare a subject who disobeyed clear orders." The grip on Alexander's throat tightened painfully.

Lucille cleared her throat.

"What?" Julius let go of Alexander and flung around.

"As I see it, in a way this boils down to a property dispute." Lucille averted her gaze from Julius and looked directly at Alexander now.

Hearing her refer to Catherine as mere property made Alexander's blood boil. But he didn't argue, hoping that whatever Lucille was about to say would help defuse the situation further. At least he was no longer subjected to Julius' death grip.

"How so?" Julius barked.

"Well, you claimed the Blood Bride as property of the Council. Alexander claimed her as his consort, a process that is known to begin upon a couple's first meeting. His bond is stronger, and should take precedence. Yet that doesn't change the fact that a debt is being owed here."

"Explain!"

Alexander balled his fists. If Lucille suggested he share Catherine with Julius, he was going to rip her head off along with everyone else's. Sister or no sister.

"Well, as per our laws, Alexander owes you a Blood Bride—any Blood Bride—and the debt will be repaid." Lucille bowed her head as a show of respect and awaited a response.

"You're not actually considering this ridiculous suggestion, are you?" Gillian's voice was shrill with anger. "Take his bloody head off!"

Julius turned and glared at Alexander again; the latter didn't flinch or show any sign of weakness.

"I've waited two thousand years for an experience like this," Julius spoke in a low growl. "You youngsters have no idea what it's like to walk this wretched earth for so long."

Alexander didn't dare to make a move or even respond, for fear of provoking Julius into further violence.

"Still, I suppose, time teaches you patience. Lucille's solution is agreeable to me, but know I won't wait forever." Julius addressed Alexander now. "If you don't deliver within a reasonable time frame, you may find me on your doorstep again. And at that time, there will be no mercy. If you can't deliver me the blood I want, I'll take an equal measure of yours."

Alexander never broke eye contact as long as Julius spoke. He took care not to show emotion: not fear, not relief at the proposed solution.

This would buy them time.

"The solution is agreeable," Alexander said.

"I don't believe it." Gillian threw her hands in the air and turned to leave.

Julius turned around and left the room within the blink of an eye. His guards followed, leaving behind only Lucille and Michael, who had remained at a safe distance throughout the entire confrontation.

"Thank you," Alexander said.

"I was only interpreting the rules, brother."

He smiled at her. Rules or otherwise, she'd taken the risk of opposing Julius, which was significant.

"Thank you anyway."

Lucille left as well, as did Michael, who would likely need to feed to heal his wounds. This meant only Alexander and Catherine remained.

"Whoa, that was intense," Catherine said, while reaching out for Alexander's arm.

He embraced her, held her tight. "I'm sorry you had to experience this."

Catherine's heart was still racing; Alexander could hear it clearly. He closed his eyes as he continued to hold her. Slowly but surely her body seemed to relax, bringing her heartbeat back under control. It occurred to him that although he still hadn't fed, her blood didn't call out to him with as much intensity as before. He could still smell it keenly, of course, but the ritual seemed to have dulled his thirst for now.

"Are you going to do it?" Catherine asked.

"Deliver him a Blood Bride?" Alexander said.

"Yes."

He remained quiet for a moment, while mulling it over. His aim first and foremost had been to keep Catherine safe. Now that they were bonded for life, her happiness would depend on his safety as well. In a way, he owed it to her to fulfill Julius' demand.

"I may not have much of a choice," he finally said.

Catherine didn't respond. She was still human, despite everything. The prospect of Alexander capturing and delivering some random woman to Julius would no doubt be horrifying to her.

Short of removing Julius as Principis of the Council, there was no other choice, though. And even then, he might no longer have the authority to officially punish Alexander, but he wouldn't hesitate to take matters into his own hands. The older vampires got, the more they felt they were above the law.

Alexander pulled back and looked into Catherine's captivating green eyes. He wouldn't have hesitated to kill Julius to protect her. But would he take such drastic action to protect a stranger?

The beginnings of tears started to collect in the corner of Catherine's eyes. Alexander ran the back of his finger across her cheek. He knew the right thing to do now.

"I'll do anything to keep you safe. And I'll do anything to make you happy. For now, Julius is off our backs, but once the time comes for him to collect his debt, I'll handle it however you want me to."

Catherine smiled through her tears. "I'm sorry. It's been a long day—night—whatever."

Alexander nodded. He repositioned his arms, one around her back and one along the bottom of her thighs, and lifted her up. She instinctively held on with both her arms around his neck and rested her head against his shoulder.

Just as they crossed the reception room and entrance, and started climbing the stairs, the old longcase clock on the upstairs landing started to strike one, two, three, four, five times.

Catherine must have been exhausted, after having been up the entire day as well as night. It would be a while before their schedules would align, so that their waking and sleeping times would coincide.

Alexander made his way through the hallway, straight to the master suite, and laid her down against the pillows.

"Not like this," she argued, suppressing a yawn.

Catherine gestured at him to sit with her, then rested her head in his lap and closed her eyes. He ran his hand through her silken hair until moments later, her breathing slowed and she drifted off into a peaceful slumber.

That was how they stayed, all morning, and well into the day. Their first day together as a wedded couple couldn't have started better. With Catherine resting and Alexander looking over her.

One major battle had passed; they'd won the right to live as man and wife. But Alexander had lived too long and seen too much to dare to predict the future beyond that. They'd figure out how to handle Julius and his unpaid debt in time.

First though, he'd guide Catherine on her way into this new life of hers. He caressed her hair again. Funny, how natural this felt, when actually, they barely knew one another. He couldn't wait to learn everything about her as she eased into it all.

"Did I fall asleep?" she mumbled groggily.

Alexander smiled. It wouldn't all be easy, especially for her at first, but he was convinced they'd find a way through.

Their bond was strong. And now they'd have forever to get to know each other.

EPILOGUE

So much had happened in these last two weeks, and for Cat, everything had changed.

She'd gone from a single, mostly carefree twenty-something right into a relationship so deep and committed, she couldn't imagine her life without it anymore. Alexander made her happy, like nobody ever had before.

But she hadn't just gained; she'd lost as well.

Her life in that little apartment in Shepherd's Bush with Shelly was over. She would never return there. Now, this huge mansion in the most desirable part of London was her home.

Similarly, that job she'd started—the internship at Sotheby's—had ended the moment she'd stepped into Alexander's house after her first auction.

She wouldn't work there anymore.

The next time she'd step into Sotheby's would be by Alexander's side, as a buyer. What would Ms. Pryce say to that?

In two short weeks, Cat felt like she'd changed so much. No longer the naive girl who fumbled over her words when an attractive man approached her—she had grown and matured.

Catherine sat down at the polished mahogany writing table in what was now her office and picked up a pen and a sheet of paper. This was her last job, before she could give herself fully to her new life.

As soon as she put the tip down on the first line, the words started to flow onto the page as if they had a mind of their own.

Dear Shelly,

Ever since our goodbye on the day I moved out, you'll have questions.

You'll probably wonder where I am, and whether I am safe. Rest assured, I am.

Everything is fine, and I am happy.

I couldn't tell you this at the time, for reasons that will become clear by the end of this letter. Remember I told you about that man, Alexander Broderick, who I met at the Halloween party? We are a couple now.

It all happened so fast, and yet I don't feel rushed at all. There isn't a doubt in my mind that everything has turned out exactly the way it should have.

Alexander's Blood Bride

Although I wish I could have spent more time with you, I am glad to be where I am now.

There are so many things I ought to explain to you, even if I have only just begun to understand them myself.

The supernatural is real, bizarre as it sounds. There are things out there that go beyond what modern science or even religion could explain.
Alexander is one of them, and in a way, now so am I.

This city, with its rich history and culture, has always been home to any number of creatures society at large doesn't know about. Sure, people used to tell stories, which over time have turned into myths, but most of us don't believe them. Now, I must say that I do. I can no longer assume that just because I haven't seen something in person, it doesn't exist.

One thing is absolutely certain though; vampires are real. There really are immortals out there who drink blood to survive. No, they don't kill; not anymore. They've even got a whole shadow government to make sure that they don't. They take great care to protect their secret, which is why I couldn't tell you all this so far.

Funny, isn't it? Two girls like us happened to walk into a Halloween party hosted by vampires? What's even funnier to me is that I am the one who has ended up here, surrounded by wealth and power. I never saw myself as strong, confident. The first time I walked into this house, I felt so out of place. Now it is starting to feel like home.

I have a man who adores me more than I could have dreamed of for myself. As much as I've given up to be with him, he risked more, including his own safety, to keep me safe. A small part of me still wonders if I'm worthy.

But every time he looks at me, his eyes tell me that I am.

One day, I hope you get something like this; perhaps not with a vampire, but with a regular guy.

Alexander's Blood Bride

It's the connection that counts. This is what love feels like. You deserve to find it too.

For now, this really is goodbye. Spending time together really isn't an option; you wouldn't be safe.

Alexander and I had to fight for the right to be together. Just knowing about this underworld of sorts is dangerous and there are people—other vampires—out there who are just waiting for us to slip up. As long as we follow the rules, we'll be safe, though.

When things calm down, maybe we will meet again, but I can't make any promises about the time frame. The truth is, now that I am part of this different world, the passing of time will take on a new meaning for me. It'll no longer be fleeting, but rather more steady and constant.

All I can do is hope, and wait for the right moment.

Live your life, be happy, find love.
All the best.

Love,

Your best friend, always, Cat

Cat put the pen down and stared at the now filled sheet of paper. One solitary tear threatened to escape her lid and roll down her cheek, but she caught it just in time with the back of her hand.

Then she took a deep breath, picked up the paper, folded it, and sealed it inside an envelope which already had Shelly's name written on the front.

This was it. The final goodbye.

Cat opened the drawer of her writing desk, and placed the envelope inside, on top of the one labeled "Mom."

Of course she'd never send these letters; that would put the people she loved, as well as herself, in grave danger. But it felt nice to be able to express everything she wanted to in writing. Just to get it off her chest.

She shut the drawer and with it, rid herself of any remaining melancholy. Then she got up and left the room. Down the stairs, through the entrance hall and reception, she had already learned the way through this house.

Inside the library, Alexander was already waiting for her in one of the old leather arm chairs.

"Done?" he asked.

She stood in front of him and smiled. "Yes, that was the last one."

"I wish you didn't have to do this, say goodbye to

everything you've known. But the letters really helped me when I was just turned."

Cat reached out for him and he immediately took her hand, tugging at it gently. She stepped up even closer to his chair and straddled him, wrapping her arms around his neck.

"Will that ever happen?" she asked.

Alexander circled her shoulder with his index finger. "What, whether you'll be turned?"

Cat nodded.

"There's no real need, as long as we're together. As long as I'm alive, you will be too. Our bond ensures it."

"I know, but still," Cat said.

Immortality no doubt came with its own host of downsides. She recalled the way he'd looked at the painting that hung above the bed in the master suite on their first meeting. This house on a sunny midsummer's day—that was something nocturnal beings would never get to see. Was it all worth it in the end?

Alexander shrugged. "If you want. Your wish is my command."

Cat didn't respond, not with words anyway. She leaned down and let her lips do the rest.

She knew he didn't want to change her; that her humanity was what had attracted him in the first place. She just loved to hear that he would, if she asked him to.

He responded eagerly to her kisses; his passion drew her in closer. His hand tightened around a fistful of her hair. She loved this harmony of gentle affection and intense passion that threatened to make him lose control.

"I love you," she whispered in his ear.

Alexander's body went tense and he got up, still carrying her in his arms. "I love you too," he growled, as he carried her up to the master suite within the blink of an eye, like only a vampire could. There, he showed her exactly how much.

These were still the early days of their relationship and who knew what the future might bring. But as long as she had his love, and he had hers, they would be fine.

- THE END -

Michael's
SOUL MATE

CHAPTER ONE

Michael checked his watch and scanned the room. Little groups of people stood scattered around the tastefully lit hotel lobby, drinks in hand. Some were making small talk, others had paired up to dance toward the other end of the establishment, beyond the bar. Some had even left, no doubt to take their celebrations upstairs to one of the many vacant rooms.

Unusually, he hadn't felt the need to participate in the goings on. Dawn was still many hours away, but something compelled him to call it a night already. Frankly, he had even begun to feel a bit bored.

It was a regular Friday night in early December. The party had been fine, though Michael hadn't appreciated the gaudy decorations everyone seemed so fond of around this time of year. The people in attendance had been fine, too. Nothing particularly exciting, but he couldn't find fault with any of it either.

Still, something was off; he hadn't been able to feel comfortable. A growing feeling of unease filled his chest and he could not ignore it any longer. What exactly had sparked his restlessness, he wasn't sure.

Michael said his goodbyes, nodding at the odd

acquaintance among the crowd of strangers, then made his way toward the exit.

"Aw, won't you stay a little longer?" A leggy blonde, who he had chatted to a little earlier, intercepted Michael on his way out. Her eyes were big, almost pleading as she spoke, her movements slightly uncoordinated.

Ordinarily, he might have considered her request, even if she was a bit too intoxicated for his liking. He liked his intimate partners to be alert, otherwise there was no joy in it for him. Still, she was beautiful, well dressed. Exactly his usual type.

But tonight, he just wasn't interested.

"I really must be off. I have some work—"

"You work Saturdays?" The woman cocked her head to the side and started twirling a lock of her hair around her index finger.

Michael paused. He wasn't used to being questioned on the validity of his excuses. Luckily, vampires had ways of dealing with that sort of thing.

"I'm afraid so," he spoke, while staring into the woman's eyes. The change came over him easily. He was still young in vampire terms, but his mental abilities were well developed.

The woman's demeanor changed almost instantly. The uncertainty in her eyes vanished. She became still and was now completely captivated until he released her from his influence.

"Okay." She sounded monotone, like she wasn't aware

that she had responded out loud.

"Why don't you stay a little longer? The night is still young. Enjoy yourself," Michael suggested.

The woman blinked once, then continued to stare into his eyes.

"Go on," he urged. That was when he broke eye contact, consciously severing their connection.

She blinked again, then turned around and headed straight for the bar counter without turning back even once. Michael made his escape before anyone else could stop him.

He buttoned up his woolen overcoat as he stepped outside. It was a starless night; the dense cloud cover had made sure of that. There was a certain electricity in the air, which to him suggested it might be about to start snowing.

Michael took a deep breath and closed his eyes. Yes, something was definitely coming. Could that be what had made him feel off for most of the night?

The frosty air surrounding the bar he'd just left seemed heavy with a great many aromas. Things that humans might never notice; for example, the scent of what remained of the fallen autumn leaves from that one tree down the street.

Michael turned to face the opposite direction. Chinatown was at least a mile away, but he could smell the restaurants from here.

He was tempted to stretch his legs a little and sprint home as fast as only a vampire could, but the roads were still too busy. He couldn't risk someone watching him as he seemingly disappeared into thin air. The Council didn't take kindly to vampires exposing themselves to humans at the best of times. Ever since the big showdown between Michael's friend and mentor Alexander and Council leader Julius, they'd been under extra scrutiny. Julius would jump at the chance to punish Michael for supporting Alexander.

Things had really changed a lot in a short period of time, and not entirely for the better.

Michael opened his eyes again, resigned to the fact that he would either have to hail a cab or walk home at an excruciatingly slow, much more human-like pace.

He started to walk roughly in the direction of Hyde Park. If he found a quiet spot, he might still indulge himself in a little fun. As he crossed the busy street ahead, his nose caught a whiff of something unexpected, something metallic.

Blood.

His instincts took over. He turned on his heel and sped up a little as he followed the smell. A low whimper urged him to speed up even further, but he couldn't risk going any faster if he didn't want to make a spectacle of himself.

There was a dark passageway in between two large office buildings. He made his way through and found himself in a quiet courtyard, which housed a number of large garbage bins. A woman's foot peeked out from in between them. No human would have been able to see it in the dark, but Michael could.

Her breaths were labored and becoming shallower, and her heartbeat was slowing. Michael pushed one of the bins aside and kneeled beside the woman, who lay face-down on the ground.

It was obvious to him now; she was barely clinging on to life. He carefully turned her onto her back. Her lips had a purple tinge and her skin looked dry and unusually pale for a human.

The two dark marks on her neck spoke volumes.

She'd been drained.

For but a split second, her eyelids fluttered open. She seemed to see him and opened her mouth to speak, but no sound came. Then she slipped back into unconsciousness.

Michael tensed up. He ought to leave, pretend he never found her. The last thing he needed was for someone to find him here, standing over a dying woman who had clearly been attacked by one of his own. But he couldn't bring himself to leave.

How pretty she was, how fragile, as she clung to her last shred of humanity.

Why had she ended up like this? Killing was against the rules. And discarding a drained body out in public where it could so easily be discovered? That was sacrilege.

His mind raced. Too many questions, not enough answers.

Michael gazed down at her face; the slightly parted lips, despite their unnatural color, still looked full and luxurious. As did the rest of her, actually. She made a beautiful corpse. Such a waste. This woman would have been a sight to behold before someone had decided to take her life for themselves.

He ran the back of his index finger along the side of her face. She twitched slightly, seemingly in reaction to his touch, causing him to pull away again.

No, he would not leave her, discarded among these bins of office refuse. This wasn't the end she deserved.

Michael closed his eyes and tried to focus. Her heartbeat had become irregular, as though her body was giving up the fight. If he didn't hurry, there wouldn't be any life left to save.

Before he fully realized what he was doing, Michael nicked a vein in his wrist and pressed the newly created wound against her lips.

"Drink," he whispered.

She was too far out of it, so he couldn't compel her to listen, but that wouldn't stop him.

Then, he picked up one of her arms and brought it to his own lips. He waited for what felt like forever. Was she too far gone already?

"Drink or you'll die!" he urged again, fully aware she likely couldn't even hear him.

Still, as more and more of his blood trickled out of the gash in his wrist, there was a subtle change in her. Her heartbeat seemed to strengthen. Her breaths became more controlled.

And then, out of nowhere, her free hand jerked up to

grab his wrist and press it tightly against her mouth. Finally, she drank in deep gulps as her body tried to recover what it had lost.

That was his cue.

He bit into the wrist he'd been holding already and allowed himself the smallest of tastes. That completed the cycle. The Ritual was done.

She became still again and let go of his arm, her hand flopping down onto her stomach. Her eyes had remained shut throughout; she probably hadn't even realized what had just happened.

He'd barely realized it too; he'd been acting purely on instinct. Now, as he stood up and inspected the smeared blood on his wrist, it hit him. He'd performed the Ritual. He'd created another vampire—tried to, anyway.

That was something he'd vowed he'd never take as lightly as his own maker had.

She wasn't out of the woods yet; in fact, he wouldn't know if she'd even survive the change until the following night, but for some strange reason, he'd jumped in and impulsively made the biggest decision of his immortal life so far.

Things would never be the same again.

———•———

Michael sank into one of the leather armchairs in the library and rested his head in his hands.

Neither Alexander, Michael's friend and mentor, nor

his human consort, Cat, had said a word when he reached home carrying an unconscious half-turned human in his arms. Their expressions had spoken volumes. Now that she was safely tucked away in one of the bedrooms upstairs, Michael braced himself for the lecture he was about to hear.

"You brought a fledgling into this house. This house which you share with a human! Do you have any idea what you've done?" Alexander leaned forward and balled his fists. Cat walked up behind Alexander's chair and rested her hand on his shoulder.

"I couldn't very well leave her there to die in the street!" Michael was sorry for the situation he'd put everyone in, but what else could he have done?

Alexander shook his head. "You realize she's going to wake up thirsty. And Catherine..." He reached up and placed his hand on top of Cat's. "She's a Blood Bride. You know what that means. Her presence can be too much to resist for a grown vampire. A newborn won't be able to help themselves!"

Alexander was right, of course. It had taken a good while for Michael to learn to control his urges after Cat had first moved into the house. And he had been turned decades ago.

"Michael has a point too, you know," Cat spoke softly.

Michael looked up in surprise. He hadn't expected Cat to take his side. After all, she was the one who had the most to lose if things escalated.

"You're new to this. You've never been around a newly made vampire before. They can't control themselves at the best of times!" Alexander argued.

"As you said, I'm a Blood Bride. Even ancient vampires seem to have a hard time controlling themselves once they catch a whiff of me." Cat shrugged and winked at Michael.

"It's dangerous. He's brought danger into our house!" Alexander gestured in Michael's direction.

"He couldn't just leave her to die, though."

The couple shared a look.

Michael shook his head as he thought back to the scene in the alley. How he had first discovered the woman.

"What was I supposed to do?" Michael asked.

Alexander's eyes were on him again. He pressed his lips together, clearly still displeased with Michael's actions, but he didn't respond. Perhaps he didn't have any answers either.

"You'll have to teach her everything I taught you," Alexander said finally.

Michael nodded. "I know."

"Catherine's safety depends on it."

Cat smiled subtly at Michael. At least she was on his side.

Michael had been skeptical when Alexander had first taken Cat as his consort. Especially since the leader of the Vampire Council himself, Julius, had wanted her for himself. Michael hadn't understood Alexander's reasoning for taking a risk so big. Of course, he'd sided with

Alexander anyway; loyalty was important to him and he owed Alexander his life.

Now, when it was time for Alexander to support Michael's choice, it seemed that Cat's influence was the one thing tipping things in his favor. How ironic.

"I will make sure she doesn't harm anyone, especially Cat."

Cat nodded at Michael as she squeezed Alexander's shoulder. "It'll be fine. You worry too much," she said.

"I hope so."

"I promise I'll not let anything happen to her," Michael said. Although his promise was aimed at Cat, it was equally true for the mystery woman that lay in one of the bedrooms upstairs. He'd brought her here—helpless, like a wounded animal. He was responsible.

Alexander's words had affected him deeply. Should he have left her behind? No, that would have been utterly wrong. For the woman, as well as for the safety of their own kind. What if she'd been discovered there? What if human authorities had figured out who—or what—had killed her?

Michael didn't have a choice, and if necessary, he could justify himself to anyone. But that didn't mean that this would be easy. He tensed up at the prospect of what was to come.

Michael's own initiation into immortality had been difficult, at least until Alexander had taken him under his wing. He owed it to his woman to make her turning as easy as possible. But there was no way of predicting how she'd take it.

This little argument among friends was nothing in comparison to what might yet occur.

CHAPTER TWO

She was sore when she woke up. Her muscles seemed tight to the point of being cramped, as though she had gone to the gym the day before. Not that she recalled ever going to a gym. Her thoughts were fuzzy, like she'd woken up in the middle of an intense dream, the details of which eluded her.

She opened her eyes and blinked a few times while waiting for her eyes to adjust. The room was dark, but she could still see her surroundings clearly.

The four-poster bed didn't look familiar, and neither did the decorative rosette in the center of the ceiling.

Where am I?

She winced as she lifted her upper body and rested on her elbows. Every inch of her felt like she was covered in bruises. Worst of all was her head. The shooting pain behind her eyes caused her vision to blur slightly with each heartbeat. Still, she was overwhelmed by all that she saw.

Beautiful period furniture, luxurious paintings, heavy embroidered drapes. Despite the lack of direct light, she could see the carved frame of the painting across the room in exquisite detail. She wasn't wearing glasses, was she? Surely, she should have felt the weight of them on the bridge of her nose. There was nothing there, though she felt compelled to confirm the same by touch.

She was certain that this wasn't her room.

She gently lowered herself down against the fluffy pillows again and closed her eyes. What did *her* room actually look like? Those details were much fuzzier than the sharp reality that surrounded her.

If this isn't my room, then how did I get here?

She heard a couple of muffled voices, perhaps originating from next door. Two men, having what sounded like an agitated conversation, though she could not make out the exact words. She didn't recognize either of their voices.

The more she thought about it, the more uneasy she grew. How had she ended up here?

Her heart started to beat faster, so fast that she should have been out of breath and perhaps faint. Instead, she somehow felt… stronger. Could that even be?

Everything still hurt, of course, like she'd been hit by a bus. Could she have been in an accident before someone brought her here?

She pressed her lips together and fought through the intense pain as she lifted herself again and slipped out of bed. As she set herself down onto the lacquered wooden floor, it was like an electric jolt passed through the soles of her feet and all the way up through her legs and torso. It wasn't cold as such, nor was it unpleasant, but it was somehow different than any floor she'd ever walked barefoot on.

The voices next door had calmed down a bit, like their

debate had turned into a more restrained, controlled conversation. As she listened for more, she could hear the other sounds that filled the strange house she was in. Ticking, of a clock perhaps. Rustling leaves. Creaks and scratches which she could not place nor identify.

And the scents that surrounded her were different from anything she'd ever experienced too. She could pick up everything, from the lacquer of the floor, to the fabric softener used on the sheets and the rubber soles on the pair of shoes in the corner. She could even smell the plaster and wallpaper on the walls, which was strange. She'd never paid attention to the scent of wallpaper before.

She shook her head. What a strange place this was, where everything smelled somehow more intense than normal. What did her own home smell like? She couldn't recall. She felt like Alice in Wonderland, exploring a place where the strange was normal, and she seemed to be the odd one out.

Who am I?

She wandered across the room to an elegant rosewood dresser and looked at herself in the mirror. Her reflection was the first thing that looked somewhat familiar in here.

Who am I?

She leaned forward and studied her features. Smooth skin, silky hair—this wasn't how she usually woke up, was it? No sign of puffiness around the eyes, not a single tangle in her shoulder-length locks. And what was she wearing? A long cotton nightgown, rather old fashioned. That couldn't be hers, could it?

It was like she had been groomed to perfection before being put to rest in here. Creepy.

Anna, nice to meet you! She herself had said those words not too long ago, smiled, and stretched out her hand at someone. But at whom? Whom had she introduced herself to?

Anna rubbed her eyes and then studied herself again. No, that was all she had. The only memory she could conjure was of her first name.

If she couldn't remember who she was or where she was from, the least she ought to do was find out where she was now. Anna took a deep breath and straightened her back. Surely and steadily, her muscles seemed to relax a bit. Every step loosened her up a bit more.

Anna approached the door and paused to listen for those voices again before turning the handle. It seemed safe enough. The two men seemed occupied with each other. She would be careful, and they probably wouldn't even hear her.

As she pressed her hand down, she flinched at the horrible creak of the handle. Then, to her relief, she found that the door was unlocked; she was able to push it open and create even more of a racket. These people, whoever they were, should really do something about their noisy doors!

As soon as she pushed it open a bit more, she found herself blinded by the bright chandelier hanging in the center of the hallway ahead. *What the hell? Who puts bulbs this bright into a chandelier?*

She squinted as her eyes adjusted. It took a few painful moments before she could focus properly on what lay ahead.

The hallway was more of the same luxury she'd found in the bedroom. Paintings and expensive looking wallpaper adorned the walls, and there was a cornice edging the ceiling and a rosette just above the chandelier. Whoever lived here had made the place look less like a house and more like a palace. Anna couldn't decide if it was tasteful or kitsch.

She carefully moved forward, tiptoeing so that she wouldn't tip off the men she'd heard talking earlier. Come to think of it, they had now stopped talking. Had they heard her?

She rested her hand against the wall and listened. The opening of a bottle, followed by the rush of liquid as it poured out. The sound was unmistakable; she'd heard it so many times before in her line of work.

That was it. She had worked as a waitress. Anna clearly saw a glimpse of her own hands, opening bottles and pouring glasses of champagne. She opened her eyes and still found herself alone in an empty hallway, though. Like she'd just imagined that sound.

She rubbed her temples, attempting to dull the ache. Clearly, whatever had happened to her had made her lose her mind. Hallucinations, fragmented memories. Would it all come back to her soon, like it did in the movies?

Those same men started talking again and Anna breathed a sigh of relief. As long as they carried on chatting, they would hopefully be oblivious to whatever she was up to. No way was she going to let herself get caught sneaking around a strange house without first figuring out where she was and what she was up against. She had to make sure she was safe first, before confronting any of these people.

Who knew, perhaps they were the ones responsible for her fragile condition in the first place! Perhaps they'd attacked her before bringing her here?

Anna bit her lip and a rush of warm liquid burst through her skin and into her mouth. Blood.

Strangely, the wound she had just created was the only spot on her body that didn't currently hurt. She tiptoed forward toward a mirror further up the hallway.

Her bottom lip was stained bright red. She leaned forward to get a better look. There wasn't any sign of a cut or split. She licked the blood away and found that her lips were full and flawless, much more so than normal. Then she opened her mouth and inspected her teeth. White, straight, perfect.

But the canines…

She held her breath and touched her teeth with the tip of her finger. Razor sharp and longer than what seemed possible. Was this some kind of joke?

Had these freaks kidnapped her and done some kind of

cosmetic dentistry on her? She shook her head. This must be yet another thing she was only imagining. Her mind was playing tricks on her, but she wouldn't let it get her down. She had to stay focused on the one thing that was important: figuring where she was and why she was here. And perhaps she could even find a way out.

The voices grew louder the further she tiptoed up the hallway. Finally, she found herself at the top of an impressive wooden staircase leading to the lower level of the house. They were down there somewhere. Just as Anna was about to take the first step down, a whiff of something irresistible caught her attention. Perfume? Food?

She turned around and scanned the other hallway, leading in the opposite direction of the landing. That was where it had come from. Anna took a deep breath and closed her eyes. Better than the bakery she'd walk past on her way home from work. *Cobbled streets, dark facades, except for a modern looking building with large windows that would produce the most amazing scents. Vanilla, chocolate, cinnamon...*

Anna opened her eyes again. Another clue. Whatever her life looked like, she lived somewhere near a bakery. Perhaps all of her memories would come back soon enough.

She wasn't sure how long she'd been reminiscing for. The scent had dissipated, leaving her once again alone atop the stairs. Down below, she heard the distinct click and deafening creak of a door. As nice as everything looked, simple maintenance clearly wasn't a priority in this house.

Footsteps echoed against the walls downstairs. Anna hid behind the balustrade and covered her ears to drown out the noise. It might have been smarter to retreat back to her room, but she simply had to catch a glimpse of whoever's house this was. She squinted to see through the bright light overhead. That was when she saw him.

A dark-haired man in an elegant black suit cut straight across the hall downstairs.

"You take care of it, you hear me, Michael?" he said.

"Of course, Alexander," another man responded, just out of view.

Anna pressed her lips together. Was that about her? Was this Michael fellow meant to take care of *her*?

The man left, and the double doors shut behind him with an almighty racket. Anna breathed a sigh of relief once it was over. Her poor ears. Were all of these people hard of hearing? Did they not notice how incredibly loud everything was in here?

She got up and rubbed her back. Still a bit sore, but her body felt a lot better than it had when she'd just woken up.

Anna was about to take the first step down to explore more of the house, perhaps even make a run for the door, when a figure appeared in the corner of her eye down at the end of the staircase.

"I'd been wondering when you'd wake up," the man said.

Anna flinched, only to find that she'd backed into a wall and couldn't go further. Within the blink of an eye, he had joined her on the upstairs landing.

Two pale blue eyes looked down at her briefly before glancing in the direction of the hallway she'd just come from.

He was tall and flawlessly handsome. His pale skin seemed to glisten slightly in the bright light that surrounded the two of them. If she hadn't just woken up with a wiped mind and a full-on body ache in a strange house, she might have found him attractive. Maybe.

There was something familiar about him, but she could not place him.

"Who are you? Where am I? Why am I here?" Anna asked.

The man's eyes darted back and forth between the hallway and her face. "How about we talk somewhere more comfortable. I'm Michael Odell, by the way. What's your name?"

Anna took a deep breath and studied his face. He couldn't even look her in the eye while he spoke. He was hiding something. Maybe he'd let his guard down if she played along just a little bit.

"Okay, Michael. I'm Anna." Her hand itched to shake his, just to see what he'd feel like in this strange heightened state she was experiencing, but she resisted the urge.

This wasn't the time to give in to temptation. First, she needed an explanation.

CHAPTER THREE

Michael could tell Anna had only grudgingly agreed to head back into her newly appointed bedroom with him. As they walked down the hall, he'd tried to explain everything he knew about the attack and what had followed, failing miserably.

"I'm not sure I understand," Anna said. "What exactly happened?"

Michael could hardly stand looking at her. Something about this woman—Anna, no last name, as she'd introduced herself—threw him off balance. He'd lost not just his *game,* but his entire sense of self around her. It was infuriating.

She was beautiful, but that was hardly a valid reason to lose himself in her presence.

"As I said, when I found you, you were in a bad way. There was really nothing I could do, other than perform the Ritual," he stammered.

Gone was the confident vampire who could walk into any bar, any party, any social function at all, and not just fit in effortlessly, but steer any interaction in his favor. Conversation, flattery, and seduction had not just been words in his vocabulary, they were all part of the same art Michael had sought to master over the years. Beautiful women were his *thing,* along with gourmet meals and fine wines. In his human life, he'd never succeeded at obtaining the high flying lifestyle he so craved, though not for lack of trying. It wasn't until Alexander had taken him in that he had found everything he'd been searching for. In immortality, he seemed to have the world at his feet.

But right now with Anna, none of it mattered. It was like his slate had been wiped clean. He couldn't even hypnotize her to save face. He felt completely and utterly inept.

"What are you telling me?" Anna demanded and stared at him with arms folded. "I don't remember any of this."

"I..." Michael tried to focus, but his mind didn't cooperate. Instead of feeding him the necessary words to make her understand what had happened while she was unconscious, all he could think of was old memories.

Don't fly too close to the sun, you might get burned—these words rang in his ears, decades after he'd last heard his father say them. His parents had been the more practical, down-to-earth sort, who never understood his more materialistic ambitions. And although the context was quite different now, these words had never seemed more relevant to Michael than right at this moment.

Michael looked into her amber eyes, briefly, before looking away again.

"You basically died. Now you're reborn."

"I don't understand. What have you done to me?" She'd tensed up as she glared at him. Michael couldn't tell if her reaction was the result of fear or anger.

He shook his head; he wasn't explaining it quite right. "You're immortal. You're a vampire now."

"Vampires don't exist," Anna argued. "You must think I'm stupid."

Michael's frustration peaked. "Wanna bet? Anyway, you don't have to take my word for it. Go on, look at the facts."

Anna started pacing around the room. "Facts! How ridiculous. I wake up here alone with no memory of how I got here or where I'm from, hearing voices through the walls, with weird pointy things stuck to my teeth and you're trying to tell me… I don't believe it!"

She stopped in front of the mirror. "It's all a trick, it has to be. See! I can see my reflection, right there."

Michael sighed. This was never easy. But at least most people were somewhat lucid when they underwent the Ritual. They remembered, even if they didn't understand what they'd gone through.

Anna didn't even seem to remember who she had been in her human life.

"It's a lot to take in. I understand. You'll feel better once you feed," Michael said. He was trying his best to stay calm, he really was. By God, as attractive as she was, this woman really knew how to push his buttons.

"Feed? Don't tell me you expect me to drink blood next! Look, mister. I don't know who you think you are, but I'm not participating in this perverted little game of yours. I want to go home, right now!"

You're going to get burned, the little voice in Michael's head insisted. He shook his head, trying to silence it.

"By all means then, I'll take you home right now. Remind me, where exactly *is* home?" Michael snapped. He regretted his outburst as soon as he saw Anna's face.

She retreated and sat down on the bed and rested her head in her hands. Clearly, she had no idea how to answer his question.

"Look, I'm sorry. That wasn't fair," Michael said.

He approached her and hesitated a moment before touching her shoulder. He wanted to help her so badly, but at the same time, he was frustrated beyond belief.

She flinched and shook him off.

"I just don't get it. Is everyone insane around here?" Anna said.

Michael sighed and sat down next to her, making sure he kept a safe distance. "You could say that," he mumbled, more to himself than her.

Her hand trembled as she reached for her fangs, touching first one, then the other. She let out a soft *ouch* when she nicked her finger tip, causing it to bleed.

"I know it doesn't seem like it, but I did what I thought was best. You had been attacked. I found you when you were moments away from death, and I didn't know what else to do," Michael spoke softly. He was trying to convince himself of his words, as much as her.

"Assuming I believe you—which I *don't*—please explain everything again. I'm immortal? What does that even mean?" Anna turned to face him, then put her wounded finger against her lips and licked away the blood.

It was mesmerizing to watch.

Michael shook his head. He had to snap out of it. It was deeply inappropriate to think of her that way. "Uh, yeah. Of course. Well, it's much like the stories, except for the bit about having no reflection. You'll be awake at night, you need blood to survive, you won't age…"

Anna stopped and looked at her index finger, which was once again unmarked, as though she'd never wounded herself at all. Michael watched her from the corner of his eye.

"Sunlight, garlic, holy water, stakes through the heart, those are the only things that'll harm me?" Anna asked.

Michael let out a laugh, then quickly recovered. "Sorry. Well, sunlight will definitely kill you, garlic and holy water, not so much. A stake through the heart—that's very old school. I'm not sure what that'll do, maybe sting for a while?"

Anna frowned and turned to face him. "So I'll have to murder people to survive?" she asked. Her eyes were wide, giving her face a certain innocence. She had only looked this helpless back when she'd briefly regained consciousness back in that filthy alley.

Michael shook his head and tried to reach for her again, causing her to recoil.

She didn't trust him. Not that he could blame her.

"No, we don't kill. It's against the rules."

"So how do you drink blood then?" she asked.

"Well, as you get to grips with your new powers, you'll be able to hypnotize humans. They won't feel a thing."

She looked away from him and stared at the floor in front of the bed. "Okay…"

Michael relaxed a bit. Perhaps she was ready to accept the truth now.

"And the other guy I saw downstairs, he's a vampire too?" she asked.

"Yeah, Alexander. He found me when I was still a fledgling. Taught me everything I know."

She nodded and continued to stare at the floor in silence. Neither of them said a word for at least a minute.

Anna took a deep breath. "You lads are insane. There's no other explanation." She straightened her back and folded her arms again.

Michael opened his mouth to say something, but he had nothing. He rested his elbows on his thighs and shook his head. He'd done what he could. This woman was incredibly stubborn. She'd have to figure out the truth for herself.

He got up and walked toward the door.

"Wait, you're not leaving me, are you?" Anna called out behind him.

He gestured at her to wait. Realizing that actually he didn't need to follow the usual precautions that he took around humans, he broke into a sprint, straight to the kitchen downstairs. He grabbed a few cold cuts and a steak from the fridge, depositing the whole lot on a plate. Whether she liked it or not, Anna needed to feed. Hopefully she'd realize this as soon as she saw the meat.

He was back in her bedroom within the blink of an eye. He'd hoped that this little display of his superhuman speed would convince her, but when he looked at her, still sitting in place on the bed, he didn't see recognition in her eyes. Whatever he'd just tried to demonstrate, she hadn't noticed anything strange about it.

Michael wished he could ask Alexander for advice, but that wasn't an option. He'd taken Cat away for the week, in an attempt to keep her safe, and he was still angry with him to boot. Michael was on his own. They'd all ended up in an impossible situation together, thanks to his impulsive decision to turn this woman.

All he could hope for now was that Anna would see the truth and come around to accepting her new situation before Alexander returned. Otherwise... Well, otherwise Michael wasn't quite sure what would happen. He'd have to fix this situation he'd created. If Cat wasn't safe in the same house as Anna, he'd have to relocate her somehow.

And the entire conversation he'd just tried to have with Anna suggested was that she wasn't easily convinced of anything. How would he convince her to leave with him without creating a scene? What a headache.

Michael held the plate in her direction. "You must be hungry. Please, help yourself."

Anna eyed him suspiciously, then glanced down at the

food. Her eyes rested on the raw steak.

Michael remembered clearly what it had been like when he was freshly turned. Every sense was almost painfully heightened. She wouldn't be able to resist the juicy meat, not for long anyway.

"It's raw," she said.

"You're very observant," he said, then immediately regretted his tone.

She glared at him, then looked back down at the plate.

"It'll do you good. If you don't believe me, that's fine. Try it and you'll find out for yourself," he added, doing his best to sound patient. It was difficult, nigh impossible. He wanted nothing more than to force her to eat it already. Why couldn't she just take his word for it?

After a few more seconds of indecision, Anna finally seemed to give in. She took the plate from him and sniffed the meat, closing her eyes as the scent of blood no doubt overwhelmed her senses. When she opened her eyes again, they had turned a deep shade of red.

Blood lust. Finally.

That was how Michael had reacted too, when he had awoken a newly created vampire and stood face to face with his first meal. Only, there had been no one to guide him, no one to provide him with a safe meal option. He'd acted purely on instinct and almost killed the man he'd tried to drink from. It had been a disaster.

"Eat. Trust me," he urged.

Anna didn't hesitate any longer. She scarfed down

everything on the plate, even licking off the juices that ended up on her fingers.

"Weird. I've never been much of a meat eater," she mumbled.

Michael took the plate from her and observed her as she pulled her legs up onto the bed and curled up against the pillows.

"So… sleepy…" she whispered.

Michael continued to watch her for a moment. That was what had happened to him too. It was quite a shock to the system, digesting your first meal after the change. Perhaps things between them would improve once she had more of a chance to rest.

She was quite something, even if she was his fledgling and he was her maker. Feisty, too. If only the circumstances of their meeting had been different…

"I'll be downstairs if you need me," he said.

"Mhmm."

Michael didn't look back as he left the room, pulling the door shut behind him. Out of habit, he checked the large grandfather clock on the landing. It was just before nine o'clock. Ordinarily, he'd be getting ready to go out by now. Not tonight, though.

His nights of carefree and unapologetic hedonism were over.

Michael had never been particularly responsible, but going forward, he wouldn't have a choice. And that realization worried him, possibly even more so than the prospect of having Anna argue with him some more upon waking up.

CHAPTER FOUR

Once again, Anna woke up to the sound of muffled voices. But it wasn't two men this time; instead, it was a woman and a man. And she could hear them more clearly, so much so that she could follow the whole conversation word-for-word.

"What do you want?" the male voice, which Anna recognized as Michael's, asked.

"Council business. Where is my dear brother?" the female demanded.

"Out. He took Catherine with him. I'm afraid you'll have to put up with me instead."

Anna held her breath as she continued to listen. It was obvious from his tone that whoever this woman was, Michael not only knew her, but knew her well enough to dislike her.

"Very well. It has come to our attention that some—shall we say—*outsiders* have arrived in the city. If they're even aware of our customs and laws, they are blatantly ignoring them. *Humans* have been affected."

That last bit made Anna's ears perk up even more. She was no longer content waiting around in this bedroom, she had to see this visitor for herself. The way she had emphasized the word 'humans' was very strange indeed. Could it be that this visitor also believed in the nonsense story Michael had tried to tell her earlier, about the lot of them being vampires?

"You don't say," Michael responded. His sarcasm wasn't lost on Anna, and she couldn't even see the two of them yet. She hurried out of bed and sneaked out the door as fast as she could. Thankfully, Anna's body ache had mostly subsided as she'd slept, allowing her more stealth and speed than before.

"In fact, would it be safe to say one such human is here right now?" the woman spoke up again.

Suddenly self-conscious, Anna paused just before reaching the top of the stairs. No, she had come this far, she would take a look at this new stranger for herself. It was bad enough that Michael and the other man were deluded about who or what they were, but now this woman seemed equally out of touch with reality.

"Is dear old Gillian still surveilling us then?" Michael asked. "Either way, there are no humans here."

Anna kneeled down and peeked through the balustrade, only to find Michael already staring at her. His expression didn't change one bit; the man had the perfect poker face. A perfectly handsome, infuriating poker face.

Seeing how he had already anticipated her curiosity annoyed her. How arrogant he was.

"The Council has eyes and ears everywhere, as you well know," the slender, dark-haired woman said. She stood with her back toward Anna, her shoulders pulled back, suggesting amazing posture. Anna was almost disappointed she couldn't catch a glimpse of the woman's face.

"Well, Lucille, I don't know what to tell you. If there were a human in here, I'm sure you would have smelled her… or him." Michael maintained eye contact with Anna as he spoke, making her feel uneasy.

Look away, or you'll tip this Lucille woman off! Anna frowned to make her point.

Finally, Michael did stop staring at her.

Anna breathed a sigh of relief. She wasn't sure why he was affecting her. These people were clearly nuts. If only she could get out of here and head home. Inconveniently, she still didn't remember where *home* was exactly, or she might have been able to make a run for it.

"Very well, have it your way. You'll know where to find the Council if you come across any of these unwanted visitors, as well as their victims. I don't have to remind you that Julius expects your loyalty now more than ever. And that goes for my brother as well."

Michael nodded. His expression had softened slightly, making him look just a little less arrogant than before. Still, Anna wasn't sure what to think. These people were weird, untrustworthy.

Lucille nodded and pushed the two double doors open wide as she left. They had barely swung back into position when Michael stood up on the landing in front of Anna.

"Oh!" She took a step back and tried to regain her composure. How had he moved so quickly? "Who was that?"

"Lucille Amboise. Julius turned her around the same time as Alexander, so they consider themselves siblings."

Anna wanted to argue. *Turned her.* Ridiculous. Michael was really intent on dragging this fantasy out as long as he could manage. "And what is this Council she kept referring to? What do they want with me?"

"The Vampire Council, led by Julius. Well, they make sure that we follow the rules. Like I said before, we're not supposed to—"

"Yeah, not supposed to kill, right?"

"Right." Michael smiled and looked right at her for a moment. As soon as he did, something weird happened inside her chest. Was it nerves? Excitement? No way was she going to allow herself to develop a soft spot for a lunatic!

"It appears that the Council is on the trail of the vampires who did this to you. They take that sort of thing very seriously."

"So not only have you turned me into a *vampire* to *save me*, it was *vampires* who put me in the position to need saving in the first place? Funny how there are all of a sudden a lot of vampires running around London." Anna folded her arms and cocked her head to the side. She didn't have much patience left. Not for him, or his nonsense.

Michael shrugged. "Don't believe me, it hardly matters at this point. Answer me one thing, though: that bloody steak did make you feel better, didn't it?"

Anna pressed her lips together tightly. She wanted to prove him wrong so desperately, but the worst part was that he was right. She did feel better now, and the steak hadn't been as disgusting as she'd thought either. Both those realizations annoyed her to no end.

"Perhaps I just needed more rest," she said at last.

"More rest. Sure." Michael shook his head slowly, then raised both his hands up in the air. "Look, between you refusing to believe a word I'm saying and Lucille turning up and interrogating me, this is turning into quite the trying evening. Perhaps it's best we talk about something else."

What else was there to talk about, though? She'd woken up feeling better, but there was still so much she didn't understand about her current situation. And she didn't even remember the necessary details to allow her to leave yet. She was stuck here, with him, until she could formulate a plan.

"I'm going downstairs to the library for a drink. You may join me if you like." Just like that, Michael had cut their conversation short.

"Wearing a nightgown?" Anna called after him, as he made his way down the stairs at a breakneck speed.

"Check the wardrobe in your room. There might be something in there," he said as he continued sprinting downstairs and to the left, just out of Anna's sight. God, how he annoyed her.

Within moments, she had returned to the bedroom—the one place in this house that was starting to look somewhat familiar—and found something passable to wear. As she undressed, she couldn't help but check herself out in the mirror. She'd changed. It didn't seem possible, but somehow, her body had smoothed out somewhat. Curves that had been there for as long as she could remember had firmed up. Imperfections had been wiped away.

She barely recognized her reflection, something which she might have explained away with the memory loss that she'd woken up with. Only, she clearly remembered what she used to look like. In excruciating, painful detail.

And it was those details, those little things she had found fault with before, which were missing now.

Gone was the cellulite, the odd marks and scars, even the stretch marks. Caps could explain the pointy teeth, perhaps a chemical peel had been responsible for her glowing complexion. And her hair? That could have been brushed and styled while she'd been unconscious.

But there was nothing in the world that could change her body to this extent, was there? There was no cure for stretch marks or cellulite. These two things plagued even skinnier girls. Anna was a lot of things, but even in her changed form, she still wasn't skinny.

Could it be that perhaps Michael's explanation wasn't so far-fetched after all? Could she actually have been changed into something supernatural...? Super-*human*?

It still seemed impossible, and yet it would explain a lot. Her sensitive hearing—she'd been able to overhear entire conversations taking place halfway across this massive house. Her changed physical form—pointy teeth and impossibly perfect skin. And her appetite for raw meat.

Anna shook her head and pulled on a pair of pants and a pullover she'd found in the wardrobe. These didn't look or feel like they were hers, but they would serve their purpose and make her feel just a little bit less vulnerable. It was awkward having to talk to a stranger wearing nothing more than a nightgown, even if it was nearly floor length and quite modest.

She took a deep breath and glanced at her reflection one last time before heading downstairs. She hoped that whatever drink Michael had been referring to would be something familiar, and not, God forbid, some unfortunate soul's blood.

On the way down, she caught a glimpse of the grand standing clock which towered over the landing. It was almost four o'clock. But inside the house, with its heavy drapes and brightly lit interior, Anna had no sense of time at all. If she hadn't noticed the thick cover of darkness outside as Lucille left, she wouldn't have known if it was four in the afternoon or in the morning.

She had obviously never been downstairs and had no idea of the layout, but her feet carried her automatically through the grand reception room with its elegant period settees and armchairs toward a heavy carved door that led to the library. Inside, Michael awaited.

He looked up the second she'd pushed the door open.

"There you are," he said.

Without warning, he picked up an empty glass from the table beside his leather armchair and flung it in Anna's direction. She was about to duck out of the way and let loose on him, when she realized that she had caught the glass, effortlessly, in her left hand.

"You threw a glass at my head!" she complained. "What the hell were you thinking?"

Michael's lips fluttered almost imperceptibly, as though he was suppressing a smile. "You caught it. Still unconvinced of your changed state?" he asked.

Anna wanted to bite her bottom lip, but then remembered the sharp teeth and resulting bleeding from earlier and stopped herself. How smug he was. Unfortunately, he had a point.

"Fine." She'd barely said the word, and a bottle zipped through the air in her direction. She still wasn't prepared, but at least it hadn't startled her as much as the glass. She caught it by the neck in her other hand.

"Pour yourself a drink. We have a lot to talk about." Michael said.

Anna scrutinized the label. It looked old, expensive. She walked across to the empty chair next to Michael and put the glass down. Then she opened the cap of the bottle and became overwhelmed as the aromas hit her. Woody, earthy, hints of sweetness and spice. It was brandy, that was certain, but she'd never smelled a vintage quite like it.

"Whoa," she mumbled, then glanced sideways at Michael, who was observing her, half full glass in hand.

"Your senses are much stronger now," he remarked.

She poured some of the amber liquid into the glass, which she now recognized as an expensive antique as well. To think that he'd just thrown it across the room like it was nothing. Rich people! What if she'd dropped it?

"How is this even possible," she whispered as she brought the glass to her lips.

The moment the brandy hit her tongue, she knew that somehow it was. Everything she'd rejected before had to be true. She wasn't quite sure how and why she'd ended up here, beyond what Michael had tried to tell her. She didn't even know exactly what her life had looked like earlier—she just knew that things would never be the same.

CHAPTER FIVE

Thank God.

Michael closed his eyes and took a sip from his glass. He hadn't been completely sure that it would work, but his reckless little stunt seemed to have convinced her. At the very least, it had planted the seed of doubt in her mind and caused her to stop arguing.

They sat in silence as Anna savored every last drop of the brandy. It was Alexander's stash, but he wouldn't mind. Not if it helped in getting Anna ready to deal with her new condition and most importantly, control her urges around Catherine once the two of them returned home.

And although vampires weren't affected by alcohol like humans were, sitting together and sharing a drink had a certain therapeutic value.

Michael had gone about it all wrong. Instead of taking a moment to understand that this woman had woken up confused in a strange house, surrounded by strangers, in a body that possibly felt as strange to her as everything else, he'd tried to force her into believing him.

Of course that hadn't worked.

His own transformation had been the exact opposite. Michael had woken up a vampire on his own, without a maker to guide him. Though he did remember what had happened during his last moments as a mortal, he had nobody to explain things. Everything, from the increased strength and speed to the boost to all his senses, he had discovered for himself.

That was why he wanted to spare Anna the confusion and pain of making mistakes. And in doing so, he'd cornered her and not given her the chance to process things. Now he knew that both approaches were equally wrong. He was ready to pull back. If it was space and freedom she needed, he was willing to give it to her.

What was the rush, anyway? They were immortal. Time didn't have the same meaning to their kind as it did to humans.

Anna leaned toward the side table and poured herself another drink.

"Refill?" she asked.

Michael lifted his glass to demonstrate that he still had some and continued to observe her. She had an elegance about her that he'd only just allowed himself to notice. The way she poured the drink—stopping at exactly the right level both times—suggested she'd performed the same action many times over. Perhaps this offered a clue to her human identity?

Anna wasn't his usual type; she wasn't easily impressed by anyone, least of all him. The clothes he'd found her in were simple, with not a designer label in sight. That told him that either she couldn't afford expensive clothes and accessories, or she didn't care for them.

Basically, she was his exact opposite. Michael himself

loved to surround himself with beautiful things. The luxury he lived in now compensated for the simple lifestyle he'd left behind upon being turned.

He clearly recalled the first time Alexander had brought him here, into his beautiful and unapologetically luxurious villa. Where he had reacted with instant awe and appreciation, Anna seemed to look at it all with a much more skeptical eye. Just the way she'd inspected the bottle and the old cut crystal snifter spoke volumes.

"Have you started remembering more?" Michael asked.

She shrugged. "I don't know. It's all very fuzzy."

Michael took her response as a sign she wasn't ready to discuss it.

So they continued to sit in silence for a while.

"There was a guy with red eyes," Anna said finally.

Michael straightened himself and leaned toward Anna, waiting for more.

She turned to face him, her eyes wide with fear. "I wasn't the only woman there."

"Where? What was the place like?" Michael asked.

Anna looked away at nothing in particular and blinked a few times.

"Don't know," she whispered. "It was dark."

Considering the state she was in when he found her, it was probably for the best if she never remembered everything that happened to her. Still, she was the only one who could offer clues regarding who these vampires were and where they were hiding out.

They were interrupted by the library door swinging open. Lucille had returned, this time unannounced and without invitation. *Bloody great.*

"I knew it," Lucille snapped as soon as she saw Anna. "I knew you weren't being totally truthful with me earlier!"

Michael rolled his eyes. "You asked if there was a mortal in the house. I only answered your question."

Anna gave him a concerned look. Lucille was unpleasant company, but she wouldn't do anything to harm a fellow vampire. They hadn't broken any rules; the strange vampires who had attacked Anna were the ones who should be worried.

Michael patted Anna's hand briefly in an attempt to reassure her, then immediately withdrew. A funny sensation had passed from her hand into his. It was unnervingly intense, but *so* tempting. He avoided eye contact with her and faced Lucille again in an attempt to divert his attention away from Anna. This wasn't the time to give his carnal desires free reign. She was his fledgling, for Pete's sake.

"Alexander should really ask for his spare keys back," Michael muttered under his breath.

Lucille scoffed. "As if I need keys to come in here."

Michael got up and offered her his seat. "Since we're all here now, why don't you make yourself comfortable? I'll get us another chair."

Lucille eyed Anna suspiciously. "What does she know?"

Michael grabbed the chair that stood in front of the

large desk at the back of the library and placed it near Anna. The entire maneuver was over within the blink of a human eye.

"Painfully little, I'm afraid. She's been suffering from a spot of memory loss since the attack."

"I'm right here, you know!" Anna protested. "I can speak for myself."

"I apologize," Michael mumbled, then gestured at her to continue.

"I was just telling Michael that I remember a man with glowing red eyes," Anna said.

Lucille glanced at Michael. "That's hardly groundbreaking. They were drinking her blood, after all."

Anna shrugged. "As you might imagine, I'm a bit new to this. Only trying to be helpful."

Michael sighed. "Red eyes are a sign of blood lust in vampires. Happens whenever we're thirsty," he explained.

"Ah." Anna shrugged. "Well that's all I remember for now. And that they had captured more women."

Lucille nodded. "Fine." She faced Michael again. "Now, if you don't mind sharing with me where you found her?"

"My name is Anna," Anna interjected.

Michael suppressed a little smile. It was obvious that Lucille's abrasiveness had rubbed Anna the wrong way. They had one more thing to agree on there.

If he had a choice, he wouldn't even be entertaining Lucille. Sadly, one had to humor the Council's Enforcer, especially when she arrived on Julius' orders. Plus,

Alexander owed her, meaning Michael did as well.

"Don't know the address, but I can show you the place," Michael said.

Lucille nodded. "Dawn is still a few hours away. No time like the present."

Michael shot Anna a reassuring look. "We won't be long."

"Wait just a minute! You're not thinking of leaving me here?"

"I don't think—" Lucille started to argue.

Anna got up, both hands raised in protest. "Unacceptable. I'm coming with you."

Michael shrugged. He'd had a good taste of how stubborn Anna could be when she'd first woken up. It was unlikely that he could talk her out of it.

"She's not ready!" Lucille complained.

"You're not hungry, are you?" Michael approached Anna, who now stood tall with her hands on her hips.

Anna shook her head. The way her hair fell around her face, she looked fierce. Determined. Sexy. Michael averted his gaze instantly. His thoughts were inappropriate. Plus, he couldn't allow let himself get distracted in Lucille's presence.

"See? No problem. She's already eaten today," Michael told Lucille.

Lucille's concerns were valid, since Anna had no idea of the temptation the outside world offered. But how much trouble could she really get into with two strong vampires accompanying her? If anything happened, they'd take care of it.

"Whatever." Lucille didn't sound convinced.

It didn't matter to Michael if she was. Just hours into her new life, Anna already was a force to be reckoned with. It pleased him greatly that Anna's rebellious nature was now aimed at Lucille and not at him anymore.

"Follow my lead," Michael whispered to Anna. "You'll be safe."

"Of course I'll be safe. I'm immortal now, aren't I?" Anna grinned.

Michael was about to interject that immortal didn't mean invincible, but decided to let it go. They'd have plenty of time to go through the finer points of being a vampire later.

Together, the three of them left, sprinting through the city faster than the human eye could see. Luckily, moving at superhuman speed was the one thing that came easy to newly turned vampires. Deliberately slowing things down to fit into human society? Not so much.

It didn't take them long to reach the courtyard where Michael had found Anna only hours earlier. At this time of night, the streets were empty enough that their activities went unseen.

The smell of blood still hung heavy in the air.

"Holy shit," Anna said, covering her mouth. Her eyes glowed red. "Is that me? My blood?"

"Told you she wasn't ready," Lucille said, folding her

arms.

Michael shot her a nasty glance. "Not much of it was left, but yes."

Anna wrinkled her nose and inhaled deeply. "How could you resist it? Oh my God, how did you not tear me to pieces and drink the last drops?"

Michael glanced over at Lucille, who had wandered off to start investigating.

"It takes a little while, but you'll learn to resist it too."

"Okay, but why would you want to?" Anna rambled. "I mean, it smells so… delicious. Why wouldn't you want to just give in?"

Anna breathed in deeply again and sharply turned her head away from him. Her body seemed to have tensed up as she stared in the direction of the main road, just a dozen or so feet away. Michael followed her line of sight. Footsteps approached. Human footsteps.

"This isn't the time," Michael said.

Anna snapped her head in his direction for just a split second, then turned away again. "So tempting. I can smell it."

Michael reached for Anna's arm. "Lucille. If you don't mind…"

Lucille joined him and held Anna back from the other side.

"Don't you say it," Michael warned her under his breath. He did *not* need another lecture right now.

For a tense thirty seconds or so, the three of them

stood in silence, Michael and Lucille holding Anna back, until the human had passed their position and his footsteps faded.

"Whoa. Okay." Anna's body relaxed underneath Michael's grip. "I'm okay."

Her eyes were once more the same warm amber color he had tried to avoid catching a glimpse of for most of the night. The threat was over.

"I'm sorry, I don't know what came over me," she muttered.

Lucille let go of her and silently went about her business again, inspecting bits of paper and other assorted rubbish strewn around the spot where Anna's body had been dumped.

"It's perfectly normal. You'll get used to it," Michael tried to reassure her.

"I could have. Oh God." Anna covered her face with her hands. "If you hadn't stopped me, who knows what I would have done."

I know exactly what you would have done. The same thing I did during my first night.

Michael didn't respond. Airing his own dirty laundry in front of Lucille wouldn't help anyone.

"You don't need us anymore, do you?" Michael called out to her.

Lucille shook her head and continued to ignore the two of them.

"Let's just head back home, what do you say?" Michael

suggested.

Anna nodded and took his hand. He looked down, but didn't comment on it or pull away, no matter how intense the buzzing that traveled from her palm into his was. A whole barrage of conflicting emotions tugged at him. If this was what holding her hand felt like, what would it be like to take things further? No, she was his fledgling. It was wrong to think of her as anything else.

He tried to shut down his straying mind and focused on just one thing: if she needed to hold his hand to feel safe, he owed it to her to comply. Her safety was his responsibility, after all.

Neither spoke another word as they broke into a sprint together. They didn't stop even once until they made it back to Kensington Palace Gardens and Alexander's mansion.

CHAPTER SIX

They still stood hand in hand on the gravel driveway right in front of the house when Anna came back to her senses. Their little excursion back to the *scene of the crime* had overwhelmed her. The smell of her own blood, and then the footsteps that promised her a meal thousands of times better than the raw steak she'd eaten earlier…

It was a lot to take in. And yet, she didn't want to think about any of that.

She looked down at Michael's hand, which still surrounded hers. He had made sure she hadn't done anything she would regret. As intensely thirsty as she'd felt in that strange courtyard in the city, she wasn't ready to take a life. The guilt would kill her, she was certain of it.

What a night. Although only a few hours had passed, it now felt like years ago when she'd first woken up inside the house. She was a vampire now.

Anna still could hardly believe it. She might have rejected the idea further if she hadn't felt the blood lust Lucille and Michael had been talking about. Had her eyes turned red too, like that man who had attacked her? The memory was so faint, she could just see those eyes staring at her, boring their way into her soul through the surrounding darkness.

You will come with me, the man had said. She'd heard him

clearly, but his lips had never moved. Was that the hypnosis thing Michael had been talking about earlier?

"You want to go in?" Michael asked.

Anna looked around. The gravel drive they stood on was lined by neatly kept hedges, beyond which there lay a sprawling lawn. The frost on the blades of grass sparkled in the starlight. It was magical.

Would all this make up for never seeing the sun again?

She wanted to believe so. It was too late for regrets. She glanced up at the house, with its large pillars surrounding the impressive front entrance. Above, ten windows marked the upper floor, each of them surrounded by carved stonework. Did one of these belong to the bedroom she'd woken up in? Or had hers been located toward the back?

"I have an idea," Michael said.

Anna glanced up at him and was captivated by how the soft light bounced off his chiseled cheek bones. In this light, his skin seemed to be glowing faintly. Was that how she looked too?

"What idea?" she asked, then stared at his lips, waiting for them to form a response.

He winked at her. "Trust me?"

She pressed her lips together. Should she say yes? What did she have to lose?

She nodded and was instantly whisked away, toward the side of the villa, beside a tall oak tree.

Michael jumped up into it, catching hold of the first

branch that hung at least twelve feet off the ground.

"Follow me," he said.

No way can I make that, Anna thought. But she took a deep breath and jumped, and to her surprise, found that she was hanging just next to Michael. He swung his legs up and got up on top of the thick branch, then climbed up into the next one, and then the next.

She followed right on his heels until the very top. From there, Michael leapt across to the roof of the house and turned around, waiting for her to catch up.

Anna looked down. This tree, which looked to be at least a hundred years old, was huge. She was so far off the ground, the old her would have been terrified. *I was afraid of heights,* she thought. *But now I have no more reason to be.*

She didn't hesitate anymore and jumped across the gap. It was effortless.

"That's amazing," she mumbled to herself.

Michael gestured at her to join her as he sat down on top of the ridge at the top of the roof. She did, then followed his line of sight across the front gate to the substantial villa across the road, which adjoined the park.

The view was breathtaking. She'd never seen anything like it.

In the distance, lights twinkled in the distance as they moved around the pathways in the park. Perhaps they were people out for early morning walks or cycle rides. Off to their right, Kensington Palace stood proudly in its manicured lawns, bathed in an orange-red glow. They would have turned off the main illumination of the palace as well as the other landmarks in the city hours ago, but she could still see the building clear as day thanks to what must be its emergency lighting. From here—a good 500 feet away—she could see every detail of it. Right down to the crack developing in one of the window sills on the second floor.

"Wow," she said.

Michael took her hand and pointed further ahead, to the other end of Hyde Park. "You can see the Marble Arch from here."

He was right. Although it was quite far off, the sight of it blew Anna away.

Anna pointed even further away, just more to the south. "Those lights beyond the buildings, that's what, Buckingham Palace?"

"It is indeed."

She turned to face him. "Thank you."

"Ah, forget it. I just wanted to show you the good parts of being turned. That's all."

Anna had misjudged Michael earlier. Not that he'd given her much choice. Michael hadn't shown much tact after she'd just woken up, but perhaps that wasn't his fault. This situation they found themselves in was new to the both of them.

But this little gesture of his proved that he actually did care. She'd been shaken by her experience earlier, and this had done a lot to make her feel better.

He looked over at her, letting his eyes linger on hers for a moment too long.

Anna felt a sense of familiarity now that she looked into his eyes. Like she'd seen him somewhere before, even if she had no actual recollection of it. That was silly though, obviously. Her memory or lack thereof was playing tricks on her.

She scooted a little closer to him. He wasn't so bad after all. And damn, the subdued light from the stars above made him look even more handsome. If that was even possible.

Earlier, he'd kept their eye contact to a minimum. He'd even avoided physical contact, until their outing earlier. Now, her hand rested on the roof just beside his, their little fingers touching. He didn't pull away, and neither did she.

And he continued to stare into her soul, making her heart beat faster. Was that her heart, though? Did vampires even have heartbeats?

She felt giddy and lightheaded. No matter how quickly he'd brushed it away, she was certain that this gesture meant something more than he was willing to admit.

"Do you come here often?" she asked, then grinned when she realized the cliché.

Michael smiled subtly. "Often enough to recognize a new face."

This man had an infuriatingly gorgeous smile. To go with his infuriatingly gorgeous face.

Anna's thoughts were swimming. She found it hard to focus on anything but the curve of Michael's lips.

"It's not so bad, this new life," she mumbled.

His smile widened.

She leaned in, closer and closer. His scent filled her nostrils. Intoxicating and seductive, like an expensive cologne.

Michael similarly leaned toward her until their faces were only an inch apart.

And just like that, without planning to, really, Anna pressed her lips against his.

The heartbeat in her chest seemed to speed up to a high frequency buzz. Her chest filled with—she wasn't quite sure with what. Excitement. Nerves.

Arousal.

She felt alive, like every one of her was synapses firing at an intensity she wouldn't have thought possible before. Her whole body was electric, every inch of her skin highly sensitized.

Michael reached for her, slipping his hand behind her neck and cradling her as he returned her kiss. Their tongues collided and fireworks seemed to erupt behind her closed eyelids.

It was so beautiful, she had to fight back tears.

And just like that, it was over. Michael withdrew his hand and pulled away.

Anna opened her eyes in distress. Why? Why did he stop?

"I'm sorry, this isn't fair on you," Michael stammered. He refused to look her in the eye.

Had she misread the situation completely? Had he not just brought her here to this incredibly romantic spot and showed her all the beauty that lay at their feet? Had he not just tried to convince her that immortality wasn't as scary and alien as it had seemed to be at first?

Did he not care for her?

"I'm sorry?"

"I shouldn't have done that," he said, shaking his head. "I'm your maker. It's inappropriate."

Anna didn't know what to do or where to look as he got up, dusted off his trousers, and took a few steps away from her. She'd faced rejection in the past, but nothing like this. He'd been *into* it just now, hadn't he?

"I don't understand," she mumbled, and wrapped her arms around herself protectively.

"Look." Michael reached for her shoulder, then stopped about an inch away. "I'm really sorry. I got carried away in the moment. This isn't right. I've taken advantage of your situation and I shouldn't have. This is your first night as a vampire, and you don't need to be wrapped up in all this."

Anna frowned. Taken advantage? What the hell was he talking about?

"I kissed *you*," she said. "If anyone took advantage—"

Michael shook his head. "No. I'm sorry. I'm going to go inside now. If you need anything, I'll be in the library."

Anna's throat tightened, making it impossible for her to respond. Before she had the chance to regain her composure, he'd walked across to the edge of the roof and climbed down, possibly to enter through a nearby window.

Unbelievable.

She didn't recall ever being faced with a guy acting this hot and cold around her, but then of course she wouldn't. She didn't remember much of anything.

What did it mean?

Anna pulled her legs up, wrapped her arms around them, and rested her chin on top of her knees.

A lot had happened today, and perhaps some peace and quiet was exactly what she needed. Not that it was particularly quiet up here. She could hear traffic, as well as the occasional siren, miles away. She tried to focus on the rustling of fallen leaves being carried by the odd winter breeze in the park.

That kiss, though. Holy hell. Despite the awkwardness of his sudden departure, and the confusion he left her in, she couldn't get it out of her mind.

Was everything just more intense now that she was no longer mortal? He had overwhelmed her, turned her into a mushy mess of emotions and sensations that felt completely alien. Considering she didn't have her memory back yet, this was essentially her first ever kiss now. She hated that it had to end so soon.

Although it was probably for the best. She had enough to worry already about without adding relationship issues into the mix.

If a little kiss felt this amazing, then what was sex like?

Anna groaned. She'd be a lot better off banning these speculations from her mind. He wasn't into her, or at the very least, he didn't consider her *ready*, whatever that meant.

And she wasn't about to throw herself at some guy she'd known all of what—ten hours? Most of those hours she'd been passed out. How could she even know what kind of guy he was?

Plus, she wasn't that kind of woman.

She might not remember the finer details of her old life, but she was certain of that fact.

Plus, he wasn't even into her. Or was he?

CHAPTER SEVEN

Stupid, stupid, stupid!

Michael paced restlessly around the library. No matter how much Alexander seemed to like this place for its calming influence, Michael couldn't find any peace.

He'd slipped up and given in to old habits.

Anna had hardly gotten the chance to get used to her new life, and he'd jumped in headfirst and let his cock do the thinking for him. Not only would it make things awkward going forward, it was downright inappropriate.

Michael had heard the old stories of vampires who turned women for their own pleasure, and he'd always rejected the thought. To his mind, a maker was equivalent to a father figure, or at the very least, an older sibling of sorts, making what had happened downright wrong.

He was an admirer of the female form, sure, but he wasn't underhanded or dishonest about it. He'd never forced himself on anyone.

And yet, up on the roof he'd taken advantage of his position. As her maker, he was an authority figure of sorts. Anna didn't have anyone in this new life except for him. That didn't give her much of a choice but to indulge him if he went too far.

Of course, Michael hadn't consciously tried to, but the more comfortable he'd gotten around her, the more easily he had slipped into his regular moves. She was an attractive woman, so he'd tried to seduce her. Now he couldn't forgive himself for it.

He should have known better.

The grandfather clock upstairs struck seven times, signaling that sunrise was dangerously close. He balled his fists as he left the library. As much as he wanted to stay away from Anna for a while, he couldn't risk her getting caught unaware in the sun and burn to death.

As he approached the stairs, he heard movement on the upper floor. Perhaps she'd felt the urge to head inside already. Newly made vampires had good survival instincts, though some felt the warning signs more keenly than others.

"Just making sure you're inside for sunrise," he called out.

No response.

Michael made his way up the stairs and through the hallway, only to find Anna waiting in the doorway of her room.

She averted her gaze from him. Clearly their earlier encounter had made her feel awkward too. If only he could express how sorry he was... Instead, he stood in front of her now with nothing to say.

"So I should stay here all day?" she asked, fidgeting with the bottom hem of her borrowed pullover. He took a step back, making sure to respect her personal space.

"You'll be safe in here. All the windows in this house

have blackout blinds," Michael said.

He stole a glimpse at her, top to bottom. The outfit she'd found was far from stylish, but somehow, she made it look good.

Enough with the inappropriate thoughts already!

"Oh, if you want, we could buy a few things for you to wear tomorrow… You know, until you remember where you lived before and we pick up your things," Michael suggested.

Anna shrugged. "Whatever you say."

She suppressed a yawn and went inside, shutting the door behind her without looking back even once.

What a mess. Just as Anna had finally started to warm up around him and accept the things he'd told her, he'd trampled all over her budding trust in him.

Throughout the day, sleep eluded Michael, who continued to toss and turn until his body felt the arrival of dusk. He couldn't stop thinking about Anna, obviously. How she'd tried to act strong and confident, when he had first tried to explain what had happened to her. And how vulnerable she'd been once she realized she didn't have control of her new urges.

He never planned to become someone's maker, but once he no longer had a choice, he'd been determined to do the best job he could. And then of course he had betrayed his own intentions and ruined everything when he kissed her.

It should have never happened. But now that it had, he couldn't undo it, neither could he ignore the effect it had on him.

Their kiss had been unlike any he had shared with anyone before.

The pull he felt toward her was so intense, he'd found it impossible to resist her. And when their lips connected, it had released a whole host of alien feelings within him.

He loved women and had bedded so many over the years that he had lost count. But he wasn't a selfish lover; what he loved the most during any of his encounters was the pleasure he was able to give to his partners. Those special little things he could do that human men couldn't.

A woman's face signaling the peak of her orgasm was the most rewarding thing he'd ever seen, and it was those moments that he'd kept chasing during the past three decades of his renewed life. His own physical satisfaction had always been an afterthought.

But with Anna, during that short kiss, he'd felt something deeper and more primal. He'd felt the need to make her his. And he also felt like a pervert for it.

Never before had he felt any desire to possess a woman.

How could he face her now? How could he keep himself in check as they trained her new abilities? She had so much to learn, and nobody else to teach her.

On his bedside table, his phone came to life and started

to ring.

Michael leaned across and read the caller ID. Alexander.

"Yes?" he answered.

"Just checking in. Lucille had left me a message. Has she been by the house?" Alexander said.

Michael closed his eyes. "Yes, she's investigating the rogue vampires who attacked Anna."

"Anna?"

"Yes, that's her name. She's suffering from memory loss, but she remembered that much."

An awkward silence followed. "Look, I wanted to apologize for my reaction earlier," Alexander started.

Michael shook his head. "It's all right. Since I have you on the line, I might as well tell you how things went last night. You know she didn't even believe me she'd been turned at first? It took quite a bit of convincing."

"Interesting. You sound strange, is everything all right?" Alexander asked.

Michael took a deep breath. "Actually… I suppose I owe it to you to say it out loud. This whole business of becoming someone's maker has turned out to be quite the headache."

"How so?"

Michael frowned. Was Alexander genuinely asking or could he detect a hint of Schadenfreude in his voice?

"She's… she's a handful."

"So were you."

"This is different." Michael sighed.

"Perhaps you don't realize how difficult you were."

Alexander wasn't getting it, obviously. How could he? But who else was there to ask for advice?

"Actually, *she* isn't strictly the problem. Not since she started believing me. But I fear I may have betrayed her trust and I don't know how to recover from that."

Alexander paused for a moment before responding. "What exactly do you mean *betrayed her trust*?"

"I kissed her." Michael turned onto his side and covered his eyes with his free hand. Although they'd been through a lot together, Alexander and he, this was still embarrassing to admit.

"So? Did she not like it?" Alexander asked.

Michael was stunned by his reaction. "What? That's not the point. I abused my position. I crossed the line! I'm her maker, for God's sake!"

"Honestly, when you first came home with her I had trouble understanding your reasoning. All I could see were risks. Perhaps you didn't just want to save her out of the goodness of your heart—perhaps something else motivated you?"

"Really; *that's* what you think of me?" Michael couldn't believe his ears. He had his flaws, like any man or vampire did. But he wasn't that deplorable. Did Alexander really think he would go out of his way to bring home some woman to be his concubine?

"Don't misunderstand me. I'm not judging you. I have

my vices just as you have yours. Answer me this: how did it happen? The kiss, I mean."

Michael did his best to suppress his outrage at Alexander's earlier statement and thought back to last night. "It had been a difficult few hours until she finally believed a word I was telling her. In fact I believe what finally convinced her was when she first felt actually thirsty. Lucille and I had to restrain her or she would have hunted down a nearby human. Once we got back, she was despondent about losing control, so I took her up onto the roof."

"Your special place. Remember how many nights you used to spend up there when you were newly turned?" Alexander reminisced.

Michael nodded. "Yes. Well, I thought it might help her gain some perspective. We sat together, admiring the view. Then it happened."

"You like her."

"What? Now you're just being ridiculous! I don't—" Michael protested.

"Think about it! How many women, vampire or human, have you taken up to the roof?"

Michael didn't even need time to think. The answer was simple. "None."

"Exactly. That's the point I was trying to make. Your other reason for wanting to save her life. You felt something when you first saw her."

So that was what Alexander had meant. It made sense

for him to draw those conclusions, especially since he had found Cat to share his life with. Michael's own thoughts had gone in an entirely different direction. "Right. Well, I still don't think it appropriate for me, as her maker, to—"

"Will you stop? From what you're telling me, this woman seems to know her own mind very well. If you did anything wrong, she would have reacted accordingly. She is your equal now. She could have defended herself."

Michael shook his head. He'd seen Alexander with Lucille and Julius. They had their flaws, but they were a family, with distinct roles.

"Would you have ever kissed Lucille like that?" Michael asked.

"Why would you—no, she's my sister!"

"Exactly my point. And Julius, would he ever have seduced Lucille?"

"Michael, this comparison does not stand. You are not Julius and Anna is not Lucille."

"Why not? I'm her maker. She is my fledgling."

Alexander sighed on the other end of the line. "There is a difference. The dynamic between Julius, Lucille, and me is unique to our situation. Julius made us as his children, hence he set the tone for our relationship. You're creating a big moral dilemma where there isn't one. If you like her, and she likes you, then what's the problem?"

Michael shook his head again. He wasn't ready to accept it. Even if Alexander's perception was much more relaxed, Michael's wasn't. A maker was a maker, and a lover was a lover. He wouldn't accept a crossover between the two. The more he thought about it, the bigger the knot in his chest. It was wrong. Immoral.

"My friend, stop worrying so much," Alexander said. "The most important thing right now is for you to calm down and focus on Anna's training. Get her to bring her impulses under control so Cat and I can come home, and worry about everything else later."

Finally Alexander said something Michael could agree with. "Okay. I'll do my best."

"I know you will."

"I'll be in touch." Michael sighed as he hung up the call.

Alexander was right; Anna's training was the most important thing right now. Nobody—least of all Alexander—had ever said this was going to be easy.

Michael got out of bed and listened for any sounds elsewhere in the house. Nothing. If he hurried, he could go out and get Anna some real food. Once she was satisfied, they'd start working on desensitizing her to human activity.

CHAPTER EIGHT

Anna woke up with the overwhelming metallic scent of blood in her nose. It had entered her room and tickled her nostrils, dragging her against her will from the deepest slumber. She didn't recall what she'd been dreaming of, just that the color red had entered her mind barely a moment before she'd become alert.

Now that she sat up straight in bed, she was even more aware of it. It was irresistible.

She quickly put on a robe and rushed out of her room.

The hallway was empty.

Within moments, she had found her way down the stairs all the way to the library. Inside, Lucille and Michael were already waiting.

"Are you thirsty?" Michael asked, raising one of those same antique crystal glasses from last night toward her. It was filled with the most beautiful deep red liquid Anna had ever seen.

"Is that…" She didn't finish her sentence, just inhaled, and was instantly hit by a bout of lightheadedness.

"Blood," Lucille said in her usual monotone voice. The woman couldn't be more unpleasant if she tried.

Anna ignored her and headed straight for Michael, accepting the glass and gazing down into it. Her own reflection in blood red greeted her, along with swirls of black shadows which gave the impression that the glass was a lot deeper than it actually was. It was as though the liquid had sucked the light out of all of its surroundings, like a black hole, and the sight was both exciting as well as terrifying. It attracted Anna like a moth to a flame.

She had no control over it.

Without thinking about it any further, she put the glass to her lips and drank. The second the stuff hit her lips, she was in heaven. The high was intense, like she imagined certain drugs might have been. It was unlike anything she'd ever experienced.

Now oblivious to her surroundings, Anna gulped all of it down until the glass was empty. Her eyes were closed, not that she'd consciously closed them. She stood still and enjoyed the rush that passed through every part of her body. This was the pinnacle of pleasure. Better than an orgasm, better than last night's raw steak, better than the best Belgian chocolate, better than even that absolutely wonderful expensive brandy she'd tasted the night before.

She wasn't sure how long she'd been standing in ecstasy with the empty glass in her hand. By the time she opened her eyes, she found that Lucille looked even more bored than she had before, and Michael had started studying his mobile phone.

Weird, watching a vampire doing something that natural and seemingly human.

And where was *her* phone? That would give her some clues regarding her old life, surely.

"She's back," Lucille observed.

Anna ignored her and focused on Michael instead. Their kiss, followed by his sudden rejection, had confused her deeply. Now that the effects of the blood were starting to wear off, the embarrassment and awkwardness she'd felt last night returned with a vengeance.

Michael looked up without making proper eye contact. "Wonderful. Now that you've fed, we can consider going out."

Lucille got up and folded her arms. "We've received some tips which could possibly point to your attackers."

Anna turned to face her. "Where are they hiding?"

Lucille shrugged. "That remains to be seen. But there has been some suspicious activity around the derelict power station in Chelsea."

Chelsea? That was a very upmarket part of the city. Why would anyone want to start trouble there of all places?

Michael put his phone in his pocket. "Very well, let's investigate."

Anna hesitated. Was it a good idea for her to go out and possibly end up attacking some random passerby like what had almost happened last night?

"Ready?" Michael asked.

Anna hesitated and scanned the room. Lucille had already left, leaving the two of them alone. "Wouldn't it be risky for me to come?"

He shook his head and smiled at her briefly. "You've fed on human blood now. It'll be fine. The first step to resisting temptation is to feed regularly."

That was *human blood*? Anna wasn't sure how to feel about that. Sure, it was her natural source of food now, but the thought still freaked her out a bit. Someone had been hurt and made to bleed to feed her.

"Don't worry, they didn't feel a thing, nor will they remember," Michael said.

Anna looked up at him. When their eyes met, she could see nothing but warmth in his. Perhaps he really did care. But then why had he rejected her last night?

"Fine. Let's go," she said.

It didn't take the three vampires long to reach Chelsea by cab. And despite the close proximity of the human driver, Anna was able to keep her urges under control. Michael was right. That glass of blood she drank before setting off had made all the difference.

How often did vampires need to feed to stay in control? This was just one of the many questions she still had about her new reality. Hopefully she'd get the chance to speak to Michael in private at some point, without Lucille's presence adding to the awkwardness.

"So this is it," Lucille said as she pointed to the fenced off industrial complex. Large chimneys on all corners of the building towered over their little group.

On the road, cars and pedestrians passed them by, oblivious to the potential danger. They were three vampires, among a sea of humans, and yet they managed to blend in perfectly.

Michael scanned the fence. "Let's find a way in. There are too many onlookers for us to simply jump across."

Lucille nodded and marched down the road, while Michael and Anna inspected the perimeter of the lot in the opposite direction.

Anna tried to do her bit, but she found it hard to focus. There were still so many scents in the air that tried to pull her in all directions. It had been easy enough to see the variety in the human population before she'd been turned, but only now did Anna realize just how varied their scents were. It was almost like being faced with a colorful buffet, in which every dish looked and smelled more appealing than the one that came before.

"I've found it," Michael whispered. He'd spoken just loud enough that Lucille had heard him from the other end of the street, but quiet enough that none of the humans had noticed.

Anna tried her best to drag herself away from all the distractions and joined Michael in front of an innocuous breach in the chain link fence. He stepped aside and allowed Anna to enter first.

Lucille followed, and finally the three of them were inside the abandoned yard in front of the old power plant.

It was obvious that it had been out of use for a long time. The yard was overgrown with weeds and had been used as a dump to discard unwanted household appliances and other garbage. Still, the place had a strange beauty to it which Anna probably would have never noticed as a human.

She gazed up to the roof of the abandoned power station. How amazing would it be to climb all the way to the top of one of those chimneys? The views would be amazing from up there.

From the corner of Anna's eye, she saw Lucille approach the front of the building, where one of the previously barricaded doors had been broken open. Inside, a shadow moved past the opening, startling Anna.

"There's someone in there," she whispered, pointing at the entrance.

"Probably a squatter," Michael remarked.

"But if those vampires are hiding here…" Anna wondered aloud.

"Vampires would never let themselves be seen so easily. They're probably long gone by now."

Anna hoped he was right, but still kept a distance behind Michael, as the two of them followed Lucille inside. It would take some time for her to become as fearless as her two companions.

Although it was pretty dark inside, Anna could see her surroundings in astounding detail. Indeed, there were some people inside, squatters like Michael had assumed. A few of them had made beds for themselves using cardboard, newspapers, and discarded clothes.

Lucille ignored them and walked further into the

building, but Anna caught a whiff of something she couldn't ignore.

The scent was so familiar, and yet she couldn't place where she'd last smelled it. She followed it to an empty squat. After she pushed some newspapers aside with her foot, she found what she was looking for. A plain black messenger bag. *Her* bag; she was sure of it.

"I don't believe it," Anna muttered as she picked it up.

It looked slightly worse for the wear, but she recognized the way it felt to the touch, the scuffs on the buckle that had developed over time, and even the nearly invisible coffee stain on the strap.

Michael appeared by her side. "What is it?"

"This." Anna turned and held up the bag. "This is mine."

Michael leaned forward to inspect it. "It has your scent."

Anna's heart was beating faster. Would the contents of this bag help her figure out more about her life? Only one way to find out.

She opened it and found that it was mostly empty. No wallet, no phone. If those things had still been in there when the bag was found by whoever's squat this was, they were long gone by now. She rummaged around inside. There were just some chocolate wrappers and a pack of tissues.

Then she found the zip to the inner compartment. Inside was a solitary business card. She picked it up and almost instinctively held it to her nose. Yes, this was unmistakably hers.

She remembered the moment she'd first received the stack of fresh new business cards from the printer.

Anna felt Michael's eyes still on her as she turned the card over, revealing the most important clue yet:

Anna James Catering

Underneath, there was a phone number as well as a website address, though unfortunately, no physical address.

"Where are the two of you? I found something significant," Lucille's voice called out from somewhere much deeper inside the building.

Anna and Michael shared a quick look. This trip had already paid off as far as Anna was concerned. Who knew what other clues lurked in the depths of this abandoned industrial complex.

They joined Lucille, who had found what looked like some sort of control room. Inside, she was poring over old blueprints of the facility, pointing to the center of it. "There. If I were a newcomer in this city, and I was up to something I wouldn't want to draw attention to, that's where I'd do it."

Michael leaned forward and also studied the plans, but Anna couldn't take her eyes off her old business card.

It wasn't as pristine as in her memory. Something had changed, but she couldn't put her finger on what it was.

She cleared her throat. "I think I'd like some time alone to think," she told Michael, as Lucille looked on with one eyebrow raised.

"That's understandable," he said, glancing over at Lucille. "I'll take you home then."

Lucille rolled her eyes, but didn't say anything.

"No, no, I'll just take a cab back," Anna mumbled. "It'll be fine." It had to be, right? She'd been able to control herself on the journey here, so why would the way back be any different? She couldn't expect Michael to babysit her wherever she went; she'd lose her mind.

"I must insist. I'll accompany you."

Lucille put one hand on her hip and shook her head. "Michael, I understand that you've got a shiny new toy, but this is important. We're not done here yet."

Did Lucille honestly just refer to her as a *toy?* Anna couldn't believe her ears.

"Excuse me?" Anna snapped.

"You're new to this, I understand," Lucille started, then glanced across at Michael. "But believe me, I know his type very well. His dedication will wear off once another woman catches his eye. You might as well learn to stand on your own two feet early on."

"I'm not—I mean, things aren't like that!" Anna protested. Why bother, though. Who did Lucille think she was, anyway? She didn't know the first thing about what kind of person Anna was; she'd never allow herself to be used like that. Not that it was any of Lucille's business.

Michael crossed his arms as he faced Lucille. "Before you disrespect me, you might want to consider whether or not you want my cooperation in your little investigation."

Lucille shrugged. "I can just have Julius summon you and compel you to help me. It makes no difference to me. But remember that you're on shaky ground with him already."

Michael glared at her, and Lucille glared back.

Anna, meanwhile, turned away from the two riled up vampires and left. She didn't care what these two got up to next, she was going back to the house to research her own past. That was her priority. Nothing and no one would be able to stop her.

CHAPTER NINE

———•———

Anna had every intention of heading straight back to the mansion when she left the derelict lot. She'd even hailed a cab and started to talk to the driver, when some peculiar new sensation overwhelmed her. The more she spoke with him and made eye contact with him, the more she felt a strange new presence in her mind. He was in there with her, or was she in his mind with him? It was hard to tell the difference.

"Say, do you have a phone?" Anna asked the man.

"Sure, love," the cabbie responded, his voice monotone, as though he didn't realize what he was saying.

"Show me." Anna stretched out her hand. "You don't mind if I borrow it for a bit, do you?"

The man didn't hesitate, just handed his device over. "Not at all. Glad to help."

Anna smiled at him and opened the rear door of the cab, taking a seat inside. "Just wait here for a bit, I'll let you know where I want to go in a second," she said.

So this was the hypnosis thing Michael had been talking about. It was a lot easier than she'd thought. In fact it came almost completely naturally to her. No way was a hardened London cabbie going to hand his phone to just anyone who asked for it. She could have so easily stolen it; not that she was planning to.

Anna held her breath as she typed in the website address from her old business card. It was basic, just a couple of pages of information, but no address. She read through the whole thing, studying it in detail. Slowly, memories of herself writing these words came back to her. She'd been full of excitement and hope at the time. Setting up her own catering business had been a longtime dream.

Something wasn't quite right, though, as though that memory had been tainted by a negative event.

It hadn't been a success, she thought. *I couldn't make it work.* A sense of disappointment filled her chest, as though she'd just now made the decision to give up on the business.

She looked down at the card, with its dog-eared corner and slightly faded text. She'd started off with a stack of 200 brand new business cards and this was the only one she had left.

And since the website hadn't pointed her to her home address, this clue seemed to be a dead end.

Anna looked up through the side window. The small shops on the other side of the road didn't look familiar. Her bag just happened to end up inside that building. As far as she knew, she'd never been here before.

"Just take me to Kensington Palace Gardens like I said," Anna instructed the cabbie.

She handed him his phone back through the coin slot in the Plexiglass partition between them.

"As you wish, dear." He started the engine and pulled out into traffic.

Anna sat back and listlessly looked out the window. This had been a waste of time. The memories she'd gained had only brought her down.

What would she have done in the past to cheer herself up? Anna closed her eyes and tried to remember. It was like all of her memories were right there inside of her head, but something was blocking them and keeping them from her.

Chocolate.

Anna opened her eyes. The scent hung heavy in the air. Molten chocolate. Hints of vanilla and cinnamon, and the smell of freshly baked wheat tying it all together.

"Pull over here, will you?" she said.

The cabbie did as asked.

She rummaged around in her pockets for money to pay him, but there was none. In her eagerness to start investigating the business card, she'd forgotten to ask Michael for some. "How much do I owe you?" she asked.

The cabbie turned around and smiled at her. "This one's on the house, love."

Anna smiled back at him. She could really get used to this hypnosis business. "Thank you so much. You've been very helpful."

He just kept on looking at her with a vague smile on his face. *Now what?* Was he just going to hang around here, stuck in a trance?

"You best be on your way back to where you picked me up and wait for your next fare," Anna said.

He nodded and put his hands back on the steering wheel.

Whew. She didn't want to consider the possibility of this man hanging around here endlessly, waiting for her like a lost puppy.

Anna got out of the cab. It pulled away almost immediately after she shut the door.

Now that she was outside, those familiar scents she'd just picked up on had only intensified. She started to follow her nose up the street, dodging other pedestrians, until she felt compelled to turn off into a smaller street.

The cobbled street underfoot felt familiar. This was a part of the city where she'd spent a lot of time in the past. She continued on, zigzagging through the tighter streets until she had reached her destination.

The shiny, modern building stood out starkly against the historic buildings all around. This bakery had been a part of her walk to and from work for quite a while. Being back here provided a sense of belonging and nostalgia.

She looked around, hoping for further clues. Which way was home?

Anna then closed her eyes and tried to figure it out by scent. The sweet aromas emanating from the bakery covered everything else. She simply couldn't make out what was under them.

But Anna wasn't easily discouraged. Instead of giving up, she started to systematically walk through the streets surrounding the bakery in a grid pattern. Sooner or later, she would see something familiar, she was sure of it.

This went on for ten minutes or so, until she inadvertently walked into an alley with a dead end. The graffiti covered buildings surrounding her seemed abandoned; broken windows marked the upper floors, some of which were boarded up. No way was this place going to provide clues as to where she lived.

Anna was about to turn around and continue to explore the neighborhood, when a tall, slender figure materialized in front of her.

"Will you look at that," the man said.

He looked old; just how old, Anna couldn't be sure. His skin was papery and almost translucent. His deep black eyes stood out starkly against his otherwise faded appearance.

"Do I know you?" Anna stammered. She could barely stand looking at the man. The moment she made eye contact, it felt like the man's hand had penetrated her chest and started to squeeze at her heart. It was painful, terrifying, otherworldly.

He approached her and looked her over top to bottom like one might inspect cattle at an auction.

"This is unexpected, to say the least."

Curiosity had brought her here, but Anna was over that now. She wanted desperately to run, yet her feet refused to move.

"Who are you?" she tried again.

The man smiled, revealing an entire row of razor sharp

teeth. His longer canines gave him away as a vampire, but the rest of him was unlike what Anna had seen in Michael or even Lucille. He didn't look entirely normal, even for a vampire.

Anna opened her mouth to question him further, but she was unable to make a sound.

"Take her." The man stood back and waited as two figures, entirely dressed in black, flitted out of the windows above and flanked Anna.

She tried to turn around to leave, but they had grabbed her by the arms so tightly she couldn't move at all. Within seconds, a hood of some sort ended up on her head, cutting off her vision completely. Even in this new form, she felt as helpless as a human would have been.

They lifted her up and started to carry her, presumably into the building they'd just come from. The only senses Anna had left were smell and sound. Wherever they were taking her, it smelled damp and moldy, as though someone had discarded a lot of rubbish here and left it to rot. Occasionally, the ammonia-laden scent of urine overpowered everything else.

She could hear doors open and close, as well as echoes of the same. But her assailants were so light on their feet that she couldn't hear their movements at all. Not a single footstep, neither a breath nor heartbeat. They were silent as death. The only sounds she could hear were the ambient noises of the city: traffic, sirens, the deep rumble of the occasional underground train.

Michael had explained that vampires didn't harm other vampires, so these must be the rogues that had attacked her in the first place. It was the only logical explanation; that was why their leader had recognized her. In trying to locate evidence of her old life, she'd been discovered by the very creatures she'd tried to escape.

The further they carried her, the quieter her surroundings became, until she couldn't even hear the traffic anymore.

Finally, they pushed her forward into an empty space and shut a heavy door behind her. Anna clawed at the hood on her face and tore it off as quickly as she could.

The view that greeted her was unexpected; the room was narrow and long, with a curved ceiling like a tunnel, but there was nothing at the end of it, just a solid wall. The only way out was the heavy metal door that she'd just heard shut behind her. She still couldn't hear a single sound other than her own breaths and movements.

Where was she?

They had overpowered her so easily. Despite her changed form, formidable strength, and additional powers, she was helpless to stop her captors this second time around, either. Anna found herself alone in the dark, cut off from the outside world. The walls surrounding her were thick and solid. She'd found as much as she'd explored them by touch.

How long she'd been in here? She wasn't quite sure. Every so often a deep vibration rocked the walls around her—a tube train, perhaps?

Yesterday she'd felt the sunrise just before it happened. She couldn't explain it really, but it had compelled her to get off the roof just in time. She didn't feel that way yet, so it still had to be dark outside. Or perhaps she was so far away from the sun that she wouldn't be able to feel the coming of dawn.

The darkness wasn't as disorienting as it would have been to a human; what bothered her more was that her brand new super sensitive hearing couldn't pick up on anything useful either. Her five senses were useless to her now. Although she tried her best to stay calm, the walls seemed to want to close in on her.

"Let me out!" she screamed.

There was no response, just her own dull echo.

"People will be coming to look for me!"

It was no use. Either they weren't within earshot, or they were ignoring her.

For the first time in two days, she was completely and utterly alone.

Michael would come to look for her, though, wouldn't he? Then again, she hadn't gone home like she'd told him. So how would he even find her here?

She sank down onto the ground, resting her back against the cold concrete wall, and wrapped her arms around herself. She had nothing and no one right now, only what was in her thoughts.

It wouldn't be helpful to worry about whether Michael could track her down somehow, so she diverted her attention to something else. Their relationship.

As distasteful as Lucille's remarks had been, some of what she'd said could explain why Michael had rejected her after she'd kissed him.

If he wasn't the committed relationship type, then getting into some kind of romantic relationship with a woman he'd just turned into a vampire would be the last thing he'd want. She had nowhere else to go. She didn't even remember where she lived before he took her home.

So if they ended up together, he'd be stuck with her in the same house. That would be beyond awkward.

Of course he hadn't reciprocated her kiss.

How stupid and naive she'd been.

He hadn't wanted her dead—that was why he'd saved her. And he'd been trying to teach her about what it meant to be a vampire, because he felt responsible for her safety now. But he didn't want anything more than that.

Why would he? He was immortal, and he could hypnotize any woman in the world to be with him. Why would he want to tie himself to some newbie who had willingly walked into a bloody trap and let herself be captured by the same people who had tried to kill her in the first place?

Ugh. She'd been so reckless and stupid. Instead of getting out of that cab to investigate this neighborhood, she should have gone home and come back to this area with Michael later.

As awkward as it felt to admit it to herself, she should have asked for help.

Anna rested her head on her knees and closed her eyes.

Her future was out of her hands now. All she could do was wait.

CHAPTER TEN

Michael was furious. How dare Lucille disrespect him like that in front of Anna? What business did she have, meddling in their relationship?

Of course, he'd had no choice but to stay behind as Anna left, because Lucille was right. Julius would have very little patience for him if he didn't cooperate with a Council investigation. And so he was even more frustrated.

Why did Lucille need him for this, though? They didn't get along, and he hadn't even seen the rogue vampires who had created this mess. He had no further intel to share. What use could she possibly have for him?

At the same time, he worried about Anna finding her way back home on her own. The blood she'd drank earlier should keep her from doing anything rash, but you really never knew with a young vampire like her. In his first days, he had raised a whole lot of hell on his own. If the likes of Lucille and Julius had found out about all his transgressions from back in the day, he probably would have been put to death.

She was his responsibility. Not just to make sure she didn't attack anyone, but also for her own safety. If the vampires who had attacked her found her wandering around the city alone, they might see her as a threat.

The more he thought about them, the angrier Lucille's

remarks made him.

"You had no business talking to her like that," Michael finally said.

Lucille stopped inspecting the large incinerator she'd identified as a perfect vampire hiding place.

"What?"

"That I'd move on to someone else. I'm her maker. That's not something I'm willing to take lightly."

"Her maker. Right." Lucille shook her head and climbed inside the hatch.

Michael didn't move. Just because she was in there didn't mean he had to follow. "What are you trying to say?"

Lucille stuck her head out and glared at him. "I've walked this earth a lot longer than the likes of you."

"That doesn't give you the right to convince my fledgling that I'm going to just abandon her at will."

"What exactly is your problem? That I advised her to be independent or that I told her the truth about what you are? In any case, I thought you'd welcome the help. Nobody likes a clingy fledgling."

"It wasn't your place. And you have no idea *who* I am," Michael corrected her.

Lucille rolled her eyes. "So you like her. Whatever. Now, if you'll stop arguing for a moment, come see this."

"I don't *like* her! I'm responsible for her. There's a difference!"

Michael swallowed his anger and approached the hatch.

It was no wonder she'd roped him into this stupid investigation. Anyone as abrasive as Lucille probably didn't have very many allies, and certainly no friends.

What vampire in their right mind would want to befriend the Council Enforcer anyway? It was much too risky to keep that kind of company.

"What is it?" he asked impatiently.

She pointed at the deep gashes on the inside of the hatch. "What do you think?"

"How would I know? Someone scratched the door?"

"Someone was locked in here and tried to fight his way out." Lucille smiled to herself.

Michael frowned. Her reality was vastly different from his own, if this gruesome discovery actually pleased her this much.

"These marks are quite deep. A human couldn't have done this," Lucille remarked as she followed the gashes in the reinforced metal. "Someone locked a vampire in here."

Lucille climbed out of the incinerator and wandered off with a spring in her step. Michael remained, scratching his head. She was unnervingly cheerful. Looking at the marks Lucille had just inspected, he felt horrified, not excited.

He was about to comment on her bizarre behavior when a sharp pain pierced his chest. *What the hell?*

He closed his eyes, just as a second bout of pain and horror hit him. They had made a terrible discovery, but that was no reason to have a visceral reaction like this. Something horrible was happening somewhere else, he just knew it.

"Lucille," he called out as he stumbled out of the same hatch.

"Lucille!"

"What?" Her voice was muffled.

"Something is wrong!" Michael said.

Lucille returned to his position and scrutinized him.

He found it hard to explain what was happening, so he just gestured at his own chest. "I feel something. Here."

She cocked her head to the side and frowned. "You feel the Bond?"

"The what?"

"The Bond. The connection between maker and newborn. Is something wrong with her?"

"How would I know, I've never been anyone's maker before!" Michael argued. *Shit*. Was that what he was feeling? Was Anna in danger? He really shouldn't have let her out of his sight.

"What exactly is it that you feel?" Lucille asked.

"Like someone is trying to tear my chest open and rip my heart out." It sounded overly dramatic now that he'd said it out loud. But it was still the most accurate description he could come up with.

"We should go." Lucille didn't give him the chance to respond before grabbing him by the arm and dragging him out of the building at superhuman speed.

Outside, Michael could breathe better, but he was still overcome by dread.

She pulled her phone out of her pocket and started tapping away at it. "The house seems secure."

"You're surveilling Alexander's house now?" Michael asked, as he looked over her shoulder at the various video feeds on her screen.

Lucille glanced at him sideways. "After what happened, Julius didn't exactly give me another choice."

That's how she'd known about Anna's arrival. And here he'd thought Gillian or some other disgruntled vampire had taken it upon themselves to spy on them. This made a lot more sense.

"So if the house is fine, then where is Anna?" Michael wondered aloud.

"What if she never made it home?" Lucille asked.

"Where else would she have gone? She doesn't remember much from before the Ritual. Not even where she lived." As soon as Michael had finished talking, he started to doubt his own words.

"Perhaps she remembered something," Lucille offered.

Michael nodded. That was possible. Her memory had slowly been coming back.

"So how do we find her?" Michael asked.

Lucille didn't answer, neither did she stop walking. They returned to the gap in the fence and climbed through it. Lucille led the way toward some shops further up the road. Except for a restaurant and a small supermarket, the rest of the shops had already closed for the night.

"What are you thinking? How do we find her?" Michael

repeated himself.

Lucille pointed at the parked cars, one of them a black cab. "Good old fashioned canvassing."

Michael frowned. Anna had left over half an hour ago. What were the chances that this guy knew anything? Lucille's idea was better than nothing, though.

As they got closer to the cab, Michael examined the driver. He was just sitting there, with both hands on the steering, looking straight ahead. All the other people around here were going about their usual business: talking on the phone, checking their watches as they rushed on by carrying bags of groceries.

This guy was doing nothing at all, and yet he didn't even look bored.

Lucille knocked on his window, but he didn't react.

"He's been hypnotized," Michael observed.

Lucille turned and shot him a disapproving look. "You taught her how to hypnotize people already? Why would you do that? She doesn't even know how to feed herself yet!"

Michael raised his hands in defense. "I did nothing of the sort! She must have figured it out on her own."

Although hypnosis was a talent all vampires possessed, it didn't come easily to most fledglings. Anna really was something special, and he couldn't help but feel a sense of pride. This wasn't the time to dwell on how special or how talented Anna was, though.

She was in danger, and this human was their best

possible lead.

Michael approached the driver's side window of the cab and knocked on it again. "We need your help." His tone was firm as he spoke, and his focus was entirely aimed at infiltrating the man's mind with his own. He was quite young in vampire terms himself, but he also had somewhat of a talent for mind control.

Sure enough, the cabbie turned his head and looked Michael directly in the eye. "Of course, what do you need?"

"Did you pick up a woman from here earlier—curvaceous, wavy, dark blond hair, and light brown eyes? Where did you drop her?"

The driver frowned and his eyes went distant again, as though he was reliving the moment. "We were going to Kensington Palace Gardens, when suddenly she made me pull over. I was going to wait for her, but she told me to head back here and wait for my next fare."

Michael and Lucille exchanged a look. That's why she'd never made it home. But what had inspired her to abandon the idea of heading back to the house?

"Can you take us there?" Michael asked.

The cabbie smiled and nodded. "Of course. Happy to help."

Michael opened the rear door of the cab for Lucille, and then joined her inside.

"I can't believe a newborn could have done this," Lucille grumbled. "I've been in this city a long time, and cab drivers have always been some of the most suspicious and difficult humans I've had the displeasure of dealing with."

Michael looked out the window as the taxi pulled into the road and suppressed a sigh. One needed people skills in order to deal with difficult humans, something which Lucille sorely lacked.

"I suppose she's not just any other newborn," Michael remarked, mostly to himself.

"We shall see." Lucille folded her arms and looked out the window at her side.

Michael glanced at her, then shook his head. He'd never understand Lucille. Was she jealous of Anna? Did she dislike her for some reason? Or was this just her default behavior?

They sat in silence as the cab zipped through the dense traffic of the city, until it came to a halt somewhere on Cromwell Road, which was particularly busy.

The cabbie turned around to face them. "This is it."

Michael nodded and grabbed for his wallet. "How much?"

"Oh, I must have forgotten to switch on the meter. It's fine. I hope you two find what you're looking for."

Michael focused his thoughts again, this time aiming to release the mental connection between himself and the driver. That was where Anna must have gone wrong; that was why the man had still been under her spell even after he'd dropped her off. He'd teach her how to do it properly, if only he could find her and take her to safety first.

As soon as they got out, Lucille started to walk.

"What have you got?" Michael asked, as he caught up with her.

"She was here," Lucille said as she scanned the street ahead. "Her trail is still fresh."

Michael inhaled deeply, but he couldn't pick out Anna's scent in the muddled chaos that surrounded them. Shops, cafés, restaurants, and crowds of people confused his senses.

He understood now; Lucille was a talented tracker. That was what made her so valuable to the Council.

She didn't seem to have any difficulty picking out Anna's scent, and started to walk again.

They continued up the road for a little bit, and then turned off into a smaller side street.

Lucille paused for a moment at the next intersection. "It gets confusing here," she mumbled.

Michael looked around. None of the surrounding buildings or streets seemed particularly interesting. And yet there must have been something here to attract Anna's attention.

"She's been in all of these streets," Lucille said. "Almost like she's been walking around in circles and doubling back on herself."

"She was looking for something," Michael concluded.

Lucille nodded. "It'll take too long if we rely on my

sense of smell alone. It's your turn."

Michael raised an eyebrow.

"Follow the Bond," she urged.

Michael closed his eyes; doing so seemed to strengthen his connection to Anna. Although he could still feel that something was very wrong, he couldn't easily pinpoint where the feeling originated. It didn't help that in closing his eyes, he kept *seeing* her. The way she looked at him up on the roof, just before they'd kissed. It broke his heart to consider the possibility that he might never see her again.

"I can't tell where she is," he said.

"Try harder!" Lucille said.

Michael opened his eyes and glared at her. "I am! It's not that easy."

Lucille observed him for a moment, then pursed her lips. "Okay, I have an idea. Close your eyes again."

Michael did as asked, and almost instantly, Lucille started dragging him forward by his arm. "You just let me know if we're getting warmer or colder,"

Michael was about to protest that this wasn't a game, when suddenly he felt it. The tension in his chest seemed to grow marginally. "Okay, warmer."

CHAPTER ELEVEN

It didn't take Michael and Lucille all that long to locate the spot where Michael's connection to Anna was the strongest. There was just one problem: they'd ended up in the center of a cobbled road with no sign of Anna anywhere.

The buildings surrounding them looked innocuous enough, but every time they approached one of them, Michael's sixth sense suggested that Anna wasn't inside.

"What if she's underneath us?" Michael kneeled down and placed his hand flat on the cold ground. Sure enough, he could sense her more keenly from there.

There was a manhole cover near their position which wouldn't be difficult for even one vampire to lift up.

"She could be in the sewer," Michael said.

"That's not all that's down there," Lucille said. "London has a very extensive system of tunnels. That would explain why these buildings don't feel right to you."

Michael nodded. It made sense. He picked up the heavy metal disk and cast it aside, then he jumped down into the darkness below, landing squarely on his feet in a puddle.

The water didn't take long to penetrate his shoes and the legs of his trousers. Ordinarily, getting soaked in human filth would annoy the hell out of him. But if he found Anna and stopped the terrible threat that seemed to loom over her, it was worth the sacrifice.

The only problem was that he still couldn't pick up on her scent down here. The stench of human excrement and garbage was too overwhelming.

Lucille landed next to him and marched straight ahead. Perhaps her nose had picked up something his couldn't.

They continued for ten, twenty feet, then Lucille stopped in her tracks.

"Listen," she said.

Michael shook his head. He couldn't hear a thing.

"We better go," she whispered.

Before he could question her, or they could retreat, Michael saw why Lucille had become spooked all of a sudden. The two vampires that appeared before them looked very different from any Michael had seen before. Their eyes glowed in the dark as they bared their sharp fangs.

"You shouldn't be here," the one on the left hissed.

"This is our domain," the other said.

"We made a mistake, our apologies," Lucille said, trying to placate them.

Michael shot her a confused look. This didn't sound at all like the Lucille he knew and disliked. What had gotten into her?

Anna was here somewhere. Couldn't Lucille just tell these two what was what, that they were breaking Council laws by holding one of their own? Couldn't they fight these two idiots?

Michael opened his mouth, but Lucille rested her hand on his arm to silence him. They exchanged a look and he decided against better judgement to follow her lead. The safety of his fledgling was on the line, but she had been in the business of enforcing Council law much longer than he'd even been alive. Perhaps she knew best.

"What's your business here?" the other vampire asked.

Both of them stood slightly hunched forward with their fists balled, ready to fight if necessary.

"We were just looking for a place to stash prey. You know how it is." Lucille gestured at the tunnel surrounding them. "But seeing as this spot is taken, we'll be on our way."

The two rogue vampires exchanged a look, then surged forward.

Lucille took Michael's hand and dragged him back toward the manhole they'd entered from. They fled as quickly as they could, jumped up onto street level and sprinting north toward the park.

Michael was quick, but Lucille was even faster, so with her dragging him along, they ran so quickly they could not be seen by human eyes. They only stopped once they'd reached a spot in the park surrounded by trees where they weren't overlooked by anyone.

"What the hell was that? Those were the vampires we'd been looking for. They took Anna!" Michael protested.

Lucille just shook her head. "It's not so simple. Those

weren't ordinary vampires like you or me."

Michael frowned. They did look unusual, but still. They should have at least tried harder to rescue Anna.

"They're Soul Eaters." Lucille turned to face Michael. "They don't just drink blood, they drain their prey completely. Every kill makes them stronger, and over time, they've evolved into what they are now!"

What the hell was a Soul Eater? Why had he never heard the term before?

"So what? You're almost four-hundred years old, and I'm not a bad fighter either. Together we might have defeated them!" Michael argued.

"They would have torn us to shreds. Trust me." Lucille paced the clearing in the trees, back and forth, her arms folded. "Let me think."

Michael looked back in the direction where they'd just come from, but it didn't seem like they had been followed. Any vampire worth his salt would have caught up with them now, and if these two were really so strong, they wouldn't have had any trouble at all.

"So call more of your Council people. We'll defeat them with sheer numbers." Michael suggested.

"Still too risky."

"Well, we can't just do nothing. I'm sure Julius won't be happy if word gets around that anyone can just move to London and ignore the laws, whether they're Soul Eaters or not. It'll make him look weak," Michael said. The longer they waited, the more danger Anna would be in. If they had intended to kill her when they fed from her, they might want to finish the job now. If every mortal soul gave these monsters more strength, then what would happen if they took an immortal soul?

If they couldn't overpower them, then they had to trick them or outsmart them somehow. Although Julius was the wisest vampire Michael knew, he couldn't trust him to help if he didn't benefit from it somehow. Not after the incident with Cat…

That was it!

Michael took a deep breath and retrieved his phone from his pocket.

"What?" Lucille asked. "Have you thought of something? Who are you calling?"

"Alexander," Michael said.

Lucille's eyes widened. "Of course. Cat's blood!"

Michael smiled. They'd had a bit of a slow start, but throughout the night, Lucille and he had actually started to work as a team. The sparkle in her eyes told him she was on the same page.

"Hello, Alexander?" Michael started. This wasn't going to be an easy conversation, but it was unavoidable. Even Lucille seemed to agree on that.

"What's wrong?" Alexander asked, who must have picked up Michael's urgent tone.

"Those vampires who had left Anna for dead, they're so-called Soul Eaters."

"Ah." Alexander's reaction suggested he knew a lot

more about the topic than Michael did.

Lucille stepped forward and grabbed the phone from Michael's hand, switching it to speaker.

"Brother, they've taken the newborn," she said in a matter-of-fact tone.

Alexander sighed on the other end. "How many?"

"Two that we know of," Michael said. "We can't let them have Anna. They'll kill her!"

"Even with Council reinforcements…" Lucille started.

"Alexander, I need your help to get her back," Michael interjected.

"My friend, after what you've done for me last month… What do you need?" Alexander asked.

"We won't be able to defeat the Soul Eaters in direct combat, but if we had, say, a *secret weapon*…" Lucille said.

"Sister, you're not suggesting—"

"By all accounts, it ought to work. And she wouldn't need to be here. We could just use a little sample—" Lucille continued.

"I'm not ready to involve Catherine in this! The risk is too huge!"

"Just a few drops would do it," Michael said.

"Brother, you've got the most extensive library outside of the Council itself. Don't tell me you don't know what Soul Eaters are capable of. And to think we have two running wild around London? That's not just unacceptable, it's dangerous. Sooner or later, they'll catch wind of Catherine's identity and then, it might be too late.

Right now, we have the advantage."

Alexander kept quiet for a few moments.

"I can guarantee that this will do wonders for your relationship with Julius," Lucille added. "He'll take it as a sign of loyalty to his leadership."

Michael and Lucille exchanged a look. *He had to agree, right?* This was the only play they could reasonably make.

A rustle broke the silence on the other end. "I'll do it," Cat said.

"It's not safe," Alexander interrupted her.

"It never will be as long as Julius is angry with us. A little goodwill from his side could go a long way."

"Will you both hang on for a moment?" Alexander asked.

"Sure," Michael said.

He stared at the floor as the call went mute. Alexander and Cat had their own conflict to resolve. They'd made their case, and the matter was out of their hands now.

The line rustled again, making Michael perk up.

"Meet me at the house. I'll bring a sample of Catherine's blood. But after this, we'll be even, you understand?"

Michael breathed a sigh of relief. "Yes, Alexander. I understand."

"And dear sister, I need your assurances that you won't disclose the finer points of tonight's plan to Julius. If he thinks I'm handing out vials of Catherine's blood, he will want some for himself and that can't end well."

Lucille shook her head. "I won't say a word. I swear it."

"Thank you, my friend," Michael said.

The line went dead. Lucille and Michael shared a look.

"Thank you," he said.

She brushed his gratitude away. "I didn't do it for you. Imagine what will happen to me if it becomes known I've let a bunch of Soul Eaters run rampant under my watch. My position in the Council would be compromised."

Michael nodded. *Sure.* If that was how she wanted to play it, fine. He still didn't like Lucille very much as a person, but their partnership tonight had taught him that she was a powerful ally to have. Without her help, Anna would be doomed, and as a result, so would Michael.

He'd never planned to become someone's maker, but now that he was, he couldn't turn his back on her. If she didn't survive, he wouldn't be able to just shrug it off.

The Bond between them was too strong.

CHAPTER TWELVE

Michael and Lucille had returned home and waited in the library for Alexander to show up.

Michael sat in one of the two leather chairs as Lucille paced back and forth. Dawn was still hours away, but he grew more restless with every passing minute.

Finally, Alexander burst in, causing Michael to jump out of his chair.

"You made it. Let's go," Michael said.

Alexander gestured at him to sit back down. "Hang on. We must prepare ourselves, or we'll lose."

Michael pressed his lips together. Of course, mentors had a nasty habit of being right, and Alexander was no different. But the tightness in his chest hadn't let up all night, and he was at the end of his tether. *What if they were too late? How would he live with himself?*

"You brought the blood, yes?" Michael said. "What else do we need?"

Alexander approached one of the ceiling height bookcases that lined the wall. "It's here somewhere. Ah!" He reached up and retrieved a tatty old leather binder and brought it to the large mahogany desk that stood at the other end of the library.

Michael joined him and watched as he carefully unfolded the fragile documents inside to reveal plans and diagrams, hand-drawn on discolored paper.

"What are these?" Michael asked. "And how did you come by them?"

"Just an auction find. Never mind." Alexander inspected sheet after sheet until he paused on one marked 'Kensington.' "Here it is. These are plans from the 1920s and '30s, when they tried to streamline the London Underground system."

"We came across the two Soul Eaters in the sewer, though, not in a rail tunnel."

Alexander nodded. "It's all connected. Have a look here." He pointed at a section of tunnels marked in black ink. "These are part of the Underground network. Those dotted sections are part of the sewer. Was this roughly the spot where you had your confrontation with the Soul Eaters?"

Lucille leaned across the table and pointed out the exact location. "Here."

"Right. Well, if you look a little bit further north from there, there the two systems link up via a ventilation shaft."

"I could feel Anna's presence strongest over here." Michael pointed at a spot further south in the sewer line. Looking at the plans now, it made perfect sense. There was a dead end section of maintenance tunnel that crossed underneath the sewer. That was probably where they had imprisoned Anna.

"That's our target," Alexander said as he picked up the old plans and carefully folded them up again. "We'll have to create a diversion and then trap them once they turn up to investigate."

Lucille nodded and smiled. "The two of us can take of that, brother. They'll recognize me, and we can douse you in Cat's blood to disguise you as my prey. They won't be able to resist."

Michael straightened himself. "That'll give me the chance to slip into the other tunnel system from the ventilation shaft and get Anna."

"When is your backup coming?" Alexander asked Lucille.

"I can have them in position within a moment's notice. Then they'll capture the rogues at our signal."

"Good. Michael, you take this—" Alexander handed him a little vial. "Just in case."

Michael didn't need to open the small bottle to know what was in it. He nodded as they shared a look of understanding. It was deeply flattering that Alexander would trust him with a little sample of Cat's blood. Michael put it away deep in his pocket, fully expecting to return it to Alexander by the end of the night.

The three of them shared a look. It seemed like a solid plan. Certainly better than Michael's initial impulse of just heading down there by himself and fighting the two strange vampires to the death. With a bit of luck, they'd return home with Anna before long.

"I do believe we're ready," Alexander said. "Where are the weapons?"

Lucille gestured at him to follow her, but he stayed behind with Michael for a moment.

"It's going to be fine. Your woman will be fine."

Did Alexander just refer to Anna as 'his woman?' Michael frowned.

"Don't tell me you're still going to deny it?" Alexander asked, a coy smile playing on his lips. "Catherine was the first to notice it. Your expression when you talked about her gave it away."

Michael shook his head. "I'm her maker. That's all."

"I'll let you in on a little secret. Sure, there's a bond between maker and fledgling, and you would have sensed if she was in danger, but not like this. I can see you're in physical pain because of it. This something else, something deeper."

"That can't be. And it goes against everything—" Michael protested.

"Oh, hush! Deep down, you know I'm telling the truth. All that stands in your way is your misguided belief that your relationship is somehow inappropriate, when really, your situation is a lot more common than you'd think. Now let's go and get her back, or I will have potentially compromised Catherine's safety for nothing!" Alexander urged.

Michael pressed his lips together and swallowed, hard. Had he really been that far off the mark? Neither Alexander nor Lucille seemed to bat an eye at the chance of something more intimate developing between Michael and Anna. It would be so much easier to just let go of all the guilt he had developed since their one and only kiss. He took a deep breath and followed Alexander into the reception room, where Lucille waited with the weapons.

Fine. If they—especially Anna—made it out of this mess alive, he would confess his forbidden feelings to her. And then it would be up to her to decide how to move forward.

It would have been easy for Anna to lose hope.

She'd been stuck in this dead end tunnel for hours, with nothing to keep her company but the periodic rumble originating from nearby Underground trains. She had become so used to the interval at which the trains passed that she'd started anticipating them.

Maybe a dozen or so trains ago, she'd felt some strange sensation, as though she wasn't entirely alone anymore. It was like she could feel Michael's presence, but that reassuring feeling had passed very quickly, leaving her alone again. Was this another one of those vampire sense things, like the one warning her of the rising sun? More likely she was starting to lose her mind already.

But if he did turn up, and Anna did get out of here, she would insist on a heart-to-heart with Michael. She would tell him that it was fine if he didn't want any sort of romantic relationship with her; she'd understand. They could just forget about the kiss and everything, and pretend it never happened.

The sad fact was that he was the only one she had now, and she couldn't bear for things to be awkward all the time. If they were going to be just friends, fine. They would never cross that line again.

Anna paced around her cell, investigating every inch of wall for the hundredth time, which only confirmed what she'd already known: she was trapped and there was no way out.

Then without any warning, the door to her cell swung open, revealing the creepy old vampire who had approached her out on the street.

She took a step back and bumped into the wall behind her.

Her captor smirked and seemed to float slowly in her direction. Could she make a run for it? Something told her he was only slowing things down in order to toy with her. He'd catch her without any problem if she tried anything.

"What do you want with me?" Anna asked.

He let out a chuckle. "Oh, dear child. How do I explain?"

By just telling me already, Anna thought. Her throat felt tight as her heartbeat sped up more and more.

He was only a couple of feet away from her now. "I am not one to leave unfinished business," he whispered, then leaned forward and inhaled deeply. "Ah. The smell of youth."

Anna kept her breaths and movements to a minimum.

She didn't want to provoke him. *Unfinished business?* They'd left her for dead, so was he going to finish the job now?

"Please don't kill me," Anna whispered. "Harming another vampire is against the law."

The man laughed. "Your innocence amuses me."

Anna frowned. She'd blurted it out without thinking. *So stupid.* If this guy cared one bit about Vampire Law, he might not have captured her the first time around.

"Then why not keep me around, if my presence amuses you?" she tried again.

He slowly shook his head. "I'm afraid that would be against *my* code."

Anna didn't dare ask what his code prescribed; she feared she already knew the answer.

"The male and the female who came snooping around. Acquaintances of yours?" the man asked.

Anna's heart jumped a few beats. So Michael *had* tried to find her already. She *had* felt him nearby.

"I don't know who you're talking about."

The vampire bared his teeth. If this was his way of trying to intimidate Anna, it was working.

"Don't play games."

Anna shook her head. "I swear, I don't know them."

"Do you swear on your life? On theirs?" he asked.

Anna pressed her lips together and averted her gaze. That was what she got for bluffing.

"As I suspected. Now, perhaps we can converse openly. I would very much like to learn more about these city dwellers."

What was the point?

"I really don't know very much about them," Anna said, which was much closer to the truth.

"Why did they save you? Were you their property?"

What a bizarre question. The way Michael, Lucille, and even Alexander seemed to live was quite different to the reality this strange vampire inhabited.

"No, they just don't kill humans." Anna frowned.

"Well, that's something new. Why wouldn't they kill humans? How do they gain strength?" The vampire moved around the dark cell, as though he was pacing, but his feet still didn't quite touch the ground.

"Are you certain they didn't keep you as a servant? I hear some Nightwalkers do that, enslave humans to run daytime errands."

Anna folded her arms. Perhaps she had said too much already. "Frankly, I don't remember much of my human life."

The old vampire smirked again as his deep black eyes focused on hers. "Of course you don't, child. I had made sure of that already."

So it was all *his* fault? The loss of memory hadn't been due to any injury or trauma, but hypnosis?

"Then why don't you undo whatever you did before, so that I may remember and answer your questions properly," Anna suggested.

Her captor paused and scratched his chin with white

spindly fingers. "I suppose there's no harm in trying."

Anna's heart beat a little faster again. Could it be so easy?

He grabbed her cheek, digging into her skin with long, claw-like fingernails. His eyes locked onto hers with a stare so intense she couldn't look away if she wanted to.

"Anything you had been made to forget, you shall remember it again."

Anna blinked involuntarily when she felt his presence enter her mind. It was unpleasant to have all this darkness, all this evil in her mind, but she could do nothing to defend herself.

She was frozen in place, unable to stir a single muscle or formulate any thought, beyond what he wanted her to.

Then, just like that, her mind was hers again.

"Well?" the vampire demanded. "What can you tell me about those two busybodies who came looking for you?"

Anna tried her best to answer his question, but she couldn't say a word. Her memories came rushing back, overwhelming her as she tried to process them. All of her old life: her worries, her fears, her ambitions and dreams.

She had wanted to run her own catering business, but when that didn't work, she'd gone back to work for her old boss. She'd picked up odd jobs, waitressing at parties and temping in restaurant kitchens. She'd worked sometimes two shifts a day, saving up money as well as knowledge.

She didn't have very many friends and certainly no boyfriends. The most intimate she'd gotten with anyone over the past couple of years had been that awkward kiss on the roof she'd shared with Michael.

Living in a modest single room in a house share allowed her to put as much of her earnings into savings as possible. Even if she made it out of here and went back there to pick up her belongings, she would end up with very little indeed.

She'd never achieved any of what she'd set out to.

"Tell me, or you'll regret it!" the vampire shouted.

She'd never really *lived*. And now she would die.

CHAPTER THIRTEEN

Michael was as ready as he would ever be. He waited in the shadows near the manhole from where Lucille and Alexander had already descended into the sewer. They were to perform their role in Anna's rescue—create a diversion—while he was going to wait here until the coast seemed clear enough to look for her.

From the moment Alexander had camouflaged himself with Cat's blood, Michael and Lucille had found it hard to resist the scent. These Soul Eaters would find it even more irresistible, since they were supposedly more bloodthirsty and guided by primal instincts.

As a result, Michael did not need to wait long.

Underneath him, a muffled commotion pierced the silent night. Footsteps fled north, just as planned; that would have been Lucille and Alexander. Something, presumably the Soul Eaters, chased after them, making more of a whoosh than the usual sound of footsteps he was expecting. Perhaps their increased power had afforded them the talent of levitation.

He waited for another minute or so, when he could no longer resist. As he was on his way down the manhole, the tension in his chest surged all of a sudden.

Anna was in very sudden, very real danger.

He ran through the sewer, ignoring the splashes of

dirty water landing all over his clothes, until he found the way through the ventilation shaft Alexander had pointed out on his old plans. From then on, the way was much drier and cleaner.

As he left the shaft and climbed into what seemed to be an old, now defunct part of the London Underground network, Michael paused to listen for any noises suggesting he'd been found out. Nothing. There was no movement anywhere around him, as far as he could tell. The tunnel ahead was empty, save for a few old signs abandoned on the ground.

He continued on much more slowly, trying to focus most of his energy on Anna. She was nearby, he could feel her so clearly.

Finally, he stopped in front of a heavy steel door with a crank handle in its center. Anna was in there, he would bet his life on it. He grabbed the crank, prepared to give his all to open it, when he found that it was already undone and the door opened with a simple push inward.

Inside, a pair of fearful eyes awaited. Anna.

Behind her stood a strange white-haired man Michael had never seen before. He looked even more bizarre than the two Soul Eaters they'd found in the sewer earlier that night. Older, more deformed, and more monstrous.

"Welcome, young one," the strange vampire said.

Anna tried to run toward him, but she couldn't move. One of the man's hands was on her throat, tightening visibly around her esophagus.

"Run," she whispered, barely able to make a sound.

Michael stood firm. He was not going to give up on her so easily.

"Run, dammit!" Anna repeated herself, her voice even more choked as the man squeezed her throat.

"She's cunning, this one. I like her." The man grinned, flashing his sharp teeth, then turned to gaze at Anna's neck. "Shame she must die. And once I've taken care of her, you'll be next."

Michael's entire body tensed up. No way. He would not let that happen. He slipped his hand into his right pocket and closed his fingers around the small vial Alexander had given him. Although he never expected to need it, he was glad to have it now. This would be his secret weapon, his only hope of defeating this ancient Soul Eater.

"You will do nothing of the sort," Michael said.

The strange vampire turned his head in Michael's direction again and glared at him. "You think you can stop me, young one? I am the embodiment of a thousand souls!"

"But that's my woman you're holding. I'm ready to fight." Michael glanced at Anna, who looked as surprised at his words as he was. They'd just slipped out before he had a chance to think things through properly.

"No matter, she's mine now. I finish what I start."

Michael stood firm with the bottle in his fist. Would Cat's blood be strong enough to disable the Soul Eater temporarily? Or would it just make him more violent?

Anna's position at the further end of the tunnel was less than ideal. But perhaps, if he threw the vial and broke it against the wall…

"Don't. He'll kill both of us," Anna whispered.

Michael looked into her eyes and all he could see was fear. The vampire turned to face Anna again, readying himself to drink.

This was Michael's last and only chance. He pulled the bottle out of his pocket and threw it as fast as he could against the back wall of the tunnel, smashing it into a million pieces and vaporizing the blood everywhere.

The Soul Eater's eyes turned red immediately as he turned his head to look for the source of the overwhelmingly delicious scent in the air.

Michael saw Anna, frozen in place, her throat now freed of the ancient vampire's grasp. She was shivering, her eyes deep red, as she tried to resist the urge to follow the blood herself.

Michael surged forward, holding his breath to minimize the effect of his diversion, and pulled Anna backward through the open door, slamming it shut behind them.

He turned the wheel as fast as he could, securing the bolts inside the door.

"Are you all right?" he asked, once he was done.

Anna was panting heavily, still shivering through her entire body.

"What. Was. That," she gasped.

"Blood. It's not important. He didn't hurt you, did he?"

She reached for her throat and swallowed a couple of times. "Not yet."

Her eyes turned their normal shade again, and she looked quite a bit weaker than before. Newborns needed more nourishment than mature vampires; she was probably due her next meal already.

"Let's get out of here, before that *thing* breaks out," Michael said, looking back at the door. It was so thick and heavy, hardly a noise filtered through. It seemed like the Soul Eater was still distracted by what little blood Michael had thrown against the wall.

"Sure," Anna said.

Michael watched her as they made it through the maze of tunnels and out into the fresh winter air. She remained quiet as they walked the streets, as though she was lost in thought, then suddenly paused at the next intersection.

"What is it?" Michael asked.

Anna pointed to the right. "There. That's where I lived."

"You remember? That's wonderful! Do you want to go pick up a few things?"

Anna stood frozen in place. For someone who had just unraveled the mystery of her recent past, she didn't seem even a little excited or pleased about it.

Michael continued to observe her. Why wasn't she happier? What was wrong?

She finally shook her head and started to walk away from the building she'd just pointed out. "There's nothing there for me anymore."

Michael frowned. "Wait! Don't you have anyone to say goodbye to, or personal items you want to take back to the house?"

Anna shook her head.

"I lived for my work. My biggest ambition was to run my own catering business. I'd even given it a try, as you might have figured out from the old business card we found. But I just didn't have what it takes, so I gave up everything—friends, relationships—and focused only on gaining experience and educating myself. I never succeeded." She sighed deeply. "It all seems so pointless now."

As Michael faced her, the sadness in her eyes nearly broke him.

"I don't know what I'm going to do now," Anna said.

He put his hand on her arm. "Remember up on the roof, that feeling of having the world at your feet? You can do anything. If you finally want to live that ambition of yours, you can do it so much better now."

Anna frowned. "I can? But I'm no longer human."

"You're faster, stronger, and smarter than you've ever been. And your senses are a hundred times more powerful than they were; you're now able to taste and smell things you would have never even noticed." He smiled nervously. "Do you think I would have lived in a mansion back when I was human? I was a bum who never amounted to much until I was turned."

"What about our limitations? I won't be able to go out during the day."

Michael brushed away her concerns. "Do what you can at night, and hire human staff to run errands during the day."

Anna turned and looked back at the street where she used to live, then turned and pointed at a cobbled street to their left. "There is something we can take back to the house."

"Tell me."

Anna shook her head. "It's best if I show you."

She waved at Michael and resolutely marched ahead until moments later, they stopped in front of a glass-fronted modern building that looked out of place among the Victorian and Edwardian buildings that surrounded it.

"These people make the best cinnamon rolls I've ever tasted," Anna said, gazing longingly at the switched off sign. "Do you think we could sneak in?"

Michael couldn't suppress a grin. Despite just having described herself as a rather serious workaholic, Anna did have a hidden wild streak.

"Listen," Michael said.

She did, and smiled when she heard it. "They're already at work inside."

Michael nodded. "While we absolutely will pick up some cinnamon rolls, it's time you had a very different sort of meal as well."

Anna's eyes widened. "I don't want to hurt anyone."

Michael shook his head. "You won't, I'll make sure of that. We'll take only as much blood as you need." He gestured at her to follow him, which she did, through a narrow alley that led to the backside of the bakery. They hid behind a large garbage bin and watched in silence.

A couple of men dressed all in white were in the midst of unloading a van full of raw ingredients. Anna and Michael gave them a few more minutes to complete the job, only then did they reveal themselves.

"Morning, lads," Michael spoke firmly, attracting their attention.

"Hey, this area is off limits!" one of the men protested.

Michael turned to Anna and nodded at her. "Hypnotize him. I know you have the talent."

Anna smiled briefly, then walked up to the man, whose demeanor changed immediately. Michael, meanwhile, invaded the other man's mind, rendering him harmless as well.

Then he stood back and watched in amusement as Anna compelled her subject to grab a box of cinnamon rolls from inside the bakery. As soon as he returned with their prize, Michael joined her and pointed out the right spot on the side of the man's neck.

"Bite him here. Drink. Count to five. Let go," he instructed.

Anna smiled nervously and took a deep breath. "Here goes nothing."

As it turned out, she need not have worried. Moments

later, they released the two men from their influence and watched as they went about their business without a single memory of what had just occurred.

CHAPTER FOURTEEN

What a night. Anna could not believe what all had happened in such a short time. Within a couple of days, her entire life had been turned upside down.

She slipped her hand into Michael's as they made their way back to the villa, so that soon after, they found themselves in exactly the same spot as the night before.

"It *is* beautiful here," Anna said, admiring the view of the house and its surrounding gardens, just as she had done last night.

Thanks to everything Michael had told her back in her old neighborhood, she had started to feel a bit more positive about the future. Perhaps she had gotten it all wrong; those old regrets were just that: old. They didn't matter anymore. Now that she had an eternity to look forward to, she could do whatever she liked.

Michael winked at her. "Race you to the top?"

Before she had the chance to agree, he was gone already. There was no way she could catch up, but she gave it her all and charged at the tree, climbed up the branches, and jumped up onto the house in record time.

Once she reached the roof, Anna found that Michael was already waiting for her with the box of cinnamon rolls in his hand. He gestured at her to sit down and opened the box, holding it in her direction.

She picked up one and inhaled deeply. Of all her old memories, it was this combination of scents which offered the most comfort; these were her guilty pleasure, her one indulgence in an otherwise lackluster existence.

"You really do love these cinnamon rolls, don't you?" Michael teased.

She opened her eyes and smiled. "Just try one. You'll understand."

He didn't, though, he just kept staring at her. His expression had turned from playful to completely solemn, which suddenly made Anna nervous.

"I should explain myself," he said.

She averted her gaze, letting it rest on Kensington Palace in the distance. This was where things had gotten awkward last night. "Look, if you just want to be friends, that's fine," she said.

Michael rested his hand on her arm. "I promised myself that I would tell you everything if we made it through the night in one piece. Suddenly I'm having trouble finding the right words."

Anna put the cinnamon roll back into the box and folded her hands in her lap, waiting for Michael to start talking. Whatever he was trying to say, it seemed important.

"I have always held the belief that the bond between maker and fledgling is sacred. That it is always meant to be platonic, more like a family relationship than anything else."

Anna's heart started to beat a little faster. So she had been right. He was trying to let her down easy.

"Then tonight, when it seemed like I might lose you forever, I achieved clarity. I made a terrible mistake, and I'm sorry."

Anna blinked a few times, trying her best not to feel awkward or hurt. She had prepared herself for exactly this conversation while she'd been locked up. So why did it now feel so wrong to hear him say these words?

"It's okay," she whispered.

"I'm not finished," Michael said, running his hand through his hair. "I was wrong trying to dismiss my feelings for you. You made me feel things I've never known."

Anna turned to face him. This wasn't what she thought he was going to say!

His eyes evaded hers and also focused on some spot further away in the park that lay in the distance.

"I couldn't bear the thought that something might happen to you, which is funny, since we've only just met." Michael glanced at her briefly. "I think… And if this is completely out of line, please do stop me. But I think I have come to love you."

Anna was stunned. She was expecting a lot of things, but not that. A declaration of love from Michael the supposed playboy vampire was the last thing she could have foreseen.

Her heart did a little happy dance inside her chest, even

if the entire situation was completely bizarre. Then again, over the last 48 hours, it had just been one bizarre event after another, so in a backward way, this development should actually make sense.

"I've also not felt like this, ever," she said.

His eyes locked onto hers. It was actually a bit funny seeing him this way. His demeanor since they'd first met had ranged from confident, to arrogant, to downright confusing, and she'd had trouble figuring out who he really was. But right now, she could tell that he had opened up. This was the real Michael, baring his vulnerabilities to her.

"So if you would forgive me for my strange behavior last night, I would very much like to start over," he said.

He was really rather cute like this. She pressed her lips together, but could not suppress a smile. "I would. I mean, I do. Let's start over."

She had only just finished speaking when he leaned forward, cupped her face, and pressed his lips against hers. It was magnificent, this do-over of their first kiss. Even with all of her memories restored, she still could not remember a time that she had ever felt so alive.

Her instincts had been right, he *did* care. He just had an incredibly crappy way of showing it. That was all going to change now, though; his confession promised as much.

Anna wrapped her arms around Michael, exploring him by touch and finally giving in to those illicit thoughts she'd been having about him. Their tongues danced around one another in a feverish frenzy. The fireworks she had felt the first time around paled in front of the pleasure his touch gave her now.

Before she knew what was happening, she found herself floating in his arms as they swiftly descended down the side of the roof and into a nearby window. Michael rushed her through the upstairs hallway, straight to one of the many bedrooms.

She briefly looked around only to note that she had never been in this room before. It must be his.

Now on her back on the bed, she watched as Michael unbuttoned his shirt. Was she ready for this? She'd thought of it after their first kiss and rejected the idea. *Not that kind of woman,* she'd said to herself.

All bets were off now. She wanted him. He wanted her.

What difference did it make who she had been in her mortal life? She was a vampire now. Powerful, strong, guided by instinct and pleasure.

She could have her cake and eat it too. And after getting to know Michael just a little bit, she was confident she would not be judged. The whole world lay at her feet now, as Michael had said. Anything she wanted, it would be hers for the taking.

Right now, all she wanted stood in front of her, only halfway done with the buttons on his shirt. *Too slow!*

She reached for him, almost clawing at the soft fabric. He understood, and with a naughty grin on his face, ripped it off in one swift move.

"Now do me," she demanded.

In the past, she might have felt insecure, but the way he was already looking at her, with lust darkening his normally light blue eyes, was all the reassurance she could wish for. He got onto all fours on top of her, leaned down, and grabbed the collar of her pullover with his teeth, then, without breaking eye contact, he tugged it off.

Anna gasped as the fabric split at the seams. How effortless it looked. Could she do the same? She pushed him back, fighting the barrage of goosebumps that spread over her naked skin as she felt his firm, chiseled chest underneath her hand. She would have plenty of opportunity to touch him. First, she wanted to play some more.

He stood back at the foot end of the bed, and she got down on her knees in front of him, pushing her fingers into the waist of his trousers and giving them a firm pull. They came off in shreds just as easily as her pullover had done.

This sort of strength she could get used to.

She dropped her own jeans and stood back, admiring him as he did the same to her.

They circled each other like animals prepping for a fight. It wasn't conflict they were after, though. Their end game would be so much more satisfying.

It was Anna who pounced first, jumping Michael and clinging onto him with her legs around his waist. They kissed again, more violently than before.

They had endless energy to spend, immense tension to

release.

Their bodies felt right together, hers slightly softer than his, but still more toned and powerful than she'd ever been before. Perhaps it was for the best that she was discovering all this with him to guide her. By now, she might have broken and bruised a human lover.

"You're beautiful," he whispered in her ear.

"Mhmm," she responded, as she nuzzled the crook of his neck and bared her teeth. Was this how vampires made love? She wasn't sure, just that it felt right.

He groaned, his low voice sending a shiver down her spine.

"You're tasty," she remarked, as she pulled back and licked her lips. She hadn't meant to hurt him, much.

His eyes narrowed and he grabbed her firmly by the back of her neck, guiding their lips together again.

"Let me see. Yes, that's rather nice, isn't it?" he mumbled, in between kisses.

Then, abruptly, he threw her off, back onto the bed, and approached on all fours again. His movements were smooth, deliberate, like a large feline stalking its prey. She felt her heart flutter as she waited for what he would do next.

He was on her within a split second, his weight pressing against her naked body, as his hand tore at her underwear. She was completely naked now, completely his.

Anna couldn't suppress a moan as his hard manhood pressed against her aroused sex. It was going to happen at last. She would discover just how extra sensitive all her senses had become.

When he entered her, she screamed. Along with all her past worries, her inhibitions had gone too.

He chuckled into her ear as he lowered himself into her. They became one. One pulsating, thrusting, moaning, and grinding mess of limbs.

The bed shook with every move of theirs, the paintings rattled on their fittings; even the chandelier in the center of the ceiling made its presence known in rhythmic jangles.

If this house had been any less solid, this furniture any more delicate, they might have destroyed it all. Not that Anna in particular cared much. All of this stuff was replaceable.

But this moment they shared now was priceless.

Her skin was tingly, on fire, and cool to the touch all at the same time. Every touch of his, every caress or squeeze, seemed to soothe her *and* send her nerves into an overwhelming overload of pleasure. She couldn't take it anymore, and she couldn't stop.

Then she felt it: the beginnings of her release. The pressure built and built until she could neither scream nor stay silent. Anna closed her eyes and dug her fingernails hard into Michael's back.

He never slowed or showed any sign of fatigue, he just kept going. The fireworks were back, bigger and brighter than ever before. What she saw behind closed lids was the perfect representation of her arousal as it built to bursting point. A volcano erupting, bright lights and fire everywhere.

She opened her eyes again and watched Michael as he closed his and groaned loudly, signaling his own release. It was like she could feel his pleasure as her own. She held him against her, admiring the smoothness of his skin with her fingertips.

"That was amazing," he whispered.

"It really was," she agreed.

What was even more amazing was that they had both orgasmed, and yet neither seemed tired at all. Dawn had not yet arrived; they still had time before they'd lose their energy.

Anna smiled subtly as she looked up at him.

He reciprocated and caressed the side of her face with the back of his hand.

"How about we do that again, and this time, I'll be on top?" she said.

His smile widened, exposing his fangs. "My thoughts exactly."

And that was exactly what they did, taking turns until the clock down the hall struck seven and Anna's body began to slow. The higher the sun rose outside, the duller their energy levels became. Finally, they ended up next to each other, with Michael's arm around Anna's shoulder, both sated and content.

Before she drifted off, Anna reflected once more on everything that had happened.

Just like that, she had gone from dejected and full of regret over the way she'd lived her human life to full of hope for the future. And she had found a lover to share this bright new future with, something that had eluded her during her human life.

Despite the twists and turns, everything had turned out all right.

CHAPTER FIFTEEN

It had only been one day since he'd confessed his true feelings to her. Michael turned his head and glanced at Anna, who lay beside him. His heart sped up at the sight of her.

One day down, eternity to go.

She was still sleeping peacefully, recouping from the excitement of the past few days. Being nearly killed by Soul Eaters, then turned into a vampire and captured by those same Soul Eaters again, had undoubtedly taken its toll.

Michael couldn't help but smile at her. How innocent she looked, resting with her eyes closed. Her calm expression was a stark contrast to the willful Anna he had come to know during the previous days. The one who was always ready to question her own reality, or him.

He realized now that he loved both versions of her equally. She would keep him on his toes. They would never have a dull moment together.

It was strange, how it felt like he'd known her for so long, when actually she had only come into his life a few days ago. To think that he'd tried to resist her charms at first seemed ludicrous now. He'd felt *guilty*, when the real tragedy would have been to let this opportunity get away.

For thirty years, he'd used this city as his playground.

He'd seduced and courted numerous women, priding himself in his abilities as a conversationalist as well as a lover. But with Anna, everything had changed.

He was well out of his comfort zone with her. He couldn't just coast by on autopilot and expect that she wouldn't call him out on it. Being in a relationship was completely new to him. At the same time, her entire immortal life was still new to Anna.

They had so much to discover together; the possibilities were endless. Despite all his escapades, he'd never slept with another vampire before last night. It had been a revelation to share his body with an equal. But their connection had been so much deeper than just sex alone.

He was still her maker; he still felt responsible for her safety as well as her training as a new vampire. But added to that, he had new desires and hopes for her: that he could keep her happy. That she could live to her full potential and follow her dreams.

Whatever she wanted, he would be there to support her in every way he could. He hadn't told her this in so many words, but he would make sure to do that in time.

He carefully got up and stretched his stiff limbs.

"Where are you going? Don't leave," Anna whispered, her eyes still closed.

"I'm just getting something to eat. You stay here and rest," he said.

She did not respond; perhaps she had just talked in her sleep.

As he scanned the room for something to wear, he had a sudden realization. Everything *was* new for them. But this place was old, and it wasn't even his. Perhaps it was time to take what had happened as a sign to make a few more changes in his life.

No longer would he live here in Alexander's shadow. The latter had Cat to take care of, whereas Michael now had Anna.

Getting something to eat now became second on his list of priorities. He grabbed a robe from the closet and retrieved his phone from his torn trousers on the floor.

Then he dialed Alexander's number as he quietly sneaked out of the room.

"Hope I'm not disturbing you. I was hoping we might have a chat, face-to-face," Michael said.

"I'm glad you came by, especially since you had to leave Cat alone in hiding." Michael glanced at Alexander, who had taken a seat in the armchair next to him in the library.

Alexander nodded. "No problem. Though let's not make a habit of it. I would very much like to move back into my house now that the main threat has passed."

Michael nodded. Fair enough. That tied in perfectly with what Michael wanted to discuss.

After his experiences with Anna, Michael felt like he understood his friend and mentor better too. He hadn't been able to relate when Alexander paired up with Cat and rebelled against Julius and the Vampire Council to protect her.

Now he understood things perfectly. He would do the same for Anna.

Still, he decided to broach the topic slowly.

"What's going to happen to the Soul Eaters?" Michael asked.

Alexander sighed. "They're Julius' problem now. Perhaps they'll be put to death for their crimes."

Michael brought his glass to his lips and savored the taste of the brandy as he swirled it around his mouth. Julius would have to take firm action; anything less would be seen as a sign of weakness by anyone looking to contest his leadership of the Council. Either way, Michael was glad he wouldn't have to deal with those two anymore and Anna would be safe.

"And the other human victims?" Michael wondered aloud.

"We were too late for them; they were probably killed even before you performed the Ritual on Anna. When we caught the two Soul Eaters down in the sewer, they bragged about disposing of the bodies in the river. Lucille will verify if they were telling the truth. Thankfully, she's quite a talented tracker."

"So I've noticed. I wouldn't even have known where to look for Anna without her."

Michael felt Alexander's eyes on him and turned his head to find his friend already grinning at him. "Don't tell me you and Lucille are friends now?"

Michael made a face. "I wouldn't go so far. But at least I know now that we *can* work together if necessary."

Alexander nodded, his expression still equally smug. "Whatever you say."

A few minutes passed in silence, giving Michael the chance to work up the courage to discuss the one thing he'd been holding back so far. His motives were pure, but he wasn't sure if Alexander would take it that way.

"I've been thinking," Michael began.

Alexander didn't speak; instead, he took a sip from his glass and waited.

"Perhaps it's time we move on—Anna and I."

Alexander frowned. "Whatever do you mean?"

"Well, it's not that I don't appreciate your hospitality, you know I do…" Michael also took a sip, not for courage as much as to buy some time to formulate himself properly. The last thing he wanted was to come across as ungrateful.

"But you want to leave?" Alexander asked.

"I just think it's for the best. Anna is still learning to control her urges, so I wouldn't want her to be a threat to Cat. We could also use some time alone together, to figure out how our lifetimes together are going to look."

Alexander's expression relaxed once more. He nodded in silence.

"You both will appreciate the extra privacy I'm sure. I know we will," Michael joked.

"Just know you'll always be welcome here, my friend," Alexander said.

"I do. Thank you. I probably wouldn't have lasted a decade without your guidance and help."

They shared a smile and raised their glasses.

"A toast. To immortality. And love," Michael said.

"And to family," Alexander added.

"To family."

They shared a little smile and each took a sip.

"I must say I wasn't expecting this, not yet," Alexander said. "Where are you going to go?"

"We'll stay in the city. Lucille tipped me off to some serviced apartments that would be perfect. And with the investments I've been making lately…"

"Anna's idea?" Alexander asked.

Michael shook his head. "I haven't even told her yet. But I have a feeling she will appreciate a place she can make her own. Figure out what this new life is going to mean for the two of us."

"It'll be an adjustment."

Michael wasn't sure if Alexander was talking about the two of them, or himself.

"Just don't be a stranger. And if you ever need anything…" Alexander's voice trailed off as he emptied his glass in one last sip.

"Thank you, my friend. Now, I'd better head back upstairs, see if Anna is up yet."

Alexander nodded and got up as well. They shared a short, if slightly awkward hug. "Any time."

- THE END -

Lucille's
VALENTINE

PROLOGUE

Ever since Lucille had hauled the criminal known as Marek before the Council, she could not wait for the trial to begin. She had so many questions and very few answers. Her curiosity was what made her such a driven investigator.

Marek was a Soul Eater; that much was clear. But how had he become so powerful? How old was he? How long had he been killing humans indiscriminately without appearing on her radar?

Obviously, he had only just started his reign of terror in London a few weeks ago, when a human had been found on the brink of death by one of their own. The vampire Michael had turned the unfortunate female, and Lucille had worked together with the unlikely pair to track down Marek and his henchmen.

It had been a triumphant victory for her, and earned her much praise from Julius, Lucille's maker and leader of the Council.

Tonight was finally going to be the night. The trial of Marek and his associates would begin.

He stood accused of reckless conduct that risked the exposure of the vampire race to humanity as well as attempted murder of a fellow vampire. Julius had wanted to add on more charges, but decided against it on Lucille's advice. They had caught him on the gravest crime possible. The Council took the safety of their kind extremely seriously. And randomly draining humans and leaving them for all the world to find was the most callous display of overt vampirism the city had seen in over a century. The only way the Council could have come down any harder on Marek would have been if he'd videotaped himself drinking his victim's blood and posted it on the Internet.

So it wasn't the outcome of the trial that Lucille was interested in; the case was clear and the punishment obvious; Marek would be sentenced to death, and depending on whether they were complicit or only following orders, so would his two associates. Lucille was more interested in any possible justifications Marek would give during the process. Any information at all that would shine a light on his motivations and history.

Lucille would be lying to herself if she didn't admit that Marek's immense power had intrigued and even impressed her a bit. He had been a formidable adversary.

Additionally, there was something about the vehemence with which Julius sought to punish Marek that had set off her investigative instincts. There was something more to their relationship than the Council leader had led on.

"Are you ready, my child?" Julius interrupted her thoughts.

"Yes, of course." Lucille looked up and nodded at her

maker.

The most powerful vampire in the world, as Julius liked to refer to himself at times. It was true in a political sense. His claim for the Council leadership had gone unchallenged for centuries. Though Marek had shown powers that outshone Julius manifold. Was that his reason for disliking the Soul Eater so much?

He returned her nod and beckoned her to come closer.

"It'll all be over soon. Before long, Marek will no longer be able to threaten our way of life."

Lucille scrutinized the smug grin on Julius' face. He was definitely hiding something.

"Have you come across him before?" she asked.

Julius glanced at her, his face suddenly serious again. "We've known of the Soul Eaters that live outside the Council's realm of influence for centuries. You know this. Never before have they ventured into London, though."

None who were this evolved, no. Though Lucille had dealt with plenty of killers before.

That hadn't answered her question, but Lucille decided not to pry. Due to their history, Julius had a soft spot for her, but it would be unwise to exploit their relationship just to get answers out of him. Perhaps she was just being nosy. What business was it of hers whether or not Julius knew the Soul Eater from another time?

"I will call in the elders," Lucille said. "Once everyone is here we can begin."

Julius shot her a quick smile and rubbed his hands

together. "Very good, my child."

Lucille left the main hall and rounded up the other six members of the Council. Although she was already four centuries old, the elders, as the term suggested, were all much more senior. At least a millennium old, each one of them. Together, they represented the far corners of the world, both ancient and modern. As the six venerable vampires entered the great hall, Lucille found herself captivated by their movements. Some seemed to levitate rather than walk, but each demonstrated a smoothness and elegance of movement that Lucille herself could not replicate if she wanted to.

Vampires, those that had the capacity to outlast the age they were born in, got better and more impressive with age.

They sat on the six chairs arranged in a semi-circle around Julius' throne. Three to his left and three to his right. There were further chairs inside the main hall facing the throne for any other vampires who wished to observe the trial. The center of the hall had been kept free for the accused.

Lucille signaled at Dominic and Cameron, the two guards stationed beside the large entrance doors, to let the audience in.

Whispers and footsteps echoed against the tall ceiling of the cathedral as about three dozen vampires shuffled inside and found their seats. Then, Julius raised his right hand and the crowd became silent.

"We are gathered here for the trial of Marek the Soul Eater and his two progenies, who shall remain unnamed," Julius spoke in a firm voice.

A whisper traveled across the audience once again.

"So it's true."

"A Soul Eater!"

"I can't believe it!"

Lucille rolled her eyes. The sort of vampires who frequented Council trials were not her usual choice of company. Then again, not many people were.

Julius cleared his throat and silence prevailed once more. "Bring in the prisoners!"

Lucille watched as the double doors swung open and two more Council guards rolled in a cage on wheels that gleamed under the chandelier in the center of the hall. The Silver Vault, as it was known, was only used during trials of the most notorious, dangerous criminals. Obviously, Marek posed a flight risk; his powers were greater than those of anyone in this room. Perhaps he was even stronger than Julius himself.

Marek's two associates were led in wearing cuffs right behind the cage.

The audience was deadly silent as the three accused were positioned in the empty space between the council members and the rest of the crowd.

Julius cleared his throat again and got up from his throne.

"Marek. You know why you are here. You are to stand

trial—"

Marek shook his head. "Julius, please refer to me by my full title."

Lucille frowned. Julius and Marck did seem awfully familiar, the way they spoke to one another.

Julius' eyes narrowed. "Very well. Marek, son of Lilith. You are on trial for—"

Lilith. Only the most ancient of vampires held the title son or daughter of Lilith. Julius held this title himself. That meant Marek was an ancient? A contender for a seat on the Council?

"The rest also, if you don't mind. I've worked too hard these past millennia for my achievements to go unnoticed."

Lucille found that she was holding her breath. Marek had guts to interrupt Julius twice in front of an entire room full of his subjects. Then again, he probably knew as well as any of them that his life would soon be over, so he had nothing much to lose.

"Son of Lilith, Master of a Thousand Souls." Julius folded his arms and stared darkly at Marek. How long would his patience last?

"Thank you." Marek grinned, showing off a row of razor sharp white teeth.

During the brief contact Lucille had had with Marek, he had not struck her as one of those vampires who grew weary of immortality and longed for it all to end. Yet here he was, taunting Julius and grinning like a madman on what could very well be his last day walking this earth. It wasn't just unusual, it was unnerving.

Julius ignored Marek's remark and started listing his offenses, during which Marek seemed to grow even more cheerful. He was obviously proud of everything he'd done.

Lucille found herself tuning out Julius' monotone voice. It was all stuff she'd heard before. Killing humans, leaving their bodies, risking their exposure, blah, blah.

Instead of listening to him rehashing the same old accusations, she took the time to really observe Marek. His strange appearance had fascinated her from the moment she'd first laid eyes on him.

Vampires didn't age normally, but in the case of Marek, he seemed marked by every century he'd lived through. The casual observer might mistake his transparent skin, his slender body, and papery voice for signs of frailty. Lucille knew otherwise. It had taken a dozen guards to subdue Marek and restrain him for transport back to the Council prison.

The two younger Soul Eaters who stood toward his left now looked much more powerful, but actually did not even possess half of Marek's strength. Lucille found it difficult to control her curiosity. She knew of vampires who'd killed humans; she had locked up many of them over the years. But these three were different. They didn't just kill, they had figured out a way of absorbing a victim's essence—their strength and life-force. Not just their blood.

Was it magic?

She could not make sense of it on her own, and seeing as Julius seemed in no mood to share whatever information or previous knowledge of Marek he had... She would talk to Alexander about it as soon as the trial was over. Perhaps her brother and his vast library of old books could shed some light.

Lucille rested her gaze on the younger Soul Eater who stood nearest to the Silver Vault. He seemed unafraid, like his maker, smiling subtly and staring at nothing in particular, until suddenly he looked up right into Lucille's eyes.

A shiver travelled down her spine, but she did not let it show.

If you want to live, you'll stand down.

So he was a telepath, and a rather talented one too, if he could communicate with her halfway across the large hall.

Lucille did not take kindly to threats. Her hand instinctively reached for the dagger she kept in a sheath attached to her belt. She snapped open the clasp that held the blade in place and tightened her fingers around the grip.

She looked back at Marek, who had started to laugh. A quick glance at Julius revealed that he was starting to lose his cool. He spoke faster now, lecturing the three accused on the codes of conduct the Council lived by and promoted. His eyes were wild, his expression even tenser than before.

Lucille looked back at Marek, who had now reached for the bars on his cage, tightening his long, bony fingers around them. The scent of burning flesh filled the air as his skin reacted to the metal. An ordinary vampire would not be able to bear it, but Marek showed no sign of being in pain. Instead of letting go, he held on tighter, tugging at it until the bars started to give way.

Lucille jumped forward, her dagger drawn, and was instantly joined by the guards who had been positioned at the doors. The crowd gasped in horror as Marek's form became blurred, his body twisting and whirling around so fast that even Lucille's perfect vision could no longer focus on him. His laughter echoed through the Council chamber, growing louder and louder until it became deafening.

She reached the cage, but Marek was no longer inside. Instead, he seemed to be levitating far above the ground, still turning at lightning speed, like a whirlwind. Now what? She didn't have his talents or his powers; she could do nothing but watch.

Lucille turned and saw that Julius was frozen in place in front of his throne, his fist raised in the air in protest, lips opening and closing, without any sound coming out.

She had never seen him stumped like this.

At that moment, the stained glass of the large rosette shaped window above Julius' throne shattered as Marek's floating form surged against it and broke through. He was gone within the blink of an eye.

"Go after him," Julius hissed, before repeating himself much louder and forcefully. "Go after him at once!"

Lucille turned and found that Julius had moved from his throne. He now stood just a few feet away from her near the Silver Vault, with Marek's two followers slumped in pools of blood at his feet. After the initial shock of Marek's grand display, Julius had recovered and taken swift action and punished them with death. Their still twitching hearts lay on the ground beside their lifeless bodies.

"Yes, master," Lucille mumbled. It had been extremely difficult capturing Marek the first time around. This time, she would need a miracle.

CHAPTER ONE

Valentino Conti dealt in death.

He knew it, and those unfortunate creatures he was after found out soon enough.

But for the past month and a half, he had been tracking something else, something much more depraved than everything he'd already seen in his illustrious career. Something that managed to send shivers down even his spine.

That was why he was here tonight, on this cold, dark January night. He navigated the corridors deep inside Waterloo train station leading to the video surveillance control room, which was normally off limits to outsiders. It was through sheer tenacity, as well as a heavy dose of Mediterranean charm and a significant sum of money, that he had found a way in with one of the camera operators.

He waited at the agreed spot and checked his watch. The woman better be on time. If this lead panned out, it would be by far his most important achievement yet.

Valentino's hunt had started, like so many other quests, with a short anonymous message on an online forum about the supernatural. To the casual observer, these websites looked like the paranoid ravings of horror movie obsessed teenagers, but Valentino and those in his line of work knew better.

Someone had spotted a creature in London that was so bizarre the mere description of it had inspired Valentino to get on a plane and investigate it himself.

Years spent as a hunter had taught him not to be too presumptuous. Nightwalkers—or vampires, as they were known in the common tongue—came in all manner of forms. Some seemed almost normal—human, like himself. Others were obviously otherworldly.

Either way, the description he read had reminded him of old stories his grandfather had told him when he was just a little boy, of a Nightwalker so powerful and evil, he even inspired terror in his peers.

Upon arriving in London, he had heard of a string of deaths attributed to a new serial killer. It hadn't been too difficult to come by autopsy photos of the victims; such items had a way of leaking to the press or even private collectors.

Despite how the authorities and the media had spun it, Valentino was certain the deaths were the result of vampire activity. But since the crime scenes had not been discovered yet, he couldn't prove any of his suspicions.

Footsteps approached, and soon, the skittish looking woman in uniform came into view. She checked that she wasn't being followed, then nodded at Valentino to join her in one of the corridors leading off to the right. It was obvious from her entire demeanor that she had never done anything like this before. She was scared.

"There's no cameras in here," she whispered.

Lucille's Valentine

"You've got the footage?" he asked.

She glanced over her shoulder again, then retrieved a folded printout from her pocket. "They've installed some new security features. I couldn't risk it with the pen drive. But I did manage to print off a still," she said, thrusting the paper into Valentino's hand.

It was disappointing not to get the original video, but a still was better than nothing. He nodded at her and handed her a sealed envelope.

"It's all there," he said.

"Thanks. I really must be off now." She turned on her heel, ready to leave, then paused. "The image, it's a little blurry, but it's the best I could find. Some kind of camera glitch, perhaps. The man you're after, he looks a bit distorted. Hopefully it's good enough."

It was too late to change his mind. He'd already handed her the rest of the payment, and he was a man of his word. Whatever was on that printout, it would have to do.

"No problem, darling. If you find anything else, do get in touch." He shot her a quick smile.

The woman gave him a brief nod, then made a quick exit. It was unlikely he'd hear from her again.

Valentino waited until she was out of sight before unfolding the piece of paper she'd given him. The sight of it took his breath away.

So this was who—or rather, what—he was hunting.

The figure was humanoid in form, if you ignored the spindly arms and legs. Its robes seemed to cling to it in a strange fashion as well, almost giving the appearance of black clouds or shadows. If you looked carefully, it seemed to be floating; its feet didn't appear to touch the ground.

Of course his insider had felt it was some kind of optical illusion, a malfunction in the camera equipment that had made the footage look so creepy. People outside his circles often preferred to remain in denial; he'd learned that the hard way a long time ago.

She had no idea what he was hunting and that was just as well.

Valentino knew better than to presume the same, though. The anonymous tipster whose forum post had brought him to London had been correct; this was a very peculiar creature indeed. And the image he saw in front of him bore an uncanny resemblance to the sketches his grandfather had shown him when he was just a boy. At the time he'd thought the old man was exaggerating; now he knew better.

How many monsters this vile could possibly walk the earth unnoticed? Valentino was certain it could not be a coincidence. It *had* to be the same one.

Valentino instinctively grabbed for the silver chain around his neck. The pendant hanging from it was the medal of St. Benedict, which had been in his family pretty much forever. He wasn't particularly religious, or even superstitious, so he wore the medal to remind him of his family's legacy rather than for its supposed powers for warding off evil spirits.

He would complete this mission for his late grandfather.

He studied the blurry surveillance photograph in front of him again.

This right here demonstrated the difference between hunting a creature in London, versus any other city he'd traveled to in the past: there were cameras everywhere. Of course, those people manning the cameras were a lot stricter about rules and regulations, but at the right price, one could procure anything.

His wallet was lighter tonight, but the price had been worth it.

A month of aimless canvassing had made him precious little progress, until tonight. In fact, he'd been close to giving up before the woman who worked in the control room had agreed to help. Now, Valentino felt revitalized.

He slipped the photograph into the inner pocket of his coat and zipped up tight. It was cold out there and he had a long night ahead of him. Tonight, he would start with the area around that particular surveillance camera. The time stamp on the image placed the creature in a back alley near Waterloo five whole nights ago.

Who knew, perhaps it had left some clues behind.

So that was his first destination. He made his way through the large station and exited.

As he progressed through the dark, wet streets, he felt the burden of this quest weigh heavily on him. His grandfather had not succeeded in catching this creature when he'd first come across it during the First World War. It had escaped and terrorized many a city and village since, and the resulting guilt had been difficult for him to live with.

Valentino was determined to succeed. If not for himself, then to honor his grandfather's memory. As it was, since the death of his father two years ago, Valentino was the last of the Conti clan still standing. A lot rested on him. Where even just a century ago, there had been multiple prominent hunter families in Italy alone, the Contis had been the last to endure. The modern world seemed to not have much room for his kind.

Meanwhile, the other side, the Nightwalker side, seemed to flourish in some parts. There had been a resurgence in vampire activity in Eastern Europe, even though the authorities had often explained any suspicious events away as cult activity. It was as though the Nightwalkers had become bolder and bolder over time. Perhaps they thought they were invincible, because there were not many able or willing to stop them.

He had to do his part to make a difference.

It was these and many more similar thoughts that occupied him as he reached the service lane beside the station where the creature had been captured on camera.

Valentino opened the leather messenger bag he always carried with him and retrieved a bottle of Luminol. Where there was a vampire, there was bound to be trace evidence of blood. He took a look around and identified a couple of dark corners ideal for the creature to attack and drain someone. One in particular, a grouping of garbage bins underneath a broken streetlights, seemed most likely. He sprayed the area surrounding the bins and inspected it for any fluorescent stains. Sure enough, there was some blood present, though not a lot. Just a fine spray pattern on the side of one of the containers. This was the kind of evidence one might find where a vampire had fed; puncturing a man's jugular to feed could result in a bit of spill-over.

But considering the area, the blood in itself was hardly definitive; the blood stains could have been the result of a human altercation, such as someone being struck hard enough to rupture skin. A big city like London had its ugly parts even without any supernatural influences.

Valentino put the spray away and took out a specially modified ultraviolet torch. Human saliva and other bodily fluids lit up under so-called black light, but their luminescence was dull compared to traces of vampire saliva.

Besides the blood splatter Valentino had just identified, there was a smear of something that glowed bright purple under his UV light. That was it. Conclusive evidence.

He took a sample, which he carefully sealed in a plastic pouch. One for the collection. Sometimes he wondered if he was wasting his time collecting samples and cataloging them in detail. He had prepared a file on each Nightwalker he had ever hunted; who knew, maybe one day all this stuff would come in handy.

Once he had labeled the sample and put it away, he took out a small, leather bound notebook and started to write. *Feeding site, alley near Waterloo station, date of attack: 3rd Jan.*

Where to next? Valentino looked around and spied an unassuming pub at the end of the road. Perhaps someone there remembered seeing something suspicious on that night, five days ago. Any establishment in a location like this would serve mostly travelers passing through. Still, the staff might have something to share.

Of course, he would be careful and only ask innocuous questions. The last time he had tried to be candid with someone who wasn't part of his world had backfired painfully.

Valentino was on his own. He could not count on anyone to help him defeat this monster.

He put the notebook away, securely buckled up the front of the bag, and resolutely marched in the direction of the lit up sign. As glamorous as it had seemed to him when he was younger, being a vampire hunter was mostly legwork and traditional detective work, only without the benefit of holding an official badge.

CHAPTER TWO

Lucille had followed the stranger from the alley, which still stank of the Soul Eater Marek, into a down-market pub at the end of the road. She had watched from a quiet, dark corner while he had spoken to the cranky bartender, who seemed unwilling to answer any of the questions with more than two syllables, and the young woman who worked the tap. It was obvious from the increasingly strained and tense body language of everyone involved that the stranger had not been able to get the information he was after.

Who was he?

His accent was unmistakably Italian, even if his English was very close to perfect. So perhaps he wasn't from here. In a cosmopolitan city such as London, that did not narrow things down.

Lucille had watched him earlier out on the road as he had scraped off some sort of substance from the side of a garbage container and put it in a bag. Now, realizing that the staff was no longer open to conversing with him, he sat down at an empty table with a pint and started scribbling away in that little notebook of his.

She would have to do a walk by and read his notes over his shoulder at some point. It could, of course, be a coincidence that during the same week as Marek's daring escape from the Council chambers, some stranger had come along and started nosing around the exact place Lucille had come to investigate. If only Lucille believed in coincidences.

No, this man, with his strange equipment and affinity for sniffing out dark blood-stained corners, was definitely after the same thing as she was. He smelled human, so he wasn't back-up sent in by one of the other Council elders. That left only one possibility: he was a hunter.

Lucille had heard of vampire hunters active mostly in Eastern Europe, where she presumed Marek had traveled in from last month. They hardly ever came to London; why would they? The Council, and Lucille as their Enforcer, worked hard to keep vampire activity under wraps here.

But now, it seemed Marek's presence had attracted at least one of them.

The Council generally forbade the killing of humans, but if he got in her way, she might not have any other choice.

Lucille continued to watch as the man put down his pen and stared at the bar. If she wanted to sneak a peek at his notes, she had to hurry before he put them away.

She got up, empty glass in hand, and walked slowly and deliberately through the few tables that separated her dark corner from the vampire hunter's position. It took barely a second for her to read the page of notes. Funnily, they were in English, not Italian, as she would have expected, considering his accent. This truly was the age of globalization.

There wasn't a lot in there that Lucille didn't already know. He'd found a feeding site, obviously; that was why he had taken a sample. But the thing that surprised her was that the man had written down the date on which he thought Marek had been there. How could he possibly know that? *She* hadn't known that.

All she had been able to do was narrow down the time of the attack to 3-6 days ago. That was what her nose had told her, anyway, based on the deterioration of the blood stains Marek had left behind. Her estimation was as accurate as a human's might be, trying to decide the age of stale milk left out in warm weather. What methods did this hunter use that she was as yet unaware of?

She caught herself staring at the man's back and was forced back into action when she heard his heartbeat speed up just a little. He had sensed her presence.

Just as he turned his head to see who was looking at him, she had passed him by and reached the bar.

"Another, please." Lucille pointed at her empty glass, then at the bottle of her choice that stood on the shelf opposite her.

She wasn't much of a drinker, unlike her brother Alexander, who enjoyed his glass of brandy every night as though it was a sacred ritual. She didn't even like the taste of most drinks, certainly not those many women in this age seemed to favor. Everything was too sweet, too sickly.

The bartender glanced at her with a hint of bemusement in his eye as he poured her another Laphroaig single malt. Obviously, he thought it was an unusual choice for someone who looked like her. Then again, he had no way of knowing he was serving a nearly four-hundred year old vampire instead of the twenty-three year old young woman whose body she occupied.

She put the money on the bar without saying a word and was about to turn when she spied movement in a reflection on the bottles behind the bar.

"I'll have whatever she's having," the hunter said in his smooth Italian accent.

Lucille had learned how to blend into human society a long time ago. There was no way for him to know who—or what—she really was. She was just an attractive woman drinking alone in a dodgy bar near Waterloo. And despite his unusual and lethal calling, he was still a man. Her best option would be to play along.

"Suit yourself, but it's an acquired taste," she said, smiling subtly.

He was a fine specimen, this hunter. A chiseled jaw, full, sensual lips, and sun-kissed skin. She might have had a taste, if he was just a regular guy and not her sworn enemy.

But when she looked up into his eyes, something she saw in them tugged at her, constricting her chest and making her take a step back. *It can't be. It's been centuries.*

"It's best not to make assumptions about a man's taste," he said, letting his gaze rest on her lips.

Seriously. This guy was hunting the most dangerous vampire Lucille had ever come across in her four-hundred years of walking this earth and he thought it wise to flirt with her right now? They were on opposing sides, but she was outraged all the same. Did he not take his work seriously at all?

Lucille avoided eye contact and shrugged. "That goes for women's tastes too."

The bartender poured the hunter's drink but kept quiet otherwise. His disapproval of the hunter was obvious, though; he was probably still irritated by his nosy interrogation earlier.

"Salute! How do you say…" He raised his glass in Lucille's direction.

Again, best to just play the part. "Cheers!" she said.

"Ah yes, cheers."

They both took a sip, which Lucille savored. Peaty. Just like it said on the label.

"Wow, this sure is something else," the hunter remarked. He sniffed the glass, then swirled the remaining dark amber liquid around in it.

"Told you." Lucille straightened herself. What was she doing? The look in his eyes made her feel uncomfortable, almost threatened. Perhaps she should let him know she wasn't interested and get on with her work.

"I like it, though." The hunter smiled and stuck out his right hand. "Valentino Conti. Pleasure to meet you."

His name rang a bell, like she'd heard it before. Lucille

reluctantly accepted his greeting. His skin burned against hers almost painfully. So warm. So alive. It occurred to her that in trying to hunt down Marek, it had been a while since she'd last fed.

"Lucille Amboise. I really should be off, though," she said.

Valentino raised an eyebrow. "But you've only just bought a drink. And your hand was so cold I'd worry about you freezing to death out there."

Lucille stared down at her glass. An excellent point about the drink. She should just hypnotize him. Get it over with. But what if he had some kind of technology to counter it? She would give herself away.

"You're absolutely right, of course. I suppose I'm just nervous," she said. It was only a half-lie. There was something about him that had made her uneasy, and it hadn't been the fact that he would try to kill her if he knew what she was. It was those eyes, those warm, infuriatingly friendly eyes that sought to bore a hole in her soul.

The eyes that seemed to belong to someone who died a very long time ago.

"Aw, I did not mean to make you nervous. Why don't we have a seat and chat," he suggested with a smile.

Lucille looked at the table he was gesturing at, the one he'd sat at while she was spying on him, and shrugged. "I suppose I can stay a little while longer."

Perhaps if she got him talking, she could figure out more about what he was doing here and what else he had found out. She wasn't the sort to lose her nerve easily. How hard could it be to practice her poker face for little while longer and see what she could learn?

"Are you a regular here?" Valentino asked as he pushed her chair in for her.

Lucille looked up and cocked her head to the side. "Are you asking me if I 'come here often?'" she teased.

The man laughed. "I see, that came out wrong. The truth is I'm looking for a man who might have been in the area a few days ago."

Lucille pressed her lips together. He had a strange technique. Going from flirting with her to questioning her about Marek in just a short exchange.

"On the third, to be precise."

"Friend of yours? The man you're looking for, I mean." Now it was her turn to start interrogating.

Valentino smiled and shook his head. "Not exactly."

"Well I'm just not entirely sure why I should help you. I know nothing about your motivations. What if you wish to harm this man?" Lucille argued and took another sip.

The hunter observed her, then followed her example, putting his glass down on the wooden table when he was done.

"Let me ask you something: Do you believe in destiny? That perhaps we were meant to meet here tonight because you could help me find what I'm looking for?"

Lucille frowned. She couldn't make out if he was still prying for information or flirting again. Very strange technique indeed.

"Not everything can be explained by science," she responded.

Valentino nodded. "Indeed. Well, perhaps not yet. Anyway, this man I'm looking for is dangerous. I'm just trying to keep people from harm."

Okay, so it was still an interrogation.

"You're trying to save the world, is that it?" she said.

He laughed again. Lucille folded her arms. She hadn't even tried to be funny. Jokes were not her forte.

"I suppose you could put it that way. You don't believe me, do you?"

Lucille shrugged. "Whatever helps you sleep at night."

Valentino pulled out the leather notebook from his messenger bag and placed it on the table in front of them. Then he flipped to a different page than Lucille had seen when she read over his shoulder earlier.

"I believe a murder has been committed just down the street from here. And the man I'm looking for did it."

He held up the book, showing her a pencil sketch of a group of garbage bins, the ones where he'd taken his samples earlier. Off to the side of the bins stood two dark figures; one had the other by the throat. Blood splatters were scribbled on in red ink.

"How do you know this?" Lucille asked. "Are you with the police?"

Valentino shook his head. "The evidence is right there for anyone to find."

Lucille picked up her glass and emptied it. "Well, why don't you show me?"

The hunter stared at her face while she did her best not to look into his eyes again. "Has anyone ever told you you're quite unusual? One moment you want to leave, the next you want to go look around a dark alley for clues with me?"

"I read a lot of detective novels. Perhaps I want to see a real one in action," she said.

He smiled again and nodded. "Why not. But on one condition."

"What's that?" Lucille asked.

"You let me buy you another drink when we're done. It really is cold outside."

CHAPTER THREE

Valentino stole a glance at Lucille as they left the pub together. What a peculiar young woman. Everything about her, from the way she carried herself to her choice of Scotch signaled that she was an old soul. The fact that she had joined him out here meant that apparently she was fearless as well.

Was she part of the same underground he belonged to? The online message boards, the discussion groups that met virtually to discuss any supernatural activity they had come across. It had been one of those anonymous reports of vampirism that had brought him to London in the first place. Was she active in those circles? Or was her presence here a coincidence?

Her catlike movements as she walked alongside him toward the feeding site suggested she was strong and well trained. She definitely knew how to fight.

He wouldn't be surprised if she had some hidden weapons somewhere underneath her long coat. He had some too, after all.

When they reached the bin he had inspected on his own earlier, he pulled out the bottle of Luminol again and sprayed the area where he knew the blood to be.

She leaned in closer and followed the direction of the spray pattern with her index finger.

"Interesting."

Valentino smiled. "As I said, the evidence is right here."

Lucille stood back and stared at the ground surrounding the area. "It wasn't much of a struggle, so perhaps the victim came here willingly."

Valentino raised an eyebrow. "How do you know this?"

Lucille pointed at a very faint muddy footprint which the winter rains had done their best to erase. "If two men had fought here, they would have knocked over some of these bags of rubbish. They would have left smudged prints and scuff marks from their shoes. I don't see any of that here."

She turned to face him, her eyes narrow and darting back and forth between him and their surroundings. "Do you think the murderer might have arrived here by train? Or is he a local?"

"I think he is not the sort of man who could travel by train without drawing too much attention to himself. He is the sort who stays in the shadows."

Lucille nodded, as though she understood him perfectly, even those things he'd left unsaid. She really was peculiar, unlike any woman he'd met before.

Could he risk it?

It had been a long time since he'd ever told an outsider about his calling, and that had backfired spectacularly. Suddenly years of history didn't matter anymore, and the woman he'd opened up to because he wanted to spend his life with her had simply left.

But this right here was different; there was no history. What did he have to lose?

"There are more things between heaven and earth than most people choose to see or believe…"

Lucille folded her arms as she focused on him. He had her full attention.

"This murderer is not strictly a *man*," Valentino added.

"Why. Is it a woman?" she asked, cocking her head to the side.

The peculiar glint in her eye told him that he was on the right track. She was testing him; Valentino would bet his life on it.

"He's a Nightwalker. A vampire."

Lucille pursed her lips and glanced at the bin with the blood evidence on it, then back at him. The corner of her mouth twitched in amusement; it was so subtle he would have missed it if he wasn't paying attention.

"You're a hunter," she remarked, as though it was the most natural thing in the world.

He nodded. She knew the terminology. Unless she was the best actress he'd ever come across, nothing he'd told her so far had shocked her in any way.

"You have unusual methods. More like a forensic investigator than a hunter," she added.

He nodded again. "And your methods? Old school. More like a tracker."

Lucille smiled briefly. "I favor a more intuitive approach."

"Have you been at this long?" he asked. He was thirty-four, not old by any stretch of the imagination, but Lucille looked about ten years younger—exceptionally young for someone in their line of work. Perhaps it was a family affair for her, just like it had been for him.

"My entire life," she said.

Fine, so she wanted to keep things vague. He didn't mind. Their line of work was lonely and unappreciated for the most part. To run into another hunter was its own reward. He didn't need anything more than that for now.

"How about you make good on that promise then?" she said. "Of buying me another drink."

Valentino grinned. If she didn't look so serious he might have thought she was flirting with him.

They walked back together, and he again marveled at her smooth, deliberate movements, the strong spring in her step. It was a lonely existence; living on the fringes of society, hunting creatures that most people only acknowledged in their nightmares.

The times had changed since his parents and grandparents had been around. Mainstream society no longer believed in the supernatural, as he had so painfully found out in the past. Continuing in their footsteps had earned him a solitary life. It would be a nice change of pace to combine forces with a like-minded soul.

Plus, Lucille was an exceptionally beautiful woman. He would be lying to himself if he thought that she hadn't affected him on some deeper level. But he'd been at this too long to simply take other people at face value. He still needed to find out if he could trust Lucille.

"Right. Let's get that drink then," he said.

The conversation between them had flowed more freely from the second round on.

Now that Valentino was back at the guest house which had been his home for the past few weeks, he went through the events of the evening again in his head.

As he lay down on the bed, closing his eyes for a moment, he felt his body grow heavy. If he wasn't careful, sleep would claim him before he had the chance to finish analyzing his encounter with Lucille. He wasn't a big drinker, but in her company, he had indulged a little. The effects were only starting to wear off now, hours later.

Had he let his guard down too much?

She had been vague about her background, about how she'd found her start in hunting Nightwalkers. Instead, she'd mainly been a very good and supportive listener. And perhaps he'd ended up sharing more information with her than he should have.

It had been hard not to. Everything about her seemed especially designed to invite him in, to make him feel comfortable being his true self. Even the fact that on the surface, she seemed curt and difficult to impress. The challenge of getting closer to her had been irresistible.

The only things she'd shared were the odd hint or

remark suggesting she knew more about this vampire than she had initially let on. She'd spoken about how this monster was different from other vampires. More powerful. More devious. Above all, more dangerous.

Valentino already knew all that, but it was interesting to hear her say it. And it sparked the question: what made this vampire so fundamentally different? Was it age or something else? He was determined to get to the bottom of it, and despite some lingering reservations about his hunting partner, Valentino was certain she was the key to finding out.

They would hunt this monster together, and in the process, he hoped to find out everything there was to know about Lucille too.

———•———

She stepped out of the fog and offered him her hand. She looked different; rather than the tight black jeans and long leather coat she had been wearing earlier that evening, she was all dressed up now.

Her long gown and pinned up hair reminded her of women depicted in the works of art by Renaissance masters that Italy was so famous for. He had visited many such places with his mother when he was only a boy.

His father had taught him how to fight; his mother had taught him what to fight for.

Even the large empty room they found themselves in reminded of days past. Shiny inlaid marble flooring; dark polished wooden paneling along the walls.

He craved her attention, for those amber eyes of hers to rest on his and let him in.

He accepted her gesture, took her hand, and let his fingers thread through hers. She was cold, so much so it sent a shiver down his own spine.

But he did not let that discourage him. He wrapped his other arm around her shoulder, drawing her in closer until their faces were only a fraction of an inch apart.

He felt her breath tickling his skin. Her lips were so close to his he could almost taste them.

Her eyes shimmered under the crystal chandelier that hung overhead as she looked at him. It wasn't a casual glance; it felt as though they were truly connecting. As though she really saw him for everything he was.

That was when it all changed. Her whole demeanor had taken a U-turn. From confident and stoic, she was now showing vulnerability.

Suddenly she seemed intent on dodging his gaze as much as she had dodged his questions back at the pub.

Lucille was not an easy person to get to know, that much was obvious. She had baggage as well as barriers around her. The walls she had constructed around herself seemed awfully tough to penetrate for someone so young.

What had happened to her to make her this way?

Valentino wanted desperately to find out. He wanted to reach out to her and tell her everything would be all right. That together they could conquer whatever demons lurked in her past and move into a bright future together.

"You should keep your distance," she said, averting her gaze toward the floor.

"I've never been good at doing what I'm supposed to." Valentino smiled and tried to take her hand, only to have her snatch it away. Whatever moment they had shared just now, it was long gone.

Something had changed. As though in that brief second when she had allowed herself to be vulnerable, she had seen something in him that had scared her away.

"The Soul Eater might kill you. I won't able to forgive myself," she whispered.

"He might kill you too. We're in this together," Valentino said.

She shrugged. "I've lived a long life, it's not the same thing. Plus, it's my duty to go after him."

That remark gave Valentino pause. A long life? The girl looked to be in her twenties, younger than he was. What on earth was she talking about?

"It's my duty too. We're both hunters. He is merely our next prey," Valentino argued.

She shook her head. "It's not the same. It's not a fair fight."

He took a step in her direction and reached for her arm again, but was unable to get a hold of her. It was like she had turned to dust at his touch, only to materialize again just out of reach.

"What are you not telling me?" he asked. "I need to

know."

Lucille looked down at her hand. She was holding a dagger; its intricately decorated blade shimmered in the light. Then she looked up at Valentino again.

"There are things between heaven and earth that cannot be explained." She swiftly ran the pointy end of it across her other palm, leaving a trail of blood across her ivory skin.

He was about to shout out in protest, to grab her hand and take the weapon from her before she did anything more drastic, when he looked down and saw that her wound was gone. The dagger, too, had vanished, as though it had never even been there.

"I'm dreaming," Valentino concluded. "This isn't real."

Lucille smiled bleakly. "Just because you're dreaming doesn't mean I'm not telling the truth. If you stay and hunt this vampire with me, you will die."

Valentino paused, remembering the odd phrase she had used earlier. "What's a soul eater?"

Lucille shook her head. "Not everything can be explained. You should go, be safe, live your life."

"And what will you do?" Valentino asked.

"I will do my duty. I will kill him."

CHAPTER FOUR

Lucille paced back and forth outside the Council chambers. Julius had insisted on regular updates, which was fine and well, but that meant she would be forced to come clean about Valentino.

She was secretive by nature and did not easily share her thoughts before she was absolutely certain about them. Inconveniently, she was not yet certain about Valentino Conti.

"Something troubling you?" Dominic, who guarded the door, asked.

She pressed her lips together. Again, opening up in front of other people did not come naturally to her. And least of all with Dominic.

He'd been a guard for the Council since before Julius had appointed her Enforcer. That was over a hundred years ago now.

Unfortunately for him, he wasn't the sharpest pencil in the box. His century or more of loyal service at the Council chamber's doors had earned him no promotion, no progression at all. The only thing he had consistently done that went beyond his duties was try to flirt with Lucille.

She faced him. "Just the entire situation with Marek." This was only partially true. As much as she had been obsessing about finding Marek, she could not get Valentino out of her head either. He had not left her alone, even in her dreams.

Dominic nodded. "That was quite something, wasn't it? How he escaped. Nobody ever saw it coming."

His broad face and build gave away his Slavic heritage, even if his accent was perfectly local. The vampire society in London mirrored humanity perfectly. Sometimes it seemed that half of the people here, Lucille included, were from somewhere else.

Lucille considered his words. Nobody had seen Marek's escape coming. Why not? It was the first time Lucille had come across a Soul Eater of this caliber. She'd been unable to predict that he could break out of the Silver Vault.

"Yes. But why?" she mumbled.

"Why what?" Dominic asked.

Lucille ignored him.

What about the others? The ancients who sat on the Council, including Julius. Had they not known about Marek's immense power? It was a little hard to believe that a vampire like Marek could exist in this world without even one of the elders knowing about it.

That led her thoughts back to the day of the trial itself. She had been so certain that Julius was hiding something. That he and Marek shared some kind of history.

"You shouldn't take it so hard, you know," Dominic said. He reached out for her and tried resting his hand on Lucille's shoulder.

Lucille's Valentine

She took a step back and dodged him. Physical contact was highly overrated.

"It's my job to bring him back. I don't have any other choice," Lucille said.

"You don't have to do it on your own, though," Dominic remarked.

Lucille smiled briefly. No, she didn't. Although she wasn't normally a team player, she would have to take all the help she could get. And while her mind was full of doubts and suspicions about why none of the elders had known about the full extent of Marek's powers, who better to help her than someone who had no affiliation with the Council. Who better than a complete outsider.

Valentino Conti.

The only thing left to do was to convince Julius of her plan.

"You did what?" Julius bellowed. His loud voice echoed against the cathedral walls, filling every nook and cranny of the space with his outrage. "Why on earth would you share Council secrets with the enemy?"

Lucille stood her ground. She was used to her maker's occasional outbursts. Plus, she was now convinced she had made the right choice. At least for the time being, until she knew who she could trust inside the Council.

"He has no idea who I am. And his methods really are quite revolutionary. I truly believe that together we will be able to track down Marek before he causes more trouble, or even before he flees the city and we may never find him again."

"He's a human, how talented could he possibly be?" Julius scoffed.

"He has scientific methods and equipment I have never come across," Lucille explained.

"And what if he turns his methods and equipment on you and finds out the truth?"

"You overestimate humans, master. They very rarely notice that which they do not want to see. He wants to see me as his peer. To believe that he is not alone in his world. I'm just showing him what he wants."

"You are exposing our secrets, that's what you're doing," Julius grumbled

"I'm not telling him anything he does not already know. He is a hunter after all, a descendent of a long line of hunters. You will have heard of the Conti clan?" Lucille asked.

Julius squinted at her. "The Contis have caused us a lot of trouble over the centuries. Many friends have fallen at their hands."

"Well, he's the last one left. Please trust my judgment and let me utilize his skills."

Although Julius had stopped raging, his expression betrayed that he still disapproved of her idea.

"What if he wants to track Marek at daytime, then what will you do?" Julius probed.

Lucille shrugged. "I've thought of that. I told him I have a job so I can only hunt at night."

"And what if you find Marek together, or run into someone else who knows you and you are exposed?"

Lucille pressed her lips together and took a deep breath. "Then I'll wipe his memory. He is still human, after all," she bluffed. She was not as talented at mind control as some of her peers, but perhaps it would be enough to get by if the worst happened. Provided Valentino did not have access to some kind of high tech defense against vampire hypnosis. Special contact lenses, perhaps. She ought to ask him the next time they met.

Julius slowly shook his head, then gestured at her to come closer. She approached him, her head bowed as a sign of respect.

"My child, understand that I don't want to see you harmed. Marek is a formidable enemy, and putting a hunter in the middle of it all… It's rather risky."

He placed his hand on top of her head. His touch gave her goosebumps, and not in a good way. She only allowed it as a sign of respect.

"I will have Dominic follow you so you'll always have backup when you need it."

Lucille frowned and straightened herself. Julius really did seem concerned. Or was he suspicious? It was sometimes hard to tell the difference with him. She nodded. *Fine, send Dominic after me.*

It would be easy to get rid of him, either by

outsmarting him or placating him with the odd smile and compliment. He had been following her around like a lovesick puppy for a century now. She was certain she could control him.

"I best get back to work," Lucille said. "Marek could be out there raising all kinds of hell."

Julius stared at her in silence for a moment, then waved her away. "Be safe, my child."

Lucille nodded.

She stole a glance at the still shattered stained glass rosette Marek had escaped from, then turned on her heel and left before Julius had the chance to change his mind. As she left the double doors, she could hear him bark instructions at Dominic, followed by rushed footsteps.

Dawn was still a couple of hours away, so Lucille decided to do the one thing she had not yet gotten the chance for ever since Marek's daring escape. She would make a social call. Her destination: an opulent yet familiar villa on Kensington Palace Gardens, belonging to her brother, Alexander.

It had been easy to get rid of Dominic, just as Lucille had predicted. As soon as he realized where she was headed, he had become disinterested in following her. When she told him that her hunt for Marek would continue the following night, he had offered to leave her be of his own accord.

So when she marched through the luxurious entrance

hall and reception room, straight to Alexander's favorite place, the library, she was alone.

"Brother," she greeted the man who sat in his usual spot, one of the brown leather arm chairs, sipping brandy from an old snifter.

"Lucille, what a pleasant surprise," he responded.

She ignored the hint of sarcasm in his tone. Their relationship was cordial, but they weren't particularly close.

"Where's Michael?" she asked.

Alexander shrugged and took another sip. "He moved out last week. Wanted to get a place of his own to share with Anna. They've become very close lately."

Lucille nodded slowly. She had never understood the strange dynamic Alexander and Michael shared, living together in the same house for the last couple of decades. If Michael hadn't been such a notorious womanizer before his run-in with Anna, she might have wondered if perhaps there was something more intimate going on between the two men.

Then again, she couldn't imagine sharing her home, her sanctuary, with anybody. Man or woman. She preferred to come home to blissful silence at the end of the night.

"He'd better be careful, with Marek running rampant in the city. He might want to collect on a grudge or two," Lucille remarked.

"He's quite aware of the situation," Alexander said.

Lucille studied her brother's face.

"I was hoping for your help in this matter."

Alexander straightened himself and folded his hands. "I'm unwilling to put Catherine in any more danger, so you can forget about using her blood to bait him again."

Lucille shook her head. "Not like that; I doubt Marek would fall for the same trick twice. I was hoping to gain some insights into the history and nature of these Soul Eaters. Do you have any relevant materials in this great big library of yours?"

Alexander smiled briefly. "I might do, actually. Over there. Second shelf from the top."

He pointed at a row of old, leather bound volumes.

Lucille fetched the exact book he was talking about and started leafing through it.

"Does Julius know you have these?" she asked.

Alexander shrugged. "He's never asked; I've never told."

"You realize your collection is as comprehensive, if not more so, than the Council archives?" Lucille said. Alexander wasn't easily swayed by flattery, except when it came to his collection of rare books and documents. And perhaps the numerous paintings gracing the walls of his home, but Lucille had precious little appreciation for human arts and crafts.

He smiled again. "It's amazing what you can find when you look in places where the Council, led by our dear maker, won't look."

He was referring to human auction houses, of course. That was where he'd obtained most of his earthly possessions.

Lucille sat down in the empty chair beside her brother. "Where *is* Catherine, actually?" she asked. It had been a while since her last meal, so the temptation of being around a real life Blood Bride might be too much to bear. She might be Alexander's consort and hence off limits to any other vampire, but Catherine's blood was so potent it could tempt anyone into breaking the rules.

"She's resting upstairs. It's been a couple of months, but she is still getting used to her new nocturnal routine."

Lucille nodded. That was safe enough.

Alexander put his now empty glass down and got up to join Lucille. Together they leafed through the book which turned out to be a volume of ancient folk tales from Eastern Europe. Lucille was tempted to say something clever and dismissive, but held her tongue when she came across the first illustration. A spindly figure wrapped in a black, almost cloud-like robe, with long, thin fingers, sharp fangs, and blood red eyes. The creature bore an uncanny resemblance to Marek.

"Not just fairy tales in these books," Alexander commented; he must have picked up on her skepticism earlier.

"Apparently not." Lucille sighed and started to read the accompanying fable about a creature that lived deep underground in a network of tunnels of his own construction, terrorizing travelers and local villagers alike.

It was a tragic tale, which suggested that at least one

powerful Soul Eater had been around for centuries—a reference to Marek himself perhaps? Sadly, it was only the villain himself who'd achieved a happily ever after.

"So. Soul Eaters are invincible," Lucille remarked after shutting the old volume.

Alexander shrugged. "When pitched against poor peasants who can't defend themselves, yes, they are."

"But we're not peasants," Lucille mumbled. *And this is the modern world now.*

"It's obvious then that you need a secret weapon to defeat this foe," Alexander said. "One that the people in this book didn't have."

Lucille looked up and found her brother already staring at her intently.

"And *not* my wife, if you don't mind," he added.

"I think I might have something in mind," Lucille said, getting up abruptly. "Thank you, brother. Our little discourse tonight has given me a lot to think about. Do give my best to Michael when you see him."

Alexander stared at her for a few seconds. "Of course. Good night, dear sister."

Lucille nodded and left without a further word. The information gathered from Alexander's collection wasn't much on the surface of it, but tonight had given her some clarity: much like the creature from the folk tale, Marek did favor hiding underground; he'd even done so the last time she'd captured him with Michael's help.

Furthermore, Marek was an ancient being, set in his

ways and unable to fathom just how much human society—and its technology—had evolved over the centuries.

Valentino, with all his fancy gadgets and know-how, was to be her secret weapon.

CHAPTER FIVE

A hearty meal and strong, yet inferior, cup of coffee helped Valentino shake off the sense of unease that had hung over him since waking up. Those strange dreams that had seemingly plagued him all morning had made him restless. By the end of it all, he was no longer certain if he'd even slept at all or if he'd just been caught up in a persistent hallucination.

Perhaps something he ate? Or more likely…

It had to have been the drinks he'd enjoyed the previous night. He was not used to it, and would need to be more cautious from now on. Hunting vampires was tricky at the best of times; he would need his wits about him.

As he found his bearings inside the unassuming little cafe near his guest house where he'd enjoyed his late breakfast, he had the growing sense that once he met Lucille—after they got to work on their common goal of capturing the vampire—things would fall into place. He could not wait to see her again.

He checked his phone. No messages. Of course not, why would she message him in the middle of the day?

Lucille wouldn't get off work until at least five-thirty, giving them all evening and perhaps a fair portion of the night to start their hunt. It was fitting to hunt a

Nightwalker at night, of course; that was when they were active and you were more likely to come across them. But it did make the whole affair more dangerous. One couldn't simply flee into sunlight if things went wrong.

Still, as long as he had Lucille on his side, they were two against one. Those were already better odds than what Valentino's grandfather had faced all those decades ago. Plus, she seemed to know a thing or two about their common enemy, which would definitely come in handy.

He pulled out his notes and laid them out on the table in front of him.

After they had parted ways the previous night, Valentino had scribbled down a few more thoughts, but there were still a lot of gaps that needed to be filled somehow. Knowledge was power, especially when hunting an enemy this dangerous.

Perhaps tonight Lucille would be willing to share more of what she knew. After all, if he had his reservations about her that first night, it was only sensible to assume she felt the same. Trust was a two-way street, and it only grew slowly.

He sat back and thought again about their conversation at the pub. A lot of Valentino's memories were cloudier than he would have wanted them to be. And what about those strange dreams? Perhaps they were a sign that his subconscious was trying to tell him something that he otherwise would have missed.

One phrase stood out from the fog in his brain, one

phrase he had never heard anyone say before. *Soul Eater*.

Valentino opened a blank page in his little notebook and wrote it on the first line.

Then he opened his laptop and started to research. The message boards and websites he and other hunters frequented were part of what was called the *dark web*. Websites that didn't show up on Google and other search engines.

That made them difficult to navigate, unless you knew exactly where to look. There was no mention of that term anywhere he could find. Perhaps his mind had played a little joke on him and he had simply made the phrase up himself. Perhaps it meant nothing at all.

He sat back and ran his hand through his hair while still staring at the screen.

What the hell, why not?

Valentino opened up a new browser window and typed those two little words into Google. Faced with a million or so search results, which seemed to pertain to an anime series by the same title, he closed his laptop again. Clearly this was just a dead end. He would have seen one of these magazines somewhere, and his mind had fed the title back to him in a crazy, alcohol-fueled dream.

There would be no shortcuts during this hunt. He would have to find the monster the old fashioned way. As soon as Lucille got in touch, the search would be on.

"You made it." Valentino got up from his seat to greet Lucille.

Amazing, how she managed to look so put together and alert after a full day at work, despite their escapades the previous night. Youth had its advantages.

"Of course. No rest for the wicked." She smiled briefly. A rare treat, as Valentino had noticed during the short time they'd spent together. Except when relaxing with a glass of scotch, Lucille was obviously a serious and focused individual.

Perhaps she was warming to his company?

"Where do we begin?" she asked.

Valentino shrugged. "I have not yet worked out where the Nightwalker went after he was spotted near Waterloo."

"I'm sure we can put our heads together and come up with something. What above all else does a Nightwalker require?"

Valentino studied Lucille's face. Her skin was radiant, flawless. Her presence brightened up the surroundings of the rundown cafe where he'd spent most of the evening. Even the other customers couldn't help but steal glances in her direction when they thought nobody was looking.

"Shelter?" Valentino said.

"Right. Especially from sunlight. Luckily for the Nightwalker, London has an extensive network of tunnels, many of which are now disused. I wouldn't be surprised if he was utilizing them to get around the city unseen, as well as stay out of the sun," Lucille said. She pulled a couple of folded sheets of paper out of her coat pocket and arranged them on the table.

Valentino leaned forward and studied the faint maze-like drawings on them. Although the paper was new, signaling it was a copy, the markings beside the plans looked so old fashioned, they had probably been drawn up quite a few years ago.

"Nice. Where did you get these?"

Lucille shrugged. "I know someone who knows someone. There are quite a few public records out there if you know where to look."

Valentino smiled. So she wanted to keep the mystery going. Fine.

"Have you ever been down there, in the tunnels, I mean?"

Lucille sat back and folded her perfectly manicured hands. Had those fingernails ever seen dirt? Valentino doubted it.

"I've explored them a little. There are even underground walking tours for tourists nowadays. Since there haven't been any more suspicious deaths or disappearances in the news lately, it would be safe to conclude that our suspect is being more careful and mostly using the derelict tunnels, not the ones being used for the Underground or sewers."

It would be risky, wandering about in the same tunnels as a dangerous blood sucking vampire.

"Would it not be best to explore the tunnels at daytime? Catch him off guard and perhaps even while he's asleep? We could wait for the weekend, so you don't have to work…"

Lucille brushed away his suggestion. "You underestimate the enormity of this task. Even if we stick only to the abandoned tunnels, that still leaves a huge area for the two of us to search. The chances of running into the Nightwalker on our first try are quite slim. Plus, what do you suggest we do until the weekend? We can't afford to sit idle."

Plus, Soul Eaters don't sleep. Where had this random thought come from? And again, that same phrase: soul eater. He couldn't still be impaired from the night before, could he? Valentino took a deep breath and tried to focus.

Meanwhile, Lucille picked up the plans off the table. She arranged them and folded them in half again, before stuffing them back into her pocket. "If you're not up for it, I'll go in by myself," she said.

"No, no. That's not what I meant." Valentino sighed. She was as stubborn as she was beautiful, this one. And if he was going to be any use at all, he quickly had to snap out of whatever funk he'd woken up in today.

"So it's decided," Lucille said.

Valentino nodded. *Fine.* They'd investigate some tunnels together. For both their sakes, he hoped Lucille was right and they wouldn't stumble across an angry vampire while he wasn't at his best. Judging how she carried herself, Valentino was sure Lucille was a formidable fighter. But would that be enough?

He craved to keep her safe, to protect her, come what may. Funny, to have developed such strong feelings for a woman he had only just met.

Lucille had been correct.

After many hours inside the hidden world that was underground London, they'd found nothing to indicate that the Nightwalker had even been down here. Her hypothesis had made sense, of course, and one glance at Lucille's map also made it painfully clear just how big this task was. Still, Valentino started to wonder if this was all just a waste of time.

"Are you sure he's using the tunnels?" Valentino wondered aloud.

Lucille stopped and turned around. "It's only obvious. It's what I would do."

"Well, okay. But what makes you assume he thinks like you?" he asked.

Valentino wasn't even sure why he was questioning her. But the longer they wandered through these musty tunnels, the more he felt like she was hiding something. Every minute of silence between them had weighed heavier on his mind, and now he had reached breaking point.

"You know something. Something you're not sharing," he said at last.

Lucille cocked her head to the side and pursed her lips.

"You mean like how you're not sharing everything you know?"

So that's how she wanted to play it. Valentino sighed.

"All right. I'll tell you mine if you tell me yours."

Lucille nodded. "That's fair. You go first."

Valentino turned his head and checked the tunnel they had just walked through. It was still as empty as before.

"This vampire. We share a history of sorts," Valentino said.

Lucille nodded. "Me too."

Valentino frowned. So this was personal for both of them. "Here. I have a surveillance photo of him. It's how I tracked him to Waterloo yesterday."

He retrieved the photograph from his messenger bag and handed it to Lucille.

Her expression was unchanged as she looked at it; his appearance had not surprised her. Perhaps she'd even recognized him.

"I have hunted him before, but he got away," Lucille whispered. "His name is Marek."

Valentino nodded. *Marek*. So she did know more about him than she'd let on.

"My grandfather tried to defeat him; or at least, a Nightwalker very much like this one. It was during the time of the Great War," Valentino said.

Lucille frowned as she looked up from the photograph. "He killed your grandfather?"

Valentino shook his head. "He got away. But it was a close call."

That seemed to satisfy her, and she looked down at the still of the shadowy figure again.

"He's not a normal Nightwalker," Lucille whispered.

"You keep hinting at that," Valentino said.

"He feeds not just on the blood of his victims but on their souls," she added.

"A Soul Eater," Valentino blurted out. So his subconscious hadn't tried to trick him. The phrase actually had relevance. Perhaps she had referred to him like this already the other night.

"Yes, a Soul Eater," Lucille confirmed. "And a very powerful one as well. We won't be able to defeat him like a regular vampire."

"No?" Valentino asked.

Lucille shook her head. "The normal ways won't work on him. Silver, for example, will not hold him."

Now they were getting to the heart of the matter. If they couldn't use silver to restrain him, that would make capture very difficult indeed.

"Anything else I should know?" Valentino asked.

Lucille stared at him, the look in her eyes reminding him of one of those strange, feverish dreams he'd had of her. With this reminder came a surge of feelings he couldn't fight. How she stood there, still holding the photograph—it tugged at his heart.

Every fiber of his body was overcome by the instinct to

protect her, to give her whatever she wanted in this world. Right now, it seemed that what she wanted was to defeat Marek the Soul Eater. Good. So did he.

He reached for her and brushed a stray lock of hair out of her face. She flinched, seemingly unwittingly, but stood her ground. Then she looked at him again with those big, dark brown eyes.

"The last person who came close to me died," she whispered.

At least that was what Valentino thought he heard; he couldn't be sure. Perhaps it was just a strange flashback to one of his bizarre dreams.

She handed him the picture and straightened herself. "If we're going to catch this Soul Eater, we have no time to lose," she said, in her old, much firmer tone again.

Gone was the vulnerability she'd shown. Gone was the connection between them. Perhaps he'd just imagined it.

They were back to being colleagues. Nothing less and nothing more.

CHAPTER SIX

After an awkward first night of working together, Lucille had met with Valentino again just after sunset. Together they had planned to investigate the second grid mapped out on her copy of the old underground plans she'd taken from Alexander's collection. If all went well, they planned to cover all of Central London within the week.

As it turned out, they got lucky and found evidence of Marek's activities much sooner than expected.

Marek had only been cautious on the surface. He'd left no obvious evidence for human authorities to find, but if you looked a little further, like Lucille and Valentino had done, there was a wealth of information. It was almost as though Marek intended to be found.

The feeding sites they stumbled across were much fresher than the one near Waterloo; one had been used as recently as a day or so before. Valentino could not detect anything more than that, but Lucille had a few hidden talents.

She could *smell* Marek. She was certain she could track him down there if left to her own devices. So it was time to leave Valentino behind and get the job done on her own.

And so, as soon as Valentino showed signs of tiring, she had feigned fatigue herself and convinced him to call it a night.

Now, less than half an hour later, she was back on her own and ready to follow Marek's trail.

This had always been her biggest talent. Some vampires were good at mind control, some, like Marek himself, had acquired the art of levitation. Lucille was a tracker.

She closed her eyes and breathed in deeply, focusing all her mental abilities on just one thing: identify and separate all the various scents her nose could pick up. Tunnels were tricky in their own way. While above ground human activities often created distractions, down here, it was the pungent smell of human waste that tried to throw her off, as well as the overwhelming aroma of stale blood, courtesy of Marek's unquenchable thirst.

This was precisely the reason Lucille had forced herself to make a pit stop and helped herself to some fresh blood, just before returning to this spot.

She breathed in again, and sure enough, she was able to distinguish Marek's scent from the hotchpotch of stenches that filled the tunnel. It was a very particular smell: old, somewhat musty, with spicy overtones. It was repulsive to her now that she really focused on it. Luckily, that meant it would be easy to follow, even when mixed in with other scents.

As she systematically searched the tunnels with the help of her map, she couldn't stop thinking about the strange partnership she'd fallen into with Valentino.

He made her uncomfortable, but why? He was only

human; a man who had walked this earth maybe thirty, thirty-five years now. She had been around for nearly four-hundred.

It was that look in his eyes, she was certain of it. That look, which made him seem oh so familiar. It had been that same look that had made her forget herself and share everything she knew about Marek the first night.

It had been a very long time since someone had looked at her like that. Dominic, the clingy Council guard, did not count, of course. No, Valentino looked at her not like a meek admirer but as an equal.

Normally, she was good at banishing those old memories from her mind, but tonight, alone in this dark hole in the ground, she was painfully susceptible to them.

These reminders cut right into her core; they made the centuries she had spent as a capable and proud vampire seem insignificant and made her *feel* once again. Lucille hated it. Feelings were messy, terrible things that could overwhelm and make you lose focus.

They reminded her of how weak she used to be. How she had let him down. How she had survived into this new form and he had not.

She had grown up with the boy, back when she was still human in 17th century France. They had been inseparable from an early age, and their friendship had grown into something a lot more intimate as the years went by.

When one of the many religious conflicts that had spread across Europe during those days started to affect life in the formerly peaceful and sleepy village she called home, it changed everything. Suddenly, food was hard to come by. Disease was rampant.

Plague felled many, including her parents, and even the boy she had come to love. Yet somehow, she had survived. That was when Julius had found her and put a heartbroken and listless Lucille back together again.

Tonight, after getting rid of Valentino and continuing her search alone, she wondered if all her strength was just a veneer that hid the old her. And it was this weak and pathetic person that Valentino had once again sought to bring out in her. She couldn't let him; it hurt too deep. Plus, they had no future together anyway. A vampire and a hunter: she couldn't think of a more ridiculous couple.

No, it would be best if she cut their collaboration short and brought Marek to justice as soon as possible. That was what tonight was all about: continuing this quest alone so she wouldn't have to deal with Valentino anymore.

As she turned the corner into yet another tunnel, Marek's scent grew in intensity. She was getting closer. Lucille took a deep breath and did her best to shake off all those idle thoughts about the past. *Focus!*

She wasn't even certain what she was attempting to do here, going after the Soul Eater by herself, but she knew she needed to show strength above all. Her survival depended on it.

Lucille closed her eyes and paused, then she opened them again and scanned the tunnel ahead. It was pitch black and hard to see what lay ahead, even for a mature vampire such as herself; there simply wasn't any ambient light to help her.

Once again, a whiff of Marek's scent seemed to call out to her. He was nearby.

"Come out. I am no threat to you," she said, suddenly extremely aware of the dagger she wore in a sheath on her hip. It would do her no good if they got into a confrontation, though. He was too powerful.

"Marek—" Lucille remembered the formalities he had insisted on during the trial. "Son of Lilith, Master of a Thousand Souls!"

A dark figure approached from the shadows. His movements were smooth and effortless as he levitated a couple of inches off the ground. "So you found me."

She observed him carefully for any sign in his body language that he was prepping for a fight. He seemed perfectly relaxed. *Good.* She had come here for answers, not to be killed.

"I was hoping to speak with you," Lucille started.

The Soul Eater grinned, exposing his razor sharp teeth. "Oh? And what might the both of us have to discuss? Do explain why I shouldn't rip your heart out right here like Julius did with my two progenies?"

Lucille shook her head. Those were questions for another time. Right now, she had to focus on the task at hand.

How had he come to know about the details of how

Lucille's Valentine

Julius had killed his associates? Marek had already escaped by the time Julius had jumped into action.

"Because you have no audience. Julius isn't here to see it." Lucille flashed her own fangs briefly. It wasn't a smile as much as an instinctive show of aggression. *Don't show weakness.*

"Very well. Next time, perhaps." Marek made a nonchalant gesture, like he was in no rush.

"I get the feeling that there is more to your relationship with my master than he is inclined to share," Lucille spoke softly.

Marek's gaze locked with hers and the corner of his mouth twitched slightly.

"So you came here to get to the bottom of it all. To find out the truth?" he taunted.

Lucille nodded and averted her eyes downward. "The truth is important to me."

He let out a short laugh and approached her. "All right. It's no secret—not to me. Julius and I have known each other for a very long time. All our lives, almost."

Lucille's mind started digesting the information immediately. All their lives? Julius had never shared the details of his turning and the circumstances under which he'd started his life as a vampire. As a consequence, he had never mentioned Marek either.

"Do you intend to kill Julius and take over the Council?" Lucille wondered aloud.

"Ha! I have no need for that childish Council of yours.

We are vampires. We are eternal. We don't need to be herded like cattle. We are the wolves that roam free: we take what we want, when we want it!"

Lucille frowned. If he had no interest in the Council, then why come to London? Why risk exposure and capture by the Council? Unless… He never actually said he didn't wish to kill Julius, so perhaps that was the plan all along. Get close enough and kill an old rival, simply for the sake of taking his life, rather than gaining any political influence.

"Why stay behind and risk capture?" Lucille pried.

Marek burst into laughter. "Risk capture, you say? Dear child, I'm not risking anything. Your dungeons cannot hold me!"

He had a point, of course. It seemed that the entire period of his imprisonment leading up to the trial itself had been a charade. If the Silver Vault was no match for his powers, he could have broken free at any time. The only ones in danger had been his less powerful associates, and they'd paid heavily for their loyalty to Marek.

Marek reached out for her. His long, claw-like finger approached her face, causing her to flinch away. His pungent scent threatened to overwhelm her.

"Have you ever considered breaking free from all the constraints? All the rules and regulations your precious Council imposes on you? There is a whole world out there, and it's yours for the taking."

Lucille closed her eyes and focused. Was this the end

game, perhaps? Did Marek wish to seduce everyone close to Julius to his own way of life, and *then* kill him after seeing him humiliated?

"I have everything I need right here in London," Lucille said.

"Child, you have no idea of the possibilities. The immense power you could wield if you broke free from the shackles Julius placed on you."

"You mean the power I would gain from killing people?"

"Ah!" Marek made a dismissive gesture. "Anyone can kill. Even humans can kill if they try hard enough. There is nothing special about that."

If she kept him talking, would he share with her the secret behind his great power?

"Then tell me what's special about your way of life. What sets you apart from any old killer?"

Marek let out a hoarse laugh. "I'm afraid if I told you all my secrets, I'd have to kill you. No, you pledge your allegiance to me first, proving your loyalty with a sacrifice of some sort, and then I might teach you."

Lucille considered her options. It would be useful to learn as much as she could. But the sacrifice Marek demanded complicated matters. Considering everything she knew about him, it was bound to be a blood sacrifice. Something drastic enough that she would be disgraced in front of the Council forever.

Unless… It was risky, it was devious.

"What if I told you I could give you a hunter? The one who has been after you?" Lucille said.

Marek grinned. "I was thinking more along the lines of an immortal soul. You offer me a mere human? I can take those for myself any time I want."

"What if I told you he is the descendant of an old foe of yours? A hunter who very nearly killed you many years ago?"

"I do recall a hunter like that… It was during the Great War."

Lucille nodded. "This man I'm referring to is his grandson."

Marek approached her again, his eyes boring into hers. It was a good thing she had been truthful; he would have known if she was lying, she was certain of it.

"Interesting. And you could deliver this hunter to me?"

Lucille swallowed a lump that had been developing in her throat. Guilt? Perhaps even fear?

Would she be willing to use Valentino as bait? It was a risky plan, but perhaps it was the beginning of a plan to defeat Marek. If she gained some further insights into the workings of a Soul Eater, then all the better.

"If you like, I could lure him to you," she said.

"I would enjoy that very much." Marek grinned, exposing his fangs.

"Then we have a deal. I will deliver him to the old industrial complex near the river in Chelsea three nights from now. You know the place; you've been there before."

Lucille gave him a nod, which Marek reciprocated, then turned on her heel. She was half expecting to be stopped, to have Marek swoop down on her and kill her as soon as she turned her back, but he didn't.

He simply let her go.

Perhaps he was underestimating her; Marek was so certain of his superior powers that he did not feel threatened by the prospect of a meeting with Julius' Enforcer and a Vampire Hunter.

Or worse, perhaps *she* had underestimated *him* and their next meeting would end with both Valentino and herself dead in a pool of blood. Only time would tell.

First though, she would have to use all her cunning to convince Valentino to go along with her plan…

CHAPTER SEVEN

A knock on the door alerted Valentino to her arrival.

"Valentino. We must speak," Lucille started, as she marched right past him into his shabby room.

Valentino frowned and shut the door behind her. She looked tenser than usual. Although she had kept her hands buried deep inside her pockets, he could make out that her fists were balled. What had set her off?

"What's wrong?" Valentino asked.

"The Soul Eater. He left us a sign." Lucille retrieved her phone from her pocket and showed it to him. On it there was a photograph of an access door to one of the tunnels they had searched the other night. Only in this picture, there was some writing on top of the dirty gray paint of the door that had not been there before. The red color of the message was so distinctive, it had to have been written in blood.

Valentino Conti, you and I have unfinished business.
Three nights from now, Lots Road, Chelsea.

"I brought you a sample of it to test," she said, handing him a small re-sealable bag with a blood-soaked ear bud in it.

"This wasn't there last night! How did you find it?" Valentino studied the baggie, then looked up and scrutinized Lucille's face.

"Last night after we said our goodbyes, I felt a strange sensation. Like something or someone was calling out to me. I followed it and it led me right back to the door we entered into the tunnels from. Near the most recent feeding site," she explained. "That's when I saw it."

Her eyes were wide, concerned. This Lucille who stood before him tonight was entirely different from the confident fellow hunter he had been dealing with so far. Her experience alone in the tunnel must have really spooked her.

He got to work on the evidence, testing it with his UV torch while Lucille observed. Sure enough, the sample lit up; the blood was definitely contaminated with vampire DNA.

"What do you think it means?" she asked.

Again, two wide eyes stared at him, speaking directly to his protective instincts. He wanted to reassure her, that together they could work this out. Could they, though? The message had come as a surprise even to him.

"Clearly this Nightwalker realizes we're on its trail. Perhaps he was observing us last night. He figured out who I am and that one of my clan hunted him generations ago and intends to even the scales."

"I can guess what you're thinking, but it would be too dangerous to confront him," Lucille said.

She reached out for his hand, and her touch sent an electric shock from her skin into his. The tension between them had only grown since the first night they'd met, and Valentino felt his resolve was close to breaking.

But he had to be strong, for her as well as for himself. The Nightwalker they were after had worked out who he was. The element of surprise in their pursuit was gone now.

"I have no choice. He has challenged me. I must respond."

Lucille blinked a few times, then made eye contact with him again. Her brown eyes were almost black in this light and heavy with emotion. He placed his hand on top of hers and felt her twitch underneath him. This tension, it was mutual. He could feel it.

"Fine. But not without a plan," Lucille said.

Valentino nodded. That was fair. "Yes, we must have a plan."

"And… that's not everything," Lucille said.

"Oh?" Valentino tightened his grip on her hand, squeezing it gently. His heartbeat had sped up; he wanted to touch so much more than just her hand.

"The way I found the message. The way he led me there even though I don't remember seeing him in person. I fear my mind has been compromised."

She still looked unusually fearful.

There had to be an explanation for her strange experience; Marek might have approached her, hypnotized her into forgetting where and how she met with him, and then influenced her to seek out that message for Valentino. It was unlikely that her mind was permanently infiltrated, though.

Valentino smiled at her reassuringly. "Don't worry, Lucille. We'll come up with something."

"Do you know of any way to protect our minds? Do you know how to break the Nightwalker's hypnosis?" Lucille asked.

He shook his head. "Technology cannot help us with that. The only thing we can do is to try and avoid eye contact if we meet one."

Lucille nodded, seemingly satisfied with his answer.

Valentino sat down on one of the creaky old chairs and started to scribble down thoughts and ideas. They needed a plan indeed—a foolproof one. And since Marek the Soul Eater could not be restrained with silver chains or cuffs like normal Nightwalkers, he had to think of something a lot more elaborate. Their adversary was extremely powerful, but he wasn't invincible. Anything that could kill a normal vampire would kill him too, in time.

He reached for the pendant of St. Benedict that hung from the chain around his neck. *Think. What's the way forward here?* He had the knowledge of generations of hunters behind him. But right now, the old ways wouldn't help them. They needed something more powerful to defeat this foe.

"Ultraviolet rays," Valentino mumbled to himself.

"That's it. We will rig up a trap using UV lights. I will be the bait to lure him in, and you set off the lights."

"And what would stop him from simply running away once the lights switch on? It'll take time for the UV rays to kill him," Lucille said.

She was right, but he'd already thought of that. "We'll incapacitate him at the same time."

Lucille frowned. Clearly she did not follow. Why would she? She was an old school hunter; she wouldn't have done the same kind of research he had into how Nightwalkers functioned.

"Nightwalkers are sensitive to electromagnetic waves. If we can create a magnetic field strong enough, it will disorient him and temporarily disable his fast reflexes. Then, we can fight him. It should buy us enough time for the lights to take effect."

Lucille opened her mouth, then closed it without saying anything. Finally, he had rendered his hunting partner speechless. Valentino couldn't help but feel a bit victorious already. Her old school investigative methods and fighting skills and his inventions and research would bring this creature to its knees together. It would be a perfect marriage of old and new, the ultimate partnership.

The brainstorming part of the operation was over; now they just had to assemble the trap and put the plan into action.

He picked up his notebook and stowed it away in his bag. "The meeting is set for three nights from now. If we want to be ready for him, we'd better work quickly. We have some shopping to do."

Lucille's previously surprised expression softened until a subtle smile broke through. "This plan could actually work. I know a few places that should sell everything you need. With a bit of luck, they're still open."

They had managed to find most of what they needed for their trap within the first night. Most of the second night was spent in Valentino's small room, assembling all the bits and pieces and wiring them together. The one remaining night was spent installing the trap in their final location.

And tonight, they would find out if their work would pay off.

Things had been tight, but Valentino felt confident. Even Lucille, who had shown a bit more trepidation at first, had seemingly come around to seeing things his way.

Marek the Soul Eater was overconfident by nature, according to her. And he had no way of knowing about all the technology hunters had at their disposal nowadays. He would not see an ambush of this nature coming.

Now that everything was done, Valentino just had one remaining doubt.

"Are you sure we can place Marek exactly where we need him?" Valentino asked.

Lucille smiled at him, and he felt captivated, unable to

look away from her expressive, seemingly endless eyes.

"He's tried to influence me before; I've had him in my mind," she said. "But it seems like he doesn't want to harm me; at least not yet. He aims to use me to get to you."

Valentino nodded. "And we'll give him what we want." His voice was more monotone than usual—that was how distracted he had become by her gaze.

"Precisely. He's fixated, bordering on obsessed, and that makes him reckless. Once he gets here and realizes where you are, he will simply come to you."

That made perfect sense. Valentino smiled. He was glad to have her here. To be in this partnership.

The longer he looked at her, the more his chest swelled with hope. He had never worked with anyone other than his father during his early hunting days. She'd told him she'd always worked alone too.

Yet now, against all odds, they had made their partnership work. They had complemented each other's talents and become a team.

Tonight was the night when all their efforts came together, and they'd do what they had set out to. Defeat Marek.

Valentino was certain the trap would work; he'd tested it. And once Marek walked right into it, all would fall into place. They would need to hurry, to get into position just in case Marek turned up early. But he still could not look away from her.

"Despite everything, there's still a risk that things could

go wrong, that you get hurt. This could be goodbye," Lucille said.

Valentino shook his head. "No. Our plan will work; I know it."

Lucille briefly glanced away, and he was instantly overcome with dread. *No, don't look away! Everything will be fine as long as I can stare into those eyes of yours!*

She made eye contact again and Valentino's confidence surged. When she reached for him, cradling his face in her hands, his heart skipped a beat.

He instinctively slipped his arm around her waist. This, this was what he had wanted ever since that first meeting at the pub near Waterloo.

She maintained eye contact as she tiptoed and touched her lips against his. It was the most glorious thing. Their first kiss.

It didn't matter that they were about to embark on the most dangerous confrontation of his whole hunting career. He couldn't care less about the stakes they faced. If, by the end of the night, Marek emerged victorious and they were both dead, at least he could take solace knowing they'd lived through this moment first.

If, however, they made it, if they survived tonight, he would ensure that their partnership endured. He would ask her to come home with him; if she couldn't leave London, he'd even consider staying with her. He wouldn't let her go.

Valentino closed his eyes and focused on the sweet

taste of her lips. She was intoxicating, like a drug he'd never known he needed. He'd had his reservations about tracking the Soul Eater to London. That this mission was too dangerous, that he'd put too much pressure on himself to make up for his grandfather's one failure.

But if he hadn't, he would have never met her. He would have never experienced the joy in working with another hunter.

He would have never had this kiss, which meant everything. This connection, which went deeper than anything he'd felt before.

Thanks to Marek's reign of terror on London, he was no longer alone.

CHAPTER EIGHT

Tonight was the night, and hypnotizing Valentino was the last piece of the puzzle. Ever since finding out that he had no gadget to defend himself against hypnosis, she had known that this was what she had to do. Marek expected her to. If he found Valentino fully aware of his surroundings while she delivered him, it would just create suspicion.

Still, she battled conflicting feelings. Although they had done their best to think of all eventualities and built a very impressive trap, the outcome of tonight's encounter was not set in stone. Perhaps Marek had some talents Lucille didn't know about, which would allow him to defeat their trap.

There was only one way of finding out.

She shouldn't have kissed him, though. Kissing Valentino had been a mistake.

Hypnosis was difficult for her; it required a great deal of concentration and eye contact. And as she stared into Valentino's eyes, she kept seeing all those reminders of the past which sought to soften her heart. She had been unable to stop herself.

On top of that, she'd felt all of Valentino's emotions as if they were her own. For a moment there, when she considered that very soon, at least Valentino could be dead, she had lost herself and acted on impulse alone.

And now, the lasting sensation of Valentino's lips on hers made everything worse. She was leading him into danger. He'd agreed to act as bait, sure, but she hadn't exactly been upfront with him.

She'd hidden her true nature from him and allowed him to develop feelings for her, which she felt now that their minds were connected. She'd tricked him into thinking that he wasn't alone in this world, that she was a fellow hunter. As a result, he was ready to make a big change to ensure they could be together. His thoughts had told her as much.

For that, she was sorry.

Lucille took a deep breath. It was too late for regrets; she'd deal with her guilt once this whole sad business was over. Because no matter what the outcome: after tonight, she'd never see Valentino again.

She waited in silence for what felt like forever. Finally, she caught a whiff of Marek's scent. He was here.

"Marek, I'm here with the hunter, as promised," Lucille said as she scanned the large central hall of the old power station. Valentino stood still beside her; he was still lost in his trance.

Memories of their kiss clouded Lucille's mind. She shouldn't have done that. She was dangerously close to losing focus.

Marek approached, floating a couple of inches off the ground as he had done the last time she had seen him. His black eyes bore into hers, as though he could see directly into her most private thoughts.

"Very good. Perhaps Julius' influence hasn't completely corrupted you yet."

Funny, Julius might have said the same thing about Marek's influence. Lucille stole a glance in Valentino's direction; his expression was dazed and vacant. Her hypnosis seemed to be holding. She could only hope that he would snap out of it the very moment she needed him to fight.

Marek circled the two of them, inspecting Valentino from top to bottom. "He does bear a resemblance to that hunter who was after me all those years ago. It never ceases to amaze me how overconfident some humans are," Marek said.

Lucille nodded. "Indeed."

"What about the other part of our bargain?" Marek asked.

"How do I know I can trust you? I've delivered one sacrifice, now I must get something in return before I deliver another."

"Not ready to completely cast off your shackles yet, I see. Very well. I suppose you have done well enough to deserve some kind of reward."

Lucille took a step forward and kept her eyes fixed on Marek's face. "How does it work? What did you mean when you said anyone can kill but what you do is special?"

Marek laughed. "You are suddenly very keen, aren't you? I did not agree to be interrogated."

Lucille glanced away. "Of course not, I am just eager to learn." Eager to learn and eager to buy time. The more distracted Marek was when she initiated the trap, the better their chance of success. And if she could identify what exactly it was that turned a regular vampire into a Soul Eater, even better. Perhaps she could then prevent that sort of thing from happening in future.

The Council had its hands full already with regular criminal elements among their ranks. Lucille would prefer not to have to deal with another Soul Eater as long as she held her position as Enforcer.

"So what is my reward?" Lucille asked as she took a couple of steps in Marek's direction, leaving Valentino behind in the designated spot in the center of the hall.

"I will share with you a little secret," Marek said.

Lucille nodded eagerly. "What's that?"

Marek grinned, exposing his teeth. "You can experience great power beyond your wildest dreams. And its source is right in front of you."

That didn't help. Marek was being vague again, speaking in riddles to confuse her.

"You can give me great power," Lucille said.

Marek nodded. "You could say that. But you must deliver me an immortal soul as a sacrifice."

Again, they were back to that same old story. Perhaps Lucille should just give up on the whole idea of questioning Marek and stick to the plan. It was starting to look like he never meant to share anything meaningful with her in the first place.

"Why would I want to deliver another vampire to you, just so you can take his soul?" Lucille argued.

Marek made a dismissive gesture. "Not just any immortal soul. An important one. The most important one you know."

The nerve. How dare he ask for that? "You expect me to sacrifice Julius? What kind of a demand is that?" she complained. "Do you have any idea how much danger I'll be in if the other elders find out? They'll have my head!"

Marek shrugged. "It's the only way you'll learn about the great power I can give you. But if you don't want that, then suit yourself."

Lucille shook her head. This was it. She wasn't going to get any more useful information out of him. He was too slippery, too suspicious to share anything else before she proved herself. She had no other choice but to end things right now.

"I've brought you the hunter; that's all I'm willing to do for now," she said.

It was time. Lucille kept her eyes fixed on Marek and focused. Mind control was effortless for some of her peers, but for her, it had always been an arduous and tiring task. She was determined not to make her struggle too obvious.

She held her breath and severed the connection between Valentino and herself. He woke up instantly, opened his long coat, and grabbed the axe that had been concealed underneath with one hand, and a short sword with the other. At the same time, Lucille reached for the remote control in her pocket that activated the trap.

The resulting noise was overwhelming. Buzzing surrounded her, infiltrated her mind, slowed her down. She stumbled backwards, trying to get out of the heat of the UV lights, but progress was slow.

The stench of burnt flesh filled the air. The intense pain forced her to her knees.

When she looked up, she could see flashes of Valentino fighting a dazed-looking Marek. Blow for blow, they were equally matched. Valentino's science had panned out; the electromagnetic waves had done their bit in disabling Marek's quick reflexes. He even seemed to be standing on his own two feet rather than floating in the air.

For once, he did not look like the fearsome Soul Eater she had interacted with before, but a frail old man, struggling to stay alive.

Lucille was nearly overcome by pain as the lights continued to burn into her. With tears of blood streaming down her blistered face, she fought her way into the shadows on all fours, where finally she could breathe again.

Meanwhile, Valentino was doing a magnificent job of keeping Marek in the danger zone. He was a great fighter, for a human. Lucille grabbed for her dagger, wishing that she could help somehow. But it was too risky.

She had already endured the lights for too long; her

wounds were only slowly starting to heal. Marek, who had only just begun to smolder, looked like he could still last a bit longer.

But she couldn't just stand there and watch. Her nature didn't allow it. She circled the fighting pair until she stood behind Marek.

Across the room, one of the UV lights went out with a loud pop. The system was getting overloaded; there was no time to lose.

She raised her arm and aimed, trembling as she forced her aching muscles into submission. The din created by the large electromagnet was still slowing her down, disorienting her, but her aim was true. She flung the dagger with as much force as she could muster.

Marek never saw it coming; he had his back turned. Perhaps Valentino didn't either, until the blade found its new home buried deep into the back of Marek's neck. He let out a silent scream and fell onto his hands and knees.

Valentino acted immediately, raised his axe, and brought it down with as much force as he could. That was it, the deciding blow, which severed Marek's head. The Soul Eater slumped to the ground by Valentino's feet. The latter could only watch as Marek turned ashen, then charcoal black, then dissolved into a pile of dust, which was immediately dispersed by a draft blowing through the old building.

At that very moment, the rest of the lights blew out too.

Lucille flipped the switch again before discarding the remote. Finally. She felt like herself again.

She rushed to join Valentino in the center of the hall. It was time for the final stage of the plan.

"Are you all right?" she asked, while staring deeply into his eyes.

Valentino raised his hand and reached for her face. "You're bleeding," he said.

Lucille placed her hand on top of his and shook her head. *Not for long.*

"I'm fine. We did it. Together we defeated him," she said.

It took all of her remaining energy to hypnotize him again. Had he been any other man, she would have fed off him right this moment to regain her strength. But she couldn't bring herself to; that felt like too deep a betrayal of his trust.

"We met Marek, and I set off the trap," Lucille began. "Then we fought him side by side, remember?"

Valentino nodded. "That's how it happened."

As she told him the rest of the fictional account of their battle, she felt her heart grow heavy like before. They had won, but it felt like an empty victory.

This was it. The end.

After tonight, she would never see him again.

Once she was done, she tried to shake his hand, which he refused.

"We'll do it the Italian way, huh?" he said, as he

wrapped his arms around her and kissed her cheek. "Good job, Lucille Amboise."

"Yes… Good job," she said, averting her gaze to disguise the pain she felt.

"Now, I must go. Goodbye."

She turned around and left without looking back. The sting of tears was too fresh. If she stuck around any longer, she might lose her nerve and backtrack on her decision. And that would be bad for everyone involved.

No, this part of the job was done. She had to get back on task and report tonight's events to Julius. They had taken care of Marek against all odds; that ought to please her master. And then, things could finally go back to normal. What a relief that would be.

CHAPTER NINE

Valentino felt conflicted as he reached his modest room at the guest house. With Lucille's help, he had done what he set out to do. The monster was dead. His grandfather's unfinished business had been taken care of. This was cause for celebration, but his heart was not in it.

After all, this meant his collaboration with Lucille was over. She'd made that pretty clear when she left him at the old power station. He hadn't even had the chance to ask her out for celebratory drinks or dinner. Or even breakfast, considering the time.

Did it have to be this way? Were hunters nowadays destined to live solitary lives?

Valentino touched his lips, which still burned with the memory of her kiss.

Just as he settled into the creaky chair in the corner, a rustling noise attracted his attention. He got up to investigate and found an envelope lying by the door.

Valentino quickly opened the door and scanned the dark hallway. It was empty. Whoever had delivered the letter had already left.

He went back inside and picked up the envelope. It was made of some kind of heavy parchment. There was a seal on it, but he did not recognize the symbol on top. It was very old school, the sort of communique his ancestors might have received in the past.

Valentino carefully opened the seal with a knife and took out the folded letter inside.

The handwriting on it was as old fashioned as the paper it was written on.

He carried it back to his chair and started to read.

Mr. Conti,

The woman you have been working with is not who she says she is. You will have picked up the signs, at least subconsciously. Your instincts as a hunter do not lie. She is the enemy.

You owe it to your forefathers, the great hunters that came before you, to take a stand.

Lucille Amboise is not human. She is a Nightwalker.

Remember the oath you, as well as your ancestors, have taken.

You must end her.

Valentino's heart started to race as he read and then re-read those words.

Lies!

He flung the offending letter across the room and rested his head in his hands.

How dare this person interfere? How dare they accuse her of being the very thing they had been hunting together? Had she not proved her worth when they defeated Marek the Soul Eater together? Had she not defended the safety of the human race right alongside him? If the accusation was true, she should have died under those lights, but she'd been fine.

Who could even know about their partnership? Or even his whereabouts? He was cautious, always aiming to blend into the crowd in any new city, yet someone who harbored ill will had followed him here.

Who the hell could know so much about his activities in London?

The letter, like many such tips he and his family had received over the years, was unsigned, of course. People, even those frequenting the same circles as him, were careful about leaving behind evidence of their knowledge about the supernatural for fear of being ridiculed if it was ever discovered. That left only circumstantial clues regarding the sender of this message.

Whoever it was would have been surveilling Valentino and Lucille. Perhaps someone high up in law enforcement or politics? Someone who could have gained access to the many CCTV cameras all around London, like the one near Waterloo which had captured an unsuspecting Marek almost two weeks ago.

But what of its contents?

Surely the accusation could not be true?

Valentino pinched the bridge of his nose and closed his eyes. There was no point in letting his emotions cloud his judgment. He was a hunter, first and foremost. He had a duty to investigate any lead, even a ridiculous one such as this.

What did he really *know* about Lucille?

Precious little.

She was talented with a blade, agile, strong, and quick on her feet. She had razor-sharp instincts and great observational skills. If it wasn't for her, he might have missed out on certain clues pointing them in Marek's direction.

She had been instrumental in the plan to entrap and defeat him.

A lot of it could be explained away. Almost all of it could, except the niggling feeling he had had since the moment he'd met her that there was something she wasn't telling him.

She had a secret.

Had Valentino let his guard down too much? Had he let himself get dazzled by her beauty, by her perhaps feigned solidarity to his cause? Had he let his heart get stolen by the enemy?

He couldn't believe it. It simply wasn't possible.

Only, if this letter was true, that explained a hell of a lot.

Valentino opened his eyes and pulled out his old faithful notebook. In it, he recorded everything he knew about Lucille, aiming to uncover any evidence to prove or disprove the letter's contents.

Their chance meeting inside the pub near Waterloo could have been suspicious. Had she been there because she was also on Marek's trail? Or had she been hunting the hunter and followed *him* there?

They had downed quite a few whiskeys that first night, and yet, she may not have been as affected by them as she should have. This, of course, he could not be certain of, since he had let his own senses get impaired.

She had told him she had a job, so… *He had only ever met her at night.*

This last thought he underlined.

It was still a few hours until dawn; perhaps if he reached out to her, they could put this matter to bed quickly and easily. If he could convince her to meet him during daylight hours, that would be conclusive proof that she wasn't a Nightwalker.

And then he could burn that letter and forget it had ever arrived.

Valentino picked up his phone to dial her number. It rang and rang, but there was no answer. Perhaps she had gone to bed, like a sensible human being should be doing this time of night. Or she was avoiding him after saying her goodbyes already.

He should rest, but he was certain he couldn't relax as long as he didn't have the answers he needed. He had to try to reach her again.

This time, she answered.

———•◆•———

Lucille watched as Julius paced back and forth in front of her. They had won. Marek had been defeated, so why was he still so agitated?

"There was no way to bring him in alive?" Julius asked, after a seemingly endless silence.

Lucille frowned. She thought he would be happy that Marek was never going to bother them again. His reaction again aroused her suspicion that there was something about their relationship that neither had cared to share with her.

"He made it abundantly clear that our dungeons would never hold him. There was no other viable option."

Julius shook his head.

"It goes against our rules to kill one of our own. Death sentences are meant to be carried out only when following proper procedure."

He was saying one thing, but Lucille heard another. This was not the first time the Council, or one of its representatives, had killed a rogue vampire during capture.

The way Julius talked, it was as though she'd randomly murdered an innocent bystander when this was the very same Marek who was already to be put to death during the trial he escaped from weeks ago.

Even back then, Julius had simply executed Marek's progenies in front of everyone in attendance, as though it was nothing. Nobody had batted an eye.

Suddenly though, when *she* had done the killing—as far as Julius knew; she hadn't told him about the full extent of Valentino's involvement—he almost acted like she had done something wrong. The hypocrisy was getting to her.

"He would have never stopped," she argued. "Do you know why he was in London? Why he came here in the first place?"

Julius stopped pacing and stared at her. "We will never know now. Dead vampires can't talk."

Lucille shook her head. For such a powerful and wise ancient vampire, Julius was being rather thick.

"He was after something, clearly. You knew him well, perhaps you might have some idea what he might have wanted here?" Lucille probed. What could a powerful, ancient vampire possibly be after but more power? And what better source of power for a Soul Eater than a Council consisting of ancient immortal souls, ripe for the taking?

"Why does a criminal, one who broke our most fundamental laws, deserve so much consideration?"

"He…" Julius balled his fists and stared Lucille down

again. His eyes narrowed and a red glimmer appeared in them.

Good, perhaps if he got angry enough, he would let something slip.

"Why won't you understand? He was my brother!"

Lucille was stunned. She had not seen that coming. Despite the hint Marek had dropped that he had known Julius forever…

Vampires generally took after their makers. Julius had taught Lucille everything she knew after he had turned her. Her sense of right and wrong and her belief in the rules they lived by had been spoon-fed into her during her first decades as an immortal. And Alexander was the same; he had his quirks, but he believed in the same ideals. The things Julius had taught them.

There were some exceptions, but that was how it usually went. Some vampires went through a period of rebellion, but it was mostly harmless. Very rarely did a vampire fundamentally betray his or her maker.

Although Julius barely spoke of his early years, she had always assumed that he had been brought up the same. He had never given her any reason to think otherwise. But since Marek had turned out so drastically different, she wondered how true her assumptions really were.

"He was your brother," Lucille whispered. "And because of that you did not wish him to die?"

Julius started pacing again. "It was meant to be me. *I* was meant to end his life."

Lucille was uncertain how to respond; luckily, Julius did not give her much of a chance to.

"I suppose it is time I tell you this, my child. I wished to avenge our maker's death."

Lucille looked up at him, at his once again pale eyes, which seemed to finally show some emotion other than anger. So Marek had killed their maker and Julius felt obligated to take vengeance. That at last made sense.

"Master, I avenged him for you. At least we kept it in the family, so to speak." *In the family indeed.* Thanks to Julius' and Marek's secrecy about their true relationship, Lucille had unwittingly killed her uncle. Not that she felt remorseful about it.

Julius nodded. "In any case, what's done is done."

Lucille didn't respond, but her mind was racing again. Her conversation with Marek, the fact that he had come to London, risking life and limb for *something*... Perhaps Marek had never wanted the ancients' souls. *Perhaps...*

She thought back to something he had hinted at. That if she wanted to experience a power beyond anything she could imagine, she should deliver Julius, sacrifice him.

Perhaps he had not meant to kill Julius himself, perhaps he had intended for her to do it. What if that was the secret?

It made perfect sense.

That little clue was the missing piece of the puzzle. The difference between a vampire who simply murders his prey, and a Soul Eater. In order to become a Soul Eater a vampire must first commit the ultimate sin: parricide. Kill his or her maker.

"Lucille? Are you listening?" Julius demanded.

Lucille looked up. What had she missed?

"Yes, master?"

"The hunter is going to be a problem. A loose end." Julius folded his arms and stared right at her. This was not a suggestion, but an order.

"I took care of him," Lucille said. "He only remembers a perfectly plausible version of events, one that does not implicate me."

Julius cocked his head to the side. "That's immaterial. He needs to be eliminated."

Lucille's chest tightened. *No, he wasn't serious!*

"I can compel him to leave London, never to return. He will not bother us. Plus, he doesn't know anything except that his mission here has been accomplished. The vampire he came here to hunt has been defeated."

"You're not listening to me, child. He is still a hunter. That means he's still the enemy. Why would we willingly let one of our enemies walk away? Especially one with no attachments or family to avenge him. He *is* the last of the Conti clan, as you said. Your sentimentality in this matter is baffling to me."

"He will not be a threat to the Council. To you." Lucille kept her eyes fixed on Julius, looking for any sign that his resolve was wavering. It wasn't. He had made up his mind. And he was very close to losing his patience with her.

"I'd rather not have to repeat myself. You know what you have to do. Those are my orders," Julius insisted.

Lucille nodded, defeated. She had to concede and accept his will. "Yes, master."

In the back of her mind she had always known that involving Valentino in her investigation into Marek carried with it this very risk. But until now, she had never seriously considered the consequences.

Would she be able to carry out Julius' orders? Would she be able to take a human life, Valentino's life? She would soon find out. Julius had left her no other choice.

CHAPTER TEN

The first time Lucille's phone rang, she hadn't picked up. It was Valentino, of course. And for once in her life, she found that she had no idea how to respond to him. What would she say? How would she hide her feelings?

So she had simply turned the ringer off and tried to enjoy the resulting silence. But rather than calm her, the empty house surrounding her and the muted phone in her hand just made her feel cornered. This was not something she was used to. This had always been her sanctuary, her home. This morning, it felt like a trap.

Somehow, Valentino had found a weakness in her and awoken old emotions that had been buried for a long time. Saying goodbye to him had been the most difficult thing she'd ever done, and now, she had to end it forever.

Julius would never change his mind. He could be extremely stubborn, and defying his orders was a dangerous proposition. No, if she valued her role at the Council at all, and wanted to continue living her life the way she had done for centuries, she had to do as he said.

And beating around the bush or delaying the inevitable would not help one bit.

Lucille took a deep breath and picked up her phone to call Valentino back when it rang again.

"Valentino, I was just about to call you," she greeted

him.

The line was quiet; not silent, just quiet. He hadn't said anything yet, but Lucille recognized his breaths on the other end.

"Are you there?" she asked. "Everything all right?"

"I need to see you today. Please tell me you will come."

Lucille frowned and checked the time. Dawn was about two hours away. That was plenty of time to meet up, carry out her orders, and report back to Julius. So long as she stayed focused.

"Where are you?" she asked.

"I'm at the guest house," Valentino responded.

"I can be there in—" Lucille considered what would be a reasonable, human-like, time frame for her journey. "Twenty minutes."

The line went dead with a click. That was very much unlike Valentino. No goodbye, no standard human niceties to end the conversation. Something was definitely off.

She took her time getting ready, though when she left her place, a familiar shadow already lurked across the street, partially concealed behind the trunk of a tree.

"Dominic," she called out.

The shadow froze.

"I can see you, you know. Come out!" she insisted.

Finally, a dejected looking Dominic appeared in front of her.

"I'm sorry, Lucille. I'm here on Julius' orders."

Lucille rested her hands on her hips and kept staring at

the flustered looking man who towered over her.

"I am to follow you, offer assistance during your confrontation with the hunter."

She shook her head. Great. Not only was she being tested with the most difficult task she had ever been ordered to perform, she now had to worry about Dominic meddling in it.

"You will do nothing of the sort," she said.

"But Lucille, those are my orders!" Dominic protested.

Lucille straightened herself and stared him down. Despite everything, she was still his superior as far as Council business was concerned. "I will take care of the hunter myself. Alone. You understand? If Julius makes a fuss, I'll cover for you. But this is something I must do on my own."

Dominic turned away, but then stole a glance at her sideways. "You've never killed a human before, huh?" he asked finally.

Lucille frowned. Why on earth would he say that? Killing humans was against Council law now, but before Julius took over as Council Leader some centuries ago, things hadn't been so strict. Almost every vampire had a few skeletons in his or her closet, literally, so Dominic had no reason to believe Lucille was any different.

"Actually, Dominic, you are mistaken. I *have* killed a human before. That is why I must do this on my own," Lucille explained.

She had never directly ended someone's life, but she'd

felt responsible for so many deaths before Julius found her. The statement felt truthful enough to make her sound convincing.

"Fine, I'll do as you ask. If Julius asks for a report, I'll say that I lost you and couldn't pick up your trail anymore," Dominic said, then he reached for Lucille's arm, patting it; possibly he meant to be supportive.

For a change, she did not dodge him, even if his touch made her feel awkward. Funnily, she had felt a lot less uncomfortable touching Valentino. Was she doomed to live through eternity without ever feeling the joy of sharing a touch or a kiss again? She couldn't even imagine letting Dominic's lips touch hers; the mere idea repulsed her.

"You take care. Remember, he's the enemy. It's all in a good cause," Dominic said.

"Perhaps you were destined to sacrifice him after all."

Lucille nodded, then slipped away into the darkness, leaving Dominic behind.

So this was it. Valentino checked the time, then put the phone down. It was a good sign that she had agreed to meet him. But he wouldn't know for sure where he stood unless she stuck around until after sunrise.

They had agreed to meet here, at the guest house. But this was hardly an appropriate place for what potentially had to happen. If he had to act on the mysterious letter, he'd better do it somewhere else. The last thing he needed was to attract the wrong kind of attention by getting into a confrontation in his room.

No, he needed to convince her to accompany him somewhere. Somewhere secluded enough that they would not be disturbed. Somewhere exactly like the tunnels Marek the Soul Eater had used to hide out. Or even the old factory where they'd trapped him. And he needed a good excuse for it so he would not make her suspicious.

That was it. He would tell her he had received an anonymous tip that Marek hadn't acted alone, that there were more Nightwalkers out there that needed to be dispatched.

It was close enough to the truth to sound convincing. And if she was telling the truth, or intent on keeping up appearances, she would not be able to refuse.

Valentino picked up his leather messenger bag off the floor and checked its contents. All of it was still there just as he'd left it: his weapons, his samples, his notes.

Then he sat back and waited. It wouldn't be long before Lucille would arrive and he'd better stay focused and calm.

If the letter was right, he had to be on his guard, but if it was a bunch of lies as he expected, he didn't want to jeopardize the potential for any further relationship with her over some anonymous tip. It was a fine line to walk.

He remained there, sitting on that chair in silence until a knock on the door made him jump up. She was here.

"Lucille? Come in," he said.

She entered, and he could see immediately that she was on her guard. They hadn't known each other long, but he'd never had any trouble gauging her mood right from the start. Right now, as had often been the case, she was tense.

He got up, slung his bag across his shoulder, and met her by the door.

"I have received an anonymous tip. Marek was not the only Nightwalker that needs to be taken care of. The fight is not yet over," he said, all the while observing her expression carefully.

Lucille's eyes met his, and he was surprised at how cold they looked. Her walls were up.

"That's hardly a surprise," she said. "What do you want to do?"

He patted his bag. "Let's properly investigate the old factory, shall we? Collect some samples, analyze the evidence left behind. Perhaps we can find some proof suggesting Marek wasn't working alone."

Lucille pursed her lips. "Sure. Let's go."

Although his suggestion was sensible enough and should not have made Lucille suspicious, the dynamic between them had changed. She seemed to be miles away, as was he. The tension he felt now was no longer one of stifled attraction, but one of distrust.

Valentino wasn't sure how, but Lucille had definitely picked up on the change in him since the arrival of that mysterious letter. Her intuition had always been one of her biggest strengths as far as he could tell.

Lucille's Valentine

Or perhaps he wasn't as good a liar as he thought he was.

As they left the guest house and hailed a taxi to take them across the city to the place where their showdown with Marek had gone down, they barely spoke a word. *Just keep it up for a little while. Once the sun rises, we can stop this charade once and for all,* Valentino told himself.

But it was no use. The more time they spent in each other's company, with this painful silence hanging over them, the more on edge he felt.

And the worst part was, she could tell. He could see it written all over her face.

When they finally arrived at their destination in Chelsea, they waited for the taxi to leave and found the gap in the fence where they had entered from before. Still, neither said a word.

Once inside the old, drafty building, Valentino could not contain himself any longer. Her potential betrayal stung too deeply.

"You're not who you say you are," he said.

Lucille approached him so fast he could barely focus on her movements. He took a step backward in shock. Had that just been an optical illusion? It was very dark in here; perhaps that explained it.

"Is that so?"

Valentino fumbled with the buckle on his bag and retrieved his UV torch. He shone it straight in her face, which made her shriek and retreat instantly into the shadows. The air was suddenly heavy with the scent of charred flesh.

That was it. Conclusive evidence.

It was like his chest had been ripped open and his heart removed.

How could he have been so blind, so trusting? And now he had led her here, into this old rotten building, without much preparation at all. Worst of all, he had shown his hand; he had lost the element of surprise.

From his bag, he grabbed the trusty old axe and marched forward, while still holding the torch in his other hand. He had to find her and end this. It had been too good to be true; their partnership was now over. He was destined to take another Nightwalker's head tonight. Lucille's.

"You can't run from me. I'll just keep hunting you down until I catch you," he said.

There was a rustling sound somewhere else in the building, followed by footsteps. He knew it wasn't her. Probably some unfortunate human caught up in their game of cat and mouse. Valentino had been in this business far too long to be fooled by that. Vampires were stealthy; they did not make accidental noise.

He continued on, deeper into the building. Was she still here somewhere, or had she fled?

Something told him she would not run like a coward. They had shared a bond while hunting Marek together. A bond that had cemented itself in his heart during their first kiss.

He could sense that she was still around.

Once he reached the large hall with the old furnace, he tightened his grip on his weapon. There she was, waiting, with a dagger in her hand in the exact spot where the Soul Eater had perished.

Too bad the UV lights had burnt out during their battle with Marek. It would have been so simple to just flip a switch and end things right now.

No matter, this wasn't the first physical confrontation he'd had with a Nightwalker. He wasn't afraid.

Valentino could not believe his monumental failure. How he could have been so gravely mistaken about the woman he'd spent the last week with.

They had hunted Marek side by side. They had worked together like a team. Right up to this moment just now, when all his worst fears had come true, he would have trusted her with his life.

He would have sacrificed everything for her.

And now, they found themselves at odds. She was the enemy, just as the letter had said.

He had let down his family's legacy, everything he stood for. He had let himself get dazzled by a pretty face and the promise of a like-minded companion, and in turn failed as a hunter.

Give up now. You can't win. Valentino wasn't sure if that was his thought or hers. For how long had she been corrupting his thoughts?

He pressed his lips together and stepped forward with his axe raised. He had killed bigger, scarier vampires before. She would be no match for him.

CHAPTER ELEVEN

What were the odds? How on earth had Valentino figured everything out at the exact time Lucille had received orders to kill him? Did it even matter, though? Knowing the finer details of it all would change nothing.

Within the last five minutes or so, they had become enemies and declared war, as it were.

She started to circle him, like a wild lioness, playing with its prey. Although he was a skilled hunter, and no doubt well trained with that axe of his, she wasn't worried. She would win, no doubt.

"This isn't my first fight, Lucille. Give yourself up," Valentino warned her.

She rolled her eyes. It wasn't her first fight either. And she was accustomed to wrangling fellow vampires into submission. A human would be no match at all.

He lashed out with his axe, but she simply dodged him by stepping aside. What was he thinking? Could he not see that there was no hope in hell of him ever winning this fight?

Valentino was tenacious, she had to give him that.

Although her eyes still stung from when he shone his torch in her face, she was as ready for this confrontation as she was ever going to be. All that guilt that she had carried with her tonight had faded into the background now that her life was under threat.

How quickly things changed.

Valentino lashed out again, but she dodged him and retaliated with her own weapon. The shiny dagger with the intricately carved ivory handle had been with her for centuries. A souvenir, from a trip to the Middle East with Julius and Alexander, many years ago.

Although Valentino's reflexes were impressive, for a human, he was not quick enough to evade her. The tip of the dagger pierced his sleeve and sliced into his flesh.

Lucille inhaled deeply. *Blood.*

That must have hurt, but Valentino did not let it show. He stepped forward and swung his axe at Lucille's head, prompting her to hunch onto all fours and jump at him. In one swift move, she struck his hand, breaking his grip on his weapon. The axe fell to the ground, making an almighty racket.

She reached for his throat, and pushed him backwards into the nearest wall.

Her face was only inches away from his, her other hand raised with the tip of her trusty dagger aimed at the side of his neck. With just one jab, she could sever his carotid artery. The blade was sharp enough.

Lucille allowed herself one last look. At the handsome face in front of her. The amber eyes that had looked into hers on so many occasions this past week. The full lips she had kissed just once.

It was too painful. She averted her gaze again.

Lucille's Valentine

What on earth was she doing? Their partnership had been like a strange dream, teasing her with possibilities that she had never even considered since the loss of her first love. And this early morning, it had turned into a nightmare.

She inhaled sharply, attempting to force down the painful lump that had developed in her throat, but all that did was bring back even more messy emotions. This fight, this very moment, felt so unreal.

Lucille looked up again and saw not Valentino, but the boy she had loved all those years ago.

Startled, she dropped the dagger, and stepped back.

"I can't. You do whatever you have to, but I can't finish this. You win," she said. Her voice sounded flat and lifeless even to her own ears.

Valentino straightened himself and rubbed his neck where she had just grabbed him.

"I'm a hunter. It's my job."

She shrugged. "Whatever you say."

Lucille observed as Valentino bent down and picked up the dagger she had just discarded. The handle had not survived the fall unscathed; a bit of ivory had chipped off the bottom end. It didn't matter anymore, though. She would soon leave this world and all of her possessions behind.

"You rarely hear of vampire sightings in London," he said, inspecting the weapon in his hands. "How many others are out there?"

Lucille pressed her lips together. She might have capitulated, but she wouldn't tell him any more Council secrets.

"How do you keep your activities under wraps? Or are there so many unwanted people out there that nobody cares to figure out what happens to them when they disappear?"

She shot him an angry look. "If you must know, we don't kill."

Valentino paused. "Vampires that don't kill. Now there's something you don't hear about every day."

"There are plenty of things you know nothing about," Lucille snapped.

He was getting to her. Why was she allowing herself to be goaded into answering these inane questions? She ought to just keep quiet and wait for the inevitable. At least then her heart would stop hurting.

Valentino took a step towards her and Lucille closed her eyes and braced herself.

"If you had wanted to kill me, you could have done so on numerous occasions. What changed?"

She balled her fists and stood her ground. *Enough.* She would say no more.

"Someone ordered it, right? That's what's different now. And now you'd rather give yourself up than face the consequences of disobeying that order."

She shook her head. He would get nothing else out of her.

"Don't worry, I'm here to help," another male voice startled her. Dominic.

Bloody hell, so he had ignored her instructions and followed her anyway! Lucille opened her eyes and just about caught a glimpse of the other vampire charging toward Valentino.

Lucille did not get time to think, only act. Before Dominic had the chance to hurt Valentino, she was on him, clawing at the flesh on his shoulders and biting into his neck. A steady trickle of fresh blood entered her mouth. Clearly, he'd fed sometime tonight.

She dug her fingernails deeper into his shoulders and dragged him backwards into the next room.

Dominic should have just stayed away like she'd told him. He would regret his insubordination dearly.

"Don't you dare," she hissed in his ear. "Don't you dare attack him."

"But he was about to kill you!" Dominic argued. "And he murdered Marek. He must pay for that!"

"I was handling it!"

Lucille forced Dominic down onto the ground. Despite her smaller frame, Lucille was quite a bit stronger than she looked. Dominic was a much younger vampire and still had a lot to learn.

She glared at him and let his earlier words sink in. The realization hit her like a brick wall. He knew Valentino killed Marek even though she'd never reported that detail to Julius; fine, so he'd followed her earlier. But the thing he'd said back at her house about sacrificing Valentino…

There was no reasonable way for him to know about that. *Unless…*

"If you don't back off right this minute, I'll tell Julius that you've been colluding with the Soul Eater."

Dominic's eyes widened in shock. So she'd guessed correctly.

"I was only trying to help… I'm… I'm so sorry!" he mumbled.

"As you should be. Now bugger off and let me handle the hunter!" Lucille barked.

She got off him and Dominic reluctantly stood up and backed away.

"Go! I'm not going to tell you again!" she called after him.

Lucille waited until he was out of sight. It would be so easy to just leave as well, if only her pride didn't prevent it. She had already failed to carry out her orders and it was only a matter of time before Julius found out about it. The life as Council Enforcer that she had become accustomed to was now over.

She had let Julius down.

Footsteps approached, dragging her back to reality.

"Lucille," Valentino called out.

"Yeah. I'm here," she said as she sat down on top of a pile of rubble in the center of the room.

He approached her with his arm outstretched and her dagger in his hand.

"I can't do it either."

Lucille's Valentine

They stared into each other's eyes as she accepted the weapon. There was so much there to see. For Lucille, it was all a painful déjà vu.

"What a pair we are, huh? Sworn enemies. Yet we cannot bring ourselves to kill each other," Valentino remarked. There was a sad glint in his eyes.

"I suppose life isn't always black and white," Lucille said. Funny that she was the one uttering this phrase now. Just two weeks ago, she would have passionately disagreed with that statement. Lucille had spent centuries as a stickler for the rules.

And now, for the first time ever, she found herself stuck in the gray areas of life.

"I've never met a woman like you," Valentino said.

Lucille looked up at him again. Could she give this up? Could she give *him* up?

"This can never work," she said.

Who was she trying to convince exactly? The little voice in the back of her head tried to disagree vehemently. So what if he was a hunter and she was a vampire?

"My forefathers would be spinning in their graves if they saw us now." Valentino averted his gaze and started to pace back and forth in front of her.

"I attacked one of my own. I can't believe I did that."

"He seemed pretty surprised too," Valentino remarked.

"Oh, you noticed that, did you?"

Dominic's reaction had been almost funny, if their circumstances weren't so tragic. Still, Lucille found a little smile creeping over her face. She looked at Valentino, whose expression had softened as well. Then, her smile turned into a giggle, before erupting into laughter.

Valentino sat down next to her and joined in.

The pain, the confusion was too much to bear. Next thing she knew, her face was wet. At some point, without realizing it, she had stopped laughing and started crying.

***

The other vampire had come out of nowhere. Valentino was not prepared at all and very nearly paid the price. He also was not prepared for Lucille's reaction. Within the blink of an eye, she had taken care of the threat and dragged Valentino's assailant backwards out of view. For an experienced hunter, he had really let his guard down one too many times tonight.

Of course he'd gone after her, searching through the adjacent rooms and halls. When he found her, she was sitting on top of the remnants of a concrete support beam that looked like it had fallen from the ceiling of the old building a long time ago. As he observed her sitting there, hunched over with her head hanging down in defeat, he could not take it anymore.

He'd never planned for this moment. From the moment he'd read that letter, he'd hung on to the assumption that it was full of lies. And although discovering the opposite had shocked him deeply, he could no longer bring himself to hate her.

They spoke in fragments and statements that didn't

make a lot of sense. He'd offered her the weapon he'd picked up as a gesture of goodwill.

She accepted his gesture, her face tense with regret.

She was the enemy. He was meant to kill her.

But if she was really a monster like those he'd hunted before, even like Marek whom they had defeated together, she wouldn't have surrendered to him. She would have finished the job before he had the chance to defend himself.

He told her he'd never met anyone like her.

She responded that it wouldn't work.

They stared into each other's eyes and he wondered if she really meant it.

These were not the eyes of a dangerous monster. Evil was supposed to be ugly, repulsive, but he'd never seen any of that in her. Not when they'd worked together, and not now.

He remembered what she'd said only moments ago, that she did not kill humans. Her actions had proved as much. That in itself meant she was different.

Valentino had always been so proud of his heritage. Vampire hunters for generations. He'd grown up with stories of his forefathers' conquests. He'd gone on hunts with his father once he was old enough.

Never did he consider that he still had so much to learn.

"I attacked one of my own. I can't believe I did that," she said.

"He seemed pretty surprised too," Valentino quipped.

"Oh, you noticed that, did you?"

She laughed. It was the first time she'd really let loose in front of him. It was contagious, so when he sat down next to her, he soon found himself joining in.

He glanced at her and noticed tears streaming down her face.

Enough. To hell with the old rules.

He put his arm around her and pulled her close.

They had hit this roadblock together. While he found himself doubting everything he'd ever believed in, she was facing a similar crisis. They didn't need to face it alone.

Despite everything, they had proved their loyalty to each other already. That had to mean something.

Valentino closed his eyes and buried his face in Lucille's hair. She did not resist him, quite the opposite. So they continued to sit there in silence, in that cold, drafty old power station, their arms wrapped around each other.

If everything went wrong tomorrow, if they never saw each other again, at least they'd had this moment together.

CHAPTER TWELVE

They had stayed at the old power station until the approaching dawn had made itself known to Lucille. Neither his room at the old guest house nor her home would be safe. Julius would know to look there.

They found refuge in the one place everyone who defied the Council seemed to flock to. Alexander's villa.

The latter had not been impressed to find Lucille and a bruised stranger on his doorstep at six in the morning. But with twilight already upon them, he had not been so cruel as to send her away.

"Just for one night," she'd insisted. "Then we'll be out of your hair."

He'd shrugged and retreated back inside and up the stairs. "You'll do whatever you want anyway."

Now Lucille found herself alone with Valentino in one of the spare bedrooms, where they looked painfully out of place. Dusty, torn clothes and dirt smudged skin stood out against the opulent Regency decor Alexander loved so much.

What on earth was she doing here? With a human—no, a *hunter*—who had a prize on his head.

No wonder Alexander's greeting had been even colder than usual.

"Perhaps we should talk," Lucille began.

Valentino stopped inspecting the room and focused on her instead.

"How much of it was true?" he asked.

Lucille sighed. She knew this part of the conversation would be inevitable.

"I hypnotized you earlier. Before we fought Marek."

Valentino nodded. "I suspected as much. But which memories are false?"

Lucille took both of Valentino's hands and made eye contact with him.

She wasn't sure this would work, but she at least had to try and undo the damage she'd done to his memory earlier. It was the least she could do.

She focused all her energy on releasing those events from the past few hours that she had previously blocked access to. Once that was done, she also transferred some of her own memories and knowledge: her private interactions with Marek, and her last report to Julius.

Valentino blinked a few times and frowned. It was a lot to process, no doubt.

"Wow," he said, when Lucille severed their connection again.

She brushed herself off as best she could, then sat down, gingerly, on the edge of the settee.

"I'm sorry. I was just trying to defeat Marek. And I had to protect my secret," Lucille whispered.

Valentino shook his head. "It's not that. I'm actually surprised at how much I remember correctly."

Lucille's Valentine

"What do you mean?" Lucille looked up in surprise.

"The kiss. I half expected that to be an illusion."

"Ah." She sighed. "Yeah, that really happened. You were meant to be under my control at the time, but I fear I might have been influenced by you in return."

"But you meant it?" he asked.

Lucille folded her hands in her lap and stared down at them. Had she? The urge had overwhelmed her and made her lose control of her own impulses and emotions. Of course she'd meant it. But the secret was out now. Surely, his feelings for her would have changed?

She looked up and found Valentino already staring at her. "Did I want to kiss you? Yes. Do I think it was a good idea? No."

He shrugged. "Who is to say whether an idea is good or bad, as long as it feels right?"

She frowned. Valentino was full of surprises.

"So how did you find out about my secret?" Lucille asked.

Valentino retrieved a piece of paper from his messenger bag and handed it to her. She got up to accept it.

It was an envelope with a broken black seal on top.

Lucille stared at the offending document and found that her knees were getting weak. The seal was different from anything she'd seen before, but the paper was so distinctive she would recognize it anywhere. It wasn't just the quality, the texture of it, but also the scent. She'd received communications like this before. And they had always come from the same sender.

She opened it with trembling fingers and pulled out the parchment inside. The handwriting was equally distinctive.

Julius.

"I don't believe it," she whispered.

She crushed the paper into a ball and flung it across the room.

Valentino came up behind her and rested his hand on her shoulder. "That's pretty much how I reacted too."

She spun around and looked at the man she'd very nearly hurt, and worse, almost killed. It shouldn't have come as a surprise that her own orders to eliminate Valentino should coincide with a similar directive sent to him. Julius liked to play it safe; why shouldn't he hedge his bets?

If Julius suspected Lucille might disobey, at least Valentino might follow through and force her hand, thus ensuring that his will was done. It was only sensible, and yet it felt like a deep betrayal.

Julius never ran his own errands, so Dominic was undoubtedly involved. And he had been there at the power station, watching when Lucille laid down her weapon. Even if she could continue to blackmail Dominic into helping her, there was no hope. Julius was too suspicious by nature; he would insist on seeing a body.

"My maker sent this. *Julius* sent this," Lucille said. The game was up. What were they going to do?

Valentino frowned. "Why would your maker want to see you harmed?"

Lucille shook her head. "You don't understand. He didn't expect for you to succeed. He was just trying to make sure that I'd be forced to kill you. If not on his direct orders, then at least in self-defense."

Valentino smiled. "Seems he underestimated the two of us."

Lucille started to pace around the room, back and forth, again and again. Now what? Defying Council orders was a grave crime. He would try to punish her, and then execute Valentino anyway as an enemy to vampire kind. She had come too far to defend him already; she had to find a way not to let that happen.

"He will kill you. He might even kill me for disobeying him."

Lucille sat down on the settee again and rested her head in her hands. *Think! What's the most logical way out of this?*

"I suppose killing him is out of the question?" Valentino asked.

Lucille shot him a disapproving look. "He's still my maker. He's been like a father to me for centuries." Plus, if she did that, she suspected she'd turn into the very thing they had been hunting together: a Soul Eater.

Valentino nodded. "Fair enough. So how about we just go? Leave this place and everyone in it. He has his responsibilities here, doesn't he? So he's unlikely to come after us?"

Lucille was about to protest. London had been her home for so long, it was hard to imagine anything else. But Valentino did make an excellent point. Julius was much too suspicious about being superseded if he left the Council behind to hunt after her.

"You want me to run away with you, after everything that's happened? After everything I've done to you?" she asked.

"Perhaps I've been alone for too long," he said, with a grave expression on his face.

"You realize I've been on my own for four-hundred years, right?" she asked.

Valentino grinned at her. "Fair point. But I imagine the years pass much quicker when you're immortal."

"Touché."

"Come on, think about it. We'll make a fresh start. I'll take you home to Italy. It's a beautiful country, you'll see. And the food is amazing…" Valentino's expression fell again. "Wait, can you eat human food?"

It was Lucille's turn to grin. "Of course. But I'll still need the occasional dose of fresh blood to sustain me."

The relief was evident on Valentino's face. "Thank God. I can't imagine spending a lot of time with someone who doesn't appreciate a good meal."

Lucille couldn't stop herself from staring at him. Was this it? Was this love? Normally it annoyed her when people behaved in ways she couldn't understand. She should find his quirks irritating, but instead, he intrigued her.

She wasn't quite sure what outcome she'd intended when she refused to carry out Julius' orders. She'd been ready to lay down her life to protect Valentino, but she hadn't actually considered the possibility of *being with him*. Now that they were alone, her mind was trying to play catch up with what her heart had wanted all along.

Here he was, despite everything, trying to convince her to what—elope with him? What a strange man he was. A beautiful optimist who despite everything, was still trying to see a positive outcome at the end of it all.

Her heart surged when she thought about it. Should she risk it? For once in her life, should she stop thinking with her head and just jump into something, no matter how silly and ill-advised it was?

"You know, this might actually work," she mumbled. And if they left together, she wouldn't have to involve Alexander any longer than necessary either.

"Of course it'll work. As long as we both want it to," Valentino urged. "I know you tried to yourself, but I am not ready to say goodbye."

There it was again, that look. The one that had sought to disarm her from the start of their partnership. The one that brought with it so much baggage and uncovered so many scars she thought had faded centuries ago.

Lucille pressed her lips together.

Valentino sat down beside her and put his arm around

her, just like he had done at the old power plant. The gesture gave her shivers, in a good way. It sent a warm rush down her spine that filled her heart with hope.

Surely she didn't deserve this man and everything he was trying to offer her?

His hand traveled up her back until it reached the nape of her neck.

"What do you say then?" he whispered.

His voice, so smooth, it was like warm honey. And his scent... A lot had happened since their first kiss; would it still feel the same?

Lucille reached for him, embracing him and bringing their faces closer together.

She sought out his lips with hers and closed her eyes when he bridged the gap, kissing her with a passion they hadn't shared before.

Words couldn't describe what they shared now. This bond, this understanding. All of Lucille's worries and fears faded into nothingness and all that mattered now was that they were together. This was what she had needed all along. For someone to come and chip away at her hardened exterior until the old her re-emerged.

She was no longer Lucille, stern and cynical Enforcer of the Council of London. She was just a girl. A girl who had come from simple beginnings in 17th century France. A girl who fell in love with her best friend and then promptly lost him and everyone else she cared for.

For the umpteenth time tonight, tears streamed down

her face. Only this time, they were happy tears.

Even those memories she had buried so deeply for hundreds of years seemed to not matter anymore. This, this moment right here, with Valentino, was all that held any importance to her. She felt relieved, redeemed. She had risen from her own ashes.

Without even realizing what he'd done, this man from a world so different from her own had given her a second chance.

Their second kiss *didn't* feel the same. It was infinitely better.

CHAPTER THIRTEEN

Valentino felt like he had woken up in the middle of a dream.

In his arms was a woman unlike any he'd met before. A flawless beauty, whose complexion was so perfect it could have been carved out of the finest Italian marble. During most of their past interactions, she had shown herself to act cold as well, but this last hour or so with her had changed everything.

Her eyes were no longer guarded. Her touch was filled with heat. And her lips…

Valentino had never known a taste more intoxicating.

Had someone told him even just two weeks ago that he would find himself here, in a strange vampire's house, making out with said vampire's sister, he wouldn't even have laughed. He might have been tempted to cut the messenger's head off.

But this wasn't an illusion. What they shared was real. And as bizarre as it was, he felt strangely at peace with how things had turned out between them.

So not all vampires were monstrous killers. They needed blood to survive, but some had found more ethical ways of procuring it than simply taking human lives for it. That had made his decision to fight for a chance with Lucille a lot easier.

Lucille's Valentine

There would be a period of adjustment, of course. Save for one miserable attempt in the past to let someone into his life, he had been a loner. Women had come and gone, but none had left a lasting impression.

And the same was true for Lucille as well, who had spent centuries on her own.

But ever since she'd surrendered to him earlier tonight, he knew that this was the right way forward. Against all odds, they shared something. Call it a connection, a sense of solidarity. Love?

In addition to that, they also shared a heavy dose of something more primal in nature. Passion, lust, whatever you wanted to call it. Lucille and Valentino had heaps of it.

They'd been dancing around each other for only a week, but what felt like a lifetime of frustration was about to be cast off in a most spectacular fashion. He was ready for her.

Of course they'd done this before, briefly. The memory of their first kiss was still fresh in Valentino's memory. He'd been under her influence at the time, but even that could not taint his perception of it. He'd been wanting to kiss those shapely lips from the moment he'd first laid eyes on them. To know she'd felt the same was too precious to let something as petty as their circumstances or opposing backgrounds get in the way of it.

Every touch of hers now felt like a lifeline to keep him from drowning. The events of tonight had changed his outlook in life. Beliefs he had held on to all his life were shattered. Future plans that he had considered certainties had been discarded.

He was ready to wipe the slate clean, to break free from his past and his legacy in order to rediscover a new life with her.

Valentino closed his eyes as he let his hands roam her body. It didn't make a difference. Eyes open or closed, he could see only her. She filled his mind, his soul, his whole being.

She pulled away, just for a moment, prompting him to chase after her.

Lucille stood in the center of the room, beckoning him to come closer. He couldn't refuse if he tried.

He tore at his clothes, ridding himself of every last barrier that could get in their way.

Lucille followed his example. Even his wildest dreams couldn't have compared him for the vision of womanhood that stood before him. He wasn't sure what he was expecting, but it wasn't this. She looked radiant, alive.

"Take me. Make me yours," she whispered. Or perhaps that was just what he wanted her to say.

It made no difference. His desires or hers, they were the same.

He reached for her, only to have her dodge his touch and edge her way backward to the bed.

No, not there. He wished to have her here on the floor.

And against the wall.

And on the sofa.

Lucille's Valentine

And…

She smiled seductively, then vanished into thin air, only to reappear behind him. She wrapped her arms around his waist, running her long fingernails over his chest and stomach, stopping just short of his cock. Oh, the sweet torture.

"I'm rather used to being in charge. I hope you don't mind." Lucille kissed him just below the ear, which sent a fresh surge of desire right through him.

Valentino shook his head. "Any way you want this is fine by me."

He turned around and wrapped his arms around her. She leaned into his embrace, then immediately flinched away and let out a loud shriek. Something had caused her to cry out in pain.

"What happened? What's wrong?" he asked. Valentino's heart beat surged. What had he done? How could he make it better?

Lucille pointed at his neck and his heart sank. *How could he have forgotten about that?* Valentino reached for the chain around his neck. His pendant, the medal of St. Benedict, was made of silver. No wonder she'd reacted the way she did upon touching it.

He tugged at it in anger, breaking the chain and throwing it as far away from them as possible.

This token had been with him forever, and although he never believed in its supposed supernatural powers, it had been a support to him in the past. A reminder of his heritage and a crutch to help him follow in their footsteps. But the meaning he'd attached to it was well and truly tainted now.

His forefathers wouldn't have asked questions or tried to understand. They would have taken Lucille's head off without hesitation. He didn't want to belong to that world anymore. How could he?

"I'm so sorry," he whispered as he pulled Lucille back into his arms. "I didn't think."

She shook her head. "It's fine. I'm a fast healer."

As soon as he felt her naked body against his again, their passions flared up as though they'd never been interrupted. She dug her fingernails into his shoulders and he groaned in sweet pain. He needed to show her just how much he wanted her. His body, his heart demanded it.

It was a strange realization to know that the woman he was with right now could tear him limb from limb if she chose to. And yet that did not intimidate him; it only made him want her more.

She jumped him, wrapping her lean legs around his waist.

With any other partner Valentino would have expected a good amount of foreplay, but Lucille seemed unwilling to wait. Their desires were too urgent to be ignored any longer.

Valentino held on to her hips, marveling at the firm curvature of her ass. So this was what a warrior's body felt like. He stumbled straight across the room, until he had her pinned up against the nearest wall.

Then he entered her. Their kiss earlier had seemed like the most glorious thing ever, but this exceeded it thousand fold. Lucille moaned loudly as he started to move.

How tight she was. How perfect.

Her fingernails dug into his back now, not hard enough to pierce skin, but just right to hit the perfect balance between pleasure and pain.

It was like she knew exactly what he wanted and how he wanted it. Similarly, he seemed to know just what she needed him to do. She would like it faster, more forceful; his instincts told him so.

He did his best to deliver, burying his manhood into her repeatedly, as deep as he could go.

Her body responded by gyrating into him, egging him on, faster and faster.

Valentino's chest felt ready to burst. His throat tight. He had so much to tell her, but his actions seemed inadequate. Faster and faster he went, eliciting more moans and muttered encouragements from her lips.

He was only human, and she was so much more. Would he satisfy her?

Beads of sweat started to appear on his forehead as he fought through the beginnings of his fatigue to make her happy. Just when he thought he'd reached the end of his reserves, something made him push through and find further strength.

That was what her influence did to him. She challenged

him; made him want to be better—stronger—than he really was. This was it, the essence of his attraction to her. It was what made him fall for her despite himself.

"Oh, God, I love you," Valentino gasped. He had blurted it out just like that, without considering her reaction.

Lucille grabbed a handful of his hair and pulled his head back to expose his neck. She ran her tongue across the whole side of his neck, then stopped just below his ear.

"I love you too," she whispered.

He closed his eyes, savoring those words she said. This, of course, wasn't a fairytale kind of love. He wasn't her white knight, and she wasn't an innocent maiden in need of rescue. They had both lived a life of darkness, in a way. They were well versed in the language of violence and death.

It wasn't a surprise then that what they were doing right now wasn't lovemaking. It was feral, unapologetic, and carnal. They all but fought for pleasure, not just for themselves but for each other.

He wouldn't have it any other way.

"Drink from me if you want," he said.

"I thought you'd never ask."

As Lucille bit down into his neck, he was overcome with yet another intense sensation he'd never felt before. It was like all the orgasms he'd ever felt in his life rolled into one. It was painful and infinitely pleasurable all at once.

She pulled back and cried out. Her body writhed and

spasmed against his rigid arms. He could barely hold on.

This was everything they'd battled towards, the pinnacle, the peak of their release. Every muscle in her body seemed intent on keeping him buried inside her and squeezing every last drop of pleasure out of him.

It took him a few moments to catch his breath. Lucille, of course, had no such trouble; her stamina vastly outpaced him. Still, the sun was probably up already, and her eyes betrayed that she was getting worn out too.

Valentino carried her to the bed and got in between the sheets with her still clinging on to his neck. Finally, as they were enveloped by the soft mattress, he felt her tense muscles relax.

"Tired?" he asked.

"Maybe," she said.

Although she lay in his arms now, Valentino had a feeling this would be a rare treat. Lucille didn't seem like the cuddling kind. And that was just as well, because neither was he.

She traced her fingertip along the outlines of one of the many scars that covered his hardened body. He didn't mind. He wasn't ashamed of any of it.

"Where did you get this one?" she asked.

He looked down at the star shaped mark on his chest. "Romania, 2008. While I was hunting a Nightwalker who had recently killed an entire family of locals, the police mistook me for the suspect and shot me."

Lucille nodded. "I've been shot before. It stings."

Valentino chuckled. "It did a bit more than sting. I almost didn't make it."

She raised her head, her eyebrows pulled together in concern. "I have a way around that, you know."

"What do you mean?"

Lucille pursed her lips. "Well, if we're going to do this—be together, I mean—we could make it official."

"What, like marriage?" Valentino raised himself up on his elbows and looked at her. Growing up, he wanted nothing more than to settle down with someone. To have the kind of companionship and love his parents had shared. He'd never figured Lucille would want the same.

"Well, sort of. If we do that, your life will be bound to mine. You'll still be human, but you'll live as long as I do. You'll stop aging. You'll be safe from harm." The way she looked at him now with those big, brown eyes stirred something up in him. She didn't need his protection of course, but nobody had told Valentino's instincts that.

He nodded. "If you'll have me."

Lucille smiled, the relief evident in her eyes. "I don't think I could bear if I lost you now. Not again."

"Again? You'll have to explain that one to me."

Lucille lay her head on his chest again and took his hand. "It was a long time ago. At first I thought you reminded me of him, but then I realized that you're nothing alike. I was simply reminded of a feeling I had before."

Valentino settled back into the pillows and closed his

eyes as he listened to her story.

The longer she spoke, the more he felt like he finally understood.

There were no more secrets between them.

EPILOGUE

---◆---

14th February
Valentine's Day

It was a beautiful ceremony, conducted by Lucille's brother, Alexander, in a most scenic setting.

Valentino's family had owned this villa that stood proudly on top of a barren hilltop in the Italian Alps for many generations. He had inherited it after his father's passing two years ago.

And on a clear and desolate night like tonight, it was mostly the stars overhead that acted as witnesses to Lucille and Valentino's wedding. They stood bathed in moonlight, filled with hope for their shared future.

The ritual ended with the two of them holding hands after making the blood sacrifice necessary to cement their relationship. And now when she looked at Valentino, she could she a subtle glow surrounding him. Their bond had taken. He was now hers, as she was his. In life, in death, until the end of days. Although humans couldn't see it, any respectable vampire would know that Valentino belonged to one of their own and be unable to harm him. The laws they lived by forbade it.

They shared a kiss, then Lucille excused herself to take care of the rest of the arrangements. Valentino never insisted on it, but she knew an Italian wedding was never complete without a feast fit for kings. Lucille had wanted to make sure that everything was just as it should be.

As she returned with one of the many dishes she'd procured—actually cooking the food would have just resulted in disaster—she stood and watched Valentino, who was now chatting to Alexander. It was a strange sight: the man she'd chosen to be with making friendly small talk with the one who had been a companion of sorts for the longest time, at least during the early days of their turning.

They seemed to get along, which made Lucille smile. Not that she cared if her brother approved of her choices; she was way too strong-willed for that. But it made the scene look strangely normal. A new husband chatting to his brother-in-law.

Lucille thought back to what it had taken for them to end up here. All the trials she and Valentino had been through. How she had hidden her true self from him, deceived him, and tried to use his expertise for her own purposes. How he had forgiven her for all that and convinced her to come here.

They had escaped London in the dead of night, and with it, Julius' wrath. Although Valentino would be safe from harm now that they were wedded, the same protection didn't extend to her; she still had defied official Council orders. There were consequences to that sort of thing.

Lucille diverted her attention away from her other half

and toward her brother. It had surprised her that Alexander agreed to come. After turning up on his doorstep with Valentino during their last night in London, she almost expected he wouldn't want to get involved in this whole affair. He had already angered Julius enough himself, and helping her would only fan that fire. But instead of turning her down, he'd jumped at the chance to conduct their bonding ritual.

Either Alexander had turned into a hopeless romantic since meeting Catherine, or he felt he owed it to his sister to grant her this request; Lucille wasn't sure which.

Clumsy human footsteps, as well as a rather heady perfume, alerted Lucille to a presence next to her. Speak of the devil; it was Catherine.

"It's beautiful here. I'm jealous," Catherine said.

Lucille turned to face her, though she tried her best not to breathe in too deeply around the woman. The unique quality of her blood still got to her, even though she had recently fed. She thought of something to say, something courteous. *What would Valentino do?*

"You and Alexander can always visit," Lucille said.

"Thank you. I appreciate the offer." Catherine smiled at Lucille, who nodded.

She'd never been good at these shallow niceties. Never felt like she had much time for them.

No, it was something else that danced on the tip of her tongue. Something much deeper and more meaningful.

"Was it worth it?" Lucille asked finally.

Catherine frowned. "What do you mean?"

Lucille nodded at Alexander. "You know. Becoming a vampire's consort?"

Catherine chuckled. "Oh, considering the circumstances… If I hadn't, I might have died that night Julius came to the house to claim me for himself."

Lucille nodded. That was an excellent point.

"Still. It's a lot to give up, isn't it?" Lucille said. "Your old life, your friends and family. The chance for a normal relationship with someone who can leave the house at daytime." *The constant threat of death if one of Alexander's acquaintances lost their control and tried to drain Catherine.* Lucille thought it wise to keep that last remark to herself.

"Honestly, I disagree. He's shown me things I never thought possible. Even if we hadn't been under threat, and I had to do it all over again, I would still marry Alexander."

Lucille watched Valentino, who was still in conversation with Alexander. He'd chosen to spend his life with her. Like Catherine had chosen Alexander.

"Thank you," Lucille mumbled, her voice so low Catherine probably never even heard it. She'd known exactly what Lucille had wanted to hear, though. It had helped put her mind at ease.

They were both only starting on these journeys with their significant others, though. Lucille could only hope that as time passed, Valentino wouldn't change his mind and yearn for his old life back.

He turned away from Alexander and smiled at her, and

she felt reassured. No, he wouldn't want things to go back to the way they were. Not as long as he looked at her like this.

She nodded and left the tiny little wedding party again to retrieve more dishes from inside the house.

When everything was set up, she called out to everyone. "Dinner is served!"

Valentino stepped up to her first, took her hand, and kissed it.

"You didn't need to," he whispered.

"I wanted to," she said.

"You continue to surprise me, Lucille Amboise," Valentino said.

Lucille smiled. It had taken a long time for her to get to this point. Of recognizing a chance at happiness and taking it. Thanks to Valentino, she had found what she'd been missing for hundreds of years.

Love.

They watched as their guests helped themselves to the food on offer.

Tonight was a special night, a unique night. A meal shared with select few to celebrate their union.

But this life of entertaining guests in their lavish home wouldn't be their future. In fact, they probably wouldn't spend much time living here in this old house. She might have left her job with the Council behind, but that hadn't changed Lucille's outlook in life.

The world was much bigger than London. And there

were still creatures—vampires—out there who broke the rules and killed indiscriminately.

Lucille had worried about losing her identity if she left her job with the Council. But together, she and Valentino had come to a compromise. They were not so different from one another; even before they met, they'd done essentially the same thing: brought criminals to justice.

That wasn't just a job; it was a calling. The only difference was, now they no longer had to do it alone.

- THE END -

ABOUT THE AUTHOR

---◆---

Dear Reader,

Thanks for reading Vampires of London: Books 1-3. Although at the time I'm writing this it's not even a year and a half since I released my debut series, Scottish Werebears, I'm not new to writing in general. In fact, my mom still tells me to this day about how I would make up stories, and attempt to record them in my clumsy, shaky handwriting from the moment I learned to read and write. From there I went on to write fan fiction and other stuff meant for my own eyes only.

I've always enjoyed stories of the paranormal. Vampires, shape shifters, witches and magic, all featured in the books I loved the most, even when I was still growing up. But it wasn't until much later that I got into romance. One of the first writers (a self published author just like me!) I came across was Tina Folsom, via her Scanguards Vampire series. I was hooked. From there I went on to read more paranormal romance until I found a new kind of hero I loved: bear shifters, like the kind written by Milly Taiden, Zoe Chant, and T.S. Joyce. What I love about bears is how they can be all strong and independent, a bit reclusive, and almost grumpy, but they always end up having a heart of gold (plus they tend to know their food, and we all know that a man who can cook is doubly sexy). All that (except for the shifting into a powerful bear) almost exactly describes the sort of man I ended up falling for and marrying in real life, so it's no surprise that this is what I started my publishing career with.

But no matter how many bear shifter books I've written, I've always longed to write a Vampire romance. Finally, once the Scottish Werebears series was complete, it was time to fulfill this dream with Alexander's Blood Bride. I'm really pleased with how it's turned out; it has everything I look for in vampire books. A dangerous attraction between the hero and heroine which could end in tragedy, a bunch of rival vampires wanting the heroine for themselves, forcing the hero to choose sides. And an ending that shows that even if you're seemingly incompatible (one of them is constantly battling the urge to kill the other; how much worse can it get?), you can still find happiness.

To find out more, check:

LoreleiMoone.com (And why not sign up for the newsletter to be the first to find out about new releases.)

You can also get in touch with me via Facebook (search for Lorelei Moone), or email at info@loreleimoone.com
x Lorelei

Printed in the USA
CPSIA information can be obtained
at www.ICGtesting.com
LVHW021007140624
783223LV00026B/405